Praise for the Maggie O'Malley Mystery Series

"Maggie O'Malley will not be cowered, stopped, or out-smarted as she sets out to prove the innocence of a friend facing a murder charge...*39 Winks* has it all: characters, plot, pace—from the very first line to the spectacular conclusion.

– Patricia Gussin,
New York Times Bestselling Author of *Come Home*

With twists you won't see coming, Maggie O'Malley and *39 Winks* are sure to keep you up all night!

– Julie Mulhern,
USA Today Bestselling Author of *Shadow Dancing*

"A page-turner! Smart, fast-paced and surprising."

– Hank Phillippi Ryan,
Mary Higgins Clark Award-Winner, Author of *Say No More*

"This one will have you up all night following Maggie O'Malley on her search for the truth... If you like a book with smarts, a heart, and flesh-and-blood characters, don't miss *Protocol*."

– Maggie Barbieri,
Author of the Murder 101 Series

"Gutsy and loyal, Maggie O'Malley finds herself plunged into the corrupt and chilling world of big pharmaceuticals where trusting the wrong person could prove as deadly as an experimental drug side effect. With a page-turner debut like *Protocol*, I can't wait to see what Valenti cooks up for us next!"

– Annette Dashofy,
USA Today Bestselling Author of *Uneasy Prey*

"A clever and twisty thriller that will grab you from the first sentence and keep you guessing until the very end.

– Kathleen Barber,
Author of *Are You Sleeping*

39 WINKS

**The Maggie O'Malley Mystery Series
by Kathleen Valenti**

PROTOCOL (#1)
39 WINKS (#2)

A MAGGIE O'MALLEY MYSTERY

39 WINKS

KATHLEEN VALENTI

HENERY PRESS

Copyright

39 WINKS
A Maggie O'Malley Mystery
Part of the Henery Press Mystery Collection

First Edition | May 2018

Henery Press, LLC
www.henerypress.com

Trade Paperback ISBN-13: 978-1-63511-338-9
Digital epub ISBN-13: 978-1-63511-339-6
Kindle ISBN-13: 978-1-63511-340-2
Hardcover ISBN-13: 978-1-63511-341-9

Printed in the United States of America

To my loving family.

ACKNOWLEDGMENTS

For me, birthing a second book was akin to having another child: I forgot the pain of the first time, cherished the beauty of the experience and found myself surprised at the fact that I loved my new arrival just as intensely as I loved my first.

I was blessed to have a lot of help bringing this book into the world. I owe a great debt of gratitude to so many. Think of this as the CliffsNotes version.

My many thanks—

To my family for their support and unceasing attendance at all of my bookish events.

To my intrepid, eagle-eyed editor Rachel and the rest of the Henery Press editorial team for their brilliant insights, great ideas and spot-on feedback.

To beta-readers/cheerleaders/tough-love-giver-outers Alan, Nancy, Valerie, Molly, Vince and Lisa, who took the time to read, comment, brainstorm and advise.

To Phyllis for her superhuman proofreading skills.

To medical advisors Daymen, Allan and Tabitha for helping me navigate the medical and pharmaceutical worlds.

To Susan and Craig for sharing their experiences with Parkinson's disease.

To my agent Jordan at Literary Counsel for saying yes to me as a client.

To Henery Press for their infinite support, tireless encouragement and prudent counsel.

And to my author brethren, including those at Henery Press, '17 Scribes and those I met at conferences for sharing their wisdom and letting me sit at the cool kids' table.

Of course, there were many other hands, hearts and minds who helped bring this book from concept to creation, including those who read *Protocol* and those who were present at my readings, signings and semi-regular freak-out sessions.

To all of you, I give my innumerable and inadequate thanks. I couldn't have done it without you.

As always, any errors are my own.

Prologue

Howard Wright found death in Life.

Life cereal, to be exact.

Polly found him face-first in a bowl of sugary whole-wheat squares, his surgically nipped chin resting against the bowl's milk-streaked edge. It wasn't until Polly shook his shoulder that Howard's head lolled to the side, revealing the wet red smile that ran from ear to ear.

At first Polly wasn't sure what was more surprising: that her husband had been murdered or that he had been eating Life cereal.

Howard was gluten-free.

Then again, the whole thing was very confusing. One moment Polly was dreaming about walking through her favorite fabric store, one hand running along a bolt of red cotton, the other caressing a pair of gleaming scissors. The next, she's standing over Howard, calling his name. Seeing his blood tinge the blue-white milk in his cereal bowl a pale baby pink.

Polly didn't remember screaming, but of course she did. That's what you do when you find your husband murdered. She just couldn't quite remember. Pieces of dreams, of things real and imagined, tumbled through her mind like balls through the bingo cage at St. Philothea's social hall.

B-1.

G-3.

B-4.

B-4.

Before what?

Polly didn't know.

That's the way it was when she sleepwalked. Her body moved, but her mind turned off.

No, not off. On autopilot, directing her body as she moved through the house with no awareness of the rooms she'd explored, the things she'd touched, the phrases she'd mixed into incoherent yet elaborate word salads.

She had no recollection of her nocturnal wanderings other than slivers of memory that sometimes came to her when Howard told her what she had done the night before. Of course, now there was no Howard. No self-appointed court reporter to read back her movements on that terrible night. She simply awoke, alert and tingling with adrenaline, suddenly aware of the crimson puddle on Howard's pajama top and the sharp smell of copper and fear.

She touched Howard again, watched the head wag as if admonishing her for sleeping when he needed her most. As if she were another disciple in the Garden of Gethsemane.

A thought bloomed somewhere deep in her brain: what if the killer was still there? What if he watched her as she stooped over Howard's body? What if he was hiding behind the Pottery Barn linen-blend drapes, waiting to pop out from his hiding place like a guest at a birthday party?

Surprise! I brought my special blade!

Polly felt a tickle at the base of her bobbed hair, the sensation of breath caressing nape newly exposed by that afternoon's haircut. She spun around, adrenaline sending prickly spikes along her scalp.

The kitchen was empty except for the empty husk that used to be Howard.

Polly padded quietly to the edge of the room. She tried to tread softly, bracing herself for the squeak of a board, the betrayal of delayed maintenance and poor housekeeping.

There was only silence.

Polly stood at the mouth of the doorway and listened for the intruder, head cocked like the dog in the old RCA ads. Beneath the hammering of her heart, beyond the whoosh of blood thundering through her ears, she heard a rattle. Steady. Insistent. Like blinds moved by the breeze against an open window.

Then she realized: the cane in her hand was trembling, rapping against the hardwood floor like a drumstick.

Had her body betrayed her, the tattoo of her cane beating out the code of her location? She lifted the cane and strained to hear. The silence was full. Nearly palpable. The only intruder was the disease that had invaded her nervous system three years earlier.

The scream that had been building at the back of Polly's throat died into a low toneless moan. She turned back toward the kitchen, her already diminished gait shrunken to shuffles by renewed awareness of her vulnerability. Her aloneness. The fact that she no longer knew or understood her own body.

She grabbed the cordless phone from the sideboard and dialed.

Her first call was to the police. Her second was to Constantine.

Chapter 1

Maggie bit her lip and pulled the panties harder. The lace-trimmed nylon caught on something. Maggie gave another yank. She heard the distinctive sound of fabric tearing.

"Umm, yeah, I don't think it goes like that," Valerie said over a pile of camisoles. "I think you've got it backwards. Or maybe sideways. And I don't think Alexa would like how you're manhandling Sheila."

Maggie looked at the mannequin in her hands. "Sheila" was on her head, one leg splayed toward the dressing rooms, the other facing a battery of perfume samplers. There was a bald spot at the top of Sheila's wig from Maggie's efforts at dressing her upside down. A rip ran down the back of the mannequin's leopard print underwear, revealing a shiny swath of plastic buttock.

Feck, Maggie thought, using the Irish-ized F-bomb Pop—and therefore she—always favored. It definitely doesn't go like that.

Maggie was about to flip Sheila onto her side when the phone in her pocket sounded.

"Buehler...Buehler...Buehler..."

The custom ringtone from *Ferris Buehler's Day Off* bleated from the front of Maggie's pants.

Valerie shot Maggie a warning look. "You better not let Alexa catch you on the phone. You know the rules."

Maggie nodded and moved to silence the ringer. She hit the volume key instead.

"BUEHLER....BUEHLER...BUEHLER..." her phone droned.

Valerie's eyebrows disappeared into her hairline. Maggie's cheeks grew hot. She could practically feel her freckles melting together. "I'll just get this over here."

She tucked Sheila under her arm and slunk from the display window, whacking Sheila's head on a *25% Off Storewide!* sign in the process. The mannequin's head fell to the ground and tumbled into a fluff of tulle.

Maggie gave Valerie a weak smile and hastily covered Sheila's decapitated body with hot pink netting. Valerie shook her head and walked away.

Maggie plucked the phone from her pocket and looked at the screen. Constantine. Of course.

She tiptoed behind a rack of bathrobes. "Gus," she whispered into the phone, using the nickname only she was allowed, "I told you we're not supposed to take personal calls at work."

She expected Constantine to lob back a joke, glibly ask about molesting mannequins (a regular event) or peddling unmentionables at Madame Trousseau's House of Lingerie. Instead he simply said, "Does that include emergencies?"

Maggie felt a hand close around her heart.

Emergencies? Was it Pop? Fiona?

She closed her eyes. Calm. She needed calm. "What happened?"

"Howard. He was murdered."

The hand around her heart released then squeezed again. Relief. Guilt. CPR by emotion. Her family was okay, but her boyfriend's wasn't. His aunt's husband had been murdered. Maggie sank down on the edge of the display. "When?"

Constantine blew out a puff of air. She imagined him raking his hand through his dark hair, pulling at his earlobe, going through his usual repertoire of nervous tics. "Around three a.m. My folks are in Europe, so she called me. I tried you at six, but got voicemail."

Maggie had been on her morning run then, a ten-miler over frost-hardened earth, every breath turned ghostly white by the mid-November chill. "I was building miles for that marathon in June." Maggie chewed her lip, picking off the loose skin. "How's Polly holding up?"

"She was basically hysterical." Another puff of air. "I guess it was pretty awful."

"What kind of awful?" Maggie's voice sounded small, even to her own ears. She didn't want awful. Not now. Not anymore. But she had to know.

Constantine paused. Maggie wondered if he was softening the edges of an ugly truth or weighing his thoughts for accuracy. His words appropriately calibrated, he finally said, "Someone broke into the house and slit Howard's throat. Aunt Polly found him."

Maggie's stomach clenched, sending a surge of bile perilously, worryingly, upward. She was transported back to blood and bone and mouths opened in final, silent pleas. Maggie knew all about finding the dead.

She bore down on bile and memory, pushing the fluid down her esophagus and the memories behind the Wall. She'd built the Wall, the secret place at the back of her mind where she corralled uncomfortable feelings, when she was eleven. She fortified it at every opportunity. She knew it was getting crowded back there, that she was quite possibly a hoarder of denial. She shoved that knowledge behind the Wall, too.

"Poor Polly," she said at last.

"She had been sleepwalking and woke up standing over Howard," Constantine continued, "confused about why he was slumped over, not understanding why he was bleeding. It took her awhile to snap out of it."

"Sleepwalking?" Somehow this surprised Maggie. She'd known Polly since she'd met Constantine in middle school. She didn't remember any mention of sleepwalking. Then again, sleep disorders weren't exactly small talk fodder.

"It's been getting worse. She mentioned it last time I was up there."

The guilt returned, keener this time. It had been months since Maggie had seen Polly. Or Pop and Aunt Fiona, for that matter. She'd been logging serious overtime at Madame Trousseau's. Not that her performance was testimony to that.

"Was it a home invasion? Do the police have any suspects? Is Polly okay?"

"Nothing was taken and according to Aunt Polly, 'the police couldn't find their asses with both hands.' She's trying to sound brave, but I don't know…" A pause, the sound of rustling as Constantine once again ran a hand through his hair. "She sounds scared."

That was one word Maggie would never associate with Polly. Brash, maybe. Feisty, definitely. But scared? Fear didn't seem to be part of Polly's emotional vocabulary.

But Maggie knew that murder changed things. Changed a person. Memory bubbled up again, images of blood-streaked tile and a ruined skull seeping around Maggie's mental stoppers. Maggie pushed back the images, harder. She'd deal with what happened last year later. Or never. Whatever.

She realized Constantine was talking. "Sorry?"

"I said she wants me to come up. Us, actually."

Maggie felt a flutter of panic. "Me? Us? Why?"

"Um, maybe because her husband has just been murdered and she needs to be with people she loves?"

"I know, it's just..."

It was just that she had dealt with murder less than a year ago. It was just that the thought of a bad man with a knife made her stomach feel like it was crawling up her throat. It was just that she had already been branded a meddler and didn't need to give the haters any more material.

Maggie would stay home in her nice, boring apartment, thankyouverymuch. Constantine didn't need her for this. Neither did Polly.

"Polly needs you," he said, as if reading her thoughts. "She specifically asked for you. She's not well, you know."

Maggie knew. And she loved Polly. She still wanted a hall pass. "I can't just up and leave, Gus. I have a job. Responsibilities."

Memories to run from. Feelings to avoid.

Constantine was quiet for a moment. Maggie tried to read the silence. She came up with nothing. Maybe she no longer spoke subtext. Finally he sighed. "Okay. I don't want you to get in trouble at work—or ruin your streak as an overachiever. I'll head out this afternoon, give you a call and let you know how things are going." He paused. "I love you, Mags."

"Me, too," she whispered.

She knew her reply was a cheat, a dupe for a declaration of love. She loved Constantine, first as a friend, now as more. Voicing that love would make her feel vulnerable, as if challenging the universe to take it away.

Constantine signed off. Maggie crept from her hiding place behind the rack and returned to the task at hand. Wrestling Sheila into a thong would be a good distraction from her feelings. Her failings. Maybe even Howard's murder.

She knelt down and plucked Sheila's head and body from the tangle of tulle. She jammed the head back onto the mannequin's body, wriggling the plastic cavity onto the flesh-colored nub, one hand spread across the mannequin's nippleless breasts. She turned to see Valerie watching her.

Valerie popped her gum. "Should I give you two some alone time?"

Maggie released Sheila and stood. "Ugh! This is too hard."

Valerie folded her arms across her chest. "Hard? I thought you were some kind of fancy scientist."

Maggie rubbed her neck "Yeah, well. Not anymore."

Valerie studied her for a moment, blew a bubble, evidence of her gum-chewing rebellion. "Why don't you go on break? You look beat and Sheila looks..." She assessed the mannequin. "Hung over. Besides, it's my turn to get the next bra-fitting." Valerie nodded toward a woman hovering near a dressing room, bras dangling from both hands. The woman grinned at Valerie and waved the bras festively. "I love my job, I love my job, I love my job," she muttered as she stomped toward the dressing room.

A break was just what Maggie needed. She pushed through a pink door emblazoned with an illustration of a lingerie-clad woman who looked like a cross between Barbie and Jessica Rabbit and collapsed into a pink director's chair that read *Director of Customer Delight.*

"So much for a career change," she said to the empty break room.

Valerie was right. Maggie had been a fancy scientist. Now? Not so much. Sure, she was still a twenty-something with a Master's Degree, and she'd left Rxcellance of her own accord. That was the official story, anyway.

The truth was a little more complicated. The truth was she thought she could go back to Rxcellance after she'd unearthed the conspiracies, the crimes, the deadly secrets kept by some and suffered by others. The truth was she thought loyalty was worth something. The truth was virtue wasn't its own reward. Not even close.

Rxcellance foundered. Contracts dried up. Revenue plummeted. Layoffs were euphemized into "corporate restructuring." Blame for the downturn was laid not only at the feet of the guilty but the person who had revealed their culpability. Coworkers stopped collaborating. Managers "forgot" to invite her to meetings. Invitations to after-work drinks dried up and blew away with the prairie wind. It was The Great Corporate Freeze Out.

Eventually, Maggie got tired of frostbite.

She sighed and mashed her unruly auburn curls into a messy bun. She had sworn off the corporate grind for good, but she still wanted to be successful—even if it meant effectively merchandising the Naughty or Nice Holiday Lingerie Collection. She was going to rock this job. Right after her break.

Maggie walked over to the communal refrigerator, which stood in the corner of the break room next to a small microwave and a defeated-looking coffee pot. She opened the magnet-plastered refrigerator door and rooted through the maze of expired yogurts and forgotten sandwiches, thinking about her old job and this new turn of events.

Howard Wright had been murdered. It was a terrible tragedy, but as far as Maggie could tell, no great loss for the human race. She'd met Howard a dozen times while visiting Polly and found him to be an obnoxious blowhard who treated his cosmetic surgery practice like a used car lot.

Maggie pulled three slices of pepperoni pizza from behind a four-pack of Greek yogurt. She peeled off the thin plastic casing and sniffed. Even cold, it smelled of sundried tomato, garlic and olive oil. It smelled like Pop.

Maggie shut the fridge and opened wide to take a bite. She stopped. Voices floated to her from the loading dock. No, not voices. Voice. Alexa's, loud and angry.

"Good God, Ada. Can't you do anything right?"

Maggie heard a mumbled reply then Alexa's high-pitched trill: "Speak up! Or can you only speak *español*?"

That got Maggie's attention.

She dropped her pizza slice onto the Saran Wrap and wiped her hands on her pants. She jogged toward the door that separated the employees' lounge and the loading dock and slipped through it. She crept past another illustration of an anthropomorphic lingerie-clad rabbit and peered from behind a pile of cardboard boxes.

Ada stood at the mouth of the dock, sunlight casting her in silhouette. Her head hung down. Her arms dangled limply at her side, the fingers of her right hand worrying the hem of her navy blue button-down. Behind the curtain of brown hair, Maggie could make out twin rivulets of tears streaming down her face. One runaway tributary snaked around her nose and into her mouth.

"You cut right through the fabric!" Alexa screeched. "I told you to never use scissors on the top of the boxes. Now half my inventory is ruined!"

"I think it's only the top item, Miss Alexa," Ada began, "and I'm glad to pay for it."

"Of course you'll pay for it," Alexa snapped. She pawed through the box, plucked out two eviscerated nightgowns and dropped them onto a concrete floor dotted with oil stains. "And anyone can see multiple items are ruined." She slammed the box shut. "God, you are such an idiot."

Maggie clenched her fists. *Stay away from her, Alexa*, she thought. *Go back to your spreadsheets and your graphs, and stay the hell away from her.*

Alexa stooped, her St. John's suit hugging gym-hardened curves, and put her face inches from Ada's. She regarded the younger woman, her mouth twisting from surprise into a self-satisfied sneer. "Are you crying? Are you actually crying?" She grabbed Ada's shoulder and gave it a shake. "The only reason you're here is because my husband owed your mother a favor." She released Ada's arm as if it were diseased. "I'm sure you're both illegal. God, I knew we should never have hired a Mex—"

"Alexa."

Maggie stepped out from behind the boxes.

Alexa turned toward her, the surprise on her face giving way to something else. She recovered. Smiled warmly. "Maggie. I thought you were on the floor."

Maggie crossed her arms. "I was. Then I was in the break room." She bobbed her head in the direction of the open door. "You know, within earshot."

Alexa's smile broadened, capped teeth turned sallow by the jaundice glow of the dock's sulfur lights. She smoothed her chignon. "Yes, well. Ada and I were just having a conversation about how I want the boxes opened. Poor thing has trouble with scissors." She shot Maggie a chummy, conspiratorial look. "You know how it is."

Maggie crossed her arms. "Actually I don't. Maybe you can explain it."

Alexa's mouth hinged open. She had been heavy-handed with her contouring, brown powder cutting a trough through peaches and cream. Alexa closed her mouth and forced the smile to return at significantly lower amperage. "I don't have to explain anything to you. My store, my rules, remember?"

Maggie could feel her pulse pounding in her neck. She wondered if it was visible, a tiny flutter that sent mini-shock waves through her skin. She knew she should stay quiet. She knew she should excuse herself back to the lounge and swallow her feelings of outrage and anger, right along with her pepperoni pizza.

She also knew she couldn't do that.

She was done being the good girl. The silent girl. The girl who tried to take up less space, command less importance.

"I remember," Maggie said quietly. "I just didn't think it included abusing the staff."

Alexa laughed. "Abusing the staff? Please. I was simply—"

"I know what you were doing." Her eyes met Alexa's. "Don't do it again."

A purple hue climbed Alexa's neck like a poisonous vine. "I was warned not to hire you," she hissed. "I was told that you like to put your nose where it doesn't belong, but I brought you on board because I'm kind, compassionate. Same reason I hired Ada." She put a motherly arm around Ada's shoulder. Ada moved away. Alexa swallowed her collagened lips. "Looks like my kindness was misguided."

Alexa nodded as if agreeing with herself, the idea of a virtuous benefactor wronged by an evil employee picking up steam. "But I won't have someone take advantage of my kindness, and I won't stand for insubordination." She straightened her back. "You're fired."

Maggie was surprised that she was surprised. What exactly had she expected? She had called Alexa on her cruelty and bullying and left her no room for dignity.

Not that Alexa deserved any.

The room had grown quiet. Maggie could hear the tick-tick-tick of cooling truck engines. Smell the heavy floral of the company's signature scent rolling off Alexa in waves. Maggie turned toward the break room, walking with purpose, her head held high.

"On the other hand..." Alexa called after her silkily.

Maggie stopped, pivoted. Alexa had one manicured hand on her hip, the other nestled beneath her chin in a parody of The Thinker. "I might reconsider if you apologize."

"You're saying I can have my job back if I apologize?"

Alexa spread her arms in a gesture of indulgence. "I'm not unreasonable."

Maggie looked at Ada who was studying the oil-stained floor as if it were a Rorschach test. Her fingers were back at the hem of her shirt. She had folded the corner into a tight little triangle. Denim origami.

Maggie took a deep breath. "I'm sorry," she said. A self-satisfied smile crawled across Alexa's face. "I'm sorry you're such a heartless, racist bitch."

The smile vanished. The poisonous purple returned, tendrils snaking down Alexa's chest. "You...you..." she sputtered.

"I...am leaving."

Maggie put an arm around Ada and gave her a quick squeeze, then she strode to the break room and pushed the door open. There was a small gust of wind as it slammed behind her with a gratifying thud.

Maggie stood there a moment, her heart pounding, her breath ragged, her mind spinning.

No more mannequin-wrestling. No more Alexa. No more excuses to get out of helping Polly pick up the shards of her shattered life.

Maggie was free.

She was also terrified.

Chapter 2

Maggie coasted into the driveway. The Studebaker was running on fumes. That sort of thing happened when you lived paycheck to paycheck and the next one had RSVP'd "no" to your bank account.

She put the column gearshift into Park and wiped an imaginary speck of dust from the Studebaker's dashboard. "You would've done the same thing," she told the car as she patted its cream-colored vinyl. "This aggression will not stand," she said, quoting *The Big Lebowski*.

As much as she wanted to pretend away Polly's pain, to avoid the grief she knew would cling to her like the stench of death, she knew coming to her aid was the right thing to do. Getting fired just made doing the right thing easier. No need to check the work calendar. No need to ask for days off. No need to trade hours.

Maggie tried to think of other positives of losing a job she'd had for five months, of once again having no professional pursuit to delineate not only her time but her identity.

She'd have to come back to that.

Maggie climbed out of the car and shouldered the turquoise overnight bag Aunt Fiona had given her for graduation. It was the sort of gift a mother would give, but Maggie's mother had long passed on, leaving Fiona to fill her shoes—or in her mother's case, her ballet flats.

Maggie walked up the flagstone path to the home of Camille Walsh, a friend who'd invited Polly to stay with her after Howard's murder. She'd gotten the address from Constantine, telling him she was able to negotiate some time off work. She didn't mention they wouldn't need her back in approximately...ever.

Maggie eyed the house's exterior. Unlike the Wright residence, an architectural monstrosity fronted by dual gold columns, artificially aged brick and a large turret that would look more at home on a Scottish castle than a suburban McMansion, the Walsh home was subdued and tasteful with a gabled roof, exposed rafters and four white-trimmed windows. Classic midcentury bungalow versus the Wrights' Late American Tacky.

Maggie rang the bell and stared at the wood paneled door, which had been painted a cheerful red. Overhead, clouds trudged across a leaden sky. A gust of wind terrorized an oak tree that flanked the porch, shaking bone-dry leaves from branches, leaving it near-naked like the others in the yard. Maggie pulled her down coat around her and stamped her feet. Cold came early in this part of the Midwest and outstayed its welcome. It wasn't officially winter and Maggie was already over it.

The door slid open, revealing a rectangle of cheek and eye. A silver brow sprang up and the door flew open. "You must be Maggie!" The woman shook Maggie's hand vigorously as she pulled her into the foyer. "I'm Camille Walsh. Please come in."

The woman was in her early sixties, tall and round-hipped with gray hair arranged in a smart pixie cut. Her face was free of makeup, with ruddy cheeks and lips bracketed by deep smile lines. She bestowed a wrinkle-generating grin on Maggie. "I'm so glad you could make it. Polly has spoken very highly of you."

Maggie felt a flush of pleasure. "Well, Polly's an amazing lady. And so are you for taking her in."

Camille whisked the bag from Maggie's hand and set it on a whitewashed wooden bench occupied by a trio of ceramic frogs dressed in evening wear. "Well what was she going to do, go to a *hotel*?" She said the last word like some might say hemorrhoid. "When I heard what happened to Howard—I was one of the first people she called, you know—I insisted she come stay with me. She was already terrified, having found him..." She opened and closed her mouth, auditioning potential descriptions. "*That way*. Then suddenly..." She pantomimed a magician's flourish, "she's homeless, her house transformed into a crime scene. This is what friends are for."

"You have a beautiful home," Maggie said, taking in the polished wood floor, the picture-decked walls, the cozy living room complete with crackling fire and *God Bless This Home* pillows. "Thank you for opening it to Polly. To all of us."

Camille touched her arm. "I know what it's like to lose someone, to be beside yourself with grief. Besides, this old house could use some company." Camille crooked her finger then turned on her heel. "Right this way."

Maggie followed her down a narrow hallway, her legs trying to match her hostess's long strides, which were accompanied by the rasp of fabric as Camille's yoga pants rubbed between her thighs. "Polly's in the kitchen." She paused before a door that looked like it belonged on the set of a TV sitcom. "Actually, everyone is."

Maggie stopped. "Everyone?"

Camille pushed the door open.

The kitchen was large, white, and illuminated by Edison-bulb pendants and sunlight that streamed through a large window over the sink. The room had been updated with professional grade appliances—a Sub-Zero refrigerator that looked more sculpture than food storage, dual Viking wall ovens, a Thor gas cooktop—yet maintained its midcentury charm with whitewashed cabinets, blonde-wood trim and an array of copper cookware that hung from the ceiling like stalactites.

A small group sat at a large white table, a platter of pastries between them. They swung their heads in unison to look at Maggie. Her eyes landed on Constantine and Polly before she spotted one man in a suit and another in khakis and a sports jacket.

She recognized the latter as the unofficial uniform of a plainclothes police officer. She'd had experience with cops. None of it good.

Before Maggie could imagine who these men were and why they were there, Constantine sprang from his ladder-back chair. He was at Maggie's side in two steps, encircling her in his arms. "Mags! I'm so glad you were able to get time off work."

Maggie hugged him back. "Uh huh." She licked her lips. Her tongue suddenly felt too big for her mouth. "I'm off for a while."

A long, long while.

He kissed her on the cheek, his five o'clock shadow scuffing her skin. "Come sit down. We're almost done."

Maggie skirted the table toward the small woman nestled against the wall. Polly Wright, née Apollonia Papadopoulos, looked both regal and brittle in a purple velour jumpsuit. Her bright red bob was pinned to the side with a bejeweled clip, her brown eyes rimmed in amethyst liner. She looked older than her sixty-eight years and smaller than the last time Maggie had seen her, as if shrunken by the weight of time and the toll of her husband's murder. Tragedy had a way of diminishing body and soul.

Maggie gently hugged her narrow shoulders. "I'm so sorry about Howard."

Polly's eyes, which had always shone with mischievous intelligence, now shimmered with tears. She gave Maggie a sad smile that puckered the corners of her lips. "Thank you, dear. It's been...." The smile faltered and she put a hand to her mouth. "It's been difficult."

Maggie's heart ached. Polly had always been the spirit of positivity, a quick-witted Pollyanna who spoke her mind and knighted strangers as good eggs within moments of meeting them. Parkinson's had sapped her physical strength, but not her emotional fortitude. Perhaps the violence of Howard's death changed that, her spirit ending with Howard's life.

The man in the suit cleared his throat. Polly turned toward him and dabbed her eyes with a tissue dispensed from the bodice of her jumpsuit. "Where are my manners? Maggie O'Malley, this is...this is..." She stopped and frowned.

"Sam Graham," the suit answered, half rising. He pressed a hand that felt like a bundle of cold twigs into Maggie's hand. "Attorney at law."

A flicker of alarm eclipsed momentary amusement at the man's rhyming name. An attorney. And cops. Maggie wondered what they were "almost done" doing.

Graham read the concern on her face. "I'm a family attorney. I came to go over some papers with Polly when the detectives dropped by." He gestured toward the khaki'd man at the end of the table. "Maggie O'Malley, Detective Jeff Greeley."

Maggie extended her hand. "Detective."

Greeley was small with a shaved head and wiry arms perpetually flexed like the *He-Man Masters of the Universe* action figure Constantine kept on his desk. Greeley frowned.

"Maggie O'Malley. Weren't you in the news? Some kind of crime in Collinsburg?"

Maggie's hand floated in the air a moment before she realized that Greeley wasn't going to take it. She reeled it in and pretended to smooth her hair. "I helped uncover a series of murders."

Greeley crossed his arms in front of his narrow chest. "Right. Amateur crime-solver. How...cute." Maggie felt her cheeks flame and opened her mouth to retort when Greeley continued. "I'm sure some people are impressed by your sleuthing skills, but we find that sort of 'help' an impediment." He looked pleased with himself for plucking the word from his internal thesaurus. "I hope you'll let us do our job. We are the professionals, after all."

Maggie began to finish the reply she'd begun, but cut herself off when another similarly clad man entered the room.

"Thanks for letting me wash up, ma'am," he said to Camille. "Those sticky buns sure are... sticky."

The man spotted Maggie and gaped. She did the same. She took in his sandy blond hair, the spray of light brown freckles that she had once thought was a good complement for her tawny ones. He'd gotten more muscular since the last time she'd seen him, and now he wore a *Magnum, P.I.* mustache. Other than that, he hadn't changed a bit.

He thawed first. "Maggie?"

"Austin." Her voice squeaked. She cleared her throat. "It's great to see you."

They moved awkwardly toward each other. Maggie extended her hand. Austin went in for the hug. Her arms hung by her side like Frankenstein's monster while he clinched.

Austin released her and beamed. "You look doggone terrific, Maggie," he drawled. "Pretty as a picture. What's it been? Two years?"

"Three."

Greeley cleared his throat. "You two know each other?"

Austin's grin broadened. "Sure do."

Maggie prayed he wouldn't add, "In the Biblical way."

"Let's save the reunion for another time, shall we?" Greeley said.

Austin, still grinning, made his way to his seat. Maggie could feel Constantine looking at her, his eyes blinking an optical semaphore: *What the hell was that about?* She'd deal with that later.

"As I was saying," Greeley looked at the assembled group, "we wanted to let Mrs. Wright know about a new development."

Polly leaned forward, purple jumpsuit brushing the table. "You found out who did this? Thank God."

Greeley held up his hand, traffic cop-style. "No, but we did come across some information we thought you could shed some light on."

"Me? What is it?"

Greeley jabbed a hand into his breast pocket and drew out a small notebook. He paged through then stopped, giving Polly a hard look. "We discovered that your husband booked a one-way ticket to Barbados. Do you know anything about that?"

Polly's brow knitted. "Barbados? I don't even know where that is."

"It's a small island nation in the southern Caribbean," Austin volunteered, all but raising his hand. "It also has the oldest rum factory in the world."

Greeley stared at him. Austin slouched and took another sticky bun.

"Do you know why your husband would travel there?" Greeley

asked. "More specifically, why he would book a single one-way ticket, without you—or your knowledge?"

It was Polly's turn to redden. "My husband didn't always consult me on his decisions. Howard was very independent."

"Do you think he was meeting someone there?" Greeley pressed. "A colleague? A friend...or something more?"

Polly's lips constricted, wrinkles radiating toward her nose. She drew herself up and looked Greeley in the eye. "Do you have any actual leads, Detective, or just innuendos?"

It was a glimpse of pre-murder Polly. Gutsy. Bold. Unafraid. Maggie was glad to see a flash of the old Polly fire.

"We're merely asking routine questions," Greeley said stiffly.

"And this routine is called 'The Spouse Did It'?"

There seemed to be an intake of air as everyone in the room drew in a silent gasp.

"Did Uncle Howard have any enemies?" Maggie asked, desperate to change the trajectory of the conversation. "Anyone who wished him ill?"

"Yes," Polly nodded. "Howard was a bit of an ass."

Graham coughed. "What Mrs. Wright is trying to say is that Mr. Wright had a big personality that rubbed some people the wrong way."

"More like all people," Polly mumbled.

Graham coughed louder then began hacking in earnest. His barking whoops reminded Maggie of the sea lion section of the zoo during mating season. Camille pushed a glass of water toward him.

Greeley picked up a sticky bun, fondled it, then returned it. Maggie made a mental note of the sweet roll's location so she could avoid it. "I thought Howard was a celebrity. TV commercials. Billboards. Newspaper ads," he said.

Maggie thought of Howard's ad campaigns. Taut and shiny from dipping into his cosmetic surgery coffers, Howard starred in all of his ads, trotting out before-and-after photos, offering deep discounts, treating surgery like as-seen-on-TV phenomena like binocular sunglasses and Ginsu knives.

"Howie certainly thought so," Polly said. "But he did have enemies."

"Like who?" Greeley's pen hovered over the pad, taxiing for takeoff.

"Let's see..." The topic of Howard's foes seemed to improve Polly's mood. "There's Deirdre Hart, the beauty queen. She's suing Howard for a botched facelift. Then there are the other cosmetic surgeons in town, always complaining about his ads and the way he undercuts them on price. Oh, and Kenny Rogers."

Maggie did a double-take. "Did you say Kenny Rogers?"

She tried to imagine The Gambler sneaking into the Wright residence. Did he bring his guitar? Warm up with a little "Islands in the Stream"? Ask Howard to join him in one final duet?

"Not that one, dear. Kenneth Rogers, MD, Howard's practice partner. They had a falling out. Over what, I've no idea." She paused for a moment. "I've known Kenny for a long time. I can't imagine him doing anything like this." She looked down at her hands. "But who knows what anyone is capable of?"

Maggie had more than a little experience trusting the wrong people.

Greeley stood and hitched up his pants with his thumbs. "We've been over all of this before, and we plan on interviewing these 'enemies.'" Maggie could hear the air-quotes. "You're sure you don't know anything about the ticket to Barbados?"

Polly shook her head. "Nothing."

"Uh-huh." Greeley underlined something in his notebook with gusto. "And you don't remember anything that happened before you found Howard? No strange noises? No cries for help?"

Polly folded her hands as if beseeching the patron saint of annoying questions. "Like I told you before, I was sleepwalking. Dreaming. About red fabric and...and..." She closed her eyes then opened them and shrugged. "I don't remember. When I woke up, Howard was dead."

Greeley made another note in the small book and pocketed it. "Right. Sleepwalking." He smirked at Austin. "That's not one we hear very often, is it?"

Austin shook his head vigorously. "No, sir. It sure isn't."

Constantine got to his feet and came around behind Polly, his face hard. "My aunt is getting tired. Is there anything else?"

"Anything else," Greeley repeated, stroking his mustache. Facial hair seemed to be station-issued in Hollow Pine. "No, there's nothing else other than figuring out why there was no sign of forced entry or why your aunt was covered in her husband's blood when the paramedics arrived."

Constantine's face turned to stone. "My aunt was covered in blood because she was trying to help her husband. And there's no 'sign' of forced entry because you haven't found it yet."

A little muscle in Greeley's jaw twitched. Maggie could almost see him counting silently to 10. "Well, that remains to be seen, Mr. Papaya."

"Papadopoulos."

Greeley showed his teeth, picket fence straight bisected by a broken toothpick gnawed to fraying. How had she not noticed that before? "Right. Anyway, we'll continue our investigation and get to the bottom of this."

He looked meaningfully at Polly then poked out his chest and plunked a hat on his head. Austin followed suit in a law enforcement monkey-see-monkey-do. "Thanks for your time, Mrs. Wright. Please let us know if you remember anything. We'll see ourselves out."

The men disappeared into the hall. Maggie heard the front door swing open and click shut.

Polly seemed to deflate in her chair, her strength dissolving like snow beneath a steady drumbeat of rain.

"Are you all right?" Maggie asked.

"Yes. No." Polly dropped her head into her hands and began to cry.

Maggie and Constantine placed hands on her shaking shoulders. Camille rose from the table, crossed to the counter beside the broad farm sink and rustled around in a bread garage. She returned with a miniature loaf of pumpkin bread.

For some, baked goods were the universal balm for whatever the affliction. Didn't get asked to the school dance? Skipped over for a promotion? Husband murdered? Have a cookie.

Camille divided the loaf into quarters then placed it on a saucer before Polly. "It's your favorite. No dairy, extra nutmeg, made just the way you like." She nudged the plate closer to Polly. "You need to keep up your strength. You know what happens when you don't eat."

Polly nodded and dutifully broke off a piece of bread. She popped the morsel into her mouth. The caramelized edges turned her lips the color of brown sugar. She brushed her mouth. "It's not just Howard," she said. "It's everything. The house. The questions. The police who seem more interested in harassing me than finding Howard's killer. I'm not surprised about Jeff Greeley. He's hated me ever since—" She stopped, shook her head. "I'm under a cloud of suspicion. No matter where I go or what I do, I can't help but feel that a storm is coming."

Chapter 3

Polly begged off the rest of the evening, blaming fatigue that seemed to radiate from her small frame. Graham followed suit, claiming a dinner date with his wife. Camille saw her guests to the door and checked her watch.

"Time for me to go, too." She began placing pastries in Ziploc bags. "I'm working at Running Home tonight. They used to keep me in my tower writing grants and coordinating services, but I've been doing more outreach lately." She pulled deli meats from the fridge and stacked them on a large oval plate on the sideboard. "You wouldn't think Hollow Pine has big city problems like teen runaways, but we do. Heartache isn't confined to a zip code."

She arranged two flaky loaves of bread and a cityscape of condiments next to the meat, then ordered Maggie and Constantine to enjoy the spread before sailing out the door in a red wool coat and matching tam. Mary Tyler Moore for the retirement community crowd.

The house tomb-quiet, Maggie and Constantine looked at each other. "Well, that wasn't what I was expecting," Constantine said.

"Which part—Aunt Polly sassing the detectives or their obvious interest in her?"

"The detectives' interest. The sassing didn't surprise me. Aunt Polly's always been outspoken."

Maggie thought of her own exchange with Alexa. Outspoken didn't always pay off.

"What do you think Polly meant about Detective Greeley hating her?"

Constantine shook his head. "No idea."

Maggie frowned. "Hate or not, I can see why she'd ping their antennae. Howard was Aunt Polly's fourth husband and they'd only been married, what, a few years? Plus he's filthy rich. Plus-plus she woke up standing over him covered in his blood after a sleepwalking episode."

Constantine grabbed the carafe from Camille's coffeemaker and filled Maggie's cup then his own. Neither feared insomnia from the coffee. They figured their bloodstreams were half caffeine anyway. "Don't forget about the one-way ticket to Barbados." He opened Camille's refrigerator, poked his head inside, came up with heavy cream. He handed the pint to Maggie. "Whether it was an innocent excursion or a rendezvous with a recently boob-jobbed mistress, it doesn't sound good. None of it does."

He was right. The spouse was almost always the first suspect in a murder, and the strange sleepwalking episode certainly didn't buy her any brownie points—or alibis. But Polly? Sweet, gentle, zany Polly, maker of crafts for the church bazaar? The idea was ludicrous.

"What's the deal with the other cop?" Constantine asked, cutting his eyes from his coffee cup to Maggie's face and back again. "The one who looked like Deputy Dog?"

Maggie dosed her coffee with cream until it turned white, returned the cream to the fridge and took a sip. "He does not look like Deputy Dog. And there's no 'deal.' We just used to be..." She took another sip of coffee. "...friends."

Understanding dawned on Constantine's face. "Oh my God. That's Austin Tacious, the rodeo clown!"

"Rodeo *cowboy*. And I don't know why you continue to call him that."

"You know...ostentatious...Austin Tacious? He bedazzled his jeans and wore a belt buckle bigger than his head? Well, that's how I imagined it, anyway."

"He didn't and he has a real name: Austin Reynolds."

"Reynolds. Like Burt. How macho-ly fitting. What's he doing in Hollow Pine, anyway? I thought he fled the state after you two broke up."

"He transferred to the police academy. His mom lives in Hollow Pine, which is why he probably moved here. Besides, it's a good thing he's on this case. We parted on good terms. He could be an ally."

Maggie relinquished her coffee and began bundling Camille's sandwich makings back into their receptacles. The day's events had killed her appetite.

Constantine followed her cue, clearing plates. "He's an ally only if he's still in love with you. Which, of course, he is." He loaded a serving piece adorned with bonneted fowl into the dishwasher and stuffed his hands in his pockets.

Maggie drew him into a hug, tucking her head beneath a horizontal divot on his chin created when a pebble cratered his flesh during a mountain bike accident. She thought it looked like a tiny mouth. "Even if he is still in love with me, which he isn't, I'm taken, remember?"

"I remember. I just hope he does."

Maggie scooted from beneath his arms and grabbed a yellow gingham dishcloth from beside the faucet. She ran it under warm water then dragged it over the counters like a mini-Zamboni that dispensed an icy glow. "Once the cops start following other leads, they'll realize their suspicions of Polly are insane. People sleepwalk. That doesn't make them murderers."

Constantine tilted his hand in a maybe-yes-maybe-no. "Not typically, but murderous sleepwalking isn't completely unheard of. Don't you remember that guy who killed his wife while they were camping? He claimed he was dreaming about fighting some guys and woke up with a strangled wife."

"'Claimed'? You sound like Detective Greeley."

"Well, you've got to admit the sleepwalking thing does sound a little incredible."

Maggie placed the dishcloth beside the sink and gave him a long look. "You're not suggesting that Aunt Polly is making it up."

"God no." Constantine looked appalled at the suggestion. "I'm just saying I see where the cops are coming from. The spouse is always the first suspect. Or the person who finds the body. Or the person with blood all over him—or in this case, her. Aunt Polly has all three, not to mention a sleepwalking problem. Have you seen that movie *Sleepwalk with Me*? People do crazy shit in their sleep. Eliminating her as a suspect—or not— is their first order of business. At least that's how they do it on *Law & Order*."

Some would take Constantine's comments—the glib remarks, the easy jokes—as a sign of flippancy. Insensitivity. Shallowness. Maggie knew better. She knew that he had his own Wall. His just happened to be made of gallows humor and witty repartee.

"I studied Parkinson's in school," Maggie said. "If I remember correctly, sleepwalking can be a symptom. I'll have to look it up."

Constantine stretched and checked his watch, a bright blue vintage Swatch with geometric patterns. "Research tomorrow, sleep now. The bad news is that we're in separate rooms. The good news is that we both have twin beds, which should be both nostalgic and chiropractic."

They turned off the kitchen light and walked down the hall to the foyer. Constantine hoisted Maggie's overnight bag. "Packing light, as usual. I hope you brought your Little Bo Peep outfit."

"Is that a real question or are you just quoting *Fletch*?"

He wriggled his eyebrows. "Yes."

She followed Constantine as he trudged up the staircase, a fat ribbon of green carpeted steps banked by a wall of memorabilia documenting Camille's adventures, accomplishments and interests.

A photograph of the Parthenon.

A handmade thank-you card signed by a dozen hands.

A race number declaring her third in her age group in the town's annual *I Thought They Said Rum* 5K.

To Maggie, there was more hominess in this tiny slice of Camille's house than all of the Wright residence with its crystal chandeliers, marble floors and men's club furniture. Despite the mural of Apollo that Howard had commissioned for Polly's birthday, the Wright home was 100% Howard. Maggie wondered if Polly saw it that way.

Constantine stepped onto the landing, strode down the hall and opened the first door on the left. "Your chamber, my lady."

Maggie stepped inside. The room was small and white, crowned by painted tongue-and-groove pine that came together in a triangle over a twin bed. A Jetsons-esque light dangled from the apex of the pitched ceiling, creating an ideal theatre for a shadow puppet artiste. The small bed was bordered by twin wooden tables, each hatted by a white doily.

Maggie spotted a small cage on the dressing table. She looked at Constantine. "Seriously?"

"What?" He set Maggie's bag on a blue braided rug and walked over to the cage. He removed what looked like a giant cream-colored dust bunny. "You know Miss Vanilla goes everywhere with me." He put the hamster up to his face and she twitched her nose. "Besides, I thought you'd come to realize the futility of resisting her adorableness."

Maggie felt a smile tugging at her lips. Despite her best efforts, she loved the blond rodent with the stripper name. "Yes, yes, she's very cute. But she's not staying in my room."

Constantine feigned shock. "Perish the thought. I was just giving her a change of scenery. She has quite the eye for home décor."

"Of course she does."

Constantine returned Miss Vanilla to her mini condominium, and Maggie walked to the window. She looked out into the night. The large oak, now completely denuded, stood sentry beside the window, blocking her view of everything except a patch of pin-neat yard. Maggie tried to peer around the tree to get a better view of the property, but could see nothing through the jumble of branches, one of which seemed to be giving her the finger.

"What are you looking at?"

"Just trying to get the lay of the land." She kicked off her shoes and fell onto the bed. "But suddenly, all I want to see is the back of my eyelids."

Constantine vaulted himself onto the bed, creating a mattress tsunami. "Me, too. This whole thing has been..."

"Exhausting," Maggie finished.

Constantine rolled over and gave Maggie a lingering kiss. She could feel the heat behind his lips, in the way his arms snaked around her body and pulled her closer, and she responded in kind. When she opened her eyes, she saw that he was watching her. "You get more beautiful every day. I'm not sure how you're doing it, but my bet is a painting of yourself aging hideously beneath your bed. And I'm surprisingly okay with that." He brushed his lips against hers. "I'd better head to my room. I get the feeling that canoodling is strictly prohibited chez Walsh."

He got to his feet and snagged Miss Vanilla's cage from its perch atop the kidney-shaped dressing table. "I'll be right next door," he said as he slipped through the door, "thinking impure thoughts." Then he disappeared into the amber glow of the dimly lit hallway.

Maggie closed her eyes. She could feel sleep waiting for her, the oblivion of unconsciousness biding its time until her eyes closed and her breathing deepened. But something else was waiting at the periphery of her awareness, too. She could almost feel it sliding through her gray matter, playing hide and seek among the whirls and folds of her brain.

Anxiety wanted a play date.

Maggie took a deep breath, a respiratory talisman against the power of dread. But its tentacles had already snaked through her mind and body. With every breath, they tightened their stranglehold around her heart.

She was worried. About the loss of her job. About revealing it to Constantine. About Polly's health. About the police's—scratch that, the detectives'—interest in a woman she'd grown to love and admire.

Maggie sat up and swung her legs off the bed, burying her head in her hands, hair tumbling over knuckles. Polly. Poor Polly.

Polly was more than her boyfriend's aunt. In the time Maggie had known her, Polly had become the woman who fit the mother-shaped hole in her life. Sharing confidences. Giving advice. Telling her how to keep her energy from flagging and her sweaters from pilling. Her own Aunt Fiona had filled that role when she was younger, but things had changed over the last year. Maybe because Maggie had changed, too.

True, Maggie hadn't visited Polly lately. She'd let work overshadow her life, distract her from what was important. But she was here now.

She thought of the sleepwalking, of the illness that had overtaken not just Polly's body but her life. She rose from the bed and pulled a slim laptop from her overnight bag. She logged onto the internet with the Wi-Fi password Camille had left on the dresser and began pulling up journal articles about Parkinson's disease.

It was grim reading.

Like cancer, the possibility of a cure had long tantalized researchers, as if the key to unlocking this disease had been misplaced, along with a favorite pair of sunglasses.

Two things were relevant:

1. Sleepwalking was sometimes associated with Parkinson's disease.
2. Various medications, even those not used to treat the condition, could transform typical sleepers into chronic somnambulists.

Bottom line: it was more than possible that Polly had gotten a sleepwalking double whammy, one from her medical condition, the other from her medication.

Maggie would talk with Polly in the morning, get some details about her condition, ask about her medications. Together they could unravel the mystery of her nighttime wanderings. Maybe even convince the police that she wasn't faking or driven to work out her guilt through sleepwalking like some modern-day Lady Macbeth trying to wash the blood from her hands. Eyes open, senses shut.

Maggie bookmarked pages about Parkinson's symptoms and drug-induced sleepwalking and closed her laptop. She kicked off her black pants and slipped out of her navy blouse, a sartorial molting of her Madame Trousseau uniform.

Maggie stepped into her green flannel pajamas, a Christmas gift from Aunt Polly last year, and gave her teeth a cursory brush. Then she fell into bed and tucked the quilt beneath her chin.

She wasn't sure how long she'd been asleep when she became

aware of another presence in the room.

What had awoken her? Had it been the whisper of footsteps across the deep-pile carpet? An almost imperceptible shift of wind, the proverbial flutter of butterfly wings creating a micro torrent that moved across the wedge of forehead peeking above the blankets? Or maybe it was a shadow that danced across the wall, the window, her lids, as if trying to outrun its owner?

Maggie would never know.

She simply felt her heart in her throat, pounding as if trying to beat its way through her skin, and opened her eyes wide.

The room had been full dark when she had crawled into her thicket of blankets, the blackness almost tangible the moment she had turned off the bedside light. Now the moon had risen. Fingers of yellow light pushed through the window, tinting the inky gloom with sepia warmth.

Maggie saw a disembodied face peering over her. Wide, unseeing eyes locked onto her own, and in the half-light Maggie could see lips moving as low garbled sounds tumbled out.

Maggie felt a glimmer of recognition.

"Aunt Polly?"

Polly's mouth continued to work, a nonsense monologue full of sound and fury, signifying nothing.

It was a *Macbeth* kind of night.

Maggie reached out and touched Polly's hand. Polly recoiled as if bitten by a snake and the muttering grew louder. Maggie squinted at the shadowed face above her. Polly's eyes were unblinking and unfocused as if she were in a trance. And in a way she was.

Polly was sleepwalking.

Maggie tried to remember the sleepwalking protocol. Never wake a sleepwalker? Always wake a sleepwalker? This time of night, she barely knew her own name, let alone conventional wisdom on parasomnias.

Just as she began to kick off the blankets, set on guiding Polly back to bed (she was pretty sure that sounded right), Polly turned around and shuffled slowly from the room, pulling the door half-closed behind her.

Maggie fell against the pillow and willed her heart to slow. She felt dizzy and vaguely nauseated by the steady stream of adrenaline singing through her veins.

Now she'd seen Polly sleepwalking firsthand. That was a good thing, right? She could observe her behavior and perhaps home in on its origin—and a solution.

Maggie folded the pillow in half and turned onto her side. She just needed to let the adrenaline abate, to invite sleep for an encore.

As her eyelids slid shut once again, she noticed a glint from across the room. She couldn't be certain, but she felt as if Polly were watching her through the crack of the door.

Chapter 4

Maggie awoke to the music of clanging pots and the aroma of bacon. She pulled on her skinny jeans, which seemed skinnier in the calves from a recent spate of weight training, shimmied into an oversized black sweater, then dragged a comb through her hair before bounding downstairs.

Constantine and Camille were seated at the table with a pot of coffee and a tray of pastries. It was a shrunken facsimile of yesterday's scene with one exception: the kitchen was a disaster.

Cupboards had been thrown open. Pots and pans were strewn about the counter. A lonely box of macaroni and cheese lay supine on the counter, its powdery contents dusting the surface Maggie had cleaned the night before.

"What the—?" Maggie began.

Camille offered a weak smile. "Looks like a tornado went through here, doesn't it? I started cleaning up then decided to switch gears and make breakfast." She slipped a bite of Danish between her lips.

Maggie's eyes roved the kitchen. The mess had spread like a rash across every counter and onto the floor. "What happened?"

Constantine rose, grabbed a mug from one of the open cabinets and filled it with coffee. He handed it to Maggie. "Polly, that's what happened."

Polly's nighttime visit to her room leapt to Maggie's mind. The vacant eyes. The incoherent mumbling. The face that seemed to hang like a small planet above her own.

Polly's sleepwalking excursions had taken her beyond Maggie's room.

Camille moved to the stove to turn the bacon. "Sometimes she'll just wander around from room to room. Other times..." she indicated the disaster area that had become her kitchen. "She does this."

Maggie looked at a sleeve of spaghetti pressed obscenely against a vial of olive oil. "She cooks?"

"Cooks, folds laundry, eats popsicles, you name it." Camille began transferring the bacon to a paper towel. "With mixed success."

"How long has this been going on?" Maggie asked.

Camille tilted her head. "Well, I haven't known Polly all that long. We met at church after I moved to Hollow Pine, maybe a year and a half ago, or so. The church is a supporter of Running Home." She shrugged. "All I can tell you is that in the two nights she's been here, she's walked in her sleep. The rest I've gathered from talking to her."

"She wandered into my room last night," Maggie said. "I woke up with her staring down at me. It was a little unnerving."

By "unnerving" she meant creepy. And by "a little" she meant a lot. Maggie decided to keep those tidbits to herself.

Camille loaded a plate with bacon and poached eggs and handed it to Maggie. "We studied parasomnias when I was an undergrad. The stress she's been under since Howard's murder can't be helping, especially considering what today is."

The unspoken shimmered in the air. Howard's funeral.

They were all quiet for a moment, as if the memorial deserved its own moment of silence.

Maggie had been dreading the service since she'd learned of Howard's murder. She had sworn off funerals after attending her mother's when she was twelve. She couldn't stomach the pitying looks, the hand-patting, the relentless procession of casseroles and it's-all-part-of-God's-plans.

Maggie didn't know God's plan, but was pretty sure it didn't include tuna and cheese topped with crumbled crackers.

Of course, all that didn't matter. Polly needed her, so she'd go, standing beside her friend like some kind of macabre bridesmaid. It would be the second time in as many years that she'd been such an attendant.

"How has Polly been handling the stress?" Constantine asked.

Camille hesitated. "She hasn't been herself. Then again, she hasn't been herself for a while. She's been forgetful, confused. Maybe even a little paranoid. It's worse when she doesn't eat or is late in taking her meds."

"Are you talking about me?"

Polly stood in the doorway. She was sheathed in a billowy black dress, her bright red hair tucked beneath a black birdcage hat with a small veil. Despite her heavily powdered face, a blue smudge bloomed beneath each eye. Even exhaustion had a fingerprint.

Camille's voice died and her face flushed with the guilt they all felt. How much had Polly heard?

"Aunt Polly!" Constantine rushed to take her elbow.

She shook him off. "I can get to my seat under my own steam, thank you." She made her way to the chair at the back of the table, orthopedic shoes scuffing against tile. "I may be old, but I'm not dead." She stopped short. Maggie thought she was contemplating her choice of words on the day of Howard's funeral then noticed that Polly was looking at the disaster that was Camille's kitchen. "Did I do this?" she asked.

The three of them nodded. Polly's face collapsed. "Looks like I've caused a lot of work."

They all leapt to reassure her, clucking about how it looked worse than it was and how easy it would be to clean. Polly accordioned her small frame into her chair and gazed at the debris field on the counter. Perhaps she'd forgotten the conversation she had interrupted. Perhaps she hadn't heard it at all.

Camille bustled about the kitchen preparing a plate for Polly. Her head vanished inside her giant refrigerator and reemerged with a victorious smile. She positioned a Lilliputian Bundt cake on the yellow placemat before Polly. "One of your favorites. It even has blueberries."

Polly nodded her thanks then slumped miserably in her chair. She assessed the room's damage. "I never used to do this."

"Sleepwalk?" Maggie asked.

Polly shook her head. "No, I've always been a sleepwalker, but not every night, and not wreaking havoc like this." She watched Camille as she nestled a fork against the cake and pushed it closer. "Obviously, my sleepwalking has gotten worse over the past few months. Howard used to tease me, trying to make me guess what I did and what I said." She stabbed the treat, brought a quivering forkful to her mouth, chewed on memory as well her food. "I only know what Howard told me. I could never be sure whether he was telling the truth or just gaslighting me." She laughed shrilly. Camille exchanged a look with Maggie.

Maggie sat beside Polly. "I've been doing some research. Some people with Parkinson's disease have problems with sleepwalking, and it can worsen with time."

Polly pursed her lips. "So I can thank Parkinson's for this, too?"

Red spots had appeared on her cheeks. "It's truly the disease that keeps on giving."

"It could be Parkinson's related, or it could also be caused by medications you're taking. Or both. Are you taking anything new or increasing your dosage?"

Polly thought for a moment. "No, just the Sinemet I started when my symptoms showed up, and that's stayed the same." She struggled to her feet and leaned heavily on her cane. "I do have to pick up a refill tomorrow. Maybe you could come along, speak to the pharmacist. You can put your heads together, figure out what's making my sleepwalking worse." She smiled bravely. Her lips turned flaccid, bravery leaking out. "You have no idea how troubling it is to wake up the next morning and have no idea what you've done the night before."

"I'd be happy to tag along," Maggie said.

Polly nodded, tucked two runaway strands of hair beneath her hat. "Excellent. Meanwhile, I have a funeral to prepare for." She ran tremulous hands over a too-thin body. "I hope this dress is all right. I read Tim Gunn. Guess I missed the chapter on what to wear to bury your murdered husband."

The trio watched Polly disappear through the doorway then looked at one another. The quiet seemed to grow proportionately with their discomfort, one decibel drop for every nervous fidget, each millimeter increase in blood pressure. "I'll go check on her, see if she needs anything," Constantine said. He paused. "Anything that doesn't involve a time machine."

He gave Maggie a peck on the lips and strode from the room. Camille began portioning eggs, bacon and sausage into Tupperware containers. "I'm going to head out, too. There are a few things I need to do at the church before the funeral." She deposited Tupperware in the refrigerator, swaddled pastries and tucked them into the bread box, then shrugged into her coat. She looked at Maggie. "I've been so worried about Polly. I can't tell you how glad I am that you're here." She gave Maggie a quick hug and disappeared through the door that led to the adjoining garage.

Alone in the kitchen, Maggie surveyed the disaster and considered her options: slap on some makeup (i.e. nude lipstick and a halfhearted swipe of mascara) or have another cup of coffee and a Danish and open a can of elbow grease. No contest. She grabbed her coffee cup and reached for a pastry.

Maggie's phone pierced the silence.

"Buehler...Buehler..."

Maggie jumped, nearly dropping her coffee. She told herself to take it easy, it was only a phone call. Her limbic system wasn't having it. Last year's events had made every chime of her phone feel like a message from the grave. Which, in fact, wasn't far off.

Maggie dug in her jeans pocket and produced her cell. She checked the caller ID. Work.

Strange.

She pressed to answer.

"I heard about your little stunt yesterday." Valerie said, her voice holding a mixture of surprise and awe. "Everyone has, actually. Alexa's still spitting, which is both hilarious and terrifying."

She was surprised how good it felt to hear Valerie's voice. Apart from Constantine, Maggie didn't have many friends. Valerie was one of the few who had ignored the No Trespassing sign that hung on Maggie's shoulder. "Well, I..." Maggie began.

"You did what all of us have always wanted to do. And here I thought my gum-chewing was some great revolt." She popped her gum as proof of her masticating mutiny. "Anyway, the official reason I'm calling is to tell you that your paycheck is waiting for you at the register."

A paycheck. That was good news. She needed to fill the Studebaker, not to mention her bank account. She also needed to find a job. Something else to think about later. "Can you just pop it in the mail? I'd love to stop by, catch up with you, see how Ada's doing after the blowup, but I'm out of town for a funeral."

"Oh no."

"It's for Constantine's uncle. He was—"

"No, not the funeral. Ada."

Maggie paused. Ada? Somewhere deep in her brain, Maggie could hear alarm bells beginning to peal. "What's wrong with Ada?"

There was a long pause.

"I didn't want to be the one to tell you. I actually thought you already knew."

"Knew what?" Maggie closed her eyes. She was pretty sure she didn't want to hear this.

"Ada's gone, Maggie. Alexa fired her, too."

Chapter 5

Maggie must have replied. Uttered a stream of mea culpas. Cursed Alexa. Reassured Valerie—and herself—that everything would be okay.

She couldn't be sure. The next thing she knew, she was sitting with her phone in her lap, a piece of paper in her hand. Numbers, hastily scrawled and underlined with such force that the pen sliced through the paper, had smeared between Maggie's sweat-slicked palms. She smoothed the paper on her knee and studied the digits, thinking of what to do next.

Call Ada. Apologize. Make things right.

Maggie was pretty sure making things right could be filed between "Easier Said than Done" and "Snowball's Chance in Hell." Plus there was no way she'd have time to call before the funeral.

In her mind's eye, she saw Alexa's malevolent smile, the curtain of hair that shielded Ada as she corrugated her shirt. Why did doing the right thing always seem to end up so wrong?

Maggie folded the paper into quarters and stuffed it into her pocket. She'd call later, once she figured out what to say.

Maggie changed into something sufficiently funereal and weather appropriate. Hollow Pine had pulled up a blanket of snow during the night, and Maggie's goal was to stay warm and upright as she navigated the ice-glazed ground.

She climbed into the Studebaker with Constantine, made her way to the interstate and put the Studebaker in third. She and Pop had restored the 1960 Studebaker Lark the last summer her mother had been alive. As if the action could restore her mother. As if Maggie's mounting grief could be covered in Bondo.

Maggie sighed.

Constantine glanced over at her. "You okay?"

It was the perfect invitation to tell him what happened with Alexa and Ada and her job, the perfect entrée to confession and catharsis and emotional absolution. She opened her mouth. Nothing came out. Finally she managed a "Just tired" and tried to smile. "Polly's little visit to my room kept me up," she added.

"I didn't get much sleep, either." He put on his best Chevy Chase voice. "The bed was very soft, Rusty," he quoted from *Vacation.*

Movie quotes were part of their secret language, a shared dialect in which entire conversations could be had without uttering an original word. It was the rock upon which their friendship had been built, along with an unyielding love of Dr. Pepper, *Mad Magazine*, and movies, both classic and campy. It felt good to be on familiar ground, to have some constancy despite the new status of their relationship and the turmoil surrounding Howard's murder, but she was too tired to engage in conversation, quote-based or not. Instead, she cranked up the Stude's heat and lapsed into silence.

Ten minutes later, Maggie eased the Studebaker from the snow-slicked roads of the main drag to the freezing slush that filmed the side streets. The snow had begun to fall heavily during the drive, turning the roadway white with heavy flakes that would presumably stick to Maggie's nose and eyelashes.

A few of her favorite things? Not so much.

Cars clumped at the cemetery's entrance. Maggie parked and they hurried inside to join the service, which had already begun.

Maggie went through the motions like a robot, focused on numbing herself, on not feeling the pain that usually accompanied funerals. An hour later, she stumbled from the chapel bleary-eyed and disoriented as if just awakening, and joined the other mourners at the adjacent cemetery.

It was a small group drawn together in a kind of emotional entropy, warmth rushing to fill the spaces turned cold by death. Polly was at the center, cane in one hand, prayer book in the other, leaning on Sam Graham as she stared at the wound in the earth in which her husband's body had just been lain.

The priest, an elderly man with a long white beard and tall black hat, stepped forward and began the Trisagion. Maggie knew that Howard's only God was the billable hour and that his appearances at church were just that: appearances. But Polly was a woman of faith. She wouldn't let a little thing like Howard's atheism stop her from having him laid to rest according to religious etiquette.

As the priest intoned prayers, Maggie looked at the crowd from beneath her lashes. She spotted Camille on the other side of the grave, head bent, eyes downcast. Beside her stood two other women whom Maggie vaguely recognized as Polly's friends. She was pretty sure they were in a knitting circle together. Or maybe it was a book club. One caught Maggie's eye and winked. Maggie remembered: wine club. Maggie's favorite kind of organization.

There were unfamiliar faces, as well. A leggy brunette with feline eyes and an expression of perpetual surprise. An elderly man with a bowler and a black umbrella. A middle-aged man with midwinter tan lines and eyes that hungrily roved Maggie's body, as if they had the bionic ability to see beneath the three layers she'd piled on.

Maggie pulled her coat tighter and moved closer to the huddle of family at the grave. The priest closed his book and put his hand on the frozen earth. He dug in with his short nails and pulled free a handful of frost-clotted soil. He knelt down and sprinkled the dirt in the shape of a cross on Howard's casket, then stood and reproduced the shape with his hands, the Orthodox motion a mirror image of the sign of faith that had defined Maggie's youth.

The holy man said a few words in Greek, each mourner placed a flower on the casket then walked toward the church hall, a modern brick addition that bore little resemblance to the Byzantine building it adjoined. It was the architectural equivalent of a CliffsNotes-inspired essay. The idea was generally right, but the details missed the mark.

As Polly and her friends disappeared into the long, squat structure, a man beside a grave marked with a St. Nicholas cross stepped forward. Maggie recognized the wiry, perma-flexed arms before registering the face.

"Detective Greeley, what are you doing here?"

The detective brushed off snow that had turned his gray coat into a powdered donut and flapped his arms against his torso. "I wanted to pay my respects."

Constantine gestured toward the door. "You're welcome to come in. Plenty of food and it's a helluva lot warmer inside. You could have some baklava, get a look at some of the haters my aunt mentioned."

A corner of Greeley's lip turned up. "Who am I to turn down baklava? Thanks for the invitation." He stamped his feet like a contestant at a square-dancing competition to relinquish the snow's hold on his boots and walked inside.

Maggie eyed Constantine. "Consorting with the other side, Gus?"

"You know what they say about keeping your enemies closer. This way we can see if he's scoping out potential murderers or just spying on Aunt Polly. That whole knowledge-is-power thing."

She couldn't argue with his reasoning, or with the aroma that emanated from the social hall. Broiled fish. Tangy garlic. Butter-impregnated pastries. Maggie put a hand to her rumbling belly, remembering the food she'd left uneaten on Camille's countertop. She replicated Greeley's dance of snowflake removal and stepped inside.

The building's interior belied its nondescript shell. Maggie expected to find institutional furnishings and easels topped with Kindergarteners' interpretation of that week's Gospel reading. Instead she found a large, elegantly appointed room with paneled walls, tasteful black draping, and round tables skirted by the Wrights' family and friends. Actually, Polly's family and friends. Howard may have been the guest of honor, a dubious honor in this case, but this was clearly Polly's event.

Maggie wiggled out of her coat, laid it over the back of a folding chair and yanked at her long black skirt which was making a slow but inevitable journey down her hips. Like most of her wardrobe, the skirt was a gift from Aunt Fiona who seemed to shop in the Dowdy Department at Marshalls. Not that Maggie really cared. Her body was more sport utility than fashion vehicle. On the other hand, it would be nice if Fiona chose items that were in her size. Or from this century.

Maggie grabbed a plate at the head of the buffet table and made her way through the line.

"Try the fish," a voice at her ear said. "It's the best thing here."

"You're just saying that because you made it," another voice hissed.

Maggie turned. She'd become the gingery middle of a human sandwich, flanked by the pair of women she'd recognized at Howard's graveside. Both sported the same short haircut favored by Camille. Both were clad in black crepe dresses that dusted the tops of sensible black boots.

"You remember us, honey?" the first woman said, extending a skinny elbow for Maggie to shake since her hands were occupied by food and drink. "Maria and Sophia. We met at Polly's last year?"

She had a soft, melodious voice that went up at the end of each sentence, as if she were constantly surprised by what she was saying.

"The wine club," Maggie supplied, wiping her fingers on her skirt to shake the woman's elbow. "I'm Maggie."

"We know, dear," the second woman said as she loaded a piece of fish that looked as if it required a forklift instead of a fork. "What we don't know is how Polly is getting along. She must be absolutely devastated."

The woman sidled up to a quivering vat of rice pudding and began to ladle it onto her plate. "So terrible. So tragic. So inconceivable." She paused, ladle mid-journey from vat to plate. "Of course, it wasn't like they were soul mates."

Maggie plucked a roll from the cornucopia of gluten and gave the woman a sidelong look. "Polly and Howard didn't get along?"

That wouldn't be a surprise. The match had always seemed like an odd one to Maggie. What did funny, irreverent, kind Polly see in overbearing, obnoxious, self-obsessed Howard? Maggie had always considered Howard a narcissist and, as her father would say, an arse. She supposed that made him an arse-issist.

"It wasn't that they didn't get along," Sophia said, licking a dollop of pudding from her thumb. "They never saw each other. Howard was always working or traveling."

"Or spending time with his Twinkie."

For once, Maria's sentence didn't go up at the end. Accusations of adultery were worthy of a more declarative tone.

Maggie thought of the single one-way ticket to Barbados. Greeley's innuendos. Polly's dismay and admission that Howard didn't "consult" her on much of his life.

His Twinkie.

Maggie trotted after the women and joined them at a table claimed with a tower of coats, scarves and handbags. "Howard was having an affair?" she whispered.

Sophia hiked a shoulder. "There was talk."

"He spent a lot of time with someone other than Polly?"

Maria tore off a piece of pita bread and dipped it in hummus. "He spent a lot of time with his female patients. Boobs and buns all day, it had to be tempting."

Maria's sentences had all become statements. On solid moral ground? Sure of her facts? Maggie wondered what the sisters knew and would be willing to tell.

"But you never saw him with anyone?" Maggie pressed. "Polly didn't worry?"

Maria took a bite of pita and wiped her fingers on a napkin. "It was all speculation. Gossip. He was too cozy with his receptionist or his nurse or one of the women in his ads. That kind of thing. Everyone seemed to think he was doing the kind of body work that wasn't billable."

Maggie thought back to what Polly had told the detectives. "I'd heard that some of Howard's colleagues disliked him."

"Disliked?" Sophia cackled. "More like despised. You can see the buzzards circling now."

She nodded toward the man in the hat Maggie had seen outside. He skulked near the back of the room beneath an icon of the Ascension. "They're not here to pay their respects. They're here to make sure Howard's dead."

"Now, now, Sophia," a man's voice boomed behind Maggie. "You're exaggerating."

Maggie turned to see the handsome man with the midwinter tan who had ogled her at the internment. He gave her a toothpaste commercial smile. "Dr. Michael West. You can call me Dr. Mikey."

Dr. Mikey. Somehow that didn't instill confidence.

Maggie took in the artfully mussed and highlighted hair, the fake tan, the tasseled loafers. She hated tassels. "Maggie O'Malley." She offered her hand, hoping he wouldn't click his heels together and bend to kiss it. "I'm, uh, a friend of Polly's nephew."

A friend? Maggie wasn't sure why she hedged at naming the relationship, why she avoided the b-word when talking about Constantine as if "boyfriend" were more epithet than endearment. Maybe it was the relative newness of the term for Constantine or a kneejerk dislike for the possessive that went along with "my boyfriend" and "my girlfriend." Or maybe it was the subtle pressure Constantine applied to move the relationship forward.

It wasn't that she didn't want to marry Constantine. She just...didn't want to marry Constantine. She loved him with every fiber of her being. She didn't need a piece of paper telling her they'd be together forever, a term she considered tenuous, like "organic" or "great-tasting."

Dr. Mikey leaned in and stared at her face. "Has anyone ever told you that you look like Emma Stone?" Maggie blushed. Mikey leaned back and pursed his lips as he evaluated her. "Or maybe Emma Stone with rosacea."

Before Maggie could respond, he turned to the sisters. "I hope you're not filling Ms. O'Malley's ears with rumors." He laughed too loudly. Neither woman said anything. He rushed to fill the silence, his voice game show host jovial. "It's true that there was always a fair amount of competition between Howard and me. And God knows, not everyone appreciated his, ah, approach to medicine." He put a hand beneath his chin like a catalogue model. "But he forged his own path to success, and I applaud him for that."

"Even if he took patients from you?" Maggie asked. "From what I understand, Howard was the most popular cosmetic surgeon in the area."

Dr. Mikey laughed again. "There's enough room for everyone in Hollow Pine and my practice is thriving. The point is, we're here to celebrate Howard's life and mourn his death." He arranged his face to match his statement. "Nobody should have to go through what Howard went through. It's unimaginably horrific."

He made a show of checking his watch, clucking about the time. He said his goodbyes then strode away.

Maggie looked at the women. They rolled their eyes.

"There's an I Hate Howard Wright Club, and Dr. West is president," Maria said. "Despite what he says, everyone knows that he blames Howard and his heavy-handed advertising for chipping away at his empire. It's sour grapes, plain and simple."

Maggie wondered about the poison that sour grapes could produce and who else might have cultivated bitter fruit. "I heard there was some friction between Howard and his practice partner."

"Dr. Rogers?" Sophia corralled the remnants of food on her plate then shoveled them onto her fork. "He's not here, but as far as I know, there were no problems between them."

No Dr. Rogers? That struck Maggie as odd. "Is he out of town?"

"Maybe," they said in unison.

"Is there some other reason he wouldn't be here?"

"I can't imagine any," Maria said.

Maggie decided to take a different tack. "From what I understand the I Hate Howard Club isn't just doctors. Sounds like he had problems with patients?"

"True, but it's a much smaller club." Sophia gestured toward the buffet. "There's the charter member now."

Maggie turned to see the tall, feline-eyed woman she had spotted outside. The woman was dressed in a black chiffon pantsuit with a plunging sequined neckline. Her makeup was impeccably applied, a strobe of highlight here, a chisel of bronzer there, eyes shadowed to bring out a vivid blue Maggie could see across the room. Maggie could also see that her brows were lifted in perpetual surprise, as if she were in constant danger of being run over by a UPS truck.

"Deirdre?"

"In the newly-tightened flesh," Maria said.

"I heard she had a lawsuit against Howard," Maggie said, striving for casual.

Sophia picked her teeth with the tine of her fork. "More like a vendetta. She was going to ruin Howard for, in her words, 'damaging her exceptional beauty and future pageant potential.'" Sophia regarded Deirdre, who was examining the buffet fare with the scrutiny of a state food inspector. "Miss Hollow Pine, maybe. But she wasn't exactly destined for the Miss Universe crown."

Sophia gazed into her cup, as if divining trajectory of Deirdre's pageant career in her coffee grounds. Maggie took advantage of the conversational lull and excused herself for another trip to the buffet. Now was as good a time as any to talk to the pageant queen.

Maggie approached the linen-encased table and placed two triangles of baklava on her plate. She took two baby steps toward Deidre in an investigative Mother May I and pretended to deliberate over a second helping of rice pudding.

"He had it coming," she heard Deirdre say to the woman next to her. "Karma's a bitch."

Maggie was stunned. She knew there was no love lost between Howard and Deirdre, but maligning him at his own funeral was beyond the pale. She leaned toward the ex-beauty queen to hear how else she might slander him. She felt an insistent tap on her shoulder.

She turned to find Greeley staring at her over his plate.

He leaned in. "Learn anything interesting?"

She was chockfull of interesting. "Not really." She poured on the nonchalance. "You?"

"Saw you talking to Dr. West." He spooned lemon roasted potatoes onto his plate. "And I see you're about to interview another potential enemy. Looks like you're working your suspect list."

"Just getting to know some of the people from Howard's life."

That elicited a smirk. "If you cared so much, why do you know so little about Howard, so little about his and Polly's life? How long had it been since you'd seen them, anyway?"

It felt like a punch to the gut. The guilt she had so carefully barricaded behind the Wall came tumbling out. She opened her mouth to respond. Greeley's smirk broadened. "Oh, right. You don't make it to Hollow Pine much. You're too busy traipsing around solving crimes."

Maggie reddened. Okay, so maybe she was at fault for letting relationships wither—she'd never been great at nurturing anything—but she hadn't traipsed in over a year. "Now hang on—"

"No, you hang on." Greeley stuck his finger in her face. "You hang onto the idea that there's already someone working this case who doesn't need anyone getting in the way. Got it?"

Before Maggie could answer, Greeley tossed his food into the garbage and stalked out the door, his breath blowing a cloud of vapor that encircled him like an aura.

Maggie shook her head. What was his problem? She'd said barely three sentences to him, and he had already branded her public enemy number one. Maybe she was infamous among cops for her exploits last year. Maybe he was an alpha dog who barked at anyone who came too close to his territory. Maybe whatever was between him and Polly was now between him and Maggie.

She spotted Constantine and Polly and walked toward them, ready to share her indignation over Greeley's behavior, hopeful Polly would reveal the story behind the detective's rancor. As she drew near, Maggie heard raised voices.

She expected to hear words of sympathy, Hallmark-ready sentiments made pat by repetition and lack of imagination. Instead she heard Polly's voice. Shrill. Sharp.

Maggie stopped, trying to understand what was going on. Was Polly shouting?

She saw Constantine bent close to Polly, his dark hair ruffling the veil of her hat. She batted him away, her agitation growing as her hands fluttered around her face like a bird.

"I don't care what you say, he's right there," Polly howled.

Mumbles from Constantine. His hand on her shoulder.

"Don't coddle me!" Polly's voice crackled with anger and anguish. "I know what I'm seeing." She shook off his hand, struggled to her feet. "I'd recognize that taut neckline, that chin implant anywhere."

Maggie looked over her shoulder to find who Polly was talking about. Others around her did the same.

"Are you blind?" Polly looked at the gathering crowd, her eyes wild. "Howard's crept from his grave, dug his way out of that putrid hole to infect us all." She lowered her voice. "He's been watching me, you know.

Through the TV. In the paintings. From behind the mirror. He plays games with the lights and poisons my food."

She grabbed her cane and dropped it. It clattered to the ground, rattling like a snake. Constantine picked up the cane. Polly grabbed it from his hand. "I'm getting the hell out of here. You should do the same before Howard comes for you, too."

Then she scuffed out of the social hall, leaving shocked faces and unanswered questions in her wake.

Chapter 6

Maggie and Constantine found Polly in the parking lot, walking unsteadily through the deepening snow.

She was calm, her eyes taking on that same vacant stare that Maggie had seen the night Polly had sleepwalked into her room and loomed over her as she lay in her bed.

Not catatonic. But not far off.

The upshot was that Polly was easily buckled into the car. Easily guided into the warmth of Camille's house. Easily dosed with Benadryl, procured from Polly's prescription pouch, a knit cosmetics bag adorned with smiling daisies. Maggie had hoped to find an anti-anxiety medication or an antidepressant with sleep-inducing qualities or, God-willing, an antipsychotic.

Because that's where Maggie feared they now were. The land of antipsychotics. The pseudo-sedative would have to do.

Polly obediently held out her tongue for the small gel cap, receiving it with the same reverence as Holy Communion. She chased it with three sips of water, then allowed Maggie to pour her into bed without comment or resistance.

Maggie clicked off the light and watched Polly's childlike shoulders rise and fall under her chenille bedspread. She'd be asleep in moments, and hopefully safe from whatever monsters chased her through her mind.

Maggie tiptoed down the hall to the living room where Constantine and Camille waited on an overstuffed sofa trying not to look worried. They turned hopeful faces toward her as she sank into a red leather recliner in front of the gas fireplace.

"She's resting," she said, watching blue and orange flames pretend to devour a fake log. "Between the events of the day and the medication, she should be asleep any minute."

Tension eased from Constantine's face, but didn't disappear. "What the hell happened?"

Maggie put a hand to her forehead. A headache had cropped up between her eyes. She probably had a tumor. Constantine teased her about being a hypochondriac, but she knew that cemeteries were full of people who said, "It's probably nothing."

She rose, grabbed her purse from the entryway bench and freed a film canister. She pried off the lid, shook out two Tylenols and swallowed them without water.

"What happened with Polly?" she asked, echoing Constantine's question. "My guess is hallucination."

Constantine rubbed the back of his neck. "I feel like I witnessed an invasion by a body snatcher. That was not Aunt Polly back there. I mean, she's always been a little nutty, but fun nutty. Not, you know, nuts. She was like a totally different person."

"She's not nuts, and she's still Polly," Maggie said. "Hallucinations can be a complication of Parkinson's, but it has nothing to do with psychiatric illness. Researchers think it could be due to a loss of networking in the brain that disturbs attentional and visual processing, which can lead to hallucinations. But it could be caused—or worsened—by any number of factors, from an electrolyte imbalance to medication to an infection."

"That happened to my grandmother," Camille chimed in. "My mother was ready to admit her to the psychiatric ward. Turned out she had a urinary tract infection."

"My hunch is medication," Maggie said. "Some Parkinson's meds can cause or exacerbate hallucinations. Same with sleepwalking. And it varies widely from person to person. It's possible that tweaking Polly's medication can help on both counts. Hopefully I'll learn more when I go to her pharmacist's."

Constantine rose and crouched by the gas fire, his olive complexion burnished bronze by the flames. "I still don't get it. I mean, I've never seen anything like this from Polly. Ever. She seemed so...strange."

"This isn't the first time," Camille said quietly.

Maggie and Constantine swiveled their heads to look at her.

"She's had hallucinations before?" Maggie asked.

Camille hesitated.

"It's okay," Maggie said gently. "We're just trying to find out what's going on."

Camille took a big breath. "She's been acting paranoid, like I said earlier, but garden-variety paranoia. 'Someone moved my glasses,' or 'People are talking about me.' But lately she's been angry, lashing out, talking about things that never happened and pointing at things that aren't there." She shook her head. "I just figured she had a little dementia. Now I wish I'd said something sooner. Maybe we could have done something to help her."

The rest of the evening was spent discussing Polly's condition in hushed whispers around the fireplace then at the kitchen table where Camille served *coq au vin* that Maggie praised but didn't taste. She was relieved when Camille made her way to her room, signaling the all-clear to go to bed. Finally Maggie could wonder and worry in private.

Maggie was up before the sun or anyone else in the house. She yanked on her jeans and a long-sleeved tee, then stole downstairs to the kitchen.

She rummaged in the cupboards for coffee, pushing aside vitamins, nutmeg oil, baking powder and three varieties of rice before finding magic beans. She loaded the coffe maker, pushed start, then put the kettle on for tea. Outside, predawn light scuttled across the tiny hills and vales of the yard, offering a glimpse of the cold, clear day to come. As drips of coffee pinged into the pot and the kettle warmed over eager flames, Maggie thought about the source of Polly's hallucinations and the possibilities for stopping it. She was certain she and Polly's pharmacist would come up with a plan. Science and research would provide.

She was on her third cup of coffee when her phone rang. She fished it from her pocket. Her father's ruddy face, bracketed by white sideburns and topped by a fisherman's hat, filled the screen. She put the phone to her ear. "Hey, Pop."

"Magnolia!" he boomed through the phone. "How's my wee daughter?"

Maggie cringed. She hated her full name and hadn't been wee for quite some time.

"I'm doing great!"

A half-truth? A quarter-truth? An outright lie, the exclamation point pushing the sin well past venial? Whatever the degree, Maggie was the queen of downplaying, especially where her father was concerned. For a worrier like Jack O'Malley, honesty was rarely the best policy.

"Grand, grand. And Miss Polly? How is she getting along?" Pop's voice had softened. He knew what it was like to lose a spouse, to feel not just halved with your better half gone, but decimated. Polly had been unhappily married, but that didn't stop Jack O'Malley from envying the luxury of a spouse to hate.

"She's hanging in there."

Maggie reported on her visit, shellacking over the funeral, Polly's strange outburst, the police's interest in Polly. Then she pivoted the conversation. "How's life in Greenville?"

He bypassed her hometown and instead offered a detailed description of what was wrong with this country and why reality TV was a sign of the End Times, right along with piercings and "Facelook." When he was done ranting, he threw in a couple of tidbits about how overworked he was. Pop's version of positivity.

"Sounds like the food carts are doing well," Maggie said. "Guess people like their Irish-Italian fare on the go."

Last year, O'Malley's Pizzeria had teetered on the brink of bankruptcy. Jack retooled, transforming his pizzeria into a staging location for O'Malley's Food Carts. They were an instant hit. Business was booming, leaving Jack both exhausted and delighted.

A thought occurred to Maggie. "You said you're expanding into Collinsburg, right?" Jack grunted an affirmative. "You need another employee, someone you can trust?" Another series of grunts. "I have the perfect person for the job."

Maggie described Ada, extolling her virtues, redacting pesky details like the fact that Maggie got Ada fired and that she may or may not hate Maggie for life.

Jack listened without comment then said, "Well, if you like her, that's good enough for me. I'll have to talk with Fiona. She likes to handle staffing, you know."

Maggie knew. Her aunt saw human resources management as an opportunity to inject herself into people's lives.

Fiona loved to meddle. Financial advice. Spiritual direction. Matchmaking. Especially matchmaking. Maggie recalled a particularly disastrous set-up between a waitress and a bartender, who they later learned saved all of his fingernail clippings in a large manila envelope that he periodically opened to examine with his dates. "It's good to have a hobby," Fiona had justified. "And he must have marvelous dexterity."

Maggie gave a silent, prophylactic apology to Ada. "I'll talk to Ada. If she's interested, I can have her call Fiona to set up an interview."

Her father agreed, they exchanged a few final pleasantries then signed off. As Maggie popped the phone back into her pocket, Polly appeared in the doorway.

She wore a berry-red jacket over a turtleneck of the same shade. Her black pants were nearly waist-high and cinched with a gold chain belt. Her bob was meticulously smoothed, her brown eyes darkened by a swipe of eyeliner and mascara.

She looked clear-eyed and alert.

In a word: normal.

"Good morning, Maggie," Polly said brightly. "You're up early."

Maggie got up to take Polly's arm, but the older woman made her way to the cupboard adjacent to the cooktop on her own and began preparing a cup of tea.

"How are you?" Maggie asked, studying Polly's face. She noticed the shadows beneath Polly's eyes, the pallor that gave her olive complexion a sickly cast.

It didn't look as if she'd gotten a wink of sleep, much less forty. Maggie estimated thirty-nine.

"I'm fine, dear." Polly popped a teabag into a mug and poured steaming water from the kettle, struggling first to lift then to control the heavy kettle. She replaced the teapot with a wheeze of exertion.

"So no...um...after-effects from yesterday?"

Polly maneuvered herself to the table, mug in one hand, cane in the other, and sat heavily. Her movements were slow, tremulous, but she had completed the task without help. Pride straightened her spine as she drowned the teabag beneath a spoon. "No. The funeral made me a bit sad, but it was good to see everyone."

No mention of her belief that Howard had risen from the grave. No reference to watching eyes or games involving light switches and poison. No indication that she remembered the hallucinations that had taunted her and horrified her guests.

Maggie considered bringing it up, informing her of her actions just as Howard had during her sleepwalking episodes. After all, her silence would be a kind of collusion with Polly's fantasies, another loosening of the fragile tether that bound her to reality.

But yesterday's events weren't easy to broach.

Hey, Polly, remember going around the bend yesterday?

The funniest thing happened at the funeral. Well, not funny ha-ha, but...

We have to talk.

Polly interrupted Maggie's internal rehearsal.

"Are you still able to take me to the pharmacy today?"

"Yes, of course."

Maggie decided not to mention the hallucinations. She could talk with the pharmacist about them, avoid upsetting Polly while possibly getting closer to a solution. Two birds, one stone. Besides, her courage was in short supply this morning. She went to the coffee pot to see if she could caffeinate her way to a backbone.

Constantine bounded into the kitchen. His dark hair was shower-slick, his toned torso clad with a t-shirt that read *It's Okay, I'm Here Now.*

Maggie groaned. She knew what the shirt meant. "Don't tell me you have to go into work."

He opened Camille's miniature bread garage and pulled out a bag of bagels. "Okay, I won't. But I should be back by six."

"This isn't exactly good timing." She gave him a meaningful look then surreptitiously nodded at Polly who placidly sipped her tea. "It would be great to have your help today."

Constantine looked at his aunt, his brows coming together to create a low spot between his eyes. "I know, but it's unavoidable. Believe me, I'd be here if I could. Unfortunately, I'm on call."

Maggie folded her arms. "If you're on call this much, you should be a doctor."

Constantine pulled out a bagel and wagged it at her. "Have you been talking to my mother?"

Once again, he had slipped behind the mask of the comic, the cutup, the goofball. She could hardly fault him. She was a master at playing hide-and-seek with her feelings.

Constantine began to butter the bagel. "Aunt Polly already knows about my IT emergency, and she thinks I'm a genius. Isn't that right, Aunt Polly?"

"Servers go down. Companies need them back up."

Aunt Polly. Tech-savvy and always full of surprises.

"See? I perform an important community service. It's what I always dreamed I would do, other than becoming an officer in the grammar police, which turned out to not be a thing." He halved the bagel in one giant bite. "Speaking of work, when do you have go back to selling unmentionables?"

Right. The job she still pretended to have and needed to replace.

"Oh, not for a while," she said vaguely.

"A while? Since when did Alexa lighten up on scheduling?"

Constantine's phone pinged. He dug it out of his pocket, read the face. "Looks like 'get to work now' has become 'get to work now-er.'" He sighed. "I love my job. My boss is another story." He rounded the long table, pecked Maggie on the lips then took a mouthful of bagel. "Gotta jet," he said with his mouth full. "Have a great girls' day. And don't get into any trouble."

He strode out the door.

Polly looked at Maggie, the old sparkle back in her eye. She crooked an eyebrow. "He doesn't know us very well, does he?"

Petrosian's Pillbox was located in Hollow Pine's historic downtown at the base of an anemic mountain redundantly named Butte Hill, which had been dubbed "Butt Hole" by locals.

Maggie cruised the strip that comprised the town's historic shopping area, eyes peeled for princess parking that would make it easy for Polly to get from Studebaker to store. Filling the tank on the way in had been a good call. Judging by the number of uber-early Christmas shoppers on the street, she might be stalking parking places for hours.

The gods of parking smiled upon her, and Maggie snagged a space vacated by a mother with a wailing infant and pouting toddler. The woman looked like she could use a nap. Or a drink.

Maggie parked, helped Polly from the car and plodded to Petrosian's through snow that stood firm in spite of being trampled over again and again. A bell heralded their arrival.

Maggie took stock of Polly's pharmacy. Petrosian's was like every small-town drugstore Maggie had ever been in. There was a window display of assorted toys, knock-off perfumes and impulse gift items, including a porcelain figurine of a dog dressed as a dentist.

Maggie trailed Polly down the center aisle, which seemed to be a catchall of clearance items. She passed volumizing mascara, corn pads, enema bags and giant tins of shortbread cookies from a brand that sounded vaguely Dutch. The waiting area in front of the pharmacy counter was vacant, as was the strip behind the counter. Polly leaned her cane against the *Audio Privacy Not Guaranteed* sign and spanked the silver service bell with a gloved hand. "Lev is probably in the back."

Moments later, a small bald man emerged. He had dark eyes, salt and pepper brows, and a frown that dragged his lips to his chin. Although thin, he had jowls that hung from his cheeks, furthering his hangdog appearance. He smiled at Polly then spotted Maggie. The frown returned.

Polly put a steadying hand on the counter. "Lev, I want you to meet my future niece-in-law, Maggie."

Future niece-in-law?

Before Maggie could determine if Polly knew something she didn't, a smooth tan hand was thrust into her face. "Levon Petrosian," the man said. "Pharmacist."

This said as if it not only explained his presence behind the counter, but his purpose on the planet.

Petrosian, Maggie thought. Armenian, like her friend and former coworker Zartar Nazarian. She felt an immediate, unreasonable fondness for the man. It vaporized when Petrosian turned annoyed, hawkish eyes on her.

Polly clasped hands warmly with the pharmacist. "Lev, Maggie is a pharmaceutical researcher."

Petrosian looked unimpressed. "Is that so?"

Maggie coughed. "Well, I, um, used to be a clinical research associate. I'm currently..." Currently what? Unemployed? Between bra-fittings? Desperate to scrape together some self-esteem? "I'm currently not working in the pharmaceutical industry."

"Ah." Petrosian began pecking at his keyboard. It was clear that her used-to-be status bored him.

"I've been having some trouble with my symptoms lately," Polly continued. "Maggie was wondering if my medication could be the problem. I thought you two could talk while you fill my prescription and I do some shopping." She patted flaming red tresses. "I need to refresh my color."

Petrosian's pecking paused and his eyebrows reached for his hairline, or rather where his hairline would be. "Symptoms? I'm sorry to hear that." He looked at Maggie, the corners of his lips in danger of touching his chin. "But discussing your medical history with your niece-in-law is forbidden."

Polly gave a dazzling smile. "I give you my permission." She reached across the counter and touched Petrosian's wrist. "Please, Lev. It's important. I'll sign anything you like."

Petrosian's face softened. "All right, Polly. I'll talk to your niece-in-law. And, you don't have to sign anything. We'll do it Old Country style, with our word."

Polly patted Petrosian's wrist with a trembling hand and grabbed her cane. "I'll be in Aisle 3, searching for Haute Tamale hair color." She gave her head a toss. "Or maybe I'll try Bombastic Burgundy. I could use a change."

Maggie watched her disappear behind a row of digestive aids, more than a little amazed that the crazed, ranting Polly from yesterday had disappeared, and turned back to Petrosian. She smiled. He scowled. "Um...so..." She unwound the scarf from around her neck and stuffed it into the oversized pocket of her coat. "Like Polly said, she's been having some troubling symptoms."

Lev sighed and pushed the keyboard away, resigned to the conversation. He removed his glasses and rubbed his eyes with his thumb and forefinger. "What kind of symptoms?"

Maggie told him about the episode at the funeral. Episode. The word was laughable in its weakness, as if were a show that aired Wednesdays on NBC.

Lev's frown deepened and he pulled the keyboard toward himself again. "Hallucinations aren't unheard of. Neither is sleepwalking. And you're right, both can be tied to medication." He began tapping. "However, in Polly's case, I have a hard time believing her prescriptions are at fault, especially where hallucinations or pseudo-psychosis is concerned. Medication, dosage...nothing's changed since she was diagnosed three years ago."

"What's she taking?"

More taps. "Sinemet for Parkinson's, same dosage as at diagnosis. Over the past couple of years, she was also prescribed a non-narcotic cough syrup when she had the flu and two rounds of antibiotics for...let's see...strep throat and a sinus infection. She also picked up the typical OTC meds for headache, upset stomach, et cetera. That's it."

No medication standouts. No answers, either.

"Hallucinations and sleepwalking can develop organically with Parkinson's," Lev said. "It could be a sign of things changing."

"And by 'changing,' you mean worsening."

Lev said nothing.

The disappointment was crushing. Maggie wanted the source of Polly's symptoms to be tangible, fixable, a result of medication rather than a dearth of dopamine.

Fact was, the cells in Polly's brain were dying. There would be no prescriptive rewind of side effects by a change in medication or a tweak in dosage. She wasn't just progressing through the stages of the disease—she was hurtling through them. There was nothing Maggie could do about it.

It brought back the helpless feeling that infected the summer Maggie turned twelve, the powerlessness that spread through the O'Malley home, fueled by low blood counts, the empty promises of doctors, miracle cures found in the back of magazines. It brought back why Maggie went into pharmaceuticals in the first place. Now the summer of loss and the professional ambition that had soothed those wounds were both memories.

Maggie felt Lev's eyes on her. Serious. Watchful. Appraising. "I can call Polly's doctor when he gets back to town," he said at last, "talk with him about her medication, her symptoms, see what he says. Maybe he can recommend an adjustment." He shrugged. "For some people, a small change can make a big difference."

Hope struck hard and bright in Maggie's chest. She smothered it with caution. Optimism could be a treacherous thing. "That sounds great."

Polly walked up to them and placed a box of hair color on the counter. She'd gone with Haute Tamale. She selected two peppermint patties from below the counter and paid for the prescription and items in cash. Maggie watched her count out her fives and tens, making conversation with Petrosian. Her hands shook, but otherwise seemed like Old Polly, Pre-Illness Polly, no hangover from yesterday's hallucination or whatever caused it. It was mystifying, but a relief. It had to be a good sign.

The moment they were outside, Polly grilled Maggie on their conversation.

Maggie hit the high points.

Satisfied that progress had been made, Polly settled into the Studebaker and placed a fuzzy white hat on her head. She donned matching gloves, her left hand trying to catch her right as it fluttered in her lap. She looked at Maggie. "Lev likes you."

That was like? Maggie wondered how his enemies fared. "He has a funny way of showing it."

"You don't know him like I do. He doesn't like people. Well, except maybe me. But I saw the way he spoke to you. There was real respect there."

Frowns, cold stares and outright dismissiveness as signs of affection and respect. Maggie would have to take Polly's word for it.

They made the rest of the drive in silence, Maggie watching the snow-dusted trees begin to bend with the weight of winter's first real sabre rattle, Polly snoring softly against the headrest.

Maggie pulled into the driveway and rounded the car to wake her friend—her aunt-in-law-to-be?—and help her from the leather bench seat.

The house was vacant; Camille and Constantine were both at work. Maggie turned on the fire to ease the chill caused by a lack of humanity and the presence of a cold front, then slipped into the kitchen to make more tea.

As the kettle warmed, Maggie dug out the phone number she had stuffed into her pocket the day before.

Ada's number. Actually, Ada's mother's number. Her former coworker lived with her mother and two sisters. The women had lost everything in a house fire the year before. Ada was the only one old enough—and well enough—to work.

She smoothed the paper out on the counter. It felt soft and bumpy, like a dollar bill that had gone through the wash. She traced the numbers with her fingertips, easily the twentieth time she had done so.

She dialed and prayed for voicemail.

"Hello?"

Feck.

It was an older voice, rough with sleep, turned up at the edges by the soft lilt of an accent.

Double feck. She had awoken Ada's mother.

"Mrs. Garcia? I'm sorry if I disturbed you."

"It's okay. I was feeling bad, so I lay down. What can I do for you?"

"This is Maggie O'Malley. I used to work with Ada?"

A pause. "Yes?" The voice was cooler, guarded.

"Is Ada around?"

"No, she's out looking for a job." The omission was clear: Because of you.

"Actually, that's why I'm calling. I wanted to help—"

The woman laughed. "Help? You want to help?" She laughed again, anger popping beneath it. "You already helped Ada out of a job. I am not well enough to work. My other daughters are not old enough to work.

And now we have no money for food, for medicine. No, miss, I don't think we can take any more of your help."

There was an audible click. The phone went dead.

Chapter 7

The shriek of the tea kettle snapped Maggie out of her trance.

She was clutching the phone so tightly fingernail indentations had formed in the soft flesh of her palm. She forced her hand to relax and let the phone slide onto the counter. She pushed it away, as if the phone were responsible for the knot in her gut.

It wasn't the phone's fault. It wasn't Ada's mother's fault. There was only one person to blame for how Maggie felt, and that made it all the worse.

Maggie pushed away the growing guilt and pretended a calm she didn't feel. Fake it till you make it. She finished preparing the tea, affixed a serene expression on her face and delivered the drink along with an assortment of baked goods to Polly.

"What's wrong?" the older woman asked immediately.

So much for faking it.

Maggie set the tray on a wooden coffee table sporting wheels, as if snacks would need to be mobilized at any moment. "I'm feeling a little keyed up. I probably just need to exercise."

Half-truth. Maggie was getting good at that.

Polly reached for a cookie, fumbled, then caught it with both hands. "Why don't you go on one of your runs? Lord knows I would if I could."

Illness aside, Maggie couldn't imagine Polly going for a run. Zumba? Yes. Hot yoga? Yes. A hike? Maggie knew Polly used to hit the trail with husband number two. But bona fide running, sweating through DriFit layers and desperately hoping that abdominal pain wasn't the harbinger of a bathroom emergency? That would be a no. Maggie wagered that Polly would prefer her exercise with a side of cute outfits and no humiliation.

A little more prodding from Polly and Maggie agreed to a quick run. She changed quickly and bounded back downstairs. "Polly," she said as she lunged into a quad stretch. "What's the deal with Detective Greeley?

You said he hated you. Why?"

Maggie knew it could be a sensitive topic. She also knew they may not have another moment alone together for some time. She switched to a calf stretch and watched Polly watch the fire.

Polly puckered her lips, flattened them, puckered again. "I met Jeff Greeley not long after I moved to town," she said finally. "He was an officer back then, a beat cop, with big ambitions and a big secret."

Maggie waited. When Polly didn't say anything Maggie raised an eyebrow. "Alcohol? Drugs? Gambling?"

"A temper. He was able to keep it in check at work. Home was a different story."

Maggie blinked. "Greeley was an abuser?"

"A manipulator. A bully. An emotional abuser who had convinced his wife she was worthless. I knew the signs because I'd been down that road with my first husband." She picked up another cookie, picked at it, watched crumbles fall to the plate, set it aside. "I also knew I couldn't just let it be. So I baked a pie and brought it to the Greeleys' when I knew Jeff would be at work. I told Mrs. Greeley—Lynne—to leave. That it would get worse. That Jeff would get tired of putting her down and start knocking her down. A slap followed by a tearful apology. A hand to the throat followed by flowers. That's how it starts, but that's not how it stops." Polly looked into the fire, remembering. "Turned out Jeff had already hit her. Turned out she was pregnant and terrified of what a crying baby would do to Jeff's mood. And it was always about Jeff's mood. Was he happy? Was he stressed? Would he be angry that the meatloaf had too much sauce? My visit was the push she needed. She packed her things, left a note, and moved across the country. Now the only thing Jeff has in Hollow Pine is his job and an empty house." She looked at Maggie. "And his hatred of me."

"He knew you convinced his wife to leave?"

"He knew I visited her. He knew she left right after. He wasn't a detective back then, but he knew something about deduction."

"And he's hated you ever since."

Polly took a teacup with tremulous hands and sipped the pond-colored liquid. "With the heat of a thousand suns."

"Shouldn't he be recused from the investigation? Don't people know about his past, your involvement?"

"I've mentioned it. Sam has mentioned it. But Greeley is well-liked and well-connected. Way he told it, his wife ran off with another man.

She's not around to defend her reputation. And now I have to defend myself against a murder accusation that I'm sure will come."

"But he has no evidence."

"He has insinuation and power. Sometimes that's enough." Polly returned her teacup to the tray, leaned her head against the recliner's headrest and closed her eyes. "I'm not worried. Sam used to practice criminal law, if it comes to that." She opened her eyes and looked at Maggie. "Don't you worry about a thing, dear. You go run off some of that energy. I'll hold down the fort."

Maggie insisted she stay, insisted they talk about Greeley and retaliation and what they could do to defend her name. Polly insisted she run. And when Polly insisted, Maggie complied. Her defiance seemed to be reserved for her employers.

Maggie finished stretching, made Polly promise to call her cell if she needed anything and headed out the door. Maybe the endorphins would help her forget about Jeff's abuse and Polly's powerlessness. Maybe it would help her shut out the conversation with Ada's mother.

Maggie stepped onto the porch and closed the door behind her. The temperature had dropped since their excursion to Petrosian's. Fat, lazy snowflakes had been replaced by tiny spitballs of ice that marched across the frozen earth like picketers. The wind that had assaulted Maggie two days ago returned with a grudge.

Maggie pulled on the hoodie of her thermal running jacket and flapped her hands against her arms as she bounced from foot to foot, well aware that she looked like a deranged chicken. She sprang from Camille's tidy porch into a whitewashed world.

Two blocks in, Maggie found her pace. She didn't listen to music while she ran. Not anymore. She didn't like the idea of earbuds impairing her ability to hear, for example, a murderer's footsteps behind her. For Maggie, the thrum of each footfall was accompanied by the steady beat of her heart and a low, tuneless rendition of AC/DC's "TNT," her (former) favorite running song.

I'm TNT. I'm dyn-o-mite.

I'm TNT, and I'll win the fight.

Most runners she knew did their best thinking while on a long run. That's when Maggie did her best non-thinking. She succeeded in washing her mind free of everything but the song's next lyric and a mental note to avoid a rock in the trail or steer clear of the barking Rottweiler ahead.

She was on her third pass of the song's refrain of "Oi! Oi! Oi!", eyes glued to the glazed sidewalk, when goose bumps erupted on her neck. Tiny hairs stood at attention, tenting the skin where skull met spine, starting a chain reaction of shivers that billowed down her back and across her shoulders like a blanket unfurled across a bed.

Maggie felt as if she were being watched.

It wouldn't be the first time unseen eyes had crawled over her, catalogued her moves, recorded her actions in order to set a deadly plan in motion.

Experience taught her it wouldn't be her last.

Maggie picked up speed. She swung her arms. Pictured her legs as pistons. Ignored the funny thing her heart was doing. She felt for her phone. Then she remembered: she'd left it on the charger.

Dammit.

Maggie chanced a glance over her shoulder. The frost-lined street was empty. She couldn't decide if that was a good thing or a bad thing.

She focused on her breathing, on smoothing out the hitches that made it increasingly more difficult to get oxygen to her lungs, to her muscles, to keep her moving forward. She told herself she was being ridiculous. That no one was following her. Why would they?

Except maybe those who blamed her for what happened at Rxcellance. Or the puppeteer who had once held the strings that controlled last year's fatal dance. Or Dr. Mikey who had stared at her over Howard's grave.

Maggie's heart felt as if it were beating in her throat. Maybe this was a good time to head back to Camille's.

Maggie slowed then turned sharply. She suddenly found herself tangled with another human being.

Maggie went sprawling, wind knocked out of her, legs akimbo like a newborn fawn. She put her head in her hands, overcome by a wave of dizziness.

A hand appeared from above. Panic, nameless and insistent, took hold. Maggie scrambled backwards, running shoes skidding, hands scrabbling for purchase.

"Easy, easy," a voice said.

Maggie looked up. Austin Reynolds' worried eyes peered down at her.

"You look like you're about to sprint out of your skin. Are you okay?" He pulled her to her feet.

"I'm fine," she muttered. *Paranoid but fine.*

Austin surrendered her hand and grinned. "Well, I'm glad I ran into you. Or, I guess, the other way around." The grin broadened.

Maggie groaned inwardly. Not only had she spooked herself into a panicky mess, the run-in reminded her of how she had met former-crush Ethan at Rxcellance's watering hole: teetering off slingbacks, falling into his arms, nearly pantsing him in front of dozens of coworkers.

It was like she was collecting meet-cute stories.

Maggie pulled her running jacket closer. The perspiration on her skin had already turned clammy. She could practically feel ice crystals forming. She was annoyed with herself. And annoyed with Austin for seeing her flustered. "You were hoping I'd knock you down?"

"Naw," he said in an accent that was two-part Texan, one-part Midwestern. "But I am glad to see you. Gives us a chance to clear the air."

"I didn't know there was any air to clear."

Austin toed the snow. "It just felt a little awkward running into you after all these years. I mean, it's not like we had any closure after you ran off."

"*I* ran off?" He couldn't be serious. "You were the one who hightailed it out of town."

Austin continued to worry the ground with his shoe. "I meant...you know...emotionally." It was clear that was a word he wasn't used to saying. "One day, we were kissing after the rodeo. The next, you just sort of disappeared into yourself. There, but not there. Then it was over. No fight. No explanation. Just 'we can't see each other anymore.' I needed a fresh start, time away to wrap my head around everything, so I left. Truth is, you'd already been gone a long time."

Maggie released a lungful of air she hadn't realized she was holding, blowing a white plume between them. She knew she had been a bad breaker-upper. She'd blamed lack of practice. Austin had been her second boyfriend. She wasn't even sure she could count Kyle Davis, a serial dater who had gone with nearly every girl in her high school class, as Boyfriend Number One. But that was a poor excuse. Fact was, she had freaked out. She started having feelings for Austin that could derail her commitment to school, get in the way of her goals, keep her off the treadmill of activities designed to force her to move on and never look back. So she shut Austin out, dismissing him with clichés about fish and promises of keeping in touch.

She hadn't believed any of it.

She was sorry for all of it.

"I should have handled things differently," she said softly. "I'm sorry."

Austin held out the hand that had lifted her from the ground. "Apology accepted." They shook, looked down at the ground, then up at the sky. Self-consciousness blew in like bad weather. "How's your aunt?" He held up a hand. "Sorry, your boyfriend's aunt?"

"Not well," Maggie admitted. "And the police's interest in her isn't helping. Her health is very fragile." She didn't mention the hallucination.

He folded his arms across his chest. "Unintended consequences. We're just doing our job."

"I think it's more than a job for your partner."

"What do you mean?" There was an edge to his voice.

"Did you know that Polly convinced your partner's wife to leave him because he was abusive?"

Austin's mouth dropped open. He closed it. "I have no idea what you're talking about."

"When she first moved here, Polly encouraged Greeley's wife to leave him. He's hated her ever since, and I think he's using Howard's murder as payback."

Austin rubbed the back of his neck. "I don't know anything about that. I do know the circumstances don't look good. Polly discovered the body, was covered in Howard's blood, has some cockamamie story about sleepwalking."

"It's not some story. It's real. I've seen it in action, and I think it's tied to her medical condition."

"Uh-huh."

Anger rushed through Maggie, followed by desperation. He had to believe her. If he thought Polly was faking, he'd think she had reason to do so, that the lie was the tip of an enormous iceberg of sin. "It's something she's been dealing with for a while, not some convenient invention. If you saw her while she was sleepwalking, got a look at her eyes, the way she wandered around like a zombie, you'd know she's telling the truth."

Austin nodded noncommittally, as if listening to someone describe the merits of Amway. "Maybe so, and I appreciate you trying to look out for her. She's practically family. But things aren't looking good for Polly. And it has nothing to do with Jeff."

Maggie's stomach dropped. "What do you mean?"

"Well…" Austin suddenly looked uncomfortable, as if he knew he'd said too much. He glanced over his shoulder and leaned in. "I probably shouldn't be telling you this. Actually, I'm damn sure I shouldn't be telling you this. But we found Howard's day planner. There was a note in it the day before he died saying, 'Get away from her. She's evil.' Not exactly an ad for wife of the year."

"But you don't know that he was talking about Polly!" Maggie sputtered. "He could've been talking about Deirdre, the litigious beauty queen, or one of his patients or the mistress everyone seems to think he has."

Austin looked at her. "Howard had a mistress?"

"People seem to think so. And like Polly said, Howard had more than a few enemies. I talked with a lot of people at his funeral. No one was weeping at his demise."

"Okay, okay, so Howard wasn't Mr. Popular, but you have to admit that a lot of signs seem to be pointing to Polly." When Maggie didn't say anything, he opened his coat. He dug in his pocket and pulled out a business card. "The other reason I wanted to see you is to give you my phone number."

His phone number? Didn't he know she had a boyfriend?

He read her face. "In case you think of anything? For the investigation? I wanted you to have my personal cell in addition to my office line."

Maggie's mouth collapsed into a tiny caldera. "Oh. Right."

He scribbled on the card and handed it to her. She tucked it into the strap of her sports bra, which was now glued to her body in an icy film of congealing sweat.

"Welp." He hiked up his pants. "It really was great seeing you, Maggie. I just wish it was under better circumstances."

Then he turned on his heel and walked into the gathering gloom of late afternoon.

Maggie arrived back at Camille's just after dark. She'd ended up logging five miles, not too shabby, considering the conditions. And the interruption.

The conversation with Austin ate at her. Not just his obvious mistrust and prejudgment of Polly, but also his feelings toward her. Pain over their breakup. Delight at seeing her again. Was it more than friendliness? Was he really over her? Was she really over him?

Maggie wanted to slap herself. Of course she was over him. She loved Constantine and what they were together. Her reluctance to take the next step had nothing to do with Austin and everything to do with her.

Constantine was still gone when dinnertime came. He texted a picture of the utility closet where he'd be eating his PowerBar meal.

Camille breezed in after work with fresh anise and fennel-laced Italian sausage from her favorite specialty butcher and began preparing a pasta and red sauce dinner that would make Giada De Laurentiis drool. Maggie had two servings of pasta and three glasses of wine.

She had initially refused the final pour, covering the mouth of the glass with her hand.

"Go on, have another," Polly said, the old twinkle back. "No good story started with salad and a glass of water." It was a sentiment Maggie had once seen on a wine bottle. Good advice could indeed come from anywhere.

Maggie wanted to talk about Jeff Greeley, her impromptu meeting with Austin, and her worry that the police were building their case and Parkinson's was biding its time. But Polly was in too good a mood. Maggie wouldn't ruin it by using her mouth as a pressure valve to release the anxiety she felt inside. She'd talk to Constantine when he returned. Whenever that would be.

The women stayed up chatting, then peeled off one by one for bedtime rituals and twin bed sanctuary.

Maggie dialed Valerie's cell number and cajoled her former co-worker into reading Ada's email address from Madame Trousseau's intranet list of employee contact info. Maggie dashed off a quick note to Ada, imploring her to inquire about a job at her father's food carts, begging for forgiveness for getting her fired and concluding with best wishes. An apology sandwich. Hopefully Ada wouldn't throw it up.

Email sent and guilt a bit abated, Maggie got into her pajamas and nestled beneath the covers that moved like tectonic plates over the bed's sheets. Within minutes, she was asleep.

Until she wasn't.

She opened her eyes wide in the dark, her blood whooshing through her veins.

There was movement outside her bedroom, slippered feet

schussing across carpet on the other side of the paneled door.

Maggie lay motionless, listening. The footsteps grew louder, then faded, presumably down the stairs. There was a creak. The third step, which responded noisily to any tread, groaned as if in judgment about the stepper's weight.

Maggie swung her feet from the bed and pulled the quilt over her shoulders like a cape. She grabbed her phone from the nightstand, hit the flashlight app, and glided silently to the door.

A twist and pull on the handle, and Maggie was peering into the dimly lit hall.

And looking at absolutely nothing.

It had to be Polly sleepwalking her way through Camille's house. But where had she gone?

A new sound floated up the stairs: a door rattling open, clicking shut. Maggie pointed the anemic beam of light toward the staircase and began to make her way down.

As predicted, the third stair announced her presence. She continued her descent. Moments later, she passed through the vacant living room, down the empty hall and into the deserted kitchen.

Light streamed through the window above the farm sink, full moon conspiring with fresh-fallen snow to illuminate the yard. Maggie walked to the window and peered through the glass. The yard was empty.

Maggie pulled open the door that led to the garage.

Polly was behind the wheel of her Subaru.

What?

Before Maggie could comprehend what she was seeing, the car purred to life. The automatic garage door began its journey along the metal track.

"Polly?" she called, softly at first. "Polly!" she shouted.

Maggie ran into the garage and toward the car. She pounded on the car's window, which was mucked with dirt and road salt and dried water droplets. Polly stared straight ahead, eyes focused on some distant vision, mouth slack. Maggie tried to grab the car's door handle, but it was ripped from her hand as the car lurched into gear and hurtled backwards into the driveway.

"Polly!"

Maggie dashed inside, wool sock-clad feet sliding over the kitchen's polished cherry floor. She fell, got to her feet, and ran through the kitchen door and down the hall. She shrugged out of her quilt-cloak, grabbed her purse from the entryway bench and jammed her hand inside for the Studebaker's keys, jabbing herself in the palm. Pain registered distantly, as though hearing about it happening to someone else. She closed her fingers around the keys, shoved her feet into her boots and sprinted out the front door and into the night.

The Studebaker was cocooned in a thick layer of snow. Maggie dragged the arm of her pajamas across the windshield, certain the car's ancient wipers weren't up for the job. She slid behind the wheel, slammed the car into first and stood on the gas pedal.

The Studebaker resisted, bucking until the transmission fully engaged, then slowly began to acquire speed, taking its own sweet time. Studebaker standard, restoration notwithstanding.

Maggie spotted Polly's Subaru ahead, its tail lights a soft pink through the accumulating snow. She pressed the accelerator and narrowed the gap between her car and Polly's.

Polly turned onto a tree-lined street and into a wide driveway fronting a house with a large stone turret Maggie recognized immediately. The Wright residence.

Maggie tried to come up with a good reason why Polly would drive there in the dead of the night.

She couldn't.

Maggie pulled in behind the Subaru and ran to the car. Polly was already gone.

Maggie jogged to the front door, feet wide to keep her balance. She tried the handle. Locked. She peered through the large plate glass window into the living room. Empty. She looked down and saw tiny footprints in the snow.

Maggie followed them.

The footprints rounded the house and disappeared at a large lattice-topped gate. Maggie pushed the gate open, wincing at the creak that shattered a pre-Christmas silent night.

In the Wrights' small backyard, Polly waded through the snow in her thin flannel gown. She circled the perimeter, carving tracks with her pink JCPenney slippers, making her way toward the center of the yard in a concentric pattern. Her eyes had that same unfocused look Maggie had seen a couple of nights before.

Lights on. Nobody home.

Polly was asleep. She had sleep-driven to her home and was now sleepwalking through her yard.

Maggie had read about such phenomena. After Polly's midnight sleepwalking trip to her room and kitchen-messing escapade, Maggie had scoured the internet to learn more about somnambulism. She learned that people were known to do any number of things while sleepwalking. Eat. Have sex. Drive.

Maggie watched as Polly wandered through her yard. The scene was strange. Bizarre even.

But it also provided an opportunity to prove that Polly's sleep disorder was genuine and acute.

Maggie checked the time on her phone. Ten thirty. Early enough to make a phone call.

Or in this case, a FaceTime call.

She opened the app on her phone and dialed.

Austin's face appeared. He looked alert, but confused, eyes squinting as he tried to determine who had just digitally entered his home.

"Austin, it's Maggie."

Austin looked at her blankly. Maybe he was searching his database of Maggies. Maybe he was trying to decide on the reason for the late-night contact, define it as police business or booty call.

Austin bestowed a cautious smile. "Hey, Maggie. What's up?"

"Polly's sleepwalking again," Maggie said in a rush. "She drove to her house and is wandering around the yard like a zombie. I wanted to show you. To prove to you she's not faking."

Austin's face flipped through emotions. Confusion. Shock. Concern. "Polly's at her house?"

"Yes, she sleep-drove here. I want you to see this."

Before he could answer, Maggie spun the phone around and pointed it into the yard. The air was biting at her, turning her arms into a mountain range of bumps. She'd have to make Exhibit A quick. Polly's thin flannel gown wouldn't protect her from the night chill for long.

Maggie followed Polly, who seemed to be homing in on an area in the yard. Polly stopped, swayed for a moment then dropped to her knees.

"Polly!" Maggie began to jog toward her, certain the older woman had fallen.

She stopped when Polly began clawing at the snow with her hands.

She hadn't fallen. She was digging.

Maggie watched slack-jawed as the older woman began dragging piles of snow then earth toward the knees of her nightgown. The spot in the yard was not protected by tree or shrub, but the soil had not yet frozen solid. Dirt, dark and loamy, moved easily beneath Polly's hands.

Polly stopped. She sat back on her haunches then thrust her hand into the small hole she had created.

Maggie thought of a gopher guarding its domain. A nest of spiders. A tangle of centipedes writhing beneath Polly's hands. A dozen dangers lurking below the earth, waiting to bite Polly's trembling hands.

"Polly! Be careful," Maggie called. "You don't know what's in there."

Or maybe she did.

Polly rooted around in the hole then pulled out her hand, fingers coiled around something small and shiny. One by one, her fingers unspooled. A flash. A glint. Moonlight bouncing off a reflective surface.

Polly turned her hand.

In her palm, bathed by the ambient glow of moon and snow, lay a red-streaked knife.

Chapter 8

When bad things happen, it's natural to try to trace the origin. To find the genealogy of error. The root of the problem.

No matter which way Maggie turned the night's events, she was the source.

The police had arrived in minutes. Just to examine the unearthed knife. Just to speak to Mrs. Wright. Just to take her to the station for follow-up questions about her penchant for nocturnal archeology and her guess about the nature of the rust-colored stain on the sharp blade.

"Just." The universe's great pacifier.

Austin was the first to arrive, headlights boring into snow that streaked against the night sky. Maggie and Polly waited in Polly's car with the heater cranked. Two sharp raps on the glass and he was in the doorjamb, hat in hands, toe in snow, his eyes bright with excitement. And why wouldn't he be excited? Their prime suspect had just unearthed what looked suspiciously like the murder weapon, right before his eyes. Maggie had practically slapped the cuffs on Polly herself.

Of course it was too early for cuffs. They "just" wanted to talk with Polly about how she'd managed to dig up a knife she said she'd never seen before, and how she drove a car to her home while asleep. Not that Polly could answer any of that. She had awoken in her backyard, wrist-deep in the ground, continuing to dig for God knew what.

"What are you doing here?" Polly had asked Maggie. Then seeing the earth in her hands, the mud at her knees, "What am *I* doing here?"

Maggie had eased the knife from her hand, took Polly by the arm and led her to the car, where she called Austin back after her hasty disconnect. Then they waited for whatever would come next.

The stream of police officers and crime-scene technicians slowed to a trickle. Additional crime scene tape was added, the proverbial closing of the barn door after the horse got out, and Maggie could feel the dagger-eyed looks of the technicians as they tried to reseal the sacred space of their crime scene.

Polly held Maggie's hand. "I don't understand," she said for the thirtieth time. Maggie had been counting her use of the phrase, starting at its fifth or sixth utterance, rounding up for easy figuring. "I don't understand how I got here or what this knife is."

Maggie didn't understand, either. How did Polly, who scarcely drove at all, manage to drive across town in her sleep and then, upon arrival, dig up the one place in the yard that housed a knife?

Sleep-driving was well-documented, something that could be explained, even with Polly's illness. But the knife...that was trickier. And considerably more inconvenient. The police would surmise that Polly had hidden it there after opening Howard's throat then waited to retrieve it.

Maggie knew this was impossible, not just because she knew Polly's character, but because she knew the woman didn't have the strength to kill her husband. And yet...Maggie saw Polly drive across town in the dark. She saw her drop to the ground, dig in the snow, muscle a knife from the earth—all without seeming to break a sweat. It wasn't just strange. It was disquieting. Even suspicious.

Maggie pushed the thought from her mind and began theorizing. What had brought Polly here and driven her to dig? Maybe she was under some kind of post-hypnotic suggestion. Maybe her subconscious had seen the killer dispose of the murder weapon while Polly was in the hinterland between sleep and wakefulness.

Maybe she hated doing dishes.

Of the options that sprang to mind, Maggie liked the second. The subconscious was a powerful thing. If she had seen the killer, even while she was asleep, a part of her mind could have recorded his actions then played them back later in a compulsive, unconscious drive to undo what had been done to her husband. It fit with her post-sleepwalking confusion, her trip back home. It also suggested a possibility: maybe Polly had seen the killer, even knew him. Maybe his identity was suppressed along with Howard's murder and would bubble to the top, just like the location of the murder weapon.

If that's what it was.

The possibility could mean that Polly was in danger. If she had seen the killer, had known him, he could come for her, wrap up the loose end before his plan to get away with murder unraveled.

Of course now Polly was on her way to the nice, safe police station.

And maybe nice, safe jail.

"You have got to be shitting me."

Constantine was pacing, ping-ponging between Camille's thimble collection and a pile of extra afghans stacked on a refurbished hope chest. "I leave for one night and you get my aunt arrested."

"She's not arrested. She's answering questions."

Constantine flopped into a chair and raked a hand through his hair. "Yeah, at the police station, thanks to you transmitting Polly's return to the crime scene to Officer Reynolds."

"Actually, he's a detective." Constantine looked at her. She collapsed onto the sofa across from him. "I know, I know. God, how I know. This was entirely my fault. I thought I was helping. I thought if I could just show Austin what Polly's like when she sleepwalks, he'd believe her. Start looking for the real bad guy."

"I can't believe you FaceTimed him." It was the sixth time he'd said that. She'd been counting that, too.

"Are you angry that I contacted him or that I caught Polly's knife excavation on camera?" She knew it was a stupid, petty thing to say. Part of her hoped lobbing an unfair accusation would make her feel better. It made her feel worse.

Constantine clenched his jaw, pulled at his earlobe. "I'm not angry," he said angrily. "I'm upset. I'm upset that you documented what could be seen as an incriminating act for the investigating officer. Excuse me, investigating *detective*. I couldn't care less if you contacted Austin."

Maggie flashed on Austin's face. He seemed to feel genuinely sorry for her when he arrived at Polly's house and saw her guilt-stricken face, the way her shoulder slumped and she answered his questions in a flat monotone. She wasn't just wracked with guilt. She was sick with it, the physicality of her culpability spreading through her body like a disease. "This is all my fault," she said again, choking back the sob lurking at the back of her throat. "And I'm going to fix it."

A wariness crept into Constantine's eyes. "Fix it how?"

"I need to do something other than flagellate myself with regret and fun-size Baby Ruth bars." She took four miniature crumpled wrappers from her jeans pocket as proof. "I need to do what we hoped the police would do, but now haven't or won't: examine all possibilities and chase all leads. Jeff Greeley was already determined to put Polly away because of his grudge against her. Now I've furnished him with another bar for her jail cell."

She brought Constantine up to speed about the shared and acrimonious history of Polly and Greeley, punctuating the ending with her hands on her hips. "Polly's innocent," she said, "and I'm going to prove it. Starting right now."

Constantine's face was unreadable for a moment, his olive skin darkening beneath the beard that graveled his cheeks. Then he got up, sat beside her. "I admire your fortitude—and your insanity—but I don't think that's a great idea."

"We'll keep a low profile, visit potential suspects, ask a few questions."

"What's all this 'we' stuff? I don't remember saying yes to felonious interference."

"It's probably not felonious, and I need your help."

"Probably. Now there's a comforting word." He studied her face. "I just don't think this is the way to deal with your guilt."

"And I don't think you're an expert on how to deal with feelings, especially mine," she snapped.

Constantine winced. "Ouch."

Regret was instant and insistent, burrowing under the Wall and crawling into her belly like a living thing. "I'm sorry, Gus. For Polly. For saying that. For everything."

"It's okay, Mags." He pulled her close and buried his face in her hair. Maybe trying to get close to her. Maybe hiding from his worry over Polly or his annoyance at Maggie. "You asking for help is a rarity. How can I resist?"

Chapter 9

Maggie drowned her guilt by diving headlong into investigation mode. Constantine seemed to relish the distraction, as well. It kept their minds off the fact that Polly had been at the police station for several hours. Maggie wasn't sure how long answering the police's questions should take, but she felt that it had already been too long. Much too long.

Maggie grabbed her laptop and suggested they start by looking into members of the I Hate Howard Club. Because Deirdre seemed the most overtly hostile, she won the title of Miss Primary Suspect for Now.

Maggie logged onto Facebook and searched for Deirdre Hart. She linked to her page, which was crowned with a photo collage that featured an 80s-style glamour shot and highlights from Deirdre's career as a JCPenney catalogue model, pageant queen, (two-time winner as Miss Lawn Care) and beauty consultant.

Deirdre's shrine to herself was followed by her grudge against Howard Wright. Post after post detailed Howard's incompetence, Deirdre's suffering, and her journey back to health and the pageant world. It was a typical hate-fest with hysterical posts, overwrought emojis and sympathetic replies assuring her that Dr. Wright—whom she'd dubbed Dr. Wrong, a.k.a. Dr. Hack, a.k.a. Dr. No— would pay.

"Fascinating," Constantine said. "The question is whether she took her rage off the page."

"An in-person visit could be revealing." She tapped the screen, underscoring a post advertising an instructional workshop on good posture at the Sons of Norway Lodge, a favorite spot for community events in Hollow Pine. It was scheduled for two p.m. that day.

It seemed their luck was changing.

They arrived at the Sons of Norway Lodge, a large concrete block building painted a brilliant blue and festooned with an enormous

Norwegian flag. The parking lot was surprisingly full and Maggie had to pull into a convenience store across the street to find a spot. She popped in, bought a pack of gum and walked out with a mouthful of Dentyne and a clear conscience—at least about using the parking space.

She and Constantine plodded across the street, their boots sinking into potholes filled with freezing water. The roadway had been salted to melt the snow, resulting in messy soup that would freeze ice-rink perilous by nightfall.

They stepped inside the cavernous building and let their eyes adjust to the lights, all of which were dimmed save for a spotlight on the stage. Deirdre Hart was at the center, a book on her head, hands by her side.

"I didn't think people actually did the book thing," Constantine said. He nodded toward the title on her head. "I wonder if it's fiction or non-fiction."

"Shh!" Maggie looked at the breast pocket of Constantine's coat, where a pair of pink ears had emerged. "And keep Mighty Mouse out of sight, will you? I don't understand why you insisted on bringing her. I'm surprised you didn't bring her to Howard's funeral."

Constantine stroked the hamster's tiny head. "Because that would have been inappropriate."

Maggie rolled her eyes and returned her attention to the workshop, which involved Deirdre walking from one end of the stage to the other, inviting a student to follow suit, then mocking said student for failure to exhibit a "swanlike neck" or an uplifted sternum.

The parade of walking wannabes continued for several minutes then ended with a break to attend to various biological needs. Teens and tweens, all female, trotted to the ladies' room or clustered around a cornucopia of snack foods next to a Mr. Coffee, which was working overtime.

Those drawn to the snack table nibbled judiciously on mini pretzels and mixed nuts. Maggie thought she might try that technique rather than cramming handfuls of food into her mouth. Just as a change of pace.

They approached Deirdre, an oasis of middle age in a sea of youth. She stood gracefully near the water fountain, one hand cradling a clipboard, one ankle turned out, glasses perched on her nose like the quintessential naughty librarian. All that was missing was a wind machine and the sudden appearance of a bare-chested man.

"Deirdre? I'm Maggie O'Malley."

Deirdre turned toward her. Although Maggie had seen her both at the funeral and on Facebook, getting an up-close glimpse provided a more complete picture.

Deirdre was model-thin with buoyant breasts and drum-taut skin that had been self-tanned to the approximate shade of Cheetos. Her eyes and mouth had been pulled back and up, giving her the appearance of a fish caught on a hook. Her cheeks were buttressed by implants and looked sharp enough to slice deli meat. Maggie could see where she was going with the lawsuit.

Deirdre thrust out an inflated mouth in selfie-worthy duck lips and evaluated Maggie, her eyes appraising her hair, her face, her body. "Good look for those interested in that all-natural thing. And the athletic body type is in." She consulted the clipboard. "But I don't see any Maggie O'Malley on my list."

"Oh, I'm not here for the workshop. I just wanted to ask you a few questions."

Deirdre looked surprised. Of course, she always looked surprised, thanks to Howard's handiwork. "Questions? About what?"

"Howard Wright," Constantine spoke up. "It'll only take a minute."

Maggie thought Deirdre would be upset, but it was impossible to divine any expression on the smooth, shiny face. "Talk to my lawyer," she snapped, turning away.

"We're not here about the lawsuit," Maggie said quickly. "We're here about his death. We're his family, and we're hoping you can tell us if you knew of anyone who wished him ill."

She cackled. "You mean besides me? If you're looking for a suspect, look somewhere else. I hated Howard, but he was worth more alive than dead."

"What do you mean?" Maggie asked.

"What do you think I mean?" she said tartly. "Now that he's dead, the lawsuit is, too. No verdict. No damages. No money to fix what he did." Deirdre touched her face. "This was my fourth procedure. I've done it all. Boobs. Thighs. Nose. Even my lady parts." Maggie wondered if she should offer congratulations. "I should never have trusted Howard with my face."

Maggie cleared her throat. "I, uh, I think your face looks good?" She couldn't keep the question mark out of her voice.

Deirdre rolled her eyes, likely the only parts of her face that could move. "Save the fake compliments. I know what I look like and now so does everyone else. What I don't know is why I'm talking to you people. I need to get back to work."

She turned away.

"I saw your Facebook page," Maggie said quickly. "It was brave of you to post all those pictures."

Deirdre turned back. "Brave? I was pissed, not brave. After the bandages came off, the claws came out. I posted on every social media platform I could so people could see what that idiot did to me."

"Didn't that hurt your work?" Constantine asked.

"If anything, it gave me a boost. The fall from grace followed by the old picking-yourself-up-by-your-bootstraps routine followed by my rebirth as Deirdre Pageant Consultant. That reinvention was the real makeover. Now if you'll excuse me..."

Maggie's mind whirred as she tried to think of a way to keep Deirdre talking. She lighted on the rumors about Howard's cadre of female patients. "We heard you and Howard liked to play Doctor," she blurted.

Deirdre rounded on her, the smile becoming a sneer. "That's a damn lie. The only relationship Howard and I had was doctor-patient." She put her face close to Maggie's. "Where did you hear that?"

Maggie swallowed. "Around."

"Whoever said it is just jealous." Deirdre crossed her arms over pneumatic breasts and squeezed, advertising the presumable source of envy. "And I doubt Howard's murder was a love-hurts scenario. I think Howard finally pissed off the wrong person."

"Like you?" Constantine asked.

Deirdre glared at him. "Who did you say you were again?"

"Relatives."

"I'd say I'm sorry for your loss, but I'm sorrier for mine. Even if I continue to pursue legal action, Howard's estate is going to be tied up for years." She extracted a pretzel from a small white bowl with French-tipped nails and nibbled the corner. "Howard got what he deserved, but now I won't."

Deirdre checked her watch and readjusted her cleavage. Certain that both were as expected, she turned toward the group of pageant hopefuls and clapped her hands. "All right, everyone," she called. "Time to get back to work."

The young women disposed of their snack food remnants and huddled together near the stage awaiting instruction. They looked like a herd of gazelles eyeing a lioness.

Deirdre pointed toward the EXIT sign. Someone had turned the "T" into the cross on the Norwegian flag. "We're done here. I don't want to see or hear from you again." She gave Maggie a final, penetrating once-over. "Except maybe you. There's a Miss Ginger pageant in Springfield. You'd be a shoo-in."

Chapter 10

Out in the parking lot, Constantine smirked at her.

"Not one word," Maggie said. "Not one single word."

"Not even about the bathing suit portion of the competition?"

"No."

"What about my idea of you dressing up as Raggedy Ann for formal wear?"

"*Gus.*"

"Sorry, sorry. I'm just so excited to be dating a potential beauty queen."

"It's not going to happen, so just forget it." Maggie forked snow from the Studebaker's windshield with her gloved hand and clambered into the car, flattening her bulky coat, which clung to the bench seat like a three-year-old mid-tantrum. "Now the real question: what did you think of Deirdre?"

"I think she had a good case against Howard. Put her too close to a heater and she'll melt. Plus she's a dead ringer for the Joker."

She turned the key and backed out of the convenience store lot. "She made a good point about not wanting Howard dead. Like Deirdre said, his estate will probably be tied up for years. I don't know the legalities, but it seems his untimely death could have put a crimp in her plans."

"True, although murder isn't always logical. She's a cool customer now, but I don't think I'd want to get on her bad side. Sounds like she assassinated Howard on social media. Maybe she took it real world. Who knows what she's capable of?" He cracked his knuckles. "So what now?"

Maggie thought about Polly's comment about not knowing what someone's capable of, her suggestion that her husband's practice partner and her longtime friend might be a cipher. Secret. Inscrutable. Known but not knowable.

She put the car in gear. "Now we visit Kenny Rogers."

* * *

The office of Kenneth Rogers, MD, FACS, was housed in Hollow Pine's newest medical facility, a two-story altar of metal and glass that served as a giant magnifying glass for the forest behind it. Unlike the parking lot at the Sons of Norway, the field of asphalt that spread before Pine View Medical Center was as empty as Deirdre Hart's refrigerator.

Maggie parked in front of the glass doors and killed the engine. They got out and gazed up at the vitreous rectangle.

"Howard is dead and now so is business," Constantine said. "Not exactly a compliment for his partner."

"Maybe business has been slow for a while, or maybe Rogers is taking his time getting back into the swing of things after Howard's death. Either way, looks like we won't need an appointment."

The wind gusted, pelting tiny crystals of snow against their faces, and they hurried toward the shelter of commercial construction, chins tucked into jackets. At the entrance, Constantine stopped short.

"What are you doing?" she asked.

He extended one hand. "Using the Force to open the door. Watch this." He stepped on the automated door's sensor and the glass parted. He wiggled his eyebrows. "The Force is strong with this one."

She rolled her eyes. "And so is the corn. Let's go."

AccentYOUate Enhancement Center perched on the second floor in the building's northwest corner between a medical billing business and a dermatology office. Its door was adorned with the photo of an attractive, middle-age woman and the headline, "Your body is a temple. Isn't it time to renovate?"

Constantine fluffed the nap of chest hair that peeped over the collar of his sweater. "My body's more like a 1970s split-level with shag." He put his arm around Maggie. "You're one lucky woman."

"So you've told me."

She pushed open the door.

The waiting room of AccentYOUate Enhancement Center bore Howard's singular thumbprint. Like the home he and Polly shared, the room sported gilded columns, ornate crown molding, and Greek statues flexed in various states of undress. Bulky couches seemed to bully glass tables strewn with old copies of *People* and *Us*. Everything was overdone, overwrought and over the top. Just like Howard.

Maggie wondered for the millionth time why Polly married him and for the zillionth time why Polly had stayed with him. If he made her happy, she certainly hid it. The handful of times Maggie saw them together, they seemed more like quarrelsome roommates than near-newlyweds.

Maggie made her way toward the reception desk, Constantine dawdling behind as he examined a brochure titled "So You're Thinking About Calf Implants." The receptionist pulled a glazed partition and smiled. Like Deirdre Hart, she had a look of perpetual surprise. Without Deirdre's overdone cheek implants and lip injections, however, the overall effect was more natural. "Natural" being a relative term.

"May I help you?" the woman asked. Her face said mid-thirties. Her voice said sixty years and four packs a day.

Maggie looked at the nameplate fronting the window. "Yes, hi, Barbara. My name is Maggie O'Malley and I'd like to see Dr. Rogers."

Barbara consulted her computer then shook her head. Her hair didn't move. "I'm sorry, but you need an appointment to see the doctor."

Evidently no cars didn't equal no need for an appointment.

Constantine stepped forward and gave his most dazzling smile. Barbara returned it and leaned forward. He had that effect on women. "Sorry we didn't make an appointment. Dr. Wright was my step-uncle. We were hoping Dr. Rogers could shed some light on his last days." He thrust his hand through the tiny window. "Constantine Papadopoulos, by the way."

The receptionist squeezed his fingers. "I'm sorry about your uncle, but I'm afraid Dr. Rogers won't be able to see you." She donned an expression of disapproval usually reserved for people who failed to put away their shopping carts. "His schedule is quite full, and he—"

She stopped, her eyes falling to Constantine's pocket. A look of revulsion crossed her face. "Is that a mouse?"

Constantine looked down. Miss Vanilla peered from her tiny fabric lanai, whiskers dancing. "Hamster," he corrected, "but she thinks she's a gerbil." He winked. "We humor her."

"We don't allow rodents in our medical facility," Barbara said primly, as if this might be a regular request.

"What if they have an appointment?"

A door adjacent to the reception desk opened and a man in a doctor's lab coat emerged. He was compact with mocha-colored skin and close-cropped salt and pepper hair. His eyes traveled over the three faces before him. "Everything okay, Barbara?"

"Everything is fine," she said, turning the last word into two syllables that would rhyme with Dinah. "They were just leaving."

The man gave Maggie and Constantine a quizzical look. "Did you need an appointment?"

"Actually, we wanted to talk to you, Dr. Rogers," Constantine said. "I'm Constantine Papadopoulos. Your partner was married to my aunt."

Surprise flitted across Rogers' face. "Polly's nephew. Yes, I see the family resemblance." They shook hands. "I'm sorry about Howard. He was a fine man."

"Thank you." Constantine looked down, taking the requisite beat of silence. "I wonder if you might have a moment. We have a few questions about Howard."

"Of course, of course." Dr. Rogers opened the door to the inner sanctum of his practice. The receptionist cleared her throat. "It's all right, Barbara. I won't be long."

Barbara huffed and took out her frustration on her keyboard, stabbing the Enter key with her middle finger, a selection that seemed more than coincidence.

Rogers led Maggie and Constantine through a door placarded with *Patients & Staff Only*.

"Don't mind Barbara," he said as they walked along a corridor lined with patient After photos. "She's just trying to protect me. It's my first day back from vacation, and I'm trying to dig out."

Vacation. That explained his absence from Howard's funeral—sort of. Wouldn't the sudden and violent death of a friend and business partner warrant a hasty return from vacation? Maggie left her mental check in the Suspicious Behavior column.

Rogers turned into a small office, closed the door and tucked his small frame into a red chair. The wall behind him was papered with diplomas and a smattering of personal photos depicting the doctor recreating in tropical climes, his nose striped with zinc oxide. Sunscreen. The real fountain of youth.

"Please," he said indicating a pair of tufted white chairs. "Make yourselves comfortable."

He folded his hands. "I'm really not sure what I can tell you about Howard. He was your step-uncle, after all. I assume you've already talked with the police?"

Constantine nodded. "We did, but we thought you could offer some insight into his professional life. We've gotten the feeling that Howard wasn't exactly popular."

"Where did you hear that?"

"Around."

Rogers shifted in the red chair, which squeaked in protest. "I wouldn't say that Howard was disliked. He was...misunderstood."

"By Deirdre Hart and Dr. West?" Maggie asked. "I'm Maggie O'Malley. The, um, girlfriend."

Kenny Rogers offered his hand and a tight smile. "Ah, yes, Miss Hart. There was a fair amount of acrimony, but her rancor was ill-placed."

"I've seen Deirdre," Maggie said. "Seems like she had a legitimate gripe."

Rogers spread out large hands with perfect cuticles. "Surgical results can be unpredictable, and in Ms. Hart's case, adjustments could have been made. She didn't give Howard the chance."

"Pride?" Constantine asked.

"Patience. Or lack thereof. She suffered from immediate gratification syndrome. She didn't get what she wanted right away and nothing could be done to placate her. You can't please everyone."

"Mmm." Maggie let her eyes wander over Rogers' ego wall. "What about the medical community? Other doctors? I heard rumors that Howard's willingness to undercut the competition ruffled some feathers."

Rogers placed his hands together as if in preparation for prayer. "Howard was a shrewd businessman and brilliant marketer. His methods may have been somewhat unconventional, but Howard was an undeniable success."

Maggie remembered a TV ad where Howard promised viewers that he'd suck out their thighs but not their wallets, offering a ten percent discount if they allowed him to ZipLip—an alternative to Snapchat—the procedure.

"Any objections concerning his use of social media?" Maggie asked. "ZipLipping surgeries has got to be an ethical gray area."

Rogers affixed a smile. It looked as though it had come from a box: stiff, waxy, disposable. "Not at all. It's perfectly within the confines of privacy if the patient agrees and he or she remains anonymous. Of course..." Rogers lifted a shoulder. "There were comments, judgments, among some in the medical community, but Howard brought in patients. He was famous." He flashed the hashtag sign. "Hashtag SnipTuckDoc."

"Sounds like Howard cast a long shadow," Maggie said. "Maybe one of his competitors didn't like losing out on the spotlight."

"Or maybe one of his patients changed her mind about being in it," Constantine said.

"This sounds less like an exploration of Howard's professional life and more like a hunt for suspects." Rogers' voice was sweater-vest warm, but his eyes were hard. "Shouldn't you be leaving that sort of thing for the police?"

"Oh, we are," Constantine said. "We're just...supposing."

Rogers put his hands on his knees and hoisted himself from his chair. "Well, I doubt it's going to net you anything of value. From what I understand, Howard's death was the result of a home invasion."

"The police seem to think he knew his killer," Constantine said. "No sign of forced entry."

Rogers opened his mouth. Closed it again. "I hadn't heard that." He circled the desk and opened the door with a flick of his wrist. Strains of Enya floated from hallway speakers. "In any case, I'm sure the police will find out what happened in short order. Then we can put all of this unpleasantness behind us."

Unpleasantness. As if a throat-slitting were on par with rush-hour gridlock.

Us. As if Rogers somehow shared the pain of Howard's murder.

"I'm sorry I couldn't be of more help. I'd do anything for Polly. She's..." His eyes grew soft. "She's a remarkable woman. She must be going through absolute hell."

Maggie pictured Polly at the police station, coat placed carefully over a chair, hands folded and tremorous in her lap. Rogers had no idea.

Constantine extended his hand. "Thank you for your time, Dr. Rogers. We know you're busy, and this can't be how you wanted to spend your first day back."

Rogers walked them to the door of the waiting room. "The vacation was over the moment I heard about Howard. I flew back immediately, but of course there was nothing I could do. Howard is dead. Now I have to make sure my practice doesn't suffer the same fate."

Chapter 11

Constantine and Maggie skated across the deserted parking lot, once again sheltering their faces from blasting snow that could double as a rejuvenating treatment at AccentYOUate, and dove into the Studebaker. Maggie turned the key. The car coughed then roared to life. The magic of carbureted resuscitation.

"Well, that was weird," Constantine said as he buckled the lap belt.

"Which part—that he said he flew back immediately when he heard about Howard and didn't, or that he doesn't seem particularly broken up about his partner's violent murder?"

"Either. Both. And maybe he did fly back and just didn't show at the funeral."

Maggie navigated the parking lot's snowdrifts as if they were cones on a slalom course. The Studebaker shuddered around the hairpin turn that led to the main drag. She needed new snow tires. She also needed a job to buy them. She eased up on the gas and tightened her grip on the wheel. "Neither option makes him look overly concerned."

"Or surprised," Constantine said. "A vacation makes a dandy alibi."

She looked over at him. "So, what, Rogers killed Howard out of professional jealousy?"

"Or irritation. From what I saw, being married to Howard was no treat. I can't imagine working with him would be."

Maggie considered this. "Add in Deirdre's social media hatchet job and disapproval from colleagues, and Rogers could have wanted to cut Howard out of the picture. Permanently."

"On the other hand..." Constantine stared out the passenger window, thinking. "Howard was the big name and, if you believed his ads, the biggest cosmetic surgery mover and shaker in the region." He looked back at her. "If Rogers was used to milking Howard's cash cow, he'd want to keep him in the barn."

"He didn't approve of Howard's tactics, but wasn't above reaping the rewards. Like Deirdre, Howard's death hurt him. There goes motive."

Constantine shrugged. "Not necessarily. Don't forget the falling out Aunt Polly mentioned. And speaking of Polly, did you see the way Rogers went all moony-eyed when he talked about her?"

Maggie gaped. "You think Rogers has the hots for Polly?"

"As someone in recovery as an unrequited-loveaholic, I would say yes."

Maggie blushed the way she always did when she thought about how long Constantine had thought of her as more than a friend, how many signs she had missed. "Even if Rogers loved Polly from afar, that doesn't change the fact that the major draw to his practice is gone and that he was on vacation when Howard was murdered."

Constantine reached into Maggie's glove box, produced a package of Bubble Yum and popped two pieces into his mouth. "Or so he says," he said with his mouth full. "I say we see for ourselves."

The drive to Camille's was delayed by a collision between a street deicer and a commercial ice truck, which Maggie found both ironic and annoying. Thirty minutes later, they opened the red door of the bungalow.

It smelled like an explosion at the Yankee Candle factory.

Scents of cinnamon, nutmeg and clove mingled with notes of vanilla and almond, each competing for olfactory attention. Constantine closed his eyes and inhaled deeply. "Ah, the sweet smell of normalcy. Almost makes me forget that the world has gone to hell and forgot its hand basket."

They slid out of their boots and ambled down the hall to the kitchen where the music of pots and pans drifted through the door like a private Stomp concert. Maggie pushed open the door and found Camille covered in flour and up to her elbows in batter.

"Oh, hi, sweetheart. Just thought I'd do a little baking."

"A little baking?" Constantine said. "It looks like you're planning a Hostess takeover."

Camille poured batter into a Bundt pan and wiped her hands on a towel depicting what appeared to be a barnyard board meeting. "The more worried I am, the more I bake." Her face fell like a soufflé. "You hear about Polly?"

Constantine waved away her concerns with his hands. "Yes, yes, but it's nothing to worry about. The police just had some questions about why Polly was at her house. Standard operating procedure. She should be back any minute."

Maggie wondered whether the denial was for his benefit or Camille's.

Camille put a flour-whitened hand to her heart. "Oh, thank God. I've been beside myself. Polly's so frail and with all the stress—" Her voice broke. "I just don't want her to get worse."

Constantine's hand lighted on her shoulder. "She'll be fine. Really."

Their hostess' relief was palpable—and temporary. She looked at her watch. "Good heavens, is that the time? I'm going to be late." She whisked off her white apron and draped it on a hook beneath a pink cat clock with eyes and a tail that moved in time with the second hand. "I need to get the rest of this in the oven and get to work. Can you take it out for me? Make sure it springs back when touched in the middle?"

Maggie promised to check the baked goods for resiliency then she and Constantine left her in peace to wrestle the remaining batter into tins.

They climbed the stairs and turned into Constantine's room. Constantine took Miss Vanilla from his pocket and deposited her on her hamster wheel. She ran with the urgency of an Olympic hopeful.

He turned to Maggie and looked at her expectantly. "Laptop?"

"For?"

"Spying, naturally. Thought we could pry into Kenny Rogers' life."

"You didn't bring your computer?"

"I leave work at work. No, really. I left my laptop at work when I went in for that little IT emergency. Now it's enjoying a getaway in the utility closet of an ad agency."

Maggie sighed and retrieved her laptop from its temporary home in the adjacent guestroom. She flopped onto the bed, sprawled out on her stomach and booted up the computer. Moments later, they were at the Facebook search bar.

Maggie keyed in Rogers' name and was rewarded with two hits: one for Dr. Rogers' professional page and one for his personal Facebook profile. She poked around both.

"Looks like his practice page is basically a series of shares from Howard's updates," she said.

"Maybe Facebook isn't his thing."

"Or maybe he's content to ride coattails." She clicked over to

Rogers' personal page. "He doesn't post much here, either, although he did upload a few pictures involving sand and margaritas a couple of days ago. Seems he really was on vacation."

"Any lady friends in those photos?"

Maggie pointed, clicked, repeated. Hotel. Pool. Pool. Drinks. Beach. All alone. "Survey says: solo flight."

"Probably pining for Polly the whole time."

Maggie tapped her mouth with her forefinger. "If we're talking professional jealousy—or irritation—Rogers isn't the only doc in that category." She told Constantine about her conversation with Dr. Mikey at the funeral then cruised over to Mikey's social media channels.

He, too, used Facebook and Twitter as both portfolio and coupon book. He, too, ZipLipped his procedures, grinning maniacally as he injected, suctioned and implanted.

"Unseemly but not exactly damning," Constantine said." What about the king of crass himself? Have you searched Howard's social media channels?"

She Googled.

Where Dr. Mikey had a social media footprint, Howard had a kingdom.

Live streaming on Facebook, subtweets on Twitter, high-production ZipLip videos that made up for brevity with sheer spectacle. On Thursdays, he performed the Bodacious Bosom Dance, which Maggie mentally christened Throw Up Thursdays. #Creepy.

Maggie slogged through posts about sagging chins and drooping bottoms, how to prop up wrinkles and sand away laugh lines. Occasionally, Howard mentioned Polly, but only as an adjunct to what he was doing. Wife as fashion statement and lifestyle accessory. Somehow that was just as Maggie had expected.

Maggie pushed away the laptop and rolled onto her back. "Nothing earthshattering. Not so much as a tremor."

Constantine opened his mouth to reply. There was a knock at the door. Camille opened the door without waiting for a reply.

"I was just about to leave when I remembered," she said by way of greeting.

"Remembered what?" Constantine asked, rising from the bed.

"To ask you to take the boxes to the garage."

Constantine looked from Camille to Maggie then back to Camille. "Boxes?"

"For the rummage sale." Camille waltzed into the room and began tidying: straightening wall hangings, tweaking a doily, adjusting the blinds. "A man from church is coming to pick them up this afternoon, but they're too heavy for me to carry downstairs. It's amazing how much junk two ladies can accumulate."

Maggie perked up at that. "Polly has things for the rummage sale, too?"

"We began collecting items weeks ago. Howard brought Polly's boxes over so we could consolidate efforts. This was before...before..." She waved a hand, let it drop. Tears shimmered in her eyes, then breached their lidded banks. "Before everything."

"We'll take care of it," Constantine said gently. "Don't worry about a thing."

"Thank you." Camille sniffed enthusiastically and fished a tissue from the waistband of her Lululemon pants. She dabbed her eyes and nose, then packed the tissue back into her waistband. "You'll call me when Polly gets home? Let me know that she's okay?"

"Of course."

"Polly is lucky to have family like you." Camille smoothed the quilt at the end of the bed, let her hand trail over a wooden sign that read *Love Lives Here*. "I'm lucky to have you, too." She glided out of the room, clicking the door shut behind her.

Maggie got to her feet. "Are you thinking what I'm thinking?"

"Nooner?"

Maggie punched him on the arm. "Maybe there's something in those boxes that tells us about Howard—and why someone would want him dead."

Maggie opened the bedroom door and listened. Downstairs she heard the jangle of keys, the scrape of feet, the front door opening and closing. She flung open the bedroom door and jogged down the hall to the master suite, which held court beside a bathroom decorated entirely in pink. Outside the raised panel door stood four cardboard boxes. Maggie lifted open the flaps on the one nearest her and began pawing through the contents.

Constantine watched her ransack. "Doesn't this seem a little, I don't know, snoopy?"

Maggie continued sifting. "Whatever's in here is headed for a rummage sale, not a safe deposit box. If anything, the police should've had first dibs as part of their investigation. Polly probably forgot about the boxes or didn't think they were important enough to mention. Far as I'm concerned, it's fair game."

Constantine continued to watch for a moment then shrugged and began his own mining operation.

Twenty minutes later, they had excavated two worn handbags, a mountain of clothes, three clock radios, an electric manicure set, six devotionals and eight pairs of shoes.

The shoes included a pair of loafers, men's size nine and a half, which Maggie guessed belonged to Howard. She wondered what the police would have to say about potential evidence walking off on a stranger's feet, post-rummage sale. She set the shoes aside for Austin and sat back on her haunches.

"Not much here other than the shoes," she said, trying not to show her disappointment, trying harder not to feel it. "Maybe the police can turn up some kind of trace evidence on the soles." She folded the flaps back in and hoisted a box to her hip.

"Hang on, what's this?" Constantine was head-first in a box, his voice muffled by cardboard. He poked his head out and thrust his hand upward. "I have something."

Maggie squinted. Constantine pinched a small plastic rhombus between thumb and forefinger.

"What is it?"

"Memory card." He looked at her. "Your laptop has a card reader, right?"

Chapter 12

Back in Constantine's room, they sat on the bed, laptop between them. He loaded the card into the machine. A directory of files appeared. All JPEGs.

Photos.

Constantine arched a brow. "Must have fallen out of a camera. Let's see what the shutterbug captured."

Constantine clicked the files, opening digital peepholes into someone else's life. Motorcycles. Automotive items. Camping gear. Men playing sports and drinking beer. Images of manly men and manly things with one exception, repeated again and again.

A woman. Attractive. Blonde. Curvy, with a deep and abiding love for crop tops.

She was in photo after photo. Leaning against a sports car. Smiling from atop a horse. Waving from behind a spray of flowers at a farmers' market. She was alone, smiling at the shutterbug behind the lens, in all but one photo. In that one picture, Howard's cameo was in profile as he kissed her on the cheek, his face shadowed by her wide-brimmed hat.

Constantine's face darkened. "That cheating bastard."

Maggie felt her heart drop. She wondered how long the affair had been going on. If Polly knew. If Howard started cheating before Polly felt the first twinges of illness or after Parkinson's had tightened its stranglehold.

Maggie shook her head. Right. Focus. This development was good news. She shared her perspective with Constantine.

"Good news?" he said. "I appreciate a glass-half-full point of view, but how is Howard's cheating good news?"

"The fact that there's another woman means that there's someone else with a motive for killing Howard. Jealousy over Polly. His reluctance to leave his marriage. A lover's quarrel. You name it, there are a million reasons this woman could have wanted him dead. And a million reasons for the police to investigate her and leave Polly alone."

"True." Constantine stroked a bumper crop of stubble. "The trick is getting the police to investigate. They seem very interested in Aunt Polly."

"I say we talk to her ourselves, learn about their relationship, report back to the police. I know Austin will listen."

"Because he still loves you."

"Because he's a moral human being who wants justice to be served."

"Mmm-hmm."

Maggie turned back to the photo of Howard and his Twinkie. The scene reminded Maggie of the kind of backdrops to be selected at Sears Portrait Studio. *We'll use the Philandering Frolic background and take two eight-by-tens.*

"Can you tell where the photo was taken?" she asked.

Constantine right-clicked the file and selected Properties then Details. Latitude and longitude coordinates appeared. He copied and pasted into Google Maps.

Maggie read the location that was pinned. "Three Rivers. What's that, three hundred miles away?"

"Five hundred miles and two states, but who's counting."

Maggie clicked the pin's link and found herself on the Three Rivers Visitors & Convention Bureau website. The image gallery portrayed it as a mountainy tourist town.

Constantine peered over her shoulder. "It's like the lovechild of Dodge City and the Matterhorn."

"Too bad it's so far away or we could go visit the other woman in person."

"Think it'll help Polly?"

"No way to know for certain, but it's more helpful than sitting here on our hands. With this weather, it would take us two days to get there. I'm just not sure we have that kind of time."

"Fortunately, I have frequent flier miles and a penchant for impulsive traveling." He pulled her close and nuzzled her neck. "I say we pay a surprise visit to Howard's mystery woman. Not to mention the town's *Star Trek* museum. I hear they have an incredible display of Tribbles."

Chapter 13

Last-minute travel plans meant hasty packing and an even hastier goodbye to Camille, who upon her return from work, shoved sandwich bags of baked goods into their hands as if the safety of their flight depended on oatmeal raisin cookies. She hugged them goodbye with instructions to visit the town's chalet, a tourist trap masquerading as a restaurant styled to look like something off the set of *Heidi*. "I've never been to Three Rivers, but I've heard all about the chalet," she gushed. "Take pictures!"

Last-minute travel plans also meant separate seats on an overcrowded flight. Two of Maggie's least favorite things: air travel and a surplus of humans.

Maggie struggled toward the rear of the plane, accidentally bumping the elbows of three passengers with her unwieldy carry-on, which Constantine had nicknamed her "carrion" due to its decaying plastic which molted a fine dust of turquoise wherever it was touched.

She carefully stowed the bag in the overhead compartment, waved to Constantine whose seat abutted First Class and its font of free cocktails and effusive flight attendants, and settled against the window.

She paged through the in-flight magazine, skimming descriptions of places she'd likely never go, slowly inhaling the plane's re-circulated air. It smelled like ozone, disinfectant and BO. A man arranged his own carry-on bag, slid into the seat beside her, then smiled. Maggie pretended to be fascinated by an article about Bend, Oregon.

She'd never been much for chitchat and she definitely wasn't in the mood today. She had to catch up on self-blame. Polly. Ada. Not telling Constantine about being fired. There was plenty of material.

The man put an elbow on the shared armrest and leaned over. "Business or pleasure?"

He was middle-aged, bespectacled, with a shock of unruly black hair. An aging Harry Potter without the lightning-bolt scar. Maggie considered her options: tell him she was flying to get information from the possible mistress of a murdered man, or say that she was attending a holiday family reunion. She went with the latter.

Mistake.

Mr. Armrest launched into a story about his family's last reunion in Topeka and a squabble about an inherited violin and whose potato salad was really homemade. Maggie nodded solemnly as though she understood the pain of misjudged salads.

The flight attendant went through her spiel about illuminated exits and water landings, which seemed unlikely given their landlocked location. When she finished, Mr. Armrest leaned over again. Maggie coughed enthusiastically into her elbow. "Just getting over bronchitis," she said, hoping the illness sounded serious and contagious enough to afford her a little space. She was ready to change her condition to something intestinal if it didn't.

Mr. Armrest took the hint and began his own in-flight reading journey. The plane taxied, took off and climbed toward its cruising altitude. Maggie looked out the window, seeing nothing.

She had intended on doing an examination of conscience as a warm-up, to tally up her shortcomings as a segue into brainstorming how to prove Polly's innocence and the other woman's guilt. Instead, she fell asleep.

She awoke with Mr. Armrest jiggling her elbow. "We're here," he said a bit too jauntily. "Don't worry. You didn't snore much."

Maggie wiped the saliva from the corners of her mouth then stood to hoist her bag from the bin, opening her eyes wide to appear as alert as possible.

She met Constantine at the mouth of the plane's gangway. He'd made friends with his traveling companion and they both flashed Spock's "Live long and prosper" gesture in farewell.

Maggie spotted a new *Star Trek* communicator on his shirt and felt a flare of exasperation. His aunt was very ill. They were trying to eliminate her from the suspect list and incriminate the real killer. There was a time and a place for Constantine's signature goofiness. This wasn't it.

"You're taking this trip seriously, right?" Maggie said between gritted teeth.

Constantine's face crumpled. "Of course I'm taking this seriously. Just because I joke around and talk about whether Kirk is better than

Picard doesn't mean I'm taking any of this lightly. Aunt Polly is more than my mother's sister. She's the person who taught me how to drive. Who gave me my first drink. Who believed in me when I changed from pre-med to IT. I love Polly, and I'm worried as hell about her. Just because I'm smiling doesn't mean I'm happy."

He looked at her. "You should know that better than anyone."

Maggie suddenly felt sick with shame. Of course she knew that. Not just because they had grown up together, had hurt together, had survived together. She knew because humor was one of her favorite hiding places, too. She'd let herself forget that.

She opened her mouth to apologize. Constantine's phone rang.

"Sam Graham," he said, checking the screen. They found a private alcove where a bank of old pay phones used to stand. He put the phone on speaker and held it aloft.

"Constantine." Graham's typical monotone had a hint of emotion. "I have an update for you."

Constantine clenched his teeth. Maggie could see a muscle in his jaw twitch. Updates, like news, weren't always good. "Yes, Sam. Go ahead."

"I'm afraid Polly has been arrested." The monotone dropped away, the hinted-at emotion becoming clear. "I'm afraid" wasn't just an expression. There was real fear in Graham's voice. "It's nonsense, of course. All they have is supposition. Suggestion."

And a possible murder weapon unearthed in the dead of night, Maggie thought.

"Even as a circumstantial case, it's weak," Graham continued. "I don't think I'll have any problem getting it overturned."

Constantine blanched. "You're taking the case?"

"Of course. I'm her attorney."

"But you said you're not a defense attorney. You handle wills and spills."

"I'm not just a country lawyer, Constantine." Graham's voice had dropped several degrees. "Yes, I mostly handle estate planning and the occasional tort, but I have had experience in criminal law. I've agreed to handle Polly's case as a favor to her. At her request, I might add."

"Polly's in no shape to be making those kinds of decisions," Constantine said tightly. "She's not well."

"I agree that her physical health isn't good and she's been acting a bit...erratic. But I just spoke with her and she sounds right as rain. She's competent enough to make these kinds of decisions." He paused for effect. "I'm keeping you advised as a courtesy."

The muscle in Constantine's jaw jumped again. He drew his lips into a thin line. "I appreciate you keeping me up to date, Sam. Please let me know if you hear anything else. And tell Aunt Polly I'm thinking about her." His voice cracked. He coughed to cover it.

"I will," Graham said. Then he was gone.

Maggie felt as if she had swallowed a handful of thumbtacks. Polly had been arrested. She was sick and alone and in jail. She couldn't imagine Constantine forgiving her. She couldn't imagine forgiving herself.

The guilt over working too much and visiting too little was a blip compared to what she felt now. The undertow of culpability began dragging her out to the black depths of past regrets, doing too much, not doing enough.

Her mother.

Ada.

Polly.

The penitential rite began thrumming through her head, conjuring up Catholic school drills and Mass with her father.

I have sinned through my own fault.

In what I have done and in what I have failed to do.

She wanted to beat her breast. She wanted to make things right. She wanted to go back in time to before FaceTiming Austin, before confronting Alexa, before sticking her nose into the dark, secret places of Rxcellance.

As she mentally flagellated herself, Maggie heard Constantine on the phone, first trying (and failing) to reach his parents in Italy, then calling a lawyer at a firm at which Constantine had installed a new router. Maggie half-listened as he laid out his concerns about Graham representing Polly, his suspicion that Polly wasn't well enough to make that decision.

He stabbed the phone to end the call. "Mark Weber, attorney at law. Make that *criminal* attorney at law. He said he'll talk to Aunt Polly about representing her, go over his experience and expertise in defending—" He paused. "In criminal cases. If she tells him to go pound sand, we'll have to decide whether to question Polly's competency."

He ran his fingers through his hair. "I have concerns about Graham's ability, but I'm not sure how far I want to push this."

Maggie's heart clenched. She imagined a hearing before a judge, experts trotted out to share their evaluations of Polly, Polly defending herself—or not.

The Pandora's box she'd opened with the FaceTime video seemed to have another one inside. Nesting Pandora's boxes. She closed her eyes and fought against the tears that threatened to scale the Wall.

She felt a hand on her shoulder. She turned. Constantine met her eye. The kindness she saw there made her feel even worse. How could he be so nice? Didn't he know that she was responsible for his favorite aunt going to jail, for the terrible and potentially humiliating legal fight that lay ahead? Didn't he understand the depth of her wrongs, her faults, her worthlessness?

Constantine wiped a tear she hadn't felt sliding down her cheek. "It's okay. It's all going to be okay."

A tear fell onto Maggie's jeans, dissolving the Wall in a ragged indigo blotch. "How is it going to be okay?"

"We'll get Polly the best lawyer—the right lawyer. We'll find out who killed Howard. We'll move forward, focused on what we can do to change the future instead of moaning that we can't change the past." He squared his shoulders. "The first item on the agenda: doing what we came here to do."

Maggie swiped her eye and nodded. "Go visit Howard's Twinkie?"

Constantine turned up the edge of his collar and grabbed their bags. "Go visit Howard's Twinkie."

In addition to milkmaid braids and a toothy grin, the woman in Howard's photos wore a logoed polo shirt. Maggie had pinched and prodded the picture until it was large enough to make out the words: Waxing Poetic.

A Google search yielded the website's business, complete with address, a description of services, which included waxing for those who "dare to go bare," and Yelp reviews extolling the waxers' ability to ever so gently rip out pubic hair by the root.

Constantine navigated their rented Hyundai to Three Rivers' downtown and parked in front of a sign marked "Hitchin' Post." Snow, deeper and denser than in Hollow Pine, had been shoveled down the center of the sidewalk, creating a maze that skirted the village's centerpiece, a now-frozen pond where (according to the Chamber of

Commerce website) lovers congregated to throw coins into the water as offerings to whatever deity granted cash-incentivized wishes.

They bypassed one quaint shop after another until they found themselves in front of a salon with a pink door and a female silhouette that reminded Maggie of Madame Trousseau's.

Woman as shadow. It seemed to be a theme.

They stomped the snow from their boots and opened the door. The spa was heavy on kitsch with retro illustrations accompanied by snarky speech bubbles, leopard-print furniture and plastic palm trees. Abba warbled through the spa's speakers. Maggie was perusing the spa's menu of services when the woman from Howard's photos emerged from a beaded partition in the back of the room.

She was pretty in a way that Maggie's Aunt Fiona would describe as hard. Her skin was spackled with foundation, her eyes rimmed with electric blue liner and topped with false lashes, her mouth overdrawn with a berry-hued lip liner that gave her a slightly vampire-esque look. She was older than her picture, her makeup bleeding into fine lines like rivulets into a delta.

The woman eyed them both. "Are you here for the Adam and Eve couples' wax? We stopped running the buy-one-get-one special, but you do get matching fig leaves."

"Uh, no," Maggie said. "No couples' wax for us."

The woman peered at Maggie's upper lip. "Lip wax?"

Maggie covered her mouth with her glove. "No, actually, we wanted to talk with you. I'm Maggie and this is Constantine." She cleared her throat and tried to sound confident and authoritarian. "Sorry, I didn't get your name?"

"It's Jenna." She looked from Maggie to Constantine. "What do you want to talk to me about? You're not here about that Brazilian I did for that lady last week, are ya? I told her not to move and she—"

"No, we wanted to see what you can tell us about this man." Maggie pulled her phone from her purse and opened the picture of Jenna and Howard she'd copied from the memory card. She handed the phone to Jenna, who enlarged the photo with black-tipped nails.

Jenna paled beneath her makeup, illuminating the veins beneath her skin, reminding Maggie of the Visible Woman anatomical doll Fiona had given her when she was ten. Jenna looked at Maggie, tears dangling from her false lashes. "Why?" she sobbed. "Why are you showing me a picture of my dead brother?"

Chapter 14

Maggie found her voice first. "Your brother?"

She tried to remember the picture of Jenna and Howard. The kiss. The smile. The implied intimacy of the two sheltered beneath her hat. They had seemed like boyfriend and girlfriend. Or had her mind simply filled in the blanks, manufacturing romance where there had only been filial affection?

Jenna covered her mouth and nodded. "Matt. He's been gone five years."

Maggie and Constantine exchanged looks.

"Matt?" Constantine asked.

"Gone?" Maggie asked.

Jenna sniffled and pressed fingers beneath her eyes to stem the stream of mascara and liner. "He died in a boating accident. Some days I still can't believe he's gone."

Maggie felt like someone was playing Fifty-Two Card Pickup with her brain cells. Everything she thought she knew was scattered in a spectacular spray of chaos. Maybe she could pick them up, reshuffle and reassemble them into some semblance of order. Maybe she'd never find them all.

"You're sure?" she asked, half aloud, half to herself.

Jenna rewarded her with a look Medusa would envy. "Of course I'm sure. He was my brother. What I'm not sure about is why you're showing me his picture, *our* picture." Her tears had dried into furrows of foundation on her cheeks.

"I'm so sorry," Constantine said. "It's just that we knew your brother as Howard. He was murdered last week."

Anger turned to confusion then to fear. "I don't understand."

Constantine pulled out his own phone then tapped and scrolled until he found the newspaper article about Howard's murder. Below the breathless headline was the PR photo Howard used for his ads, the one that made him look serious and doctor-y but in an approachable way that, in theory, would make it less awkward to have him professionally handle your breasts.

He handed the phone to Jenna. "We've been trying to find out who killed him, who would want him dead. He was my aunt's husband. We came across your photo on a memory card, which I think belonged to How—your brother. We didn't know anything about a Matt or a boating accident."

Jenna didn't seem to be listening. "I don't understand," she said again. "I just don't..." She enlarged the newspaper photo on Constantine's phone. "This doesn't make any sense."

"Is the man in the newspaper article your brother?" Maggie's voice was low and rhythmic, the kind of voice used to entice a wild animal to take food from her hand.

Jenna stared at her as though awakening from a dream. "Yes, but he looks different."

"Different how?" Maggie asked.

"Just different, like I said." An edge had crept into Jenna's voice. She peered into the phone as if it were a crystal ball. "But I know it's him. His two front teeth turn in a little, he's got that same birthmark on his cheek. And see that notch on his earlobe?" Maggie checked the lobe and nodded. "He's always had that. We used to say he was earmarked. We thought we were so clever. And that pose? The way he tilts his head and puffs out his chest? Classic Matt."

Or classic Howard.

"You say he died in a boating accident five years ago?" Constantine asked.

"Yes, he had gone upstate to go fishing. He went by himself, which wasn't unusual, and he didn't call for several days, also not unusual. When he didn't show up for work, we got worried. There's no phone service out there, so Dad and I drove up to check on him."

Jenna took a big shuddering breath. She plunked down on the leopard-print couch and began to massage the fabric. "It took a week to find his body. They sent divers into the lake again and again, and they didn't turn anything up. We started to think we'd overreacted, that Matt had decided to take a road trip or something. Then they pulled him out of the water." The fingers clenched the fabric, then clawed. "He didn't even look like a person anymore."

"How did you know it was him?" Maggie regretted the question as soon as it left her lips.

"Because he's my brother," Jenna snapped. "He had on his favorite fishing shirt, those terrible camo pants I always hated. It was definitely him."

Maggie pointed at Constantine's phone. "But so is this."

Something seemed to break in Jenna. She turned on Maggie, her eyes wild with pain and grief and something Maggie couldn't identify. "I don't know what kind of sick joke this is, but I've had enough. Get out."

"Jenna," Maggie began.

"Get out!" Jenna shrieked. She picked up a bottle of moisturizer that promised to ease after-wax chafing and threw it at them. Maggie dodged. It hit Constantine in the neck.

"Hey!" Constantine said.

"Get out or I'm calling the police."

"Let's all calm down," Maggie said.

"Calm down?" Jenna spat. "You come in here telling me that my brother didn't die five years ago, that he was murdered just days ago, that his name isn't Matthew. I don't know who you are or who sent you here, but I want you gone."

Maggie backed toward the door, hands skyward, stick-up style. "We don't know what's going on, either. We just want to find out what happened to Howard, I mean—"

"Out!" Jenna shrieked again.

Constantine and Maggie scrambled out the door, slamming it behind them. They heard the thud of something making contact with the doorframe, followed by the click of a deadbolt and the whoosh of blinds dropping into place.

"What the hell?" Constantine said.

"My thoughts exactly."

Constantine rubbed his forehead. "Did that really just happen? Did Howard's Twinkie turn out to be Howard's sister? And did Howard turn out to be Matthew, who's supposedly dead?"

"Yep." Maggie felt as if her head had become a balloon floating up, up, up into the ether.

She'd become unmoored, reality falling away beneath her. Everything she knew—or she thought she knew—receded further and further away as she climbed toward oblivion.

They walked in silence to the rental car and climbed wordlessly inside.

Constantine held up a hand. "Before you say anything, I move that we discuss over food. Preferably something involving gravy and the words 'chicken-fried.' I can't deal with this on an empty stomach."

Maggie couldn't agree more. She consulted Siri and Constantine turned the car north. They passed a tour group, an institutional building that introduced itself as Mariposa Rescue, signs directing traffic to Mt. Caper, the region's Nordic playground, and the chalet Camille had mentioned. Eight minutes later, they were sitting in a booth at a greasy spoon.

Constantine paged through the plastic-encased menu. "What goes best with coming back from the dead—coffee or tea?"

"I'd say it's more like faking a death, and definitely coffee."

The waitress arrived, poured coffee and took their orders. Constantine gulped, made a face, added three creamers and two sugars. "So your money's on a fake death."

"What else could it be?" Maggie prophylactically dosed her coffee and sipped. It tasted just the way she had always imagined the floor of a Jiffy Lube would. She added more sugar and creamer and pulled out her phone. "Let's see what Detective Google has to say about the Body Formerly Known as Matthew."

She input "Matthew," "Three Rivers" and "drowning." She struck gold on the first hit.

"The body of Dr. Matthew Foley was pulled from Clear Lake in Jackson County," she read from the local newspaper's online edition. "He was discovered by a pair of recovery divers who found him tangled in a patch of weeds fifty yards from his boat. Ruled an accident."

"Dr. Foley, huh? What kind of doctor?"

Maggie skimmed then looked at Constantine over her phone. "Cosmetic surgeon. He kept the old career and got a new name."

"And a new face, by the sound of it." He examined his own visage on the back of a spoon then twirled it in his cup. "Is there a picture?" Maggie nodded.

Constantine moved around to her side of the booth and put his arm around her. He smelled like soap, coffee and Constantine. In other words: amazing. She leaned against his shoulder as he pivoted the phone to examine the article's accompanying photograph.

Dr. Matthew Foley was roughly the same age and build as Dr. Howard Wright, but that's where the similarities ended. While Wright was a silver fox with gray hair, sharp features and a carefully cultivated goatee, Dr. Foley had round cheeks, a bulbous nose and light brown hair styled in a *Leave It to Beaver* cut.

"They look nothing alike," he said.

"The power of weight loss, hair color and plastic surgery. He was in the business, would know who to trust with the ultimate makeover. If he wanted a do-over, having a new appearance to go along with the new identity would certainly help."

"A new face is one thing, but how do you explain the body pulled from the lake?"

Maggie sipped her sludge. "Two theories: Howard murdered someone to act as his body double. Or...he happened across a body and made his plan serendipitously."

Constantine raised an eyebrow. "He just happened across a body when he was thinking of faking his own death."

"He could have found someone not easily missed. Homeless. Hiding. Living under the radar." They exchanged a look. They'd had experience in the disappearing invisible. "If he had hospital privileges, he could have waited for a Jane or John Doe to kick off at the hospital and steal the body."

Constantine moved his head in a half-nod but looked dubious. "I guess that's possible. I like it better than Howard as a murderer. As big of a jerk as he was, he never struck me as the violent type."

The waitress returned and placed the wrong order in front of each of them. "Enjoy!" she chirped brightly as she topped off their coffees.

Maggie and Constantine performed a quick rendition of musical plates. Constantine cut into his chicken-fried steak and shoved a slab into his mouth. "Seems strange that Howard-slash-Matthew would start his new life so close to his old one. If he went to the trouble of changing his appearance, wouldn't he move to a state far, far away?"

Maggie doused her waffles with strawberry syrup. "You'd be surprised. There have been a number of cases of people who lived a second life practically down the street from the first. I just read an article about a guy who had two entire families. They didn't know about each other until after he died and they met at his funeral. Turns out, his daughters went to the same dance school."

"Awkward."

"People like to live their double lives in close proximity because, A, it gives them a sense of control or B, because they're arrogant ego maniacs who think they're too smart for anyone to catch on."

Constantine chewed, salted his food, chewed again. "I'll give you that Howard had an ego the size of Pluto, but you're talking about double lives. This was a faked death. Or so we think."

Maggie wiped her hands on a paper napkin and reached for her phone. "Let's see if we can go from think to know."

She searched, but got nowhere. She turned the phone over to Constantine, who knew his way around the internet labyrinth. He quickly uncovered key facts.

They learned that Howard Cornelius Wright had been born in 1955, but didn't seem to start living until 2012. He had no credit cards, no library card, no gym membership, no jelly of the month club. None of the hallmarks of adulthood and targeted marketing. He also had no employment record other than his partnership with Dr. Kenny Rogers and didn't actually own the McMansion he shared with Polly. It was a rental procured through a property management company four years earlier. Around the time he met Polly.

"Howard was a ghost before he became a ghost," Maggie said. "How'd he pull that off?"

"Identity Creation 101: Steal the identity of someone who's dead, preferably a child born around your real birth year."

"Nice."

"And effective. And at this point, just a guess." He thought for a moment. "It's interesting that he changed everything but his profession."

Maggie sawed off a wedge of waffle. "It was familiar and afforded him a certain lifestyle, not to mention access to people who could help him with a face-changing touch-up. Creating a fake diploma and CV couldn't have been hard. You've seen *Catch Me If You Can*."

Constantine crossed his arms in front of his body. "None of this tells us why Matthew Foley faked his death."

"Most of the time, people fake their deaths to get away from something." She looked around the restaurant, as if the answer might be found in spider lines that crawled across the Formica tabletops or the order wheel that spun like a mini carousel with hastily scrawled orders rather than majestic horses. "A spouse. A debt. A threat."

Constantine's eyes widened. "You think Matthew Foley became Howard Wright to escape something dangerous?"

"Or *someone* dangerous. Maybe that someone finally caught up with him and the previously fake death of Matthew Foley became the now real death of Howard Wright."

The waitress bustled over, her mustard colored uniform swishing as she refilled their coffee cups. "Need anything else, hon?" She gave Constantine a wink.

"Just the check, thanks."

The waitress pulled a pencil from the folds of an elaborate, opalescent up-do. She scribbled on her pad, lines of concentration carving deep into her dermis. "Here y'are, doll," she said with another wink and a swish of a hip, then she slapped the bill on the table.

Constantine folded money and placed it beneath his cup. "I say we try to find out if Matthew Foley was involved with bad guys. What he might have seen. Who he might have told."

"And how do we find that out?"

Constantine stood and pulled his coat on. "We start by looking into the secret life of Matthew Foley."

Chapter 15

Maggie flipped the rental car's heat on high and checked her face in the vanity mirror. Her cheeks were red with cold, her eyes streaming from the wind, but she didn't have food in her teeth. There was a first time for everything. "Okay, Sherlock. Where do we begin?"

"You Sherlock, me Watson."

"You sound more like Tarzan."

"Potato potahto."

Maggie glanced at her watch. "It's one thirty. What do you think the chances of me scheduling a walk-in at Matthew Foley's a.k.a. Howard Wright's previous cosmetic surgery office are?"

"One way to find out."

Her call was answered on the second ring by a melodious voice that reminded Maggie of commercials for all-inclusive resorts. At first she thought it was a recording saying that the staff was busy and would be right with her. It wasn't until the woman on the other end said, "Hello? Is anyone there?" that Maggie responded. Unfortunately, she had just popped some of the Hot Tamales she kept in the purse into her mouth. She spit them onto her hand.

"Um, yes, I was wondering if I could make an appointment?" She exhumed a McDonald's napkin from her purse and began wiping the sticky red mess that had begun spreading over her skin like impetigo.

"Certainly," the woman said in her TV commercial voice. "Are you currently a patient?"

"Um, no. I'm interested in..." Maggie searched her memory banks for something appropriate. "Lip augmentation."

Kylie Jenner lips were all the rage, plus it wouldn't require her to strip down for any kind of assessment. Bonus.

Maggie heard the click of a keyboard. "I can get you in next Wednesday at two."

Next Wednesday? They were flying back to Hollow Pine in the

morning. Crap.

Maggie considered her options. "That sounds perfect," Maggie said, feeling a little reckless.

Make an appointment now, figure it all out later.

"And who may I say referred you?"

"Matthew Foley," Maggie said, continuing her streak of impulsivity. It was an experiment, her own clinical trial, on How People React When Told They'd Been Referred by a Dead Man.

Something seemed to be happening.

There was a long pause followed by muffled conversation directed away from the phone, then tentative keyboard clacking. "Please arrive fifteen minutes early to fill out some paperwork." Was it her imagination or had the TV voice lost some of its musicality?

Maggie thanked the receptionist and disconnected. She turned toward Constantine who had gotten into the Hot Tamales.

"So?" he said mid-chew. "You going to get all Angelina Jolie'd up?"

"Yep. Next Wednesday."

Constantine choked. "What?'

"It was the soonest they could get me in. I figured we could come back, drive if you're out of frequent flier miles."

Her half-assed plan was starting to sound quarter-assed. "Maybe I should call back and cancel."

"Can't we just pop by and ask questions, like we did at Rogers' office?"

"And tell them what? 'Hey, we think a murdered man in another city used to work here under a different identity until he faked his death and changed his face'? At best, they'll think we're nuts. At worst, they could be the reason for Foley's escape. I don't think we can trust anyone or assume anything. This snooping requires a more subtle—and sneaky—touch."

Constantine nodded. "You're right. We'll figure out a way for you to get in to see them. We have to."

The specter of Polly's situation settled between them like the Ghost of Past Regrets. He was right. They'd have to. Polly's health was poor. The options were few.

Maggie placed her hands on the dashboard and watched lacy flakes touch down on the windshield then take off again with each gust of wind. The snow here was different than in Hollow Pine. Prettier, more delicate, as if hand-hewn by an artisan dedicated to creating craft snow for tourists.

"We have to tell Austin," she said at last. "About Matthew Foley and the fake death."

"Because it sounds so believable?"

"It does sound insane," she admitted, "but it also happens to be the truth. If we tell Austin, he'll have to look into it. As weird as it sounds, the fake death could help prove that Matthew/Howard was trying to escape something or someone who caught up to him—and that Polly had nothing to do with his murder."

Constantine looked out the window.

"Right?" she pressed.

"I just don't trust those guys."

"I don't blame you." She dialed. "But we could use all the help we can get."

Austin picked up immediately. "This is Austin." He had on his professional voice. Maggie wondered if hers should match. She went with being herself, which had always proved to be an interesting—if sometimes disastrous —choice.

"We've found something out about Howard that you should know," she said without preamble.

"Um, okay. What?"

"Howard lived a previous life under the name of Matthew Foley and faked his own death five years ago."

The silence stretched between them like a chasm. "I'm sorry?" he finally said.

Maggie told him about the photos, Jenna the bikini waxer and her brother Matthew, alias Howard.

Austin laughed. "Is this some kind of joke?"

"I swear it isn't. I just talked to his sister who thought Howard was dead for the past five years. She said he looked different in the picture I showed her, but that it was definitely him. I also did some research and learned Howard Wright made his appearance on the planet not long after Matthew Foley died."

The wide silence returned. Maggie thought she actually heard crickets. "Sorry, Maggie," Austin finally said. "This is just a little...unreal."

Maggie put her hand into her purse and liberated another handful of Hot Tamales from the nearly-empty box. "Search Matthew Foley online. Dig into Howard Wright's life five years ago. Talk to his sister,

Jenna. Then tell me it's unreal."

"My partner is going to say that you're just trying to get Polly out of hot water, which seems to be nearing a boil." He'd said "pardner" as if he were in a Western.

"Well, you can tell your *pardner* if you want justice, you need the truth." She cringed inwardly. She was starting to talk in proverbs.

Austin sighed gustily. "Okay, okay. I'll look into it. But for God's sake, don't get your hopes up."

Too late. Optimism inflated like a balloon in her chest. They were finally starting to get somewhere. "Thank you, Austin. Thank you so much."

She cut the connection and bit into the final Hot Tamale. Maggie's phone "Buehler'ed" in her hand. She looked at the display. A number she didn't recognize. "This is Maggie," she said in her own professional voice.

"Maggie, this is Luann from InHance."

Maggie paused, trying to remember.

"InHance? Dr. Denning's office? You called about lip plumping"

She hit Constantine on the shoulder and pointed wildly at the phone. "Oh, hi there," she said with studied indifference.

"I wanted to let you know that we've, um, had a cancellation. The doctor can see you at one o'clock today, if that works for you."

Maggie did a mental fist pump. "That would be fine. Thanks, Luann."

Maggie hung up and grinned. "I have an appointment at Howard's old practice in an hour and a half."

"I thought they couldn't get you in until next week."

Maggie fluffed her hair and planted sunglasses on her nose. "I have a feeling it's because of those two little words."

"Cash payment?"

"Matthew Foley."

Chapter 16

InHance was located at the edge of town between a Walgreens and a Mini Pet Mart in a utilitarian building that looked more suited to tax preparation than cosmetic enhancement. The InHance logo, a tangle of curlicue letters that made up the hair of a woman—again in silhouette—provided the introduction.

Maggie straightened her coat and pushed into a vestibule canvassed with After photos.

Like those in Rogers' office, the gallery showcased a variety of enhancements—or inhancements—Maggie supposed. Unlike the photos in Rogers' office, these images had a distinctive flair. All featured young women with tumescent breasts, oversized lips and Kim Kardashian derrieres. There wasn't a Botoxed forehead or face-lifted cheek in sight. The InHance clientele was looking to expand rather than remodel their temples.

Maggie checked in with the receptionist whose serene, youthful face seemed to match her infomercial voice, and sat in a green upholstered chair next to Constantine. She picked up a magazine and pretended to leaf through it, eyes on the four other patients in the room.

There were three women and one man. The women were young and sported Instagram-worthy makeup. They sat in various locations throughout the waiting room, one by the door, another by the complimentary coffee station, another near the reception window, and yet Maggie had the inexplicable feeling that they knew one another. Hadn't two of them exchanged glances? Didn't they seem to flip the pages of their magazines in unison, their eyes on the man in the corner rather than on the pages on their mini-skirted laps?

Maggie took a sidelong glance at the man whose apparent magnetism attracted their furtive looks. He, too, held a magazine: the October *Redbook* issue with Kristin Bell on the cover. Like the others in the room, he wasn't reading. His eyes flicked between the women. Wary.

Watchful. Possessive. He turned to look at Maggie, flat brown eyes boring into her.

Maggie looked away. Suddenly the room seemed overly hot. Maggie opened her coat. She could feel her heart picking up speed in her chest. Something felt wrong. Maybe it had been a mistake to come here. Did she really expect Howard's former practice partner to dish about him, give up information that would magically unlock the secret behind the fake death and manufactured new life? It wasn't like she had a plan for transitioning from lip consultation to amateur inquisition. Why did she think she could do this? Why was she even here?

Maggie gathered her coat and stood, an urgent demand that they leave on her lips, an excuse for the receptionist, an explanation for Constantine, who was engrossed in a copy of *People*.

"Magnolia O'Malley?"

She froze.

A woman dressed in white scrubs stood at the door that led to the exam rooms, a clipboard in hand. She nodded at Maggie encouragingly. "Right this way." She nudged the door with the hip she'd used as a doorstop and it swung wide like a mouth ready to swallow any who dared enter.

Maggie looked imploringly at Constantine, who'd looked up when her name was called. He beamed and gave her two thumbs up. Maggie turned and followed the woman through the door into whatever lay beyond, her feet moving as if she were in a dream.

The hallway had the acrid scent of antiseptic and cleaner. The carpet was more worn than in the lobby, and Maggie noticed that a groove had been created down the center in a path that led from Before to After. She wondered how many times Matt/Howard had trod the beige Berber.

The woman, Nurse Diane according to her tag, ushered her to an empty room. She installed Maggie on the exam table, took her blood pressure and seemed impressed by the result. "You must exercise," she said.

"I run."

Nurse Diane nodded approvingly. "I thought so." She opened a drawer beneath the exam table and produced a bundle of blue. "Here's your gown. The doctor will be with you shortly."

"Gown?" A spike of adrenaline made Maggie's head tingle. "But I'm just here for a lip consultation."

Diane smiled sweetly. "Office policy. It ties in back." She closed the door behind her.

Maggie stared at the paper gown. She opened it. It made a loud, raspy sound like the cheap toilet paper Pop bought for the restaurant. She held it up, trying to determine which was the front. The only indication was a slight dip.

No one loved hospital gowns. There were no storefronts hawking the latest styles (cape! paper! tie-back!) or the wide selection of colors (blue! white! Pepto Bismol pink!). But still. At that exact moment, Maggie was sure she hated them worse than anyone in the universe. It wasn't just the way they felt. It was what they meant. She was going to be in some state of undress in front of a doctor.

Feck.

Maggie decided the answer to this was a big fat no and stripped to her thermal tank top and leggings before donning the baby blue gown. She neatly folded her clothes, sat back down on the exam table, decided she didn't feel like sitting and paced the room like a caged animal.

She was examining an assortment of ointments in the top drawer of the room's built-in cabinet when the door opened. Maggie leapt back to the exam table, tearing the paper liner as she landed. A man entered the room, his eyebrows jumping above his black-rimmed glasses at the ripping sound and Maggie's skid along the top of the table.

"Miss O'Malley?"

"Yes, hi!" Maggie said too loudly, thrusting her hand in an exaggerated put-er-there.

He took her hand. "Dr. Denning. Nice to meet you."

Denning asked a few questions about her lip goals, a notion Maggie found vaguely ridiculous, then he leaned against the cabinet and crossed his arms. "I understand you were friends with Matthew Foley?"

"Oh yes. We go way back." Maggie felt a flush crawling up her neck, threatening to betray her lie. Her mind raced to come up with medical conditions that cause flushing and that she could then throw out to Denning as cover. Rosacea? Fever? Menopause?

"Way back?" Denning flipped through her chart, making notes in the margins. "How did you know each other?"

"Oh..." Maggie could feel the beginning of panic. Why had she said she knew him? *Idiot, idiot, idiot*, her mind bleated. "We...uh..." Her mind whirred. *Jenna.* "I'm friends with his sister."

Denning looked up sharply from the chart. "Jenna? How?"

How, indeed.

"We, ah, we went to cosmetology school together. She specialized in waxing. I majored in self-tanner application." Other than Waxing Poetic, Maggie had never been inside a spa and rarely purchased makeup, let alone something as exotic as self-tanner. But she was pretty sure having it professionally applied was a thing.

Denning put the chart to his side and shoved his other hand in his pocket. "Cosmetology school? But Jenna got her esthetician's license years ago in another state."

Maggie opened her mouth. Closed it. Smiled. "Right, right. It was an, um, review course."

"Ah."

It wasn't clear whether he believed her. She wouldn't have believed her. She pulled at the neck of her gown and lifted the hair from the back of her neck. "About the inject—"

"Too bad about Matt and Jenna." he interrupted, stroking his chin.

Maggie tried to think whether Jenna had given any clues about something that happened to them. All she could come up with was a tragic waxing accident. "Mmm," she replied.

"I'm actually surprised you knew Matt through her. Because of...you know."

Maggie gave the sagest nod she could muster. "Right the...um..."

"The falling out," Denning supplied.

Another falling out. Seemed to be a common occurrence with Howard/Matthew, but Jenna hadn't mentioned it. Way she told it, she and Howard were practically twins, her life in tatters in the shadow of his death.

"Far as I knew," Denning continued, "they hadn't spoken in years. You didn't know?"

Maggie felt as if her face had burst into flames. "Well, I didn't know-*know* Matt," she stammered. "I just knew of him. Through Jenna. Because of the, ah, review course."

A trickle of sweat snaked down Maggie's back. She felt perspiration sprout on her upper lip. "Anyway," she began, desperate to change the subject. "I'm hoping for a little fullness—"

Denning slammed his clipboard onto the medical tray. "Tell me the truth," he hissed. "Why are you here?"

"I, I—"

Denning leaned in, his knuckles resting on the exam table's paper.

Maggie could see a tiny vein pulsing in his forehead where his hair had fallen away. "Did Nick send you?"

"Nick? Who's Nick?"

Denning glowered at her, his eyes searching hers. Satisfied she really didn't know Nick, he leaned back, straightened his tie and smoothed his lab coat. "My mistake," he said evenly. "Now, let's talk about the procedure. Obviously, this would be very beneficial for someone like you."

What was *that* supposed to mean?

Maggie felt her lips. Okay, so the top one wasn't exactly plump, but it wasn't like she was unable to apply ChapStick.

The doctor droned on about the risks and rewards of lip augmentation, his baritone monotone, his manner blasé. The change in topic from "Did Nick send you?!" to "here's how we do the procedure" wasn't just odd. It was paralyzing. Maggie sat in rapt attention listening to him drone on, watching as perspiration misted his own face, which he mopped with a cotton handkerchief produced from the pocket of his lab coat.

"Does that all make sense?" she heard him say.

Maggie nodded numbly. Her mind was still on the mysterious Nick. And her lack of lips.

Denning brought the tray closer and began to fill a syringe. "Now if you'll just lie back."

Maggie sat bolt upright. "Why? Why would I just lie back?"

"So I can perform the procedure." He said it slowly, as if she were a very young child.

"But—"

Denning looked at her. "You did come in for lip augmentation, didn't you?"

"A consultation," Maggie said, her voice reedy with panic. "I came in for a consultation."

"But I have time to do the procedure, and you just said you thought that was a great idea and wanted it immediately."

"I did?" She'd been too preoccupied to listen to his words, let alone her own. "Don't listen to me. Ha ha! I don't know what I'm saying."

He began preparing a paper towel lined tray with various implements that brought to mind medieval torture. "Now just relax."

He turned toward her with the needle in his hand. The image brought back a betrayal. A bloody confrontation. A moment that left one man dead and Maggie under a cloud of suspicion.

Her heart had picked up speed again, but her blood seemed to have turned to ice. She became aware that she was very cold beneath the paper gown. That she was alone. That a man with a needle of God-knew-what was putting his hand on the back of her neck. Presumably to steady her. Possibly to restrain her.

It had been a mistake to come here. He knew she'd lied about her connection to Matthew Foley. Probably knew why he had "died." Maybe knew he wasn't dead at all until he'd been murdered days before.

Suddenly Maggie was very sure that the man in the lab coat was going to hurt her. With the needle. With his gloved hands. With the scalpel, sharp and gleaming on the table between them. Why was a scalpel there? Dermal fillers were deposited with a needle.

Fear came alive in her, scrabbling to get out. She opened her mouth to speak, but only a gurgling sound emerged, like the nightmares in which she screamed silently over and over until her throat was raw. Did Polly have dreams like that? Did she wander in her sleep seeking help?

Maggie felt a paralysis spread through her body. She wanted to say no, to stop whatever this man was going to do to her, but she couldn't move, couldn't speak, couldn't do anything but watch as Dr. Bradley Denning leaned over her, his face smooth and unreadable, and said, "This won't hurt a bit."

Chapter 17

Maggie emerged into the waiting room. She was alive and unharmed. Well, unharmed except for her lips, which felt as if they had taken over the lower hemisphere of her face.

She tapped her upper lip gingerly with her forefinger. There was a lump beneath her cupid's bow and swelling that would have impressed Muhammad Ali.

Constantine sidled up to her. She could see the dawning horror on his face. He peered closely at her, his expression going from shock to wonder. "What does the other guy look like?"

She palpated the affected area. It felt like someone had stuffed bologna between her lips and gums. "Is it terrible?" she lisped.

"Nooooo. I feel like I'm dating a Picasso painting, that's all."

She was embarrassed about how she imagined she looked, but even more embarrassed that she had let the injection happen. Why had she allowed her emotions to take over? Why hadn't she reined them in, broken through the paralysis that froze her body and halted her tongue? Why was she so willing to let herself become a victim, even if the violation was so small?

"Let's get out of here," she grumbled.

They were halfway out the door when the receptionist called out, "Ma'am? Your bill?"

The proverbial insult to injury. Maggie plodded back to the reception window and dug out her billfold. She handed over her credit card and hoped it wasn't maxed.

While she waited—and prayed God would grant her a higher limit— she surveyed the waiting room. The previous patients had been replaced by their doppelgangers, young women, heavily made up and lightly clad. The man who was there earlier remained.

The payment made (a miracle) and thanks given (an act), Maggie and Constantine walked out the door and into the vestibule. Maggie spotted a mirror at the center of the After wall, which she supposed was to provide an incentive to go through whatever procedure was being considered. She closed her eyes then opened one to inspect the result of Dr. Denning's needlework.

Her lips looked like two hot dogs cooked in the microwave too long.

She was still trying to reconcile the face in the mirror with the one she was used to seeing when she felt a tap on her shoulder. She turned.

"It's Maggie, right?"

Maggie regarded the woman. She had a heart-shaped face, gray eyes and long tri-colored hair that reminded Maggie of Neapolitan ice cream. A tiny green star was tattooed at her right temple. Maggie felt a flicker of recognition.

"Yes." Maggie tried to smile. It felt as if her mouth were coming apart. "I recognize you, but I can't think of the context." Her words came out soft, mushy around the edges, as if she'd had three too many drinks.

"I'm Starr." The woman reflexively touched the star tattoo and smiled. "I know you from Madam Trousseau's Lingerie."

Of course. She had come in many times during Maggie's short stint there and was one of her first bra-fittings. "Strapless double-D from the Cherub collection, right?"

The woman chuckled, a deep, throaty sound. "That's me."

Maggie turned to Constantine. "Starr, this is Constantine. Constantine, Starr." The two exchanged nice-to-meet-yous. Neither seemed to notice that Maggie had failed to name her relationship to Constantine.

"You were my favorite at Madame Trousseau's," Starr said. "Nice, down-to-earth, like I could tell you anything. And here we are, running into each other in another city." She looked closely at Maggie. "You go out of town for injections?"

Maggie gave her lip an exploratory stroke. "No. I mean, yes. I mean, this is my first one. What brings you here?"

"Broke up with my boyfriend. Wanted a fresh start in a new town." It sounded like something right out of Austin's playbook. "I just got a job, and the girls there said I should come in to see about getting a little work done."

"What kind of job?"

"At the Alaska Bush," she said proudly. "I'm going to start dancing there on Tuesdays and Thursdays." She seemed to read the expression on Maggie's face because she rushed on. "It's a nice club. A real gentlemen's place. It has a Gold Rush theme." She beamed. "I get to pan for tips."

Maggie donned what she hoped was an appropriate expression as she imagined what panning for tips would look like. "Wow, that's...something else."

"Isn't it?" Starr said, as if she'd landed the job of her dreams. And maybe she had. Some women made considerable money dancing, financing living expenses, cars, even law school, in the process. "A lot of the girls come to Dr. Denning to enhance their assets. I figured no matter what happens with this gig, I can take these babies with me." She shimmied to drive home the point. "Boom. Job security."

Starr had a lot of boom.

Maggie thought about the women in the waiting room. "You say the dancers at the Alaska Bush come here for procedures?"

She nodded. "All of them."

"*All* of them?"

Starr tilted a shoulder. "It's an investment in our future." She pulled a business card from her bra and handed it to Maggie. It read simply *Starr, Entertainer*. "If you know anyone having a bachelor party or whatnot, I freelance. Just pass my info along."

"Will do." Maggie shoved the card into her purse then batted aside Luna bars, hair ties and loose change until she found an old drug store receipt and a lip pencil. She wrote her phone number and handed it to Starr. "And here's my contact information. In case you need me for any, um, freelance lingerie advice."

Maggie felt instantly absurd. Exchanging contact information had become an ingrained ritual at Rxcellance. Old habits died hard.

Starr thanked her and gave a surreptitious glance at Maggie's lips. "That's a lot of swelling for just having that done. I hear that Denning's more of a boob man than anything."

That would have been nice to know, Maggie thought ruefully.

Starr drew Maggie into a quick hug. Maggie was surprised at not just the gesture, but the emotion that escaped from behind the Wall. She suddenly felt homesick. For Valerie. For Pop and Aunt Fiona. For her old life. "It was great seeing you, Maggie. You guys live here now?"

"Just visiting a friend."

"Well if you decide to move here, I'm sure you could get a job at the Bush, too."

Maggie tried to picture herself trying to exotic anything, let alone dance. "I'll keep that in mind."

"See ya later, Maggie. Nice to meet you, Constantine." Then Starr gave a dazzling smile and glided into the waiting room with a gust of perfume, hairspray and bubble gum.

Constantine turned to Maggie. "You could always rehearse in front of me."

"You'd like that."

"Duh."

They shivered their way across the lot and into the car. Maggie claimed the driver's side. She was tempted to hazard another look at the mirror, then decided she'd had enough scares for one day.

"Aside from Dr. Feelgood's lip magic, how did your appointment go? Did he reveal anything interesting about Matthew Foley?"

"No," Maggie said miserably. "He figured out I was lying right away."

"You never were a master of falsehoods."

"Thanks. I think." Maggie pointed the car toward the airport. "I couldn't get any of the details about my connection with Matt right. Once he got suspicious, he got mad. Like, scary mad. He asked if Nick had sent me." Constantine shot her a questioning look. "I don't know who Nick is, but the thought of him sending me enraged Denning."

"Like, murderously enraged?"

Maggie shrugged. "Maybe. All I know is now I want to find out who Nick is and how he's connected to Denning. And Howard/Matthew."

Constantine's phone rang. "Hopefully that's Mark Weber telling me that Polly's delighted to retain him." He plucked the phone from his pocket and frowned at the display. "I don't recognize the—" He put his ear to the device. "Hello?"

He listened. His eyes darted to Maggie then closed. "How did it happen?" More silence. A head shake from Constantine. "God da—" He stopped. Closed his eyes. Worked his jaw. "Was no one watching her?" A nod. "I see. Uh huh. We'll be there as soon as we can." He hung up and opened his eyes. Maggie felt a prickle of fear at the pain and worry she saw there.

"It's Polly," he said. "There's been an accident."

Chapter 18

When Maggie was eleven, she took her first plane ride. She had purchased a new outfit for the occasion: a pair of white jeans, a Swiss dot blouse, a denim jacket embroidered with hearts and a pair of shoes with a miniscule heel. Her first foray into the world and wardrobe of womanhood.

Aunt Fiona had helped her pick out the clothes, marching back and forth from sales floor to dressing room with armfuls of outfits, the scent of Jean Naté After Bath Splash announcing her presence even before her black flats appeared under the dressing room door. She patiently culled Maggie selects, separating apparel wheat from chaff, maybes from no's. It was a job meant for Maggie's mother, but she wasn't there. The outfit, the haircut that followed, the pending plane trip were all in preparation to meet her mother at the Mayo Clinic where she was being treated.

This was back when they had hope. Before the chemo. Before the radiation. Before the trips to Mexico and the endless packages of miracle cures that came in the mail. Back when Maggie was excited about the prospect of experiencing a new mode of transportation, breathless with excitement over the elegant flight attendants, the tiny trays of food, the bitty little light that illuminated the book she'd brought on board.

On that trip, Maggie didn't understand the nature of worry. How it could hide somewhere deep in the brain. How it grew on a steady diet of uncertainty. How it could flow through the body like a disease, manifesting as nail-biting one day, diarrhea the next, insomnia night after night until reason unplugged from the brain and fantasies of a cure, of an escape, took its place.

It was a plane ride she would never forget.

As Maggie stared out the window at the tarmac, she was transported back to that same trip. To that same girl. Worry whispered in her ear, sticky and traitorous.

Polly's hurt.

She might die in jail.

It's all your fault.

She asked the flight attendant if she could have a drink. She was told she'd have to wait until they were at altitude. Altitude. Maybe she could look forward to hypoxia.

Maggie sagged against the headrest, paper-veiled for her protection, a stabbing pain in her heart. She wondered if it were possible for it to break. Hadn't she read about such a condition in college? Broken heart syndrome? She looked longingly at the seat beside her, which was occupied by a businesswoman and her miniature laptop. As with the flight to Three Rivers, she and Constantine were seated separately. She couldn't even put her head on his shoulder, find comfort in his arms, or seek the solace of the mutually miserable.

If he'd even let her.

If he were smart, he'd hate her, just as she hated herself. Now he'd never ask her to marry him. Not that he'd come out and asked. Not that she wanted that.

Damn it. When would they take off and give her a drink?

She touched her lips. They were fuller, no doubt about that, but they had begun to lose their boxing match feel. The post-procedure numbness had also subsided, which meant that she wouldn't drool all over herself during the plane's beverage service. Thank God for small favors.

The plane began to taxi. Maggie took out her film canister, popped Advil, re-stowed her miniature pharmacy and looked beneath the eyelid of the aircraft's window, which was half-closed as if the plane had awoken from a nap. Night came early to this part of the Midwest, too, draining color from the sky like a leech. The only contrast to the black sky was the snow. Powdery and crystalline from the rapidly dropping temperatures, it drifted over the ground like the sands of the desert or foam over the sea. Funny how two opposites could be so much alike.

There was no sleep on this flight. Two hours and zero booze later (Maggie decided that it might not be the best idea to show up to the infirmary drunk), they touched down. Constantine was waiting for her at the end of the gangway.

His face was shuttered in a way she had never seen. Was he concerned? Definitely. Anxious? Probably. Any other emotions were anyone's guess. Maggie was no expert on feelings.

They rode to the jail in silence as Constantine drove the dark, snow-packed roads in his 1977 Datsun B210. The hula dancer who graced his dashboard seemed to sag, as if the air were heavier, the weight of worry and blame and self-reproach palpable in the car.

"Constantine—" Maggie began.

"Just..." He held up a hand. "Just don't, okay?"

Maggie closed her mouth and then her heart. She folded in on herself, curling inward like the golden peel of an orange. She had never felt so heartsick. She had never felt so alone.

The county jail resembled the city's other municipal buildings: windowless and dun-colored. It crouched at the base of Butte Hill, cowering against the equally dumpy earthen mound as if it had been sent to the corner for being naughty.

The silence clung to Maggie and Constantine as they entered the building, checked in with the sergeant at the front desk and were escorted by a young officer who bore the same facial hair on his lip as the detectives. A hirsute epidemic.

The young officer, who told them way too much about how overtime worked in the Sheriff's department, herded them through a maze of doors until they reached a medical ward, where he turned them over to another officer.

Officer Number Two led them past beds cordoned off by privacy curtains. Maggie counted as they walked. Six total. Larger than she'd imagined, yet still much too small for anything serious.

"Wait here," Officer Two ordered. He turned and went back to guarding the opposite wall. Maggie wanted to exchange a look with Constantine, to telepathically smart-off about the officer, the room's baby-aspirin-orange walls, anything. Constantine had taken out his phone and was texting. Maggie slumped against the wall.

A few minutes later, she traded limbo for hell. The infirmary's physician arrived, looking as worried as they felt.

He introduced himself as Steve Le Croix. Small and fine-boned with white hair and a habit of clasping his hands behind his back like Marcus Welby, MD, Le Croix whispered all of his sentences. He was probably following HIPAA protocol, but the overall effect was of being in a library.

Introductions out of the way, Constantine started right in. "How is she? I understand she fell?"

"No one knows," Dr. Le Croix murmured, "but that's our guess. One of the guards discovered her unconscious in her cell. Could have been a fall. Could have been a stroke. We simply don't know."

"Well, when will you know?" Constantine's voice climbed several notches on the hysteria scale.

Dr. Le Croix motioned for quiet. "We are transporting her to the hospital. They can do more extensive testing there, offer more advanced care." He averted his eyes. "We'll have to arrange for security. Standard operating procedure. You understand."

Constantine's look said he didn't. Finally he said, "Can we see her?"

Le Croix gave a quick nod and drew back the curtain.

Polly lay in the bed as if asleep. Her chest rose and fell in time with a backbeat that played only for her. Her mouth hung open, revealing a large gold crown and two silver fillings. Maggie followed Constantine to her bedside and gently closed her mouth, her skin dry and papery beneath her touch.

"She's been unconscious since they found her?" Maggie asked.

"It appears to be a coma or coma-like state," Le Croix said. "She's failed to respond to stimuli. Once we get an EEG, we'll know more. We'll keep you fully informed, of course." He looked at Constantine. "You're the next of kin?"

Maggie could see Constantine weighing the question. Howard was dead. His mother, Polly's sister, was in Italy doing Francesca's Cooking Tour. He cleared his throat. "Yes."

Le Croix bobbed his head and led them from Polly's bedside. He pulled the curtain around her bed, rings clanking against rod. It was the loudest he'd been. "We'll call with updates. They'll take good care of her at St. Theresa's."

He inclined his head toward the door, a silent cue to leave, then began walking them past the parade of curtained beds. He talk-whispered about his workload, paperwork and grandchildren. Patient care didn't come up. He bid them a good evening at the elevator, as if such a thing were possible.

During the elevator ride and down the dank, dim first floor hallway, Constantine continued to observe a monastic silence. He tugged on fleece-lined gloves. He wound a scarf around his neck. He looked at his phone. Maggie cleared her throat, ready with an apology, a word of comfort, anything that would break the spell of his silence. She sensed a presence behind her.

"Well, hey there, Maggie," a voice called. She turned. Austin hooked his thumbs in his belt loops. "What are y'all doing here?"

Maggie was sure his accent was getting stronger, like some invisible hand was turning up the dial. "Polly fell. She's..." She swallowed a lump that had cropped up between her tonsils. "She's unconscious in the infirmary."

A shadow crossed Austin's face. "Gee, I'm sorry to hear that." He looked at Constantine. "I hope she's better soon, I really do."

Constantine seemed unsure what to do with this act of kindness. He clenched his jaw, reddened then muttered, "Appreciate it."

Austin unhooked his thumbs, stroked his mustache then rehooked them. "I looked into that gal you mentioned, Maggie. Howard's supposed sister?"

Supposed. Almost as good as alleged. "Yes?"

Austin shifted his weight. "She's got quite the rap sheet. Impressive, not just because of its size, but its variety. Larceny. Identity theft. Assault."

A surge of dread ran through Maggie. "Are you sure we're talking about the same person?"

Austin harvested a small notepad from his breast pocket, which contained a slew of pens, a roll of Lifesavers and what looked like a cylinder of waxed dental floss. He opened the notepad, flipped, read. "Jenna Foley, right? Sister of the late Matthew Foley, who you say became Howard Wright?"

Maggie nodded miserably.

"Well..." Austin reloaded his pocket with the notebook. "We can't find anything to substantiate that."

"Because it's a load of crap," a voice boomed from behind them.

Constantine and Maggie turned. Jeff Greeley stood before them. He smiled. He had all the warmth of a cobra. "Nice theory, though. Good distraction, too. Problem is, there doesn't seem to be any truth to it."

"Talk to Jenna," Maggie said. "She's the one who told us Howard was her brother, Matthew. She's the one who told us about how he drowned, how his body was found days later."

"Oh we would, believe me." Greeley pulled a cellophane-wrapped toothpick from his own breast pocket and began unwrapping. "We just can't seem to get ahold of her. No one knows where she is."

Maggie felt as if she was looking down a narrow tunnel, darkness at the sides, nothing ahead. "What do you mean no one knows where she is?"

The toothpick went into the mouth. "Just what I said. We called that waxing place where she works. She left without telling anyone. No one's seen her since." He shifted the toothpick. Bit down. Smiled again. "Maybe you scared her off with your wild ideas."

Maggie pictured Jenna's wide eyes, the anxiety in her voice as she forced them out the salon door. Hardened criminal or not, hearing that your dead brother was actually alive in another city only to die again (or for the first time?) had to be more than a little frightening. Jenna could have gone into hiding. Or she could have simply taken a few days off from work, or forgot to call in to let her manager know.

Somehow Maggie didn't think so. Somehow Maggie was sure Jenna had gone underground, driven into hiding because of Howard's murder and their questions.

A new thought edged into Maggie's mind. Maybe Jenna was afraid of whoever had killed Matthew/Howard. Maybe she knew he had faked his own death and was terrified that whatever had happened to her brother would now happen to her.

"It's not going to work, you know." Greeley had removed the toothpick. He lovingly wrapped it into a paper napkin as if it were a remnant from the Ark of the Covenant.

"What isn't?" Maggie asked.

"Your little ploy to distract us. Your story about Howard having a previous life as someone else."

Maggie clenched her jaw. "It's not a story."

Greeley placed the napkin in his pocket and patted. "Your aunt has done a fantastic job of continuing to incriminate herself."

"What are you talking about?" Constantine asked tightly.

"She's been talking to herself. Shouting, actually. Mostly at night. And mostly about cutting and secrets and Howard coming back from the dead."

Maggie felt herself grow cold. A seed of nausea dropped into her stomach. She could feel bile begin to climb her throat.

The hallucinations. The ranting. The declarations that Howard was alive and the ground bore the wounds of a murder that hadn't succeeded. It sounded like the kind of episode Polly had suffered at Howard's funeral. It sounded like the ravings of a mad woman.

Greeley seemed pleased with himself. He clapped Austin on the shoulder. "Time we get back to work, partner." He looked at Maggie. "We've got a case to finish building."

Chapter 19

Maggie stumbled after Constantine as he made his way toward the exit. Her mind seemed to unspool before her, stringing out the horrors that just kept coming, one after another. She felt a sudden need to vomit into the trashcan.

Outside, the night air bit into her. She welcomed the pain. She wanted more. She looked upward, seeking answers from the heavens. A crescent moon had risen, its toe slicing through a bank of clouds that, according to the local meteorologist, held tomorrow's snowfall. Scattershot stars were visible at the moon's perimeter, huddling near the satellite, seeking warmth that wasn't there, fooled by a glow that was a reflection of the sun's fire.

Silence followed them to Constantine's Datsun. He started the car, secured his seatbelt, and sat with gloved hands on the steering wheel.

In other circumstances, Maggie would remark that he looked like a racecar driver and start calling him Mario. Now she stared at her own hands, bare and bloodied at the cuticles where she had picked them clean of flesh.

"I can't do this," Constantine said.

Something in Maggie's chest constricted. "Can't do what?" She didn't want to know.

"Be mad at you." The gloved hands gripped the steering wheel. "I mean, I'm mad that you FaceTimed Deputy Dog about Polly while she was in a compromising position." He licked his lips. "But if I'm honest with myself, I knew this arrest was coming either way. They've been gunning for her since she made that 911 call. You just sped things up."

"I also got fired," she blurted. "And got someone else fired." The confession was out of her mouth before she could stop it, guilt finally boiling over, its frothy ugliness exposed.

"What are you talking about?"

"I chewed out the owner for being a racist, which she is, and got myself and the woman I was trying to stand up for fired."

Constantine shook his head. "Why didn't you tell me before? And why are you telling me now?"

"I don't know and I don't know," Maggie muttered. "I guess I couldn't stand for you to be as disappointed in me as I am in myself."

Constantine leaned over and cupped her chin in his hand. "You never disappoint me. Shock me, maybe. Horrify, occasionally. But never disappoint. You got fired for trying to do the right thing. Ditto with Polly's arrest. Polly's injury—whatever caused it—may have happened anyway, as well. Her health has been deteriorating, not just physically but mentally. You heard Greeley."

"The hallucinations have returned." Her voice was barely audible.

His eyes searched hers. "You think it's part of her illness?"

"It could be organic. It could be due to her medication. There are a lot of factors at play and it can be difficult to tease them all out." She leaned away from Constantine, chewed her fingers, then started in on her lip, which felt thick and fat between her incisors. "I'd like to talk with Petrosian again. He was waiting to hear back from her doctor about tweaking her medication. I could find out the latest and see if he has any new insights. At this point, I'll take anything."

Constantine put the car in gear. "That makes two of us."

They made it an early evening, retiring to their separate rooms after giving Camille an update on Polly's condition. At one point, Maggie wondered if they were going to have to hospitalize their hostess. She put her hand to her heart Archie Bunker-style when they informed her of Polly's comatose state, then staggered to her kitchen table, where she slumped over a leftover container of chicken salad. After she recovered, waving off their attempts to help her, she began pulling out butter, flour, sugar and spices. Maggie's salve was running; Camille's was baking.

Maggie stayed up late, researching on the internet. She stalked Deirdre Hart on Facebook, then revisited the social media properties of Dr. Rogers and Dr. Mikey. She hoped for some kind of clue, some errant admission that would indicate guilt of Howard's murder or knowledge of his past as Matthew Foley.

Nothing had changed. Nothing was revealed.

Maggie was the first to wake the following morning. She tiptoed to the kitchen, made a pot of coffee and sat in the false light of the moonlit snow. Dawn was nearly an hour away. She considered going for a run, letting the miles and the snow wash over her, dousing her anxiety with endorphins and Gatorade. Then she remembered her last run. The chance encounter with Austin. His handwritten personal number. FaceTiming him Polly's sleepwalking episode.

It didn't exactly pan out.

Maggie poured her coffee into a mug that read *World's Best Counselor*, doctored it just the way she liked it and began searching for Camille's junk drawer for paper and pen. She quickly discovered that Camille didn't believe in junk. The closest thing she found was a drawer of odds and ends neatly compartmentalized by plastic dividers segregating Post-its from pushpins, business cards from Bic pens. She pushed aside business cards embossed with butterflies, coupons for Zantac and found a pad of paper shaped like a woman's shoe. It would have to do.

Maggie tore off a stiletto-shaped leaf and began writing. By the time the sun pinked the kitchen counters, she had a page of a dozen notations—and exactly zero insights. She was no closer to knowing why Matthew had faked his death, who Nick was, where Jenna had gone and what their falling out was about. And yet, her pen kept moving. She kept writing, driven by her newest internal soundtrack.

Find Howard's killer. Save Polly. Find Howard's killer. Save Polly.

"Earth calling Maggie."

She started, flinging the pen dangerously close to Camille's collection of commemorative teacups. Constantine stood in the doorway in a t-shirt and jeans, his dark curly hair pointing in all directions, his face peppered with a two-day beard.

She rose to kiss him. He coughed into his elbow. "The current recommendation to avoid the spread of germs is to cough behind your left knee," he said hoarsely. "But I need to work on my flexibility first."

Maggie put a hand on his arm. "You're sick?"

He began hacking again, sounding as if he were about to expectorate a lung, and nodded. "Just a little cold. Probably from wandering around in the snow."

And from all the stress, she thought.

She steered him out of the kitchen and installed him on the couch. She covered him with a knit blanket "What you need is a day in bed."

"With you?" He tried a wicked grin. He looked deranged.

Maggie pressed a chenille pillow onto his chest. "Alone except for plenty of fluids."

"Anything else, Dr. O'Malley?"

"Chicken soup couldn't hurt. I'm sure Camille makes the best in the universe, give or take."

Constantine put the pillow beneath his head and grabbed Maggie's hand. "Sorry, Mags. I wish I could go with you to the pharmacy. I could barely croak out a phone call to Weber letting him know about Polly." He sagged against the pillow. "He's going to get in touch with Graham to see if they can work as co-counsels. He figures Graham might be willing, given the current...circumstances."

Circumstances. It seemed all of their conversations included euphemism and understatement. "Let me know what you find out. I won't be gone long. Meanwhile, you rest." She kissed his forehead. "Just need to go make myself beautiful."

"Too late," he said.

Maggie showered, plaited her wet hair into a French braid, then gave her eyes and lips a swipe of mascara and gloss, respectively. For reasons she couldn't identify, she wanted to impress Petrosian, to look the part of the pulled-together scientist. Maybe it was a reflex, a kind of career muscle memory borne from talking to a fellow pharmaceutical professional. But it felt like more than just a habit. It felt like she had something to prove to herself and to Petrosian.

She slid a pair of black wool slacks over her hips then slid into an emerald-colored cashmere sweater that matched her eyes. Both items purchased on forced marches through the mall, courtesy of former friend and coworker Zartar. Both heavy with memory.

When she returned to the living room, Constantine was asleep. Maggie's lips brushed his hairline, her mind on his handsome face and the kind heart that didn't blame her for Polly's circumstances or shame her because she'd lost her job. She put her arms into her coat, put on her boots and walked into the hard blue cold of November.

Maggie found her way to Petrosian's easily. She'd always had a good sense of direction, which she attributed to both her mother's natural wayfinding and her father's "direction drills," which involved Jack driving to an unfamiliar place and challenging Maggie to direct them home. He worked hard to instill self-sufficiency, to make sure she'd never need anyone. It was a spectacular success and total failure in equal measure.

As Maggie pulled in front of the pharmacy, her phone rang. She checked the screen. Pop.

"Magnolia?" Pop shouted over the clatter of pots and pans and the hum of a busy street. "I'm calling to tell you how pleased I am with that Ada girl."

"Ada's working there?" Maggie had assumed that Ada promptly deleted her email about the job opportunity at O'Malley's. She wouldn't have blamed her. Maggie's track record of helping Ada on the employment front wasn't exactly sparkling.

"Hired her on the spot," he replied. "Hard worker, knows her way around a kitchen, great with the customers." There was a muffled sound as Jack O'Malley covered the phone with his hand. "Speak of the—she just walked in. I'll let you say hello."

Maggie watched as a woman with waist-length hair unlocked the front door of the drugstore. "I, um—"

"Maggie?" Ada's voice came on the line. It was stronger than Maggie remembered. Louder. More confident. "Hey, thanks for the job tip."

"You're welcome." Maggie bit her lip. "Sorry about Madame Trousseau's."

"Don't be. I'm onto bigger and better things. Working for your dad is just the beginning."

Relief flooded through Maggie. "I'm so happy to hear that. You sound good, Ada."

Ada laughed softly. "I feel good." In the background, Maggie heard the clamor of new voices. "Looks like the breakfast crowd is getting restless. I've gotta go. Thanks again."

And then she was gone.

Maggie smiled to herself. Ada had forgiven her and loved her new job. At least something was going right.

She got out of the Studebaker and strode into the store, down the aisles to the back of the store where the pharmacy counter held an audience with an assortment of over-the-counter medications.

As expected, the waiting area was empty. She was, after all, the store's first customer of the day. She spotted Petrosian behind the counter, his sharp features illuminated by the glow of the computer screen before him.

Maggie's stomach lurched with a sudden jangle of nerves. What was wrong with her? She just wanted to ask a few questions, not request an interview. What was it about him that she found so intimidating?

Maggie cleared her throat.

"Yes, Miss O'Malley. I see you." He tapped at his keyboard, never taking his eyes off the screen.

"I just had a few more questions for you." Her words echoed against the store's hard white tiles. She lowered her voice a notch. "About Polly."

The tapping continued. "One moment, please."

Maggie clasped her hands behind her back then let her arms dangle. She stood on one foot and then the other. She bent to examine cough drops for Constantine and her back spasmed. What Camille's guest bed had in charm, it lacked in comfort. She walked past the blood pressure machine to a row of blue plastic chairs and sat erectly with her fingertips on her knees. She felt ridiculous.

Maggie unbuttoned her coat and began eyeing a tower of Almond Joys arranged like a Christmas tree next to a display of stocking stuffers. Her stomach rumbled. She had forgotten to eat breakfast. Maybe she should buy a candy bar, just to stave off low blood sugar. She rose and reached for a bar where the star would be.

"That display isn't finished," Petrosian said without looking at her. "Please don't disturb it."

Maggie retracted her hand. "Oh. I was hungry, so I thought I'd buy—"

"Here." Petrosian bent down, stood, jutted his hand toward her. It held a plain white plate of scrambled eggs and ham. Steam curled from the fluffy yellow peaks like smoke announcing the next pope. "My wife makes me breakfast every morning. Says I'm too thin." He patted his ribs then regarded Maggie's midsection. "It is you who are too thin."

Maggie started to protest. She wasn't too thin. She considered eating a hobby. And she'd just started to incorporate weight training to build muscle.

She smelled the heap of food beneath her nose and took the plate gratefully. "Thank you." She took the food back to the blue plastic chairs and sat, shoveling a forkful into her mouth. Flavors of egg and cheese and ham and spices she couldn't identify mingled on her tongue. She closed her eyes. "This is amazing."

"Family recipe. She won't even tell me, so don't bother asking." His voice was gruff, but Maggie could see the left side of his mouth tugged upward. "She puts it in a special container to keep it hot. That's the key. Cold eggs are useless."

Words to live by.

Maggie continued to pack the food into her mouth. When she finished, she noticed Petrosian looking at her, his lips verging toward a three-quarter smile. "Enjoyed?"

Maggie rose and handed him the plate. "Loved. Thank you again. That was very kind, and your wife is a wonderful cook."

Petrosian grunted, but looked pleased. He laced his hands together. "Now how can I help?"

"You heard about Polly?"

Petrosian shook his head, his mouth drooping back into his frown lines.

"She was arrested for Howard's murder then was found unconscious in her cell." She spoke quickly and precisely, hoping the newscast style would dam the dread that rose every time she thought of Polly. "No one's sure if she took a fall or fainted or what." If Petrosian was shocked, he didn't show it. He gave one grim nod then gestured for her to continue. "Her nephew and I went to visit her last night. She's unconscious, very possibly in a coma." Petrosian's frown deepened. Maggie rushed on. "Before the fall, there were reports of her ranting, talking about things that weren't there, things that didn't happen."

"The hallucinations. You mentioned them before." Petrosian removed his glasses, polished them on his lab coat, then returned them to the bridge of his beak-like nose. "I called her physician again after you and Polly came in. As you know, this whole situation—me talking to you, me calling her doctor—is highly irregular. But I did it because Polly is a friend." He folded his arms. "You'll be glad to know that Dr. Rogers has since returned from his vacation and is taking another look at her medication."

Maggie blinked. "Did you say Dr. Rogers?"

"Yes," Petrosian said slowly. "Dr. Kenny Rogers is her physician."

Chapter 20

Maggie felt as if she were in a movie, as if the camera were dollying forward for an extreme close-up of her reaction. Maybe there'd be a record scratch to punctuate it, a snap-zoom of her mouth hanging open.

"I'm sorry," Maggie finally said. "Kenny Rogers, the cosmetic surgeon and Howard's former practice partner, is Polly's doctor?"

"Has been for many years."

"But, but." She realized that she sounded like a motorboat. *But but but but but.* She swallowed her inflated lips and tried again. "I don't understand. How can a cosmetic surgeon be Polly's physician? Shouldn't she be seeing a neurologist?"

"Yes, that would be ideal."

"Ideal? Seems expected. Mandatory, even."

Petrosian inclined his head. "It would certainly be my recommendation. But Polly doesn't want to see a neurologist. She insists on having Kenny Rogers care for her."

"How on earth did a cosmetic surgeon start treating a woman with Parkinson's?"

"They were friends in college. After medical school, she began seeing him professionally. He became her general practitioner. He was a family doctor here in town for many years, then went back to school to become a cosmetic surgeon." Petrosian shrugged. "More money, fewer runny noses. I can see the appeal."

"And he continued to care for Polly even after changing his practice focus?"

"Polly trusted him. Rogers was very fond of her."

"How very?" Maggie asked, remembering the vibe from her earlier talk with Rogers.

Petrosian shifted. "Just...very."

"As in *love* fond?" She knew she was on the verge of rudeness. She didn't care.

"Some said he was in love with her, yes."

"Was or is?"

Petrosian gave a tight smile. "I wouldn't know. Interestingly, Dr. Rogers is the reason Polly and Howard were together. Polly met Howard when she went into Kenny's office for an appointment. Howard had just moved to town. He was going to open his own practice, then decided to partner with Kenny. They became acquainted and started running into each other more and more at the office. The rest, as they say, is history. Polly fell for the partner of the man who some say carried a torch for her." He looked at her, his eyes magnified by his glasses. "Love is a many splendored—and very strange—thing."

Maggie left Petrosian's in a daze.

Kenny Rogers was Polly's doctor. In charge of her care. In charge of her medication.

The red flags that had failed to appear when Maggie first looked into Polly's drug regimen now flapped wildly. Rogers could have decided that he'd had enough of sharing his practice and the woman he'd been pining for and killed Howard. He could have also tried to pharmaceutically disable Polly through her medication in order to keep her close. To keep her unwell and malleable and in need of his attention.

Maggie went stiff with anger. Manipulating someone already weakened by illness was unconscionable. Inconceivable. And yet totally possible. Maggie had questions. She was going to make damn sure Rogers answered them.

Maggie parked, took the stairs two at a time and pushed open the door to AccentYOUate. No one in the waiting room. No Barbara to pounce with her "appointments only" speech and put-on smile. No answer to her knock on the *Patients and Staff Only* door.

She knocked again, louder this time, anger growing with each rap against the wood.

An interior door slammed. A crescendo of footsteps.

The door eased open. The tip of Rogers' thinning pate appeared, followed by the rest of his head. The smile budding his lips wilted when he saw Maggie's face. He let out a small sigh.

"Ms. O'Malley. What are you doing here?"

Maggie doused her rage with a saccharine smile. "Dr. Rogers. Do you have a moment?"

Rogers glanced behind him. "Not really. I'm with a patient."

"Someone you're treating for Parkinson's?"

Rogers' mouth formed a perfect O then fell, the lines bracketing his lips, turning him into a marionette. Maggie wondered for a moment why Rogers didn't dip into his cosmetic toolbox like Howard had. "I don't know what you're talking about." He said it weakly, as if even he didn't believe himself.

"Polly Wright?" she prompted. "The wife of your murdered business partner?"

The marionette mouth clamped shut. "Yes, I've been treating Mrs. Wright for a number of years as her primary care provider. My initial training was in family medicine."

"Which made you a shoo-in for neurology."

Rogers narrowed the gap in the doorway. Maggie thought she heard low voices in the background. "I took over her care after her neurologist retired. She trusted me. Didn't want to start over with someone new."

Maggie leaned forward. "Who was her neurologist? Did he make the initial diagnosis?"

"I really shouldn't be talking with you about Mrs. Wright's medical history," he said tartly.

"You also shouldn't have hidden your relationship with her," Maggie shot back.

"Relationship?"

Was it Maggie's imagination or was Roger's breathing faster, his Adam's apple jumping with each inhalation? "As her physician," she said, watching him closely.

Rogers blinked rapidly. "Oh. Yes."

"I do think it's unusual that a cosmetic surgeon—her husband's former practice partner—is treating her." She paused. "The state medical board might find it interesting that you're treating outside of your scope of practice and treating someone with whom you have a friendly relationship. The police might find it interesting, too."

The blinking went double-time. "What do you mean?"

Maggie shrugged. "They might wonder if the relationship is strictly professional."

"Of course it's professional," Rogers sputtered. "Polly and I have been friends since college. I introduced her to Howard." He punctuated the last sentence by stabbing his finger into the air, as if playing matchmaker proved the innocence of their relationship.

Maggie examined her nails, purely for effect since she knew their condition: bare, close-cropped, fringed by ragged cuticles. "I'm just saying the police might wonder why you hid the fact that you were treating her. Cosmetic surgeon pinch-hitting as neurologist could raise some eyebrows, especially considering Polly's current state." She looked at Rogers. "She's in a coma at St. Theresa's. She'd been arrested for Howard's murder and was found unconscious in her cell."

"My God." Rogers' fingers slipped from the door. It drifted open.

"Kenny?" A voice echoed down the empty hallway. It was shrill. Familiar. A face floated to Maggie's consciousness, then drifted away.

Kenny Rogers reattached himself to the door, using it to buttress his sagging frame and seal the gap in the open door. "I didn't know Polly was in the hospital. Didn't know about any of it." He'd paled, mahogany skin turned to ash. He wiped a hand over his face. "I'll call over there, speak to the hospitalist in charge of her care about the prognosis, whether he thinks her coma is the result of a fall or the progression of her disease—"

"Or a side effect of whatever you're giving her." Maggie moved closer. She could smell his breath. Toothpaste. Coffee. Something with pepper. "Are you sure your treatment is doing more good than harm? Are you sure you're the best person to care for Polly?"

Bang!

A door slammed somewhere behind Rogers. Deirdre Hart's Cheetos-hued face rose behind his shoulder like a malignant sun. "There you are," she said. "I've been waiting for— "

She stopped when she saw Maggie, her face a flipbook of emotions: surprise, confusion, anger. "What the hell are you doing here?"

Maggie's mind stuttered. Deirdre Hart, wearer of book-hats and litigious leader of the I Hate Howard Club. What was she doing at the office of the man she was once suing? Was she there to put the squeeze on Rogers? Discuss surgical options? Borrow a cup of sugar? Maggie squared her shoulders. "I could ask you the same thing."

Deirdre gave her hair a shampoo commercial flip. "Like I'd tell you."

She pushed past Rogers and Maggie and straight-armed the door to the waiting room. "Give me a call later, Ken. We can continue our conversation when we have more privacy." She gave Maggie a long, cold look then huffed through the door.

Maggie turned to Rogers. He appeared to be eating his lips.

"What was—" Maggie began.

Rogers took her elbow and steered her toward the exit. "Sorry, Ms. O'Malley, but I really must get back to my patients. I've got a busy, busy day."

Maggie regarded the vacant waiting room. "But but but," she began, this time sounding more motorcycle-on-a-cold-morning than motorboat. "But why was Deirdre here? Is she suing *you* now?"

Rogers gave her a gentle push down the hall. A pat on the shoulder. Some noises about prayers for Polly. Then Maggie was out the door.

Feck.

Maggie thrust her hands into her coat pockets and stalked to her car.

Rogers was Polly's physician. Deirdre was at Rogers' office. Maggie didn't know what it meant, but she didn't like it.

She pulled out her phone and dialed Constantine. Straight to voicemail. Right. The man-cold.

She pulled on gloves and drummed fleece-clad digits on the steering wheel. She considered her options: go back to Camille's and rouse Constantine from his cold medicine-induced stupor, follow Deirdre (on social media or in real life), file a complaint against Kenny Rogers with the state medical board and the American Board of Cosmetic Surgery—the American Board of Plastic Surgery, too, if he was a member, or hop online and see what she could digitally unearth.

None of them appealed, except filing a complaint against Rogers, which she fully intended on doing. Later.

Now her mind was on Polly. Unconscious. Unwell. Vulnerable. It brought her back to her twelfth summer. A season of loss. Of helplessness. Of the crushing guilt that she could've spent more time at her mother's sickbed, offered more comfort, been more present.

Maggie started the car and headed for the hospital. Maybe she'd always be haunted by the past, but at least she could do something about the present.

Chapter 21

Maggie made it to St. Theresa's in record time. She pulled into a parking space beside a mound of snow that looked large enough to support ski lifts then trekked toward a white oval building that reminded Maggie of a giant Tylenol and a line from the movie *Airplane!*.

"The hospital? What is it?"

"It's a big building with patients, but that's not important right now."

She shook her head to clear her mind. No movie quotes. No hiding behind humor. She was there to hold her friend's hand and will her to consciousness. To have a few quiet moments to think about what she knew and how much she didn't.

Maggie ground ice beneath her Sorrels as she tramped toward the hospital.

Crunch. Crunch. Crunch.

She stopped to adjust her scarf.

Crunch. Crunch.

Maggie felt a cold that had nothing to do with the temperature run through her. Hadn't she just heard a superfluous footfall? A crunch that didn't belong to her, but was in close proximity, behind, to the right? Or was it diagonally up ahead?

Maggie finished adjusting her scarf, turning her head casually to the right. An old woman bustled toward the surgery center entrance, her white hair gleaming beneath a plastic rain cap. She was too far away for her footfalls to be heard.

Maggie threw a glance over her shoulder. Nothing. She looked left. More nothing. If this was summer, a tumbleweed would have bounced across the deserted lot.

Maggie felt the same embarrassment as she had the night she'd collided with Austin during her run. It was like a reflex. Hit her in the emotions, she'd spring as far as she could in the other direction.

Fear? Nope.

Dread? Huh-uh.

Magnolia Louise O'Malley was just fine.

And yet memory, unbidden, unwanted, came curling like smoke from around the Wall.

Flat shark's eyes on her body. A lock of her hair caressed between fat, greedy fingers. The feeling of being watched.

Maggie's stomach clenched. She tasted bile in the back of her throat. She swallowed, clutched her keys in her hand and stuffed the fear she felt building in her chest.

This wasn't Collinsburg. This wasn't last year. She was safe. Her nervous system just hadn't gotten the message yet.

She forced herself to slow her pace, to exaggerate a sense of calm. She sauntered into the hospital and approached the reception desk. The hospital smelled like all hospitals Maggie had visited. The top notes: sorrow, hopelessness and antiseptics.

She waited until the older man at the helm finished telling whoever was on the other end of the phone that he didn't care for Brussels sprouts to conclude his call. When he hung up the phone and asked how he could help her, Maggie requested Polly's room number. The man eyed her behind round, black-framed glasses then picked up the phone again. After several minutes of mumbled conversation and a show of her ID, Maggie was directed to Room 430. Because she wasn't a relative—"almost-niece-in-law" didn't count—she wasn't allowed direct contact with Polly. The best they could do was allow Maggie to visit the exterior of Polly's hospital room. Maggie complied. She was familiar with the beggars/choosers scenario.

She took the elevator. There was a feeling of safety as she was sealed behind the great metal doors. No one could get to her here. So why did that sound like famous last words?

The elevator opened. She exited and followed the signs to room 430, her hand absently trailing the magenta lines that had been painted on the walls as way-finders, then stopped. A guard, tipped back in a folding chair, nose buried in an automotive manual, was stationed outside Polly's door.

Right. Because Polly was a prisoner. The irony was that Polly's own body was enough to bar her escape. She didn't need a guard.

Evidently the state didn't see it that way.

The officer watched Maggie's approach over his manual. He

lowered the book with a huff of resignation. His expectation of her arrival didn't lessen his irritation.

She introduced herself, made small talk about the weather, then fetched coffee for herself and the officer from the pot at the end of the hall. The cop took the cup, sipped. When the cup reached the halfway point, he rose, dragged a beige cushioned chair from a nearby conference room, set it down a few feet away and retrieved a fresh cup for them both.

Maggie took the folding chair and made it her home for the next six hours.

Her vigil was anything but silent. She chatted with the nurses who came in to care for Polly. Asked the hospitalist, a thirty-something man with a mop of dark hair and a penchant for spearmint TicTacs, what he could tell her about Polly's condition.

Information was in short supply, as was the staff's patience. The bottom line: Polly had a traumatic brain injury. Whether she'd slipped in her cell, tripped while walking in her sleep or angered a fellow inmate by taking the last piece of cornbread no one knew. Just as no one knew when—or whether—she'd awaken.

Visiting hours ended and the changing of the guard began. The new one rebuffed Maggie's offer of hot chocolate and told her to go home, his meaty hand gesturing vaguely toward the elevator bank.

Maggie dragged her chair back to the conference room, took the elevator to the lobby, and trudged through the parking lot. Had the day been a waste? Maybe. Polly hadn't magically awakened. Maggie hadn't gotten any new insights. But at least she could say she was there for her friend—her future aunt-in-law?—even if it was outside her room.

Maggie scraped the snow from the rear and side windows of her car with the sleeve of her coat, too cold and too preoccupied to wrestle the ice scraper from the glove compartment. It wasn't until she reached the windshield, her coat skipping across its ice-pocked surface like stones over a pond, that she realized that someone had tampered with her car.

The center of her windshield had been shattered. The rock that had presumably caused the damage was still lodged in the glass. Cracks spread from the rock like a web.

Maggie brushed the snow from around the stone and looked around. The lot was empty as a graveyard, just as it had been—or had seemed—when she made her trek to the hospital doors hours before. She pulled at the stone, trying to dislodge it like a bad tooth, as if extracting it would heal the car. It held fast. The Stone in the Car. If she extricated it, would she be queen of the Britons?

Maggie retrieved her phone from her purse and activated the flashlight app. She leaned forward to focus the faint beam on the rock, and the snow responded, lifting and fluffing and making its way into her coat, leaving her feeling as cold outside as she was inside.

There was something written on the stone. Forget King Arthur. She had her own petroglyph.

Maggie squinted. The message was no mystic rune. *DIE BITCH* was scrawled across the stone's ageless face in black. No, not black. Red. The deep brown-red of dried blood.

Maggie's stomach, her faithful emotional barometer, lurched. It had become her signature. The Cramper 2000™.

She whirled her head around again, looking in earnest now for whoever had left her this message, this threat. Nothing. No one. She was alone.

Or worse, almost alone.

The fear she had tried to ignore came back larger and blacker, as if growing fat on the thoughts that had begun pinging around her brain. She quickly snapped a picture on her phone, unlocked the Studebaker, climbed in and twisted the key in the ignition. She slammed the accelerator and the car fishtailed, swimming out of the lot, a plume of white behind her.

She drove too fast, the spider-webbed glass and rock partially obscuring her vision. Shops, houses, banks, government buildings, all charmingly flocked and prematurely lit for Christmas, streaked by. She imagined her hammering heart keeping pace with each blip outside her window. *Blip. Beat. Blip. Beat.* She loosened her scarf and leaned forward, straining to see through the tunnel of white and black before her.

There had been no one in the parking lot. Few cars on her journey thus far. Yet she still couldn't shake the feeling that she was being pursued, the scent of blood attracting predators like chum.

Maggie plucked the phone off the seat beside her and dialed 911 with her thumb. The bad news: someone had threatened her and vandalized her car. The good news: it proved that a threat other than Polly existed. The killer was still out there.

A dispatcher answered and Maggie explained the rock, the message, the writing medium, which she suspected was blood. The dispatcher clucked sympathetically and promised to send an officer to the address Maggie gave.

Maggie ended the call, but continued to hold the phone in her palm. She considered calling Constantine. She knew he was awake. They had texted hours before about her visit to the hospital, him insisting he join her, her urging him to keep his germs far from his fragile aunt. But, really, what did she expect him to do? She was an adult woman with the freedom and relative safety of a car. At most, the umbilicus of the phone connection would feed her the comfort of words. She needed more. She needed to find out who would do this and why.

Maggie arrived at Camille's shaken, slicked with sweat and angry. Oh so angry. Her fear had mutated during the drive, the sense of danger overridden by outrage. Someone had dared to damage her prized possession. Someone—she ticked through the possibilities: Kenny Rogers, Deirdre Hart, an unknown bad guy—thought Maggie could be intimidated. Someone thought wrong.

She burst through Camille's front door and threw her purse on the entryway bench. Constantine was sacked out on the couch, his chest rising and falling to the *Star Trek* theme music trilling from Camille's ancient television. He lifted his head. "You're home," he said nasally. He saw her face and sat up. "What's wrong?"

"Someone put a rock through the windshield of my car."

His mouth dropped open. "What?"

"Not just any rock. A rock with 'Die Bitch' written in what looks like blood."

Shock gave way to outrage then fear and disgust. "*In blood?*"

Maggie walked into the living room with her boots on, the incident leaving her feeling rebellious, eager to do something extreme, even if it was testing the limits of Camille's ScotchGuard. "I can't tell for sure. It's not like I could analyze it in the hospital parking lot. But it sure as hell looks like it. It's still in the windshield if you want to take a look."

Constantine was on his feet in seconds, shoving his feet into boots, bolting out the door without a coat. He jogged down to the curb, Maggie at his heels. He put his face close to the windshield, examining the wedged stone and the ruined glass beneath the feeble light of the streetlamp. "You called the police?"

"Dialed 911. They said they'd send an officer."

"Good." He ran a hand through his hair. "I just...who would send you petrified hate mail?"

"Deirdre Hart, for one. Dr. Kenny Rogers, for two."

"What? Why?"

"I took a little field trip to Dr. Rogers' office."

"Without me? I don't know if you're aware of this, but a sidekick is supposed to be by your side. We also get all the funny lines." His voice was light. His face was deadly serious.

"You were sick and I was sick of feeling powerless. I had to do something." He nodded, a curt little dip of his chin. Assent that he'd heard, but not exactly agreement.

They walked back to the house and closed themselves inside the warmth and light of Camille's living room. Maggie sank into the chair next to the fireplace and began picking her cuticles. "While I was there, I saw Deirdre Hart, which is more than a little strange since she was suing his practice partner—the entire AccentYOUate practice, for all we know—just days ago."

Constantine flopped onto the couch. "Maybe she's making nice with Rogers in hope of some repair work."

"Maybe. But that's not the really weird part." Maggie rose and paced the room, picking up the various tchotchkes that cluttered Camille's mantle, end tables and sideboard: commemorative spoons, a lamb tearfully raising a "We'll Miss Ewe!" sign, a glass butterfly with the word Mariposa in fussy script. "Guess who Polly's doctor is."

"I'm thinking you're not going to say Seuss."

"Kenny Rogers, as in Howard's former practice partner, as in the man who loves Polly from not-so-afar."

"You're kidding me."

"Rogers started out as her GP. When he changed to cosmetic surgery, she continued to see him, even after she was diagnosed with Parkinson's."

"Rogers diagnosed her?"

"No, a neurologist did, but after he retired, she let Rogers take over her treatment." Maggie walked over to the fireplace and flipped a switch. Fake logs began to glow. "According to Lev Petrosian, Rogers is in love with Polly despite the fact that he introduced her to Howard."

"Petrosian told you all this? There's not some kind of pharmacist/patient confidentiality thing?"

"Not with their love life. He's been Polly's pharmacist for years and since there's only one drugstore in town, he knows everyone's business."

"Why didn't Rogers tell us that?"

Maggie folded her arms across her chest. "Why didn't Polly?"

Constantine looked at her, understanding dawning in his eyes. "What are you saying?"

"Nothing. I mean..." Maggie paused, nibbling a cuticle. "I can't imagine Polly being unfaithful, but I can imagine Rogers engineering a way to end that marriage."

"By ending Howard?"

"It's possible."

They were silent for a few moments. Constantine plucked a tissue from a box marooned in a sea of soda cans and crumpled papers and blew his nose heartily. "It's strange and more than a little concerning. Unfortunately, Polly's unable to tell us about Rogers' doctoring. In any case, I'm not sure I understand how Deirdre fits in."

"Maybe she doesn't," Maggie admitted. "The whole thing—Rogers in charge of Polly's care, Deirdre meeting with Rogers—gives me a bad feeling."

"Not as bad as a rock through your windshield."

She began attacking her cuticles again. "You have a point."

Constantine pulled Maggie onto the couch. "I hate to throw Deputy Dog a bone and I know you already called 911, but we should probably alert him of the latest goings-on."

"One rock is not 'goings-on.' It could be a one-off."

"Or it could be just the beginning. We don't know what's slated for the next delivery."

Before last year, she would have considered his concern ridiculous.

Before last year, she never thought someone would try to kill her.

"I guess it couldn't hurt, especially since he's a friend." Maggie got to her feet, crossed the room, grabbed her purse from the bench and fished out her phone. Austin was at the top of her contacts list. The power of alphabetization.

She clicked to connect, waited, got his voicemail and left a message, telling him about her earlier call to 911, threading the needle between calm and urgent, anger and fear.

She dropped the phone back into her purse and knelt before the fire, trying to dissolve the chill that had settled at the base of her spine. "How are you feeling, anyway?"

He uncapped a bottle of pomegranate juice and took a swig. His mouth was rimmed in red. Maggie had no trouble imagining what he looked like when he was a toddler. "Better. I can feel my cold dying already. I've even been productive."

"Do tell."

"I've been taking your laptop out for a spin, trying to dig up more information about Matthew Foley, a.k.a. Howard before he became Howard."

"And?"

Constantine propped his elbow on a pillow embroidered with pink and blue flowers and pulled the laptop through the detritus on the coffee table. "At first the gods of the internet only bestowed what we'd already found: Matthew Foley's disappearance, the divers' search for his body, the funeral of a man and those who mourned him, including a woman so distraught she tried to climb into Foley's casket."

Maggie made a face. "For Matthew Foley?"

"I know. No accounting for taste. I think your dad said the same thing about you dating me. Anywho…" He pounded on the keyboard. "I did discover that Foley had privileges at the local hospital, plus there were several articles about the hospital's mission of mercy to care for the underserved, which likely meant they treated the homeless."

"Which potentially gave him access to an unnamed body that might come in handy if he chose to fake his death."

Constantine took another swig of juice. "It's not like the hospital would make a lot of noise if a body went missing and they thought no one was watching. My theory is Howard was thinking about faking his death. He was lucky enough to be at the hospital when a John Doe kicked it, stole the body and took it to his cabin. Then he threw the remains into the lake where it was discovered by people so distracted by grief and the disfiguring power of water and animals that they assumed the body was Howard—er—Matthew."

"That's a lot of assumptions."

"We're living in the land of assumptions. It's not like we've had an abundance of answers."

"True." Her stomach soured. She tried to think non-acidic thoughts. "Did you find anything else?"

"I also discovered that Foley embarked on a very interesting business venture."

"For his practice?"

"Not exactly." He gave a Carnac the Magnificent bow toward the screen.

Maggie squinted and began reading. She expected a news article.

What she found was a business registry for an entity called The Alaska Bush Company, co-owned by Matthew Foley, Bradley Denning and Dominick Sorrento.

The name rang a bell somewhere deep in her mind. She closed her eyes to remember. They sprung open at the clatter of keyboard keys.

Constantine had opened a new browser window for his search. Maggie stared as the home page image loaded.

A woman in a fur bikini and tall Russian hat smiled at her from the screen. She wore a wide red smile, long false eyelashes and a G-string that would do little to keep her nether regions warm. Above her a large pink speech bubble invited readers to rush to the Bush.

Maggie looked from the screen to Constantine back to the screen. She began clicking through the website's tabs. "Is this what I think it is?"

"If you think it's women gyrating in a gold rush-themed 'gentlemen's club,' then yes."

Maggie clicked through the pages. "Alaska Bush." She looked at Constantine. "That's the name of the club Starr works at—the woman we ran into at InHance who I knew from Madame Trousseau's."

Suddenly everything clicked. Starr's excitement over her lucrative new dancing job. The young women in Denning's waiting room clad in mini-thises and micro-thats. The possibility that Brad Denning, and perhaps at one point, Matthew Foley, granted the enhancement wishes of exotic dancers like cosmetic fairy godmothers. Bippity, boppity, boobs!

"Let me get this straight," she said. "Brad Denning and Matthew Foley owned a strip club."

Constantine blew his nose again and leaned against the pillow. "Own, as in present tense. Denning and Foley are still listed as the owners, Foley's fake death notwithstanding. Of course, the site administrators probably update these records only when the business license is renewed, so every five years, give or take. And did you see who their co-owner is?"

Maggie toggled back to the business registry window. "Dominick Sorrento." She shook her head. "Who's that?"

"You're kidding, right? Dominick Sorrento?" She shrugged, shook her head again. "You know all the lines to all of the *Godfather* movies, even number three, which we both hate, but you've never heard of Dominick Sorrento, the king of kingpins?"

"Are you saying he's in the Mafia?"

Constantine threw his hands up. "I'm not just saying it. Everyone is saying it. Unfortunately nobody can prove it. He makes the Teflon Don look like Pam." Maggie gave him a puzzled look. "You know, the non-stick cooking spray? Never mind. The point is, Dominick Sorrento is a known but unproven player in the mob. Word is he's heavily involved in lots of unsavory things, including the drug trade and knee cap percussion."

Maggie folded her arms. "How do you know all this?"

Constantine thumped his chest with Kleenex-stuffed fists. "I'm a Mafia aficionado. Remember that summer I pretended to be Michael Corleone? I keep tabs on this kind of stuff, real world as well as cinematic. There's lots of scuttlebutt about Sorrento, but the feds haven't been able to touch him. Too slippery."

"You have a picture?" Maggie asked.

"I can do you better than a picture. I have video. Behold the power of YouTube."

Constantine pointed, clicked and played his keyboard. Moments later, a man's face filled the screen. He wasn't what Maggie expected.

In Maggie's mind, "Mafia" conjured up the stars of her favorite mob films. She pictured Pacino, DeNiro, Pesci, Viterelli. Men with dark hair, olive skin, brooding eyes, maybe sneering lips, for good measure.

Sorrento was mid-fifties with medium-brown hair, doughy features and clear-rimmed eyeglasses connected to a chain—the sort of spectacles television often associated with schoolteachers, librarians and matronly aunts. She threw a look at Constantine. "Looks harmless enough."

Constantine clicked the play button. "Looks can be deceiving."

They watched as Sorrento made merry at some kind of party. Maybe it was a wedding. Maybe it was his niece's first Holy Communion. Maybe it was the grand opening of a strip club. Sorrento smiled and waved and hoisted his glass as he made his way around the room. The assembled crowd was jovial, and the camera picked up young men wrestling for the lens' attention, a stately older woman who appeared to be the group's matriarch, and a tall, attractive woman who somehow seemed familiar. As he approached his guests, the crowd parted like the Red Sea, giving him wide berth, coming closer for a handshake or a cheek-to-cheek press. Maggie wondered if a Sorrento buss was a traditional greeting or the kiss of Judas. She shuddered and kept watching.

Sorrento appeared calm, almost passive, as he made the rounds.

Despite the deference of those around him, his carriage was less Mafia don than mild-mannered accountant.

Until it wasn't.

Two minutes into the revelry, a partygoer bumped Sorrento's arm as he turned to speak to the waiter. Sorrento's glass upended, dousing his fine suit with red wine.

The party froze.

Sorrento removed a cloth handkerchief from his pocket, dabbed delicately at the flowering stain, then replaced the handkerchief. "Another Sangiovese, Joe, pronto!" he called to the waiter. The revelers were silent another beat then exploded in laughter.

Sorrento smiled and turned. As his face scraped by the camera lens, Maggie caught a glimpse of his expression. Dark. Angry. Deadly. He summoned two men with a flick of his fingers. They huddled then the men disappeared into the crowd, carrying the drink-spiller in their wake. Off camera, there was a yelp, a scuffle, a collective gasp from the crowd.

Music began abruptly, beating out an up-tempo big band number. In the background, Maggie swore she could hear the sound of skin striking skin and the muffled warble of cries.

The video ended. Maggie looked at Constantine. "I'm guessing the guy who spilled on Sorrento wasn't escorted to get a refill."

Constantine exited YouTube. "Solid guess. I found this on my searches for Sorrento. I also tried to find out the reason for the party and what happened afterwards."

"And?"

"And nothing. This was posted by someone who has made it his hobby to post videos of Sorrento. Unfortunately, it's heavy on innuendo and light on proof. Maybe the drink-spiller got a talking to. Maybe he's wearing cement shoes. Same could be said for whoever posted the video. Either way, no record of charges filed. It just gives you a vibe of Dominick's personality. And power."

"Dominick. Dominick." Something new fluttered to the edge of Maggie's consciousness.

It crystalized. "Nick."

"Huh?"

"Nick," she repeated. "Right before Brad Denning mutilated my mouth, he got suspicious about why I was there."

"He had a point."

"He asked if Nick had sent me."

"Nick as in...Dominick? As in Sorrento?"

"Why not? I just don't understand how Foley and Denning got involved with him in the first place."

Constantine mulled this over. "Sorrento had a strip club. Maybe he was introduced to Foley and Denning by one of his dancers and decided to invite the docs to a mutually beneficial business relationship. A partnership in the Bush would give Foley and Denning access to patients interested in 'investing' in their dance futures, and would give Sorrento potential recruits for his club."

Maggie nodded. "A double-dip into the same talent pool, encouraging attractive, perhaps vulnerable patients to dance at a strip club, and urging attractive, perhaps vulnerable dancers to enhance their assets. An endless loop of use and be used."

"Consorting with the Mafia can be bad for your health. Maybe Howard saw the writing on the wall and tried to get out. When he couldn't, he faked his death."

Maggie frowned. "Then someone found him and made it real."

Chapter 22

Constantine opened his mouth to reply, but was interrupted by the front door banging open.

Camille stood in the foyer, canvas grocery bags dangling from her hands and forearms. "Hello, sweethearts! We have food."

"We?" Maggie asked.

"Food?" Constantine asked.

Camille bustled down the hall, followed by Maria and Sophia, Polly's wine club compatriots and the women with whom Maggie had sat at the funeral.

Maggie trailed the trio into the kitchen.

"We ran into each other in the spice aisle?" Maria said, her voice going up at the end in her signature question mark fashion.

"She was after currants, and we were on the hunt for more dill for our spanakopita," Sophia supplied. "We decided to join forces for a cook-a-thon." She deposited her bags on the counter. "I know it's late." She glanced at the cat clock for confirmation. "Make that very late. But we figured it would be a good distraction from..." She bit her lip and looked down at the polished counter.

"How is Polly?" Camille asked, brows tenting above her eyes. "Any change?"

"I visited today, but didn't learn much. Sounds like more imaging and lab work are planned. Hopefully we'll get some answers soon."

Camille gave Maggie a side hug. "We could use some answers. Good news, too. The planet needs Polly to stick around." She brushed away a tear then began extracting food from her bag: whole vanilla beans, Madagascar cinnamon, coconut flour. The items kept coming. She was like the Mary Poppins of groceries.

Camille shooed Maggie from the kitchen with a plate full of quick breads and advice about how worry never fixed anything. By the look on Camille's face, Maggie doubted whether she followed her own counsel.

Maggie walked back to the living room and sank beside Constantine. She cleared a space for the plate, deposited the bread and leaned against the afghan-clad mound of Constantine's shoulder, choosing the comfort of human contact over the fear of germs. She tried to remember the last time she felt so dejected, so hopeless. She decided she didn't want to remember.

Constantine jerked his head toward the kitchen. "Cooking therapy?"

She nodded. "I'm good at eating my feelings so it's the ultimate symbiotic relationship."

"You still shaken up by the rock?"

Maggie sat up. "Less shaken and more pissed off. Speaking of..." She checked the time on her phone. "Where's the officer who's supposed to come by and take my statement?"

Constantine frowned. "Seems like he—or she— should have been here by now."

Maggie looked out the window at the snow glimmering beneath Camille's porch light. "Bad weather can mean bad traffic accidents. Probably a busy night."

Constantine's frown deepened, but he nodded. "Back to the rock: any suspects?"

"My first thought was that it was a gift from Dr. Rogers or Deirdre Hart. The timing is just too cute. I confront Rogers about acting as Polly's physician, hint about the nature of their relationship, make threats about complaining to the medical board, then run into Deirdre, who looked guilty as hell to be found in his office. Now that I know about Howard-slash-Matthew's ties with the mob..." She shook her head. "I'm just not sure."

"Deirdre's appearance at AccentYOUate is odd, but like she said, Howard's murder was the death of her lawsuit."

"True," Maggie agreed, "but there could be more to her story."

"Revenge. Jealousy. Mob ties. There's no shortage of motives."

"Or suspects."

"No matter who succeeded in getting Howard out of the picture, one thing's for sure: you've made someone very cranky. The rock is proof."

Maggie had to agree. Someone had gone to the trouble to track her to the hospital, vandalize her car and threaten her. She'd gotten under someone's skin. But whose?

Ben Stein's voice droned from Maggie's purse. She fished it out and checked the caller ID. St. Theresa's. Her stomach somersaulted. Polly. Oh, God, something had happened to Polly.

She pointed the screen at Constantine. "Why would they be calling you?" he asked.

She shook her head. She wasn't kin. She wasn't an emergency contact. She was just the girl who had sat outside Polly's hospital room as the hours ticked by and the shadows grew long. Maybe that counted for something. She put the phone to her ear.

"This is Maggie."

"Maggie O'Malley?" a woman's voice asked, the rhythmic whir of machinery humming like backup singers behind her. The symphony of the hospital, a chorus of machines, the click of shiny shoes across polished Linoleum, sobs, appropriately muted so as to disturb no one but the anguished. It was a song she knew all too well.

"Yes?"

"This is Gwen Petersen at St. Theresa's hospital."

"How can I help you?" She measured each word. A pinch of calm. A dash of concern. None of the panic she felt building.

"There's a lady here..." The woman's flattened vowels and clipped delivery reminded her of Marge Gunderson from *Fargo*, her "there's" as "dere's", "lady" as "ledy."

"Polly," Maggie supplied.

There was a pause. "I'm not sure."

"You're calling about Polly Wright?"

A chasm of silence opened, widened. "I don't know her name, ma'am."

"We're talking about an older woman in a coma, guard outside her door?"

"She's unconscious, but she's young. And no guard—or ID. She did have a pocketbook. The only thing in it was your number."

Chapter 23

Maggie wasn't much for strangers. As a child she had been taught to avoid them. As an adult she had learned to fear them. Funny thing was, the more she tried to steer clear, the more they found their way into her life.

Last year it was through reminders for meetings she didn't arrange with people she didn't know. Now it was an unconscious woman in a hospital who possessed nothing but Maggie's contact information.

It was like the law of attraction in reverse.

She had verified that the woman the nurse had called about wasn't Polly. She was indeed calling about a stranger. Part of Maggie assumed she wasn't a stranger at all. Part of her assumed it was Starr, former lingerie customer, sometime InHance patient and current dancer at the nightclub owned by Foley, Denning and Sorrento. All of her assumed it was somehow her fault.

She didn't have time for the guilt that always seemed to be feeding on her insides. Not today.

Not now. She pushed it behind the Wall, slid into her coat and kissed Constantine goodbye, rebuffing his offer—his insistence—to come along. She didn't just want to do this on her own. She had to.

Traffic was nonexistent and she reached the hospital in minutes. Temperatures had dropped with the sun, transforming slushy ruts into grooves that circled the parking lot like a record. Maggie parked Constantine's B210 as close as she could to the building, her mind on the rock in the Studebaker's windshield and the faceless perpetrator who'd put it there as a warning, a threat, a promise of more to come.

"You never know what someone's capable of," Polly had said. Maggie feared she was right.

Maggie locked the car and skated toward the hospital, frigid prairie wind needling her face. The lot was quiet. Too quiet? Maggie found herself looking over her shoulder, more interested in what—or who—was behind her rather than ahead.

Nurse Gwen had told her to come straight to Room 217. It wasn't lost on Maggie that the number was the same as the Overlook's haunted room in *The Shining* where a woman, a gas-filled balloon of flesh and putrefaction, put her cold purple hands around Danny's throat.

Two women lying in wait. One room number. Maggie's hand went to her own throat.

She skipped the reception desk and took the elevator to the second floor. She stood outside the door. Perspiration had filmed the skin beneath her arms and between her breasts. She ventilated her coat and knocked on the door of 217 softly, her knuckles barely grazing the dimpled plastic of the textured door.

A woman dressed in pink scrubs opened the door. Maggie focused on keeping her eyes from wandering to the shape on the bed or her mind from envisioning malevolent twins in hallways and elevators of blood.

Focus. Breathe. Repeat.

"Gwen? I'm Maggie. We spoke on the phone."

Gwen smiled, full cheeks eclipsing sparkling hazel eyes. "Yes, Maggie. Please come in."

Maggie stepped inside. Unlike Polly's private room, 217 was a shared suite. Only the far side was occupied, cordoned off by a half-open curtain that gave the appearance of privacy but none of its benefits. From Maggie's vantage point, she couldn't see who was in the bed.

"She's been unconscious since she was brought in," Gwen said, gesturing toward the shape across the room. "Like I said, no ID, just a phone with a single number. Yours." Gwen looked closely at Maggie. "You a friend or...?"

The mist of perspiration had become a heavy dew. Maggie fanned herself with coat lapels. Her throat felt as if it were lined with sand. "She's my...cousin."

Gwen raised a painted-on brow. "Cousin?"

Maggie nodded eagerly, substituting truth with enthusiasm, grateful that the small town, for the most part, still operated on a handshake and one's word. "Well, second cousin on my mother's side, but we're really close. Summer camp, sleepovers, trips to the mall." Places Maggie had never been. Things Maggie had never done. If pressed for details, Maggie was ready to recount scenes from *The Parent Trap* and *Clueless*.

Gwen shifted from one orthotic shoe to the other, full cheeks flattening, newly widened eyes openly assessing. Then something in her face softened. "I'm close to my cousins, too," she finally said. "The trouble we used to get in." She hooted and slapped her clipboard.

Maggie tried what she hoped was a conspiratorial smile. "Ha ha! The stories I could tell." She cleared her throat and nodded toward the bed. "So, uh, how'd she get here?"

Gwen's face grew serious. "Uber."

Maggie's mind leapt to articles about predators who became drivers to hunt for prey. It was the perfect set-up, a vehicle of opportunity and destruction. "She took an Uber here, or the Uber driver caused her to be here?"

"An Uber driver found her unconscious on the side of the road and brought her in. She had no obvious injuries, but a high fever and an elevated white blood cell count."

"An infection." Maggie turned this over in her mind. When she'd heard "unconscious," she'd assumed head trauma, maybe an overdose, not something organic in origin. At least disease was familiar territory. "What was it? Pneumonia? Meningitis? Toxic shock?"

Gwen's mouth dropped open, surprise at Maggie's disease-naming facility. She recovered, clamping her jaw shut, tucking a strand of sensibly bobbed hair behind her ear. "No, but that's where the doctors started, too. It wasn't until they did a CT that they discovered the cause." Maggie waited. "Perforated bowel."

"Perforated bowel?" Maggie echoed. "Any ideas how it happened?"

Gwen lifted cotton candy-colored shoulders. "We don't know yet. I do know she's lucky someone found her. Wouldn't take her long to bleed to death or die from septic shock."

So many horrors. So little time. Maggie glanced at the shape on the bed, the curve of a shoulder that rose and fell with each machine-induced breath, shrouded in anonymity by hospital white. "Can I see my cousin?"

Gwen nodded and stepped aside, burying her head in chart notes, her chin-length hair falling forward to shield her eyes. The human version of a privacy curtain.

Maggie approached the bed.

It was low, below hip-level on Maggie's five-foot-ten frame, and Maggie hesitated as she considered whether she should crouch (uncomfortable), sit (disrespectful?) or stoop (always a little weird). She went with a half stoop/half crouch that brought her eye-level with the form on the bed.

The woman's face was partially veiled by the sheet as if she were covering her hair in an abundance of modesty. Maggie put out her hand and touched the sheet. It was stiff and raspy. She glanced back at the nurse. Gwen continued to proffer the perceived isolation of averted eyes and curtained hair.

Maggie pinched the tip of the sheet and pulled. She felt as if she were unwrapping a gift, the sense of anticipation, the feeling she'd soon have what she'd wanted (answers, hope, peace), coursing through her blood.

She let the sheet drop, the coarse fabric falling in a soft hiss. Maggie looked at the woman lying on the hospital bed. She expected to see Starr's Neapolitan hair.

The woman who lay unconscious before her was a stranger.

Chapter 24

The gasp was out before Maggie could stop it. She dropped the sheet. It floated down to the woman's chin like a funeral shroud.

Nurse Gwen was at her side. She looked at Maggie, her eyes as wide as Maggie imagined her own. "Are you okay?"

Maggie opened her mouth. Nothing came out. Gwen poured water from the plastic carafe, two hundred milliliters if the blue hash marks were correct, and thrust a disposable cup under her nose. Water. Universal elixir for the upset.

Gwen patted Maggie's arm. "It's scary when you see all the wires and tubes, but your cousin's still there. Don't you worry. We're going to take good care of her."

Maggie nodded numbly. Her. That was as close to a name as she was going to get.

As if reading her mind, Gwen stopped patting. "What's your cousin's name, anyway?"

Umm...

Maggie glanced back at the woman beneath the apparatus that kept her blood oxygenated, her infection weakened, and her vitals easily read. She was slight, fine-boned, with lavender-colored hair that encircled her head like a corona. Was she an Olivia? A Lisa? A Joan? Maggie had read a study that suggested people resembled their names, as if their fates were written in their names as well as their stars. "Madeline," she said suddenly. "Madeline Hepburn."

It was a name smorgasbord, a dollop of children's literature, a ladle of classic film. She knew it sounded ridiculous. She hoped Gwen would buy it.

The nurse smiled warmly. Sold. "What a lovely name." She tilted her head. "It sort of rings a bell."

Yeah, like Quasimodo, Maggie thought.

Maggie pulled her coat closed and wound her scarf clockwise

around her neck. "Will you let me know if her condition changes? If she awakens, asks for me..."

Tells you who she is and how she knows me.

"Of course. Now that we know your cousin's identity, the hospital will have some paperwork for you so that she's no longer admitted as a Jane Doe. Just stop by admissions on your way out."

"I will," Maggie said, knowing she'd do no such thing. She didn't know who this woman was. How could she possibly provide her identification? For a moment Maggie wished she had Howard's identity creation expertise.

Gwen opened the door of 217, less of a chamber of horrors than a room of questions. She patted Maggie's hand—people seemed to be doing that a lot these days—and held her eyes. "We'll take good care of your cousin. I have a feeling everything will be back to normal soon."

Normal. Whatever that was.

Maggie stepped into the hall. The sharp tang of antiseptic mingled with coffee, men's cologne and the cloying sweetness of day-old doughnuts. She looked toward the elevators then at the door that led to the stairwell.

The question wasn't just ease or exercise. It was whether to visit Polly.

Maggie decided to forgo a trip to Polly's room. She wouldn't be allowed to see anything other than the hallway outside her door anyway, and she wanted to tell Constantine about the woman in room 217.

She walked to the elevator and pushed L for lobby. As she waited, her mind grooved tracks in her gray matter over the identity of the unconscious woman, how she ended up with her contact information and a growing sensation of familiarity. Didn't she know her? Hadn't she seen her? Someone with lavender hair was sure to—

Maggie froze. At the periphery of her vision, she caught sight of a figure slipping through the door to the stairwell. Female. Statuesque. Curves straining against a taupe pantsuit. Maggie couldn't be certain, but the woman's skin seemed to have a taut Day-Glo quality.

Deirdre. What was she doing at St. Theresa's?

Maggie jogged to the stairwell. She listened at the door. Clicking heels played castanets on Linoleum. Someone was in a hurry.

Maggie threw open the door and plunged inside, skidding to a stop on the landing, momentum almost sending her down the stairs. She grabbed the rail and listened in an attempt to echolocate the clacking heels. When she remembered she wasn't a bat, she peered over the edge of the stairs.

Emptiness yawned beneath.

She looked up. Taupe-encased legs clattered upward. It was like watching Kim Novak climb the bell tower stairs in *Vertigo*.

Maggie bounded upward, taking the stairs two at a time. Her Sorrels squeaked each time rubber sole mated with vinyl flooring, and as she crested the next landing, her boot slid on a puddle, sending her hydroplaning across the three-by-three square until boot lost contact with ground and she landed squarely on her butt.

Maggie picked herself off the floor and looked up the stairs. The gap separating her and Deirdre had widened. Maggie cursed under her breath and poured on the steam. She scrambled up and up, sweat-slicked hand on railing, lungs burning, heartbeat thundering in her ears.

The gap narrowed. Then closed.

Deirdre stopped to open the door to the sixth floor and Maggie clamped a hand on her taut, taupe arm.

Deirdre turned. Except that it wasn't Deirdre.

A thirtysomething with basset hound eyes stared at Maggie, thrashing her arm in an attempt to wrench it away. The woman's shoulder-length brown hair flapped beside her head, intensifying the dog vibe. "What the—? Let go."

Maggie released her. The woman whimpered and fell against the wall, hand palpating the arm Maggie had grabbed, assessing the damage. In the glow of the stairwell's fluorescent bulbs, Maggie could see that the woman wasn't wearing a taupe pantsuit, but pale pink scrubs. A lanyard hung around her neck proclaiming her STAFF. The full horror of what she'd done crashed into Maggie like a train. "Oh God. Oh God, I'm so sorry."

The woman shrunk away, as if trying to sink into the pores of the wall. "What was *that* all about?" she cried, continuing to rub her arm as if it were a frightened puppy that needed to be comforted.

"I, I..." Maggie tried to think of a reason. She decided to go with the truth. "I thought you were someone else."

The woman clutched her lanyard like a strand of pearls. "Well, you scared the hell out of me." The woman stepped closer. Suspicion bobbed into her gray-blue eyes. "What were you doing lurking in the stairwell, anyway?"

Maggie's face burned. She wondered if spontaneous combustion could be confined to a specific body part. "I wasn't lurking. I was taking the stairs for exercise. I'm visiting my cousin."

The woman popped a hip and counted off Maggie's itinerary on her fingers. "Visiting a cousin, taking the stairs for exercise, accosting the staff. Sounds like you've had a busy day."

Maggie thought about her lies about the woman in 217— the fake relationship, the identification she'd never be able to produce—and wondered if the woman could read the deceit in her face. "Well, I—"

A phone buzzed in the front pocket of the woman's scrubs. Saved by the bell.

The woman dipped her hand into her scrubs and swiped the face of the phone, keeping an eye on Maggie. She uttered a refrain of "Oh no. Okay. Oh no. Okay." into the phone. Several stanzas later, she tucked the phone away and pulled open the door. "Patient emergency. I have to go." She smoothed the sleeve on the arm Maggie had grabbed and opened the door, propping it with a white sneaker. She gave Maggie a long, appraising look. "But I'm calling security. Something about you doesn't add up."

"You don't have to do—" The woman slipped through the door and it slammed shut behind her. "That."

Maggie hung her head. Another pearl in her crown as Queen of the Socially Awkward and Potentially Deranged. It was probably a good time to make herself scarce.

Maggie put her hand on the door handle. Behind her, she heard something. The squeak of a shoe, a shift of weight, the grate of fabric that comes with sudden movement. A shadow spilled over her. She turned to see who owned the darkness.

It was the last thing she remembered.

Maggie's mouth was stuffed with cotton, her tongue, swollen and large, colliding with something dry and coarse. Or at least that's how it felt. She unstuck her lips from her teeth and moistened her desiccated palate. She called for help. Her voice died in a croak.

Maggie tried to sit up. An electrifying pain shot up her spine into the base of her brain like the puck making its way to the bell on the strongman meter at the fair. The smell of something metallic, something earthy, wafted to her noise. Blood. She reached a tentative hand to her head and brought it to her eyes. Red. Sticky. Strung with hair.

She fell onto her side. She brought her knees to her chest as a test. Could she move? Yes. Was it painful? Hell yes. She rocked over onto her knees, the child's pose without the yoga bliss, and took a moment.

Her head throbbed with a dull ache that brought to mind hangovers at quintuple strength. She breathed in slowly, exhaled the short gusty blast she usually reserved for weight-lifting, and struggled to her feet.

The world got up with her. Maggie grabbed the cold metal of the door handle to steady herself and closed her eyes, her mind automatically cataloging the topography of flaking paint beneath her fingers.

The landing stopped moving. The growing wave of nausea that threatened to crash abated. She was going to be okay. As long as she got out of the hospital. As long as whoever had done this wasn't waiting to do it again.

Her fingers snaked to the back of her head. She explored the border of the wet stickiness and found a gash. Fresh pain tore through her head. She closed her eyes to shut out the pain, to try to remember what had happened. Fragments of memory floated in and out. A sound. A shadow. A presence. Then nothing.

Somewhere above, Maggie heard a click, as if a door were being eased shut. It was a sneaky sort of sound. A lie of a sound. A sick new feeling crawled through her belly. Maybe whoever had hurt her wasn't finished.

Maggie grasped the door handle and pulled. Nerve receptors sent a telegram to her brain. Agony. Nausea. She steeled herself as new wetness trickled down the back of her neck and her salivary glands clenched. She eased the door open, more carefully this time, and peered into the hallway. Empty, as far as she could see. Safe, as far as she could tell.

But Maggie had been fooled by the promise of emptiness before.

She wriggled through the door, too weak with pain and dread to hold it wide. She took a step. Stopped. Waited. Took another.

No one popped out from the supply closet. A shadowy figure didn't hit her from behind. She wasn't struck down in a new and improved attack.

She walked quickly now, feet tripping over each other as she sped toward the hospital exit.

Outside, artic air whipped her hair. She yanked her phone from her purse. She considered calling 911, but her earlier appeal for help had yielded sympathy but no actual officer. She dialed Constantine. Straight to voicemail. He was awake. Why wasn't he taking her damn phone call? She stabbed a button and broke the connection. She was on her own. She could handle it.

Maggie lurched to Constantine's car, her heart ticking like a Geiger counter nearing radioactive material with every step she took away from the building and into the inky night. *Tick. Tick. Tick. Tickticktickticktick.*

She locked herself inside the Datsun, cranked the engine and smashed the gas pedal beneath her boot. Her phone bleated. She fumbled for it, grabbed it and answered, ignoring both the speed limit and laws that prohibited the cocktail of cell phones and vehicles.

Constantine, his voice nasal, said, "Everything okay? I saw you called while I was talking to my mom."

There'd been a time when Maggie would do anything to avoid revealing a weakness, an injury, even when she wasn't at fault. Even to her best friend. Those days were gone, right along with the belief that everything would be okay.

Now she sobbed into the phone, telling Constantine everything.

Chapter 25

Maggie sat on Camille's couch, letting the numbness spread through her like a drug. It was a welcome sensation, an absence of feeling that she typically couldn't attain, no matter how many emotions she tried to shove behind the Wall. She reveled in the blankness.

Constantine bandaged the back of her head, which had a nasty gouge the size and shape of a strawberry (why were tumors and injuries always measured in fruit?) and bled more than Maggie felt was reasonable.

"How do you feel?" he asked, his eyes wide and worried.

"Like someone hit me on the head and left me for dead." She touched the bandage. "If they wanted me dead, why didn't they finish the job?"

"People have no work ethic these days." He brushed her hair away from the wound, looping tangled tresses over the shoulder of her sweater, and looked into her eyes. "You're okay? Like, really, truly, this-one-goes-to-eleven okay?"

"I'm fine," she snapped. She didn't feel fine. She pretty much felt the opposite of fine. Her head throbbed. Her esophagus was a slide whistle for half-digested food.

She had looked in the rearview mirror when she'd pulled in front of Camille's house, examining the size of her pupils, their retraction to the light of her flashlight app. She was pretty sure she didn't have a concussion. Mostly because she didn't have time for one.

"My guess is whoever conked me on the head was just trying to scare me, like the rock in my windshield."

"Twice in twenty-four hours is overkill, and an alarming bit of escalation. You called 911?"

Maggie shook her head and immediately regretted it. Distant bells pealed in her ears. "They never sent an officer after my first 911 call. I figured why bother."

Constantine frowned. "What about Austin?"

"What about him? I never heard back from him, either." She checked her phone to substantiate her annoyance. Missed call from Austin. Right. She had silenced her phone at the hospital. She pushed to dial, got voicemail again and left an urgent message that skimmed over the details. She didn't feel like reliving the event over voicemail. She didn't feel like reliving it at all.

Constantine fluffed a pillow, arranged Maggie on the couch like a mannequin (better than she would have arranged Sheila) and disappeared into the kitchen. He emerged with steaming mugs of apple cider and a slice of pie. "Camille is at the shelter, but the cooking triumvirate left their wares." He sniffed the pie, held it sideways to the light and wrinkled his nose. "Damn. It's mince. Basically the outcast of pies, the pie-riah, if you will." He looked for Maggie's smile at the terrible pun. When it didn't materialize, his face folded.

He dropped beside her and drew her into a gentle hug. "Oh Mags. I'm sorry I'm acting like an idiot. I'm sorry this happened. I'm sorry I wasn't with you. I'm sorry I never seem to be around when you need me."

She leaned into him, letting herself melt into his warmth, his scent. "What I need is a head transplant. I'd also take knowing who did this." Despite their closeness, part of her still couldn't admit that she needed him. Needed anyone.

"Whoever it was knew you were at the hospital, both when you visited Polly and when you got the call about the mystery woman. Speaking of...who was she?"

"A stranger. At least, that's what I thought at first."

"Meaning?"

"Meaning I didn't recognize her. Her eyes were closed and her face was partially obstructed by a breathing cannula. Then I remembered the lavender hair, her features, and it came to me." Constantine looked at her expectantly. "The waiting room of InHance."

Constantine's eyes widened. "Howard's old practice?"

"The same. Chances are she's a patient there and a dancer at the Alaska Bush Company, which happens to be co-owned by a Mafia kingpin."

"Alleged Mafia kingpin," he corrected. "And who says she's a patient? She could have been waiting for a friend."

"True, but I don't think so. It's just too coincidental, especially if you consider the fact that I gave Starr my phone number. If the woman in the hospital danced at the Bush, she probably knew Starr. Maybe Starr gave her my number."

"I'll give you that it's possible that she was a patient at InHance, maybe even a dancer at the Bush, given our revolving door theory. But it doesn't change the fact that this woman is a long way from either of them. Hundreds of miles and a couple of states, as a matter of fact. Why didn't she end up at a hospital in Three Rivers?"

Maggie frowned. "Good question. Great question, actually."

"Thanks." Constantine paused. "Why don't you ask Starr? See if she knew this girl, ask how she ended up here in Hollow Pine."

Maggie would've face-palmed if she wasn't worried about giving herself a—or another—concussion. She procured Starr's business card from her purse and dialed. The phone obediently rang. No one answered.

She clicked Messages and sent a text. No reply.

She knew that it was unreasonable to expect Starr to answer a text or a phone call immediately. Starr could be in the shower or working or charging her phone. But dread tightened its grip around Maggie's stomach.

Was Starr unable to get to her phone? Or was she *unable to get to her phone*? Same sentence. Two very different scenarios.

Constantine read her face. "Unavailable?"

"Let's hope it's not permanent."

Constantine's face went stony. "Why was the woman at St. Theresa's?"

"Perforated bowel."

He made a face at bowel. "How does one perforate a bowel?"

Maggie took a sip of cider, wondering if its warmth would thaw her numbness, wishing she had alcohol to intensify it. "The nurse I spoke with said they didn't know. Could be anything from ulcer to diverticulitis, but I'm wondering about something else."

"Like a knife wound?"

"Like an incision." Constantine looked a question at her. "Like from cosmetic surgery."

"I know this isn't a surprise, but I'm not following."

"Let's say she's a patient of Denning. In addition to lip injections that double as balloon animals, he also performs surgery. Breast augmentation. Liposuction. Tummy tucks. You name it, I saw it on his

After wall."

"You're thinking this is a when-tummy-tucks-go-bad situation?"

"Or tummy liposuction. Complications are rare, but they do happen. Just ask a lawyer."

"Did she look like she needed a cosmetic procedure?" He put his hand up. "Not that anyone would 'need' cosmetic enhancement."

"No, but none of the women in Denning's office looked like candidates for cosmetic anything. They were practically perfect."

"Maybe 'practically' was the problem. In a business where perfection is worshipped, it would make sense that dancers would chase that ideal. I guess it's not much different than models."

"Except in this case, we're talking about a potentially vulnerable group of women. Not all dancers are college students dancing for tuition. Some do it because they feel they have no other option."

"Which would make them willing to do anything to keep their jobs, including getting surgery, especially if they're encouraged by management to do so."

Constantine stretched out beside Maggie on the couch. It was barely big enough to hold one full-sized adult, let alone two, and his backside dangled precariously over the edge. He tucked his frame around hers and traced her ring finger, encircling the skin as if drawing on a band. Maggie held her breath, hoping the action wouldn't be accompanied by a proposal.

"What if the clinic has a habit of injuring patients?" Maggie motioned for Constantine to move over then eased herself into a seated position. She waited for her head to stop swimming then grabbed her laptop by the scruff. "What if we can find complaints against Denning and his clinic—Foley, too, for that matter?"

Constantine was already nodding along. "There are tons of sites that offer doctor ratings, but nothing beats the state medical board for malpractice and disciplinary records. May I?"

Maggie handed the computer to Constantine. He typed. Paused. Typed again. Sighed.

"Did you try Matthew Foley?"

Constantine rubbed his eyes and nodded. "Yes, and name variations."

"That doesn't mean they're in the clear. Doctors can amass an impressively bad malpractice record, move to another state and get relicensed there."

"Doctoring public perception." Constantine tapped the keyboard again, creating his own concerto. The screen filled with results for doctors Wright, Foley and Denning. The majority was physician self-promotion. The rest seemed to be fluffy PR pieces about charitable endeavors. Cleft palate surgery for children in the developing world. Skin cancer screenings at runaway and homeless shelters. Reconstructive surgery for breast cancer survivors. The good doctors as do-gooders.

Twelve pages in, they found two articles that mentioned Denning and Foley's joint venture with Dominick Sorrento. It, too, was complimentary, using language that suggested performing arts center rather than strip club, whitewashing scarlet letters with vanilla phrases and meaningless platitudes.

Maggie wondered how they'd managed the snow job. Money? Plying reporters and editors with free drinks and lap dances? Both? Maggie's head was pounding in earnest now. She needed sleep. And a giant do-over. "Complete waste of time," she said miserably.

Constantine began typing again. "We haven't reached the end of the internet yet. I have an idea."

Maggie rubbed her head. She wasn't sure she was up to ideas. "Hey, Gus, maybe we should just call it a day."

"Hang on." Constantine pointed, clicked, then smiled victoriously. "Found him."

"Denning?"

"Nope. Randy Harold."

"Is that a name or a description?"

Constantine smirked. "Both. A friend from college."

"I thought I was your only friend from college."

"I had four, thank you very much, including Randy."

"So what's so important about Randy?"

"He's in insurance."

Before Maggie could give her "so what?" look, Constantine was on the phone.

"Randy?" He nodded at Maggie and gave a thumbs up. "It's Constantine." A throat clear. "Constantine Papadapoulos. From Intro to Object-Oriented Programming." Maggie inwardly winced. Fun class. "Good, thanks. You still playing *Legend of Zelda*?"

Maggie endured five minutes of video game geek-out. Finally: "The reason I called is I wondered if you could look into a couple of doctors for me." He nodded. "Yeah, yeah, I did all that. Yep, zip. I was hoping you

could turn some of your software loose, see if you find any red flags."
More nodding then another thumbs-up for Maggie. "Awesome."
Constantine gave the doctors' names and his email address to Randy
then hung up and gave a fervent, if slightly pornographic, victory dance.

"I gather your two-first-named friend agreed to pitch in?"

"I helped him get through Miller's programming class, he helps us
take a peek behind the velvet curtain. These big insurers have some of
the most powerful fraud protection software in the world. If something is
awry—or askance, if you prefer—he'll find it."

Maggie hugged him. "You did good, Gus. Like always."

He hugged her back. "That's because I love you. Like always."

Chapter 26

Exhaustion pulled on Maggie like a moon, orbiting around the periphery of her consciousness with the promise of oblivion. Even her vision was Vaseline-blurry like the soft-focus filter on Sybil Shepherd in *Moonlighting* reruns.

Constantine hovered at Maggie's door, his hand lingering in hers. "You're sure you're all right?" he asked for the tenth time.

No.

"Positive," she answered.

"You want me to stay with you?"

Yes.

"No, I'm fine." She screwed her lips into the most realistic smile she could muster. Memory crouched behind the smile, waiting to be released. Every time she blinked, it intruded into her consciousness. Shadow. Pain. Darkness. And as she stood with Constantine, memory was accompanied by a new and powerful fear.

What if whoever had attacked her knew of her visit to Room 217? What if her attacker had put the lilac-haired beauty in the hospital and returned to finish the job? What if Maggie had led her assailant to the unconscious woman who lay alone and defenseless in her room?

"Hang on a sec." Maggie reclaimed her phone from her pocket and dialed St. Theresa's. She asked to be connected to Gwen, the second-floor nurse. She waited, tortured by her own thoughts and a Muzak version of Def Leppard's "Pour Some Sugar on Me." After an eternity and the first few chords of "Hysteria," Gwen picked up. She assured Maggie that, yes, her cousin was resting peacefully and no, no one had come to her room or had asked her whereabouts. She also reminded Maggie to bring Madeline's information to the hospital so that she could be properly registered. Maggie made another promise she couldn't keep and disconnected.

Maggie felt informed but not relieved. "She's okay. Or as okay as someone who's unconscious in a hospital bed can be. And I've got something else to add to my report to Austin."

"You don't seem okay. Like, even a little bit. Maybe I should take you to urgent care, or at least stay with you to make sure you don't wake up dead or something."

Maggie doubled down. She didn't need to go to urgent care. She didn't need a babysitter. A part of her knew that her insistence on avoiding medical care was out of character. Constantine constantly mock-accused her of being a hypochondriac. Yet she couldn't bear the idea of sitting in a waiting room, explaining what happened, justifying her refusal to call the police. She just wanted to sleep.

Constantine kissed her then lumbered to his own doorway. He tapped the door's raised panel with his fingers. "I'm right here if you need me. Miss Vanilla, too."

"I know, and I'm comforted by the thought of a watch-hamster." She gave a beauty queen-worthy wave and closed herself in her room.

She crawled into her flannel pajamas, slipped into the bathroom for her nightly toilette, (i.e. washing her face with Irish Spring) and fell into bed. She was asleep within moments.

That's when the dreams began.

A shadow.

A rock.

A faceless man with something large and dangerous in his hand.

And finally, a dream that she was sleepwalking, her feet carrying her down the stairs, out the front door and along the sycamore-lined street to the Wright's backyard. In the dream, she dropped to her knees, the ice-crusted snow biting against exposed skin as her nightgown fluttered upward in the wind, and began digging with her hands.

She broke through a stratum of ice, then through powdery crystals of snow. When her hands hit frozen earth, she scraped at it until her fingernails shredded and crusted with dirt.

Her hands hit something hard and metal. She wrapped her fingers around the unseen object and pulled.

She expected to see a knife in her hands, to see the same crimson-stained blade that Polly had pulled from the hidey-hole in the backyard. Instead she found a photo.

It was a candid shot of a group with Howard at the center bordered by women lined up like a chorus line, legs turned out, hands sidled beside thighs, chins just so to maximize angles and the chance for a photogenic picture.

Maggie recognized Starr, the woman at the hospital, others who seemed familiar from InHance. Every one of their eyes had been scratched out with a pen.

Maggie awoke in the kitchen. She had sleepwalked. Maggie, paragon of self-control, bastion of restraint, had allowed her body to take her on a joyride without her knowledge or permission.

The realization was unnerving.

She had no recollection of leaving her bed, navigating the stairs, eating the croissants that splayed suggestively on the counter like a centerfold.

She wondered what else she had done. She wondered how Polly lived with the constant uncertainty of where her feet took her every night.

Maggie rewrapped the croissants and placed them in the bread garage, thinking that Camille must have put them out the night before. She checked the cat clock: five thirty. Just enough time for a run.

If her head didn't feel like it would fall off.

If she wasn't worried someone would try to kill her.

Maggie made herself a cup of coffee, went back up to her room and fired up her laptop. A run through the digital landscape would have to do.

She checked her email, responded to messages from Fiona and Pop, who reported that Ada continued to blossom at work, stalked Deirdre Hart on social media, researched Dominick Sorrento and began a draft of her complaint against Kenny Rogers.

An hour and a half later, she had viewed three new cat videos courtesy of Fiona, but had achieved little else. She needed a distraction.

She logged into Netflix and reviewed the options that appealed: a new *Sharknado* film, *Orange is the New Black* and a handful of true crime shows: *Dateline*, *Snapped* and *See No Evil*.

Maggie moused over *See No Evil*. She had an idea.

Maggie grabbed her laptop, flung open her door and walked to Constantine's room. Her head reminded her she shouldn't do that and she slowed to a pace that would inspire approval from tortoises. She eased open his door. The bed was empty. Miss Vanilla was on her wheel.

She picked her way downstairs and found Constantine at the coffee pot inhaling a croissant. "There may have been a witness to Howard's murder," she said breathlessly.

"What?" he said with his mouth full.

"Surveillance video."

Constantine swallowed his wad of pastry. "But Polly and Howard didn't have security cameras. Which seems strange now that I think about it. Howard had to be looking over his shoulder since he fake-offed himself."

"The Wrights may not have had a security camera, but the market across the street from their house does. I just remembered seeing it the night of Polly's last sleepwalking episode."

Translation: the night of Polly's arrest.

"Think the police have reviewed the footage?" he asked.

"No idea. I was wondering if you could access it remotely." She handed Constantine her laptop.

He took it and sat at the kitchen table. He cracked his knuckles. "Lucky for you I'm a computer genius. Double lucky that many surveillance systems offer web-based access."

"So you think you can get in?"

"Does an IPv4 address have thirty-two bits?" She looked at him blankly. "It does. And I went through a hacking phase in college. I was even recruited by Anonymous."

"The international hacking group?"

"They prefer 'hack-tivist' organization, although I've always thought of them as digital-anties."

"Clever."

"I like to think so. Anyway..." he clicked the laptop's built-in mouse and attacked the keyboard "...hacking into web-based surveillance systems isn't like hacking into the Pentagon, which they frown on by the way. A lot of these systems are set up with temporary passwords like 1-2-3-4, which the users are supposed to change."

"But don't."

"Exactly. And I now know the password for Towne Market is—wait for it—'password.'" Constantine hit a few more keys and pressed enter. "And we're in. Cross your fingers that the footage is still there—and is clear enough to see anything of value. Some of these systems are crap."

Maggie peered at the screen, which invited them to change settings, access the account and view history. Constantine chose the latter.

He followed a series of prompts until they found themselves transported back to the day Polly found Howard's chin lolling in a bowl of Life cereal, his throat slit, his bloodless face as pale as the snow outside. The footage remained and, if the thumbnail was any indicator, was relatively clear.

A play box filled the center of the screen. Constantine clicked the cursor and fast-forwarded to late afternoon. Grainy black and white video began to dance across the screen. Customers exiting the store with bulging canvas bags. Neighbors arriving home from work. The sun slipping behind Butte Hill, nudging the street lamps awake as they blinked and stretched and cast searching fingers into the gathering gloom of dusk.

The video's timestamp ticked by the hours. One by one, residents took out the garbage, let in the cat and lidded the windows with shades pulled smartly into place.

Then a car.

Twin headlights bore into the night, turning the screen a blinding white as they swung in front of the camera's lens. The car pulled in front of the Wright residence.

Maggie squinted. "Do you recognize it?"

Constantine leaned in and stroked stubble that had turned his chin into a Chia Pet. "Looks like a Caddy. Not sure what year, but definitely a classic. And no, I don't recognize it."

The car idled at the curb for several minutes then drove away.

"Ugh." Maggie slumped against Camille's multicolored afghan. "Some witness."

"Well, it was worth a—" He stopped. The same car rounded the corner in front of the Towne Market and approached the Wright house for a second time. "Hold everything. What do we have here?"

The car pulled into the driveway. The driver doused the headlights, opened the car door and stepped into a tableau of white-washed lawn, columned manse and deserted street. Portrait of a murder.

A figure emerged, obscured by darkness, inconvenient camera angles, and baggy clothes and a hat, then loped around the side of the house into the oblivion of night. The timestamp read 2:43 a.m.

Maggie looked at Constantine. His face mirrored her own: fear, elation, hope, revulsion.

Something was happening. Something that could solve Howard's death and save Polly's life.

Five minutes passed. Then seven. Then nine.

At the eleven-minute mark, the shadow reemerged. The slow jog Maggie had witnessed when he—or was it she?—had vanished behind the house's faux brick façade had been replaced by a sprint. The shadow sped to the car, flung open the door and backed quickly out onto the street. Moments later, the car was gone.

Maggie guessed Howard was, too.

Constantine toggled the video back. "The bad news is we don't have a great view of the driver. The good news..." He paused on the tail of the car as it squatted on the Wright's driveway. "...we can see the license plate. I give you YKZ 523."

Maggie released the breath she didn't know she was holding. "The police can trace the tags, question the driver. The timing's about right, isn't it?"

"Aunt Polly found Howard a little after three a.m. The coroner put time of death between midnight and three, so yeah, this is definitely in the neighborhood." Constantine advanced the video. Save for a handful of cars, the street remained empty until the slow drip of commuter traffic began to travel down the IV that connected the Wright's neighborhood to the businesses of Hollow Pine. "Either my aunt and step-uncle ordered a late-night pizza or we just witnessed the killer's arrival and departure. The question is: who is it?"

"And why didn't the police pull this footage?"

Constantine frowned. "I dunno, maybe because they were convinced that Polly did it and didn't bother to look any further?"

Maggie's phone bleated. She checked the screen. Austin. Perfect timing.

"Sorry for the tardy response to your message, Maggie." He sounded tense. "I saw that you called but didn't realize it was urgent until I listened to your voicemail this morning. You should've called 911."

Maggie gritted her teeth. "I did call 911. I called after someone put a rock with a threatening message through my windshield and talked with a very nice woman who said that an officer would be dispatched to take my statement. That never happened, so I decided not to waste time—or breath—with another emergency number call."

"Gee, Maggie, I'm sorry to hear that." She could hear the clatter of computer keys. "This is strange. I don't see any record of your 911 call. Who did you talk to?"

Maggie closed her eyes and tried to remember the dispatcher's name. She came up empty.

"A woman. Friendly, young-ish voice."

"Probably Tammy. I'll see who was on that night and get the scoop.

Meanwhile, can you fill me in?"

Maggie outlined the blood-stained missive on the rock in her windshield and awakening in the hospital stairwell with a gaping hole in her head.

"So you didn't see your attacker?" he asked.

"No. I saw a shadow on the door, sort of felt this presence. Next thing I knew, I was picking myself off the floor."

"So you don't know if you were actually attacked."

Maggie's temper flared. "Are you suggesting that I hit myself in the back of the head?"

"Not at all." Austin's voice took on the exaggerated patience of a parent talking to an unreasonable child. "You could have fallen, had some kind of medical event. I'm just trying to get the whole story."

"You have the whole story," Maggie barked. "Someone broke my windshield then cracked my head, both of which suggest that someone dangerous—someone other than Polly—is prowling around. Where is this coming from?"

Austin exhaled loudly. "Sorry, Maggie. I'm not trying to be a pain. Jeff just wants me to be extra careful around…"

"Around what? Around me? Because we dated?"

"Because you're overly involved in Polly's case."

"Overly involved?" Maggie could hear the volume and pitch of her voice rising with her indignation. "I'm involved. I'm trying to find out what really happened to Howard because your *pardner* seems more interested in harassing Polly than finding the real killer."

"Now, Maggie—"

"Constantine and I just reviewed surveillance video from a store near the Wrights that shows someone entering and leaving their residence around the time of Howard's murder. Did you seek out surveillance footage?"

"I'm not allowed to comment on an ongoing investigation," he replied stiffly.

"That's never stopped you before."

The phone went silent. Maggie bunched up her lips. "Look," she said carefully, "I know you're a good guy. A good guy who wants to do good things. I'm guessing that you and Jeff haven't looked for surveillance footage. Maybe because you haven't gotten around to it. Maybe because you didn't believe any existed. Maybe because you thought you got your murderer. But it's there and I believe it reveals the real killer. Please, Austin, please get the footage from Towne Market. Review it. Call in the plate number on the car that idled in front of the Wrights while Howard took his last breath. Then decide for yourself if Polly did it. Just don't blindly follow orders because you think you have to."

"We'll probably need a warrant. Then we'll have to verify the footage, research the plate." She could practically hear the small print.

"You do what you have to do. And one more thing: Matthew Foley and his practice partner, Brad Denning, owned a strip club with Dominick Sorrento."

"Did you say Dominick Sorrento?" He rolled the Rs in Sorrento, setting Maggie's teeth on edge.

"I did."

"We-ell..." He drew the word into two syllables. "That's interesting, but I'm not sure it's relevant. We still haven't located Foley's sister, and by all accounts he left a devastated fiancée, a shocked community, but no unanswered questions."

"There are more questions than in an episode of *Jeopardy!*" She was practically shouting now. She tamped down her temper with a sip of Constantine's coffee, grabbed not-so-nicely from his hand. "The footage, the attack, Sorrento. Everything points away from Polly and toward whatever was happening in her husband's former life. The whole reason I was at St. Theresa's was to visit an unconscious woman who had my phone number in her purse. And P.S.: This unconscious woman is a dancer at Sorrento's and Denning's club and a patient of Denning. She's there because of a botched surgery by Denning, which she was forced into having as a condition of her employment."

Maggie didn't bother qualifying her claims with "I think" or "I believe" or "my theory is." She'd spent her whole life moderating her speech, softening the edges of her opinions, asserting herself in ways that were socially sanctioned and other-approved. The boiling cauldron of life had changed that, had changed her, firing her into something tougher, harder, less yielding. It was time to put stakes in the ground.

Austin stonewalled. "Honestly, this all sounds pretty nuts. But I can tell that you're upset. I'll send an officer to take your statement—for real this time. Then we can sit and talk about all of this..." He muttered what sounded like a very bad word... "drama that's going on."

Drama. Like the issue was who was asking whom to prom.

Maggie clenched her hands into fists and pushed down her growing frustration. "Watch the video, run the plates, look into Denning's association with Sorrento. Please, Austin. A woman's life is at stake. Maybe many women's lives."

Austin sighed heavily. "Let's get that report filed first. Then I'll see what I can do about the video. Greeley won't be happy about that. He's ready to close this one."

"And we're ready to find Howard's real killer," she shot back.

Chapter 27

The next morning, Maggie awoke to the chime of the doorbell. She scampered downstairs and found Constantine heading for the door.

"Camille's already gone. I guess that puts us on door duty."

They walked down the hall and pulled open the front door. Sam Graham stood on the other side. "Maggie, Constantine. Great to see you." His voice held all the color of overcooked oatmeal.

"Likewise," Constantine said. He rocked back on his heels. "So...what's up?"

Graham gestured living-room-ward. "May I?"

Constantine held the door and Graham strode in. He sat on the couch and looked from Maggie to Constantine and bestowed what was probably a smile. "I have good news."

Maggie and Constantine exchanged looks. "Aunt Polly's out of her coma?" Constantine asked. His voice frayed at the end of the question, the final syllables ragged and thin.

Graham frowned. "No, sorry. This is good legal news." His voice emphasized "legal" as if that trumped anything else. "I just got word from the DA's office—well, Mark Weber and I did." He frowned, his discomfort at sharing the spotlight with his co-council—no matter how voluntary the decision was—evident. "They received the forensics report on the knife that was...ah...recovered from Polly's yard."

Recovered. A euphemism as impotent as "episode" used to describe Polly's bizarre and frightening outbursts.

Constantine chewed his lip. "And?"

"They ran the blood sample and fingerprints through the system. Polly's fingerprints were on the knife. No surprise there since she handled it. But the blood wasn't a match for Polly, and there were other fingerprints *and* DNA belonging to someone else. No hit in the system, but their existence opens the door to an alternate killer, which puts a bit of a dent in the state's case."

Constantine clapped his hands together. "That's awesome!" He looked at Maggie. "Hear that, Mags? No blood match for Polly and someone else's fingerprints and DNA."

"It is good news." She tried to smile. "But it doesn't really clear Polly, right? No DNA doesn't necessarily mean she didn't commit the murder."

Graham looked at her like she'd just shot him in the kneecaps. "No, but it's a major chink in the state's armor. There's no physical evidence tying Polly to Howard's murder. It was a circumstantial case before. Now it's nothing more than a witch hunt."

"Is Howard's blood on the knife?" Maggie asked.

"It is," Graham allowed.

"So Polly digging up the murder weapon was just dumb luck?" Maggie wasn't sure why she kept blurting out negative, inappropriate remarks. This was good news. Great news. She was just having a hard time hearing it over the steady throb of her head or seeing it around the image of Polly holding the blade in the moonlight. She shoved aside the pain, the memories, the qualms that ebbed and flowed like the tide. She smiled more convincingly. "Sorry. Not a morning person. I need coffee."

Graham puckered his lips and straightened his tie. Maggie noticed the tie was patterned with tiny scales of justice. She bet he had matching curtains at home. "Polly's digging incident is quite puzzling," he said, "but it really has no bearing on the case. Just because she discovered the murder weapon, no matter how strange the circumstances, doesn't mean she operated it. I've filed a motion to have the case dismissed and Polly released. I know she's...unwell. But from what I understand, she's made some improvements."

Constantine snapped to attention. "Like what?"

"I spoke with the hospitalist at St. Theresa's a few minutes ago. He said she's showing increased responsiveness: reacting to stimuli, moving in response to instruction."

Constantine looked up at the ceiling then down at the floor. "That's the best news I've heard...maybe ever." He grabbed Graham's hand and shook it in a convincing imitation of a paint can shaker. "So what's next?"

Graham put his hands on his thighs and hoisted himself up. "I— we—file the motion then we wait. But I have a good feeling about it." He walked to the door and opened it.

"Oh, one more thing," Maggie said. Graham turned, eyes wary and expectant. "We found video footage of someone prowling around the Wright residence around the time of the murder."

He frowned. "Video? What video?"

"Surveillance from the market across the street."

Graham's frown deepened, gathering the skin around his tight little mouth. "Do the police know about it?"

"Yes," Maggie said, "but they don't seem overly eager to pursue it. They have their murderer."

"There's also the matter of Howard's previous identity, nefarious practices at his former practice and a strip club co-owned by a Mafioso," Constantine chimed in. He then filled in the blanks. Graham responded as if he'd been told what Constantine liked for breakfast.

"Interesting," he said, sounding disinterested. Graham stepped out into the cold and gathered his coat at his throat. "I'm friendly with the captain. His wife and mine are in the same book club. Murder mysteries." He shuddered. "I'll give him a call, make sure they're following up on all available leads. That video might be the nail in the coffin for the murderer and the ticket to freedom for Polly. I'll be in touch."

Constantine closed the door and swept Maggie into his arms. "Hear that, Mags? Polly's getting better and she might be coming home."

Maggie shut her eyes and squeezed him tightly. She felt a rumble at her gut. Constantine's phone.

They broke apart and he checked the screen. He thumbed the device to answer. "Hey, Randy. That was quick."

Maggie listened as Constantine offered up three "uh-huhs" and one "no way." He thanked Randy, cut the connection and pulled Maggie onto the couch.

"The good luck streak continues," he said.

"I'm listening."

"Remember those red flags Randy's insurance software is supposed to detect?" Maggie nodded. "He said it looks like Pamplona after the running of the bulls."

Maggie raised her brows. "Lots?"

"In the words of Ron Weasley, 'loads.' But not for the reasons we thought."

"So no malpractice?"

"Insurance irregularities."

"Meaning?"

"Meaning Denning's group has processed a metric crap-ton of claims for a variety of procedures."

Maggie's brain processor felt like it was chugging. "But I didn't think cosmetic procedures were covered under insurance."

Constantine looked her dead in the eye. "They aren't."

Chapter 28

Constantine got up and grabbed a nutcracker from the mantle. He popped a walnut into the elf's mouth and pressed the lever. The elf vomited the nutmeat.

"Some cosmetic procedures are covered by insurance," he said. "Your breast reductions, your reconstructive surgeries, stuff like that."

"But that's not what we're talking about."

"We're not talking about cosmetic procedures at all."

Maggie shook her head. "Then what?"

Constantine shoved another nut into the nutcracker and dispensed it into his hand. "InHance has been billing insurance for non-cosmetic procedures. Endoscopies, colonoscopies, cystoscopies—"

Goosebumps pricked Maggie's skin. "Did you say colonoscopies?" Constantine nodded. "A colonoscopy could cause a bowel perforation."

"The woman at the hospital."

"Exactly."

"There's more. InHance also billed insurance for hernia repairs and deviated septums—or is it septa?"

"Septa," Maggie said absently. "Which means that they were billing tummy tucks and rhinoplasty under procedures that would be covered by insurance." She sat on the couch. "And billing unnecessary yet billable medical procedures. All of which sounds an awful lot like—"

"Insurance fraud."

"But why actually do the medical procedures?" Maggie asked. "Why not just say they were doing them?"

"Denning wasn't alone in those ORs. There were anesthesiologists, nurses. He probably performed both the cosmetic and the medical procedures at the same time, saying that the patients had told him, 'As long as you're in there, Doc, go ahead and give me J Lo's ass.' He'd be reimbursed by insurance and collect cash from patients. Discounted or not, it adds up."

Maggie ticked off what they knew on her fingers. "Denning charges his patients—who are also dancers at the strip club he co-owns with a mobster—for cut-rate cosmetic surgery, performs routine medical procedures on them, and then bills insurance for the medical procedure and the cosmetic one, which he codes to seem medically necessary. Because he's a butt man but not a colon man, he makes the occasional mistake. Some victims of those mistakes, like the mystery woman who had my phone number, end up in the hospital." She looked at Constantine. "Maybe others end up in the morgue with no one to look into what happened."

A chill wriggled up her spine. "Insurance fraud with a side of malpractice and possibly manslaughter. If Howard Wright—a.k.a. Matthew Foley—knew, it could be reason enough to get out of the business at any cost."

Constantine ran a hand through his hair. "With Sorrento in the mix, you have an even grimmer picture. No criminal record, but word on the street is he has his hands in a grab bag of illegal activities. The whole thing sounds like reason enough to fake your own death."

Maggie popped a nut into the elf's head and crushed it. "Or cause someone else's."

They spent the day cruising the back alleys of the internet looking for something, anything, that would support their theories. They found a handful of articles that hinted at Sorrento's alleged criminal endeavors— the same Constantine had already exhumed—and little else. No hew and cry about shady practices at either of Howard's/Matthew's clinics. No mysterious deaths. No unidentified bodies.

Maggie closed the laptop, piled her hair up in a messy bun and stuck a pencil through it, careful to avoid the wound at the base of her skull. She rubbed her eyes and sighed loudly.

"You're not getting discouraged are you?" Constantine asked.

"No. Yes. Maybe."

"Well, don't. We have the connections between Sorrento, Howard and crimes worth killing for."

"But we don't know who did the killing," Maggie said. "Denning had as much of a motive as Sorrento, maybe more so. Maybe the insurance fraud was Denning's baby. Maybe he thought they weren't bringing in enough cash with their dancer makeover pipeline and decided to add double-billing to the mix. If Matthew wanted to give it up because he suddenly grew a conscience or became concerned about patient safety, he'd be cutting off Denning's gravy train as much as Sorrento's. Not to mention the fact that if Matthew decided to go public, Denning would be at risk for losing his license and serving jail time."

"Sorrento would also be facing jail time," Constantine said.

"Either way, Matthew decided to disappear into the ultimate hiding place."

"The grave."

"The question is who did the dirty work: Sorrento or Denning?"

"Don't forget about Dr. Rogers or Deirdre Hart. And there's also the little matter of the woman in the hospital," she said, "and the knife that Polly dug up in her yard."

An eleven appeared between Constantine's brows. "Which you probably should stop bringing up."

Maggie's face flamed. "Sorry. Sometimes I get carried away trying to find answers. Blame the scientific method."

"What matters is that things are looking up—relatively speaking, of course. Polly's improving, Graham and Weber are working on her release, we're getting closer to finding out how and why Matthew Foley became Howard Wright. I think this goodish news calls for a celebration." He flashed a crooked smile. "And you know what that means."

"*Lord of the Rings* roleplaying?"

"Dinner out with my best girl—if you're up for it."

"I'm always up for eating."

They chose their favorite diner. It also happened to be Hollow Pine's only diner.

Constantine squired her in the Datsun, opening and closing her door. When she told him he was being a gentleman, he tried to buckle her into her seatbelt, just to be extra attentive. Maggie laughed.

The diner was located in "restaurant row" of a tony neighborhood not far from the Wright residence. Constantine wound his way through faux-cobblestone streets, past public art that could only be described as thought-provoking, and around clusters of pub-crawlers, until he pulled to a stop beneath the iconic neon roller skating hamburger of Dinah's Diner.

They clambered out of the Datsun and hurried through the double doors of Dinah's. They were immediately assaulted by "Let's Go to the Hop." Constantine pulled Maggie into an impromptu jitterbug, which ended badly when Maggie triple-stepped into a cardboard cutout of Dinah hoisting a banana cream pie like Lady Liberty's torch.

Maggie righted the cutout and they followed the hostess to a hot pink booth bookended by plastic flamingos. Maggie sank into the booth and hid behind her menu. Constantine tapped it with his own. "I'm considering the Heinz 57 Chevy Burger and a large glass of Blue Suede Booze. What are you getting?"

"I recommend the Poodle Skirt Steak," a voice behind Maggie said. "It's perfect for someone like you. Yap, yap, yap."

Maggie turned. Jeff Greeley smiled and elbowed Austin in the ribs.

Maggie's smile evaporated, along with her good mood. "What's that supposed to mean?"

Greeley put his palms up. From the looks of them, he'd had a meal that involved barbecue sauce. "Just a little joke."

Maggie tightened her hands into fists beneath the table. It was clear Greeley hated her. Whether it was birthed the night Polly convinced his wife to leave him, due to some kind of inherent territorialism or because of the stench of controversy that seemed to follow her from Rxcellance, she didn't know. She simply knew she couldn't rock Polly's dingy of hope.

Maggie turned back to the menu and pretended to read. "Good one."

"Speaking of jokes," Greeley said.

Maggie lowered the menu again.

"We followed up on that little tip you gave us about Howard's supposed other life." He shook his head and chuckled. He poked Austin in the ribs again. Austin shifted on his feet and looked at his boots.

Maggie crossed her arms. "Yes, I know. You were having a hard time tracking down his sister."

Greeley gave an I-know-something-you-don't-know smile. "We were. Then we found her."

Maggie's heart leapt. "You found Jenna? What did she say?"

"That she had no idea who you were."

Maggie's heart dropped into her belly. She tried to prop it up. "Well, that's not too surprising. We had just met. It's not like we were friends."

"When I talked to her on the phone she said she never met you."

"That's a damn lie," Constantine blurted. "I was there."

Greeley showed his palms again. "Guess it's your word against hers."

"She hasn't exactly gotten gold stars in honesty," Maggie snapped. "You know her criminal record. Did Austin tell you about my car? What happened at St. Theresa's? The surveillance video?"

Greeley sucked his teeth. "He told me. No witnesses to the vandalism or the alleged assault. Just like the alleged meeting with Jenna."

Maggie sat on her fists so she wouldn't smack Greeley's allegedly stupid face.

"As for the surveillance video, we'll look into it." He smiled. "Just like we're looking into all of your other 'theories.'" He smiled. "I'm all about finding justice." Greeley fumbled in his pocket and produced a coin. He popped the coin into the table-top jukebox. He punched the button reading C7.

"Warden threw a party in the county jail," Elvis Presley crooned from the squat aluminum box.

Greeley grinned. "'Jailhouse Rock.' One of my favorites." Then he turned on his heel and strode away, Austin scampering behind him.

Chapter 29

Maggie stared at her Rebel Without a Bun Chicken Wrap. It was smothered in Caesar dressing and neatly bisected so she could see the crispy golden chicken and melted Swiss cheese peeking out from the tortilla.

It was one of her favorite dishes, discovered when Polly took her out to lunch to get to know the young woman who had caught Constantine's eye. The premise had been more than a little ridiculous. Constantine and Maggie had been best friends for years and Maggie had tagged along to visit Polly many times. Still, the lunch had been an important milestone, a cairn marking the new path their relationship had taken. The sandwich held special meaning that had nothing to do with its secret sauce.

Now it sat on her plate untouched.

"Why would Jenna lie?" she asked.

Constantine came around to Maggie's side of the booth, his jeans making embarrassing sounds against the vinyl. He put an arm around her. "She does have a criminal record, so she's not exactly a paragon of virtue. And obviously the whole thing with her brother had her spooked. She tried to run. When the police caught up with her, her only defense was to lie."

Maggie took a swig of Dr. Pepper. "I just wish I knew what she knew and why she's trying so hard to run from the past."

Constantine pushed his own plate away, parking the Heinz 57 Chevy burger near the metal napkin dispenser. "Fraud has that effect on people."

"You think she knows about the insurance scheme?"

"Even if she didn't, chances are she knew her brother was involved with Sorrento in some way. That could have been the source of the falling-out. Once she found out her brother had lived another life only to be murdered, it was enough to get her running."

"Her lie doesn't exactly help her credibility with the police."

He grabbed a tall glass of azure liquid that resembled antifreeze and drank deeply. "Or ours."

The evening soured by Greeley, Maggie and Constantine headed back to Camille's. Maggie kissed Constantine goodnight and dropped into bed without changing her clothes, washing her face or brushing her teeth.

She spent the next day in her sweats. Then the day after that. And the one that followed.

She didn't feel like wearing real clothes. Even when Officer Ted Del Vecchio finally came to take her statement about the damage to her car and to her skull. Even when Camille's knitting group took over the first floor of the house. Even when she and Constantine visited Polly—or when she was alone, outside of Polly's hospital room.

She didn't feel like doing much of anything.

Blame a head injury or the repeated run-ins with Jeff Greeley or the dearth of good news from St. Theresa's. Maggie had hit a wall.

"Polly's continuing to improve," Constantine would tell her, his voice veering dangerously close to pleading, and it was true. Maggie tried to let small steps toward progress be enough. After a lifetime of being satisfied with enough, she wanted more.

After the third night of their vigil at St. Theresa's, they rode back to the house in silence, Constantine at the wheel of the Datsun, Maggie mindlessly brushing the velvet nap of her "formal" sweatpants. For the first time in their shared history, they had run out of things to say, even when Polly's incremental improvement provided a modicum of material.

Constantine parked at the curb and they picked their way up the drive toward the house. Clouds had blotted out both moon and stars, rendering the sky as hushed and brooding as their mood.

As Maggie neared the red door, she saw a figure standing beneath the porch light. She hesitated, took a step, hesitated. The intruder cha-cha. Maggie opened her mouth to warn Constantine, to call out to the stranger, to scream. Her tongue turned to sand.

She raised her own hand. Later she'd say it was in greeting. The truth was she was winding up to strike. Something unintelligible and guttural fell from her lips. The figure at the door turned, knuckles poised to knock.

"Well, hey there, Maggie. Good timing."

Austin.

Maggie was instantly annoyed. Shouldn't he have called first? Didn't he know what time it was? Had he seen the panic on her face?

She gave her naked anger a smile to hide behind. "Hey yourself. What are you doing here?"

Austin nodded at Constantine and toed the ground, looking up at the blackness above. "I, um, I." He cleared his throat. "I just wanted to let you know I've been reassigned."

Maggie moved into the light. Under Camille's fluorescent bulbs Austin's face was blue-white, but Maggie could see that he'd colored deeply, freckles lost on his red face in a dermatological game of hide and seek. "Reassigned?"

He whipped the hat from his head and twisted it in his hand. "I'm off Howard's case."

Maggie wasn't sure how to respond. "Off the case? Why?"

"The official word? Greeley says I lack objectivity." He stole a look at Maggie. "He thinks the fact that we…um…knew each other from before has compromised my objectivity." He sniffed loudly. "But I think he's just mad."

"Mad about what?" Constantine was suddenly at Maggie's elbow.

Austin returned his gaze to the ground, stuffed his hands into his coat pockets. "About the whole Sorrento thing."

Maggie and Constantine exchanged glances. "Why don't you come in?" Maggie said.

Austin followed her inside like a puppy. She relieved him of his coat and pushed him into the chair by the fire. Maggie and Constantine sat across from him. She felt like Barbara Walters gearing up for a televised interview.

"What do you mean 'the Sorrento thing'?" she asked.

Austin shifted in his chair. "I shouldn't be talking about this."

She resisted the urge to remind him he'd talked about the case many times. "Whatever you have to say will stay between us," Maggie said. She looked at Constantine. He nodded. "Did Sorrento fall through? Greeley got mad and blamed you?"

Austin laughed bitterly. "That's just it. We got him. We got Sorrento."

It felt as if all the oxygen had been sucked from the room. "You got Sorrento?"

"We obtained a copy of the surveillance video. The plate on the car came back to Sorrento. Right car, right place, right time. The captain caught word of it. Heard Sorrento's name and got all excited. They've been trying to nab that sombitch forever." He looked at Maggie. "Pardon my French."

Maggie made the international sign for "not at all."

"The captain put a traffic detail on Sorrento, got him pulled over on a busted tail light, which may or may not have been busted. Brought him in and laid the whole thing out. Told him he was a suspect in a murder, blah, blah, blah."

Austin leaned back in the chair, his eyes focused on the memory replaying somewhere in the middle-distance. "Greeley and I weren't allowed anywhere near Sorrento. He was the captain's prize. He asked Sorrento if he would like to give a DNA sample, you know, to rule him out."

Austin looked at Constantine then Maggie. He hauled a pack of Dentyne from his coat pocket, slowly unwrapped a piece, popped the red rectangle in his mouth, and began chewing. He was clearly enjoying story time. "Now most collars we haul in," he continued, "would tell us to go f—um—would tell us no. We'd have to use some kind of subterfuge to get a sample. Give them a cigarette or a Coke then snag it from the trash. That kind of thing. Not Sorrento. He was so cocky he consented." Austen laughed. "He freaking consented."

Maggie felt a surge of adrenaline. "They ran the DNA on the knife Polly dug up and it came back to Sorrento."

"The prize goes to the pretty lady. They prioritized the sample—pushed it through faster than I've ever seen—and it matched."

"Sorrento's DNA wasn't already in the system?" Constantine asked.

"Nope. Neither were his fingerprints. He's a crafty one, and one arrogant SOB to consent to the sample."

"So what happened?" Maggie asked.

"We mirandized Sorrento, booked and printed him. Guess whose prints were on the knife Polly dug up."

"Sorrento's," Constantine said.

"A partial. That, along with the DNA, was enough to get the captain excited. Sorrento's been on everyone's list for a long time."

"What did Sorrento say?" Maggie asked.

"Not much. He lawyered up in a hurry. We'll have him for forty-eight hours, then he'll be arraigned. After that, it's anyone's guess. The upshot: looks like the case against Polly is going to be dismissed. The powers that be like Sorrento, and keeping a sick old lady under lock and key at the hospital is bad PR. My guess: Sorrento's in, Polly's out."

Relief washed over Maggie. Polly was going to be free, if not from her coma, from the shackles of incarceration. "So why is Greeley mad? You got the collar of a lifetime."

Austin smiled. It reminded Maggie of a chimp baring his teeth. "It wasn't the collar Greeley had in mind. He had his eye on Polly."

"After all this, he still thinks Polly's guilty?" Constantine sputtered.

"Yup."

"And now Greeley's pissed the evidence shows it was someone else, and he's taking his toys and going home?" Constantine's voice had climbed an octave.

"More like taking my toys and sending me home," Austin said.

"But you guys solved the case," Maggie said.

"You solved it," Austin said. "And I think that's what really burned him. Sure he was sore about Polly 'getting away with murder.'" Austin hooked quotes into the air. "But Greeley couldn't stand that someone else got the glory. He even blamed me for not getting the surveillance video first, even though I suggested it early in the investigation. He figures we're in cahoots, that because we're friends we conspired to free Polly and ruin his career."

Personal enmity. Professional pride. Maggie could see how Greeley convinced himself of Polly's guilt. She wondered how far he'd go to try to convince others.

Chapter 30

The next four days felt like college dead week and finals wrapped into one. Except without the studying. Or the all-nighters. Or the pizza.

It wasn't that Maggie had so much to do. It was that there was so much going on.

Minutes after Austin's departure, Sam Graham called to report Sorrento's arrest. Constantine feigned surprise with an award-winning performance. "I'd like to thank the Academy," he said after hanging up. "And Miss Vanilla. And Cher."

A day later, the hospital called to say that Polly had regained consciousness. Two days after that, Polly was on her way home, her release expedited by an excited yet chastened District Attorney, eager to get Sorrento behind bars and his next election secured.

It was a return worthy of a war hero. Constantine decked her dresser with a vase of coral-lipped roses. Maggie stocked the house with Earl Grey tea, fresh fruit and a stack of novels. Camille sequestered herself in the kitchen, baking Polly's favorite cakes, pies, cookies and muffins. The only thing missing was an interpretive dance to communicate their joy at her return. Even the weather cooperated, the sun shirking its cloudy companions to shine boldly enough to turn the ice into muddy Slurpees. It wasn't Waikiki Beach, but it was better than the icebox they'd inhabited the past several weeks.

Graham chauffeured Polly to Camille's in a large shiny Mercedes that screamed penile compensation. He pulled into the driveway, jogged around to the passenger side and opened her door with a flourish, signaling to Maggie, Constantine and Camille, who had clustered on the porch, to watch her arrival.

Polly emerged slowly. A sliver of glove. A hint of hat. Finally, Polly's face popping above the open car door. It was like watching Punxsutawney Phil on Groundhog's Day.

Maggie stood on tiptoe, balancing against Constantine to catch a glimpse of Polly's face. Polly turned toward them and gave a smile that was at once radiant and exhausted.

Graham gave Polly his arm. Together they shambled up freshly shoveled steps. Polly's progress was slow, her hesitant steps dwarfed by Graham's confident strides, her thin frame leaning hard against the HurryCane Constantine had purchased as a welcome home gift and sent ahead with Graham. Finally she reached the landing and relinquished the cane and Graham's arm. She pulled Constantine and Maggie into a dual hug and began sobbing.

Maggie lay her head against Polly's and put an arm around her heaving shoulders. Maggie usually took pains to avoid the occasions of emotion, running from her own pain or melting into the background when others cried or railed, as if any display of feeling were contagious and to be inoculated against. Today Maggie didn't mind Polly's tears. They were a celebration that told the story of a long absence and glorious return.

Polly pulled away and touched their faces then pulled Camille into a hug. Camille seemed surprised at first, stiffening against Polly's surprisingly strong embrace, then melted like ice from the eaves.

Camille ushered them all inside, invoking the specter of illness-causing chill, tantalizing with the promise of homemade souvlaki, prepared for Polly's return. They complied, stomped the winter slop from their shoes and stepped inside.

Polly looked older since her arrest. Her follicles had declared mutiny, overrunning her Haute Tamale dye job with fifty shades of gray. Her cheeks had deflated with sudden weight loss precipitated by illness and worry. Delicate bones shored up powdered cheekbones with such gusto they appeared ready to break through thin skin. Yet her eyes, sunken into their sockets, were bright and lively. For someone who had recovered from a coma, Polly looked remarkably spry.

Graham perched his client on the couch and basked in the afterglow of success. He regaled them with details of the motions he filed, the hearings he attended, the gnashing of teeth by the District Attorney's office as if he were the Odysseus of the legal world. Co-council Mark Weber didn't merit a mention. Graham had dropped the pretense of congenial collaboration, right along with any utterance of "we" or "us." Maggie smiled and nodded and tried not to roll her eyes. She preferred dull, lackluster Graham to the preening, obnoxious one in Camille's living room. Thankfully, he couldn't stay for dinner.

Once the plates were cleared and the kitchen tidied, Polly pulled herself upright. "I'm going to bed," she announced. "And how wonderful that it's my own bed." She grabbed Maggie's hand then Constantine's. "Thank you for everything. For staying outside my hospital room. For finding Howard's killer. I think part of me knew you were out there, working to bring me home, calling me to come back. It just took me a while to do it."

Maggie helped her to her room. She was surprised to see how steady Polly was on her feet, how little she trembled as they moved along the photo-dotted hallway to the room that had been christened Polly's since the night the empty husk of Howard's body had been found.

Maggie watched as Polly went through her nighttime routine, the application of cold cream beneath her eyes, a hundred strokes of the brush through the faded thatch of hair. "I need to see Lev," she said, frowning at her roots. "It's time for a touch-up and a refill."

Maggie plucked the cold cream from the dresser. "Speaking of Lev," she said, pretending to examine the label, "I had an interesting talk with him."

Polly looked up from the dental floss that ran between her fingers like a haphazard cat's cradle. "About my medication?"

"Sort of. He'd been trying to reach your doctor to talk about possible side effects." Maggie looked at Polly full on. "You didn't tell me that Kenny Rogers was your doctor."

Polly unwound the dental floss from her fingers and let it drop into a small wastebasket. "I didn't think it mattered. I've gone to Ken for years."

"But he's a cosmetic surgeon. You need a neurologist."

"Who says?" Polly sniffed. "I had a neurologist. Didn't like him all that much. When he retired, I figured I'd go back to Ken. We've been friends for a long time. He introduced me to Howard, as a matter of fact."

"And how did that work out for you?" Maggie asked before she could censor herself.

Polly's lips disappeared. "Let's just say fourth time wasn't a charm, either." She rose from the chair in front of the dresser, a fussy tufted affair in gilded satin, and sat on the bed. "I have no regrets. Howard was no prize, but I grew from the not-so-good times." She gave a small smile. "I try to avoid personal growth, but life has a way of doling it out just the same."

Maggie wanted to ask whether that growth included knowing that her murdered husband had led another life under another identity. She wanted to ask Polly if she knew a secret that was powerful enough to inspire a fake death and motivate a real murder. She wanted to know if Kenny Rogers' love for her was unrequited or returned with equal ardor.

She looked at the woman who had been like a mother, who might one day become her aunt. Polly drooped on her bed. Her eyelids were already beginning their southern migration. Polly was too exhausted for that conversation. Too fragile. Maggie decided that was another topic for another day. She'd keep the conversation firmly rooted in the here and now.

"Do you think Ken is the best doctor," she asked, "given your Parkinson's and that you're recovering from a coma?"

Polly lifted her chin. "Ken takes great care of me. In fact, I feel better than ever. I wouldn't say that jail was a spa experience, but some aspects of my health actually improved, thanks in part, to a former dietician I met who got me off wheat and sugar."

Maggie sighed inwardly. Not only was Polly entrusting her health to a doctor who specialized in reducing double-chins, she was getting nutrition advice from an inmate. On the other hand, Polly did seem to be doing better. She remembered the ease with which Polly held her fork, her ability to renounce her HurryCane if she wanted use of both hands. "I agree," Maggie said, "but you still have a serious condition and are recovering from a neurological incident. All the friendship and diet advice in the world won't change that."

Polly patted her hand. "Neither will science, my dear. Some things go beyond medication and diplomas."

She rose, peeled back the chenille bedspread and slid beneath the bedclothes. "Now if you'll excuse me, I need my beauty sleep." She touched the emollient-enhanced skin beneath her eyes then gave a dazzling smile. "Although I can't imagine anything more beautiful than being here with my family."

Maggie clicked off the overhead light and stepped into the hallway. Polly was home. She had returned from the land between the living and the dead. Her health seemed to be improving. There were still many unanswered questions, but things were headed in the right direction.

Maggie trotted down the hallway to join Constantine and Camille in the living room. Her phone droned. She stopped below a Norman Rockwell print of kids playing marbles. She checked the display.

Restricted. She raised an eyebrow and swiped to answer.

"This is Maggie."

"Hey Maggie, it's Gwen from St. Theresa's."

Crap.

Maggie had managed to visit her "cousin" a handful of times, but always in secret, stealing into her room during shift change to avoid inconvenient questions about paperwork. The hospital had called several times about registering "Madeline Hepburn," but the number was always displayed, making it easy for Maggie to screen the calls and stall for time. Maybe Gwen had blocked the number to get through and shake her down. Maggie swallowed.

"I'm sorry I haven't been in to see Madeline lately or complete the paperwork ID. How's she doing?"

"She's awake," Gwen said. "She's awake, and she's asking for you."

Chapter 31

Maggie gave Constantine a quick peck, yanked on her coat and jogged out the door to the Datsun. She was glad that Camille was already in bed. She was too keyed up to explain her late-night excursion, the mystery of the woman in Room 217 and whether it meant everything or nothing at all.

She started the car, ignored her father's recommended one-minute warm-up period and pointed it toward St. Theresa's. Maggie tried to tell herself that there was really no need to rush. The woman had been languishing there for days on end. But she was conscious now. Mobile. Who knew how long she'd be willing to stay in the whitewashed room of the hospital? Who might be coming for her now that she was able to talk?

Maggie shivered, thinking of the presence in the stairwell, the dank smell of melted snow and old Linoleum. Her fingers kept tracing the frontiers of her wound, as if practicing a form of phrenology that would reveal someone else's nature rather than her own.

She shook it off. She'd been to the hospital several times since the attack—and it was an attack, despite the lack of witnesses, dearth of proof, and Austin's incredulous tone. She wasn't about to be cowed by a faceless assailant or a nameless fear.

She parked, marched past the reception desk and smacked the Up elevator button, consciously averting her eyes from the stairwell door.

Moments later, Maggie arrived at Room 217. She raised her hand to knock softly. Gwen appeared at her elbow, chart in hand.

"That was fast," Gwen said.

"She's my cousin," Maggie said. As if that explained everything.

"We've missed you." Gwen's voice was even, but there was a testiness to her stance, judgment in the angle of her shoulders, the lift of her chin. "And Admissions is getting hysterical about the paperwork. We need proof of Madeline's identity for her medical records." *And billing,*

Maggie added silently. "They've called you multiple times."

"Another family emergency." At least this was true. She didn't mention the fact that it had been at the same hospital. "How's she doing?"

Gwen sandwiched her clipboard beneath her arm. "Actually, pretty well. Once she came around, her lucidity returned fairly quickly. Doctor says we'll discharge in a few days."

Maggie felt genuine relief that her fake cousin was going to recover. "Is she awake now?"

"She is, but I don't know for how long."

Maggie followed Gwen into the room. The overhead lights had been turned off, the assembly of machines providing the only source of illumination. The bed nearest the door was now occupied with a sleeping lump that rose from the sheets like a mountain range, straining the hospital corners and blocking Maggie's view of "Madeline."

Maggie crept past the first bed and sat in the chair near the window beneath an ecru-hued cabinet that Maggie supposed housed extra blankets and emesis trays.

"Madeline" stirred. She lifted her head and looked at Maggie.

"Your cousin's here," Gwen said brightly.

Surprise flitted through the woman's eyes then relief. She smiled. "Cuz. I'm glad to see you." Her voice was scratchy, deeper than Maggie would have imagined for a woman her size.

"I'll leave you two to catch up," Gwen said. "Buzz me if you need anything," She made one final flourishing note in her chart and floated out the door, leaving Maggie alone with the stranger.

She looked at the woman in the hospital bed. In spite of her bedhead and the twin thumbprints of exhaustion that nestled beneath her eyes like errant mascara, she was undeniably beautiful. Maggie gave a hesitant smile. "I'm Maggie."

The woman's smile tipped up a few centimeters. "I know," she said. "We're cousins."

Maggie's cheeks flamed. "Sorry about that. They wouldn't tell me anything unless we were related."

The woman closed her eyes, lash extensions forming crescent moons against milky skin. "We all do what we can to get by." She opened her eyes, hazel eyes piercing Maggie's green ones. "I'm Rose." She extended a hand tattooed with bruises from the IV that bit into her skin, a thin tube still snaking into a bag that hung above her.

Maggie touched Rose's fingertips, afraid of getting tangled with the tube. Afraid of breaking her. "It's nice to meet you, Rose."

"That's my real name, by the way. My dancing name is Roxy. I thought about going by Gypsy Rose, but most of the customers at the Bush are too young to get it." Her smile was wan, aging her beyond the early-twenties Maggie had guessed. The Gypsy Rose reference made her seem older, too. Not many of her generation knew about the famous stripper.

"You're a long way from the Bush," Maggie said. "How did you end up in Hollow Pine?"

Rose closed her eyes. "Transferred." She opened her eyes again. "That sounds a lot fancier than it is. Nick just opened the Landing Strip. A new club needs new blood, so I moved here."

Maggie breathed in sharply. "Dominick Sorrento?" Rose nodded. "He has a new club in Hollow Pine that just opened?" Another head bob.

The back of Maggie's skull began pounding again, a harbinger of bad things to come, like a bum knee predicting rain. How could she and Constantine have missed Sorrento's new club?

Rose shifted in her bed, trying to turn on her side. Her progress was impeded by the tubes that ensnared her. "He had a soft opening a few weeks ago. Or as Nick likes to call it, a flaccid opening." Her smile didn't touch her eyes.

Maggie thought of the stairwell, her worry that someone had hunted Rose even as they cornered Maggie. "Does anyone from the Landing Strip know you're here?"

"You're the only one. Ironic, since you don't even know who I am."

"How did you get my number? *Why* did you get my number?"

Rose turned her head and looked out the window. Night had turned it into a mirror, reflecting funhouse versions of them both. "I got it from Starr. She told me to contact you if something happened."

Another checkmark for Maggie's theories. "If you got hurt?"

She turned back toward Maggie. "If she disappeared."

Maggie felt her stomach dip as if she had just topped the first hill of a rollercoaster, the clack-clack-clack of the upward climb replaced by a moment of weightlessness, a sense of floating free, loosed from gravity and reality. "Starr disappeared?" she repeated.

"She transferred to the Landing Strip when I did. Then she stopped coming into work. I went by her place to see if she was there. No car out front. No answer when I knocked. No answer when I called."

The dual possibilities arose again: Starr was unable to get to her phone. Or Starr was *unable to get to her phone.*

"Maybe she went out of town unexpectedly."

Rose gave her a withering look. "That's what the cops said." She looked Maggie over. "You're not a cop, are you?"

"No, I'm a..." She looked at her hands. "I'm between jobs."

"Well, I wouldn't recommend the Landing Strip. There's something wrong with that place."

Maggie's stomach did its rollercoaster trick again. Up. Down. Flip. Flop. "What kind of wrong?"

Rose turned toward the window once again. Maggie waited a few moments. Then a few more. She wondered if Rose had fallen asleep, exhausted by her visit and the conversation. "Rose?"

Rose flinched and turned back to face her. "Starr didn't go out of town unexpectedly. She was supposed to meet me at Suds and Suds to do laundry. She said she had something to talk to me about. I waited, called, waited some more. She never showed up. I knew something had happened."

"I still don't understand why she gave you my number."

"She said you were smart. Nice to her when the other women at the store weren't." She looked at her hands, watched them open and close as if it were the best magic trick she'd ever seen. "She said if something happened, you'd know what to do."

Maggie bit down on her lip. She wanted to scream that she didn't know what to do, that if Rose needed a hero, Maggie had forgotten her cape and tights. "But why me? Why not a family member or a friend?"

Rose gave her a hard look. "Because Starr doesn't have any family. Because I'm her only real friend. Because she trusted you. Was she wrong?"

Maggie shook her head. She hoped like hell she wasn't. "I can help you find Starr. You're getting out of here soon."

Rose gave a bitter laugh. "No thanks to Denning."

"He incentivized you to get a colonoscopy? Gave you a discount on a cosmetic procedure if you went through with it?"

Rose's perfectly arched brows performed forehead calisthenics, reaching high then squatting low. "How did you—?"

"Lucky guess."

Rose's brows settled into an intermediary position. "Guesses like that, you should go on a game show." She rearranged the hospital blanket. "Denning gave us options. I went for the colonoscopy because it's minor and I wanted to get my boobs done. Turned out it wasn't so minor after all."

"Is that what Starr wanted to talk about? Things going wrong during Denning's non-cosmetic procedures?"

Rose reached for the plastic glass on the tray beside her. She brought the bendy straw to her mouth and sipped. "I don't think so. I never heard about anyone getting hurt, so mine must have been a fluke. Besides, who doesn't love free stuff?"

Maybe the insurance company that's footing part of the bill? Maggie thought to herself.

A moment ticked by, their companionable silence accompanied by the sounds of the hospital. The purr of monitoring equipment. The *sotto voce* of sitcoms set to low volume. The distant clatter of heels as staff and visitors drifted down the hall to administer healing or Mylar balloons emblazoned with Get Well in a Comic Sans font.

Maggie was about to ask Rose about where the surgeries were performed, what other medical professionals were present, when she noticed Rose's closed lids, the steady rise and fall of her chest. Maggie once again put her hand on Rose's shoulder. "Rose?" she asked softly. She got a small snore in return.

Maggie pulled her hat over her head and pulled her coat around her. She was disappointed to cut short her time with Rose, but reminded herself that Rose was still recovering from a serious illness. She'd come back later and find out what else Rose knew. And what Starr might have known.

Chapter 32

Constantine was on the phone when she returned to Camille's house. He looked up when Maggie walked in, waved and continued to play *Donkey Kong* on Maggie's laptop as he muttered periodic "uh-huhs" and "okays" into his cell.

After a few moments, he signed off and rose to kiss Maggie. "Work," he said by way of explanation. "They love me day and night." He crossed his arms. "So? What did she say?"

"Her name's Rose and she confirmed the insurance scam," she said simply. "She also said that Starr gave her my number. The kicker: both Rose and Starr dance at Sorrento's new club, right here in Hollow Pine."

Constantine's hands dropped to his side. "Wait, what?"

Maggie nodded. "I don't know how we missed that little tidbit, but Sorrento just opened the Landing Strip, which I'm guessing is either aviation or bikini wax themed. He transferred some of the dancers from the Alaska Bush Company, including Rose and Starr, both of whom I saw at Denning's office."

Constantine paced the length of the room, making long strides that powered him past an Endust-glossed sideboard, a built-in book case groaning with paperbacks and old copies of *Reader's Digest* and a coat tree topped by hat-adorned branches. He stopped in front of the coat tree, fiddled with a fedora, then relinquished it. "Sorrento's prints are all over this. From his ties to Howard's old practice to his midnight visit to the Wrights' house." He looked at Maggie. "And the attack at the hospital."

Maggie remembered Sorrento's face after the spilled wine, the look of rage and hatred. She felt fear's finger trace the niche between neck and spine, familiar as a lover's caress. She rubbed the pads of her fingers vigorously through her hair to dislodge the sensation. She had to hang onto her anger, her outrage at what had happened to Rose, what was still happening at InHance. Anger and outrage were the only emotions she was willing to welcome.

"Starr gave Rose my phone number and told her to call me if something bad happened," Maggie said, dropping her purse from her shoulder onto the couch. "Something bad did happen. Two somethings, actually: Rose ended up in the hospital and Starr disappeared."

"And if someone disappears around Sorrento..." The unsaid hung heavily in the air.

Maggie retrieved her purse and probed for her phone. She rescued it from its vinyl folds and resuscitated it with a swipe of her finger. "I'm calling Austin."

"But he's off the case."

"Off the case, but not off the force. Rose said she talked to the police but didn't get anywhere. Maybe Austin can turn up the heat."

Her call went to voicemail. Maggie wondered if he was screening her calls. She left a message then dropped onto the couch, fighting against a sudden fatigue that made it difficult for her to plot her next moves: go to Starr's home, look into her life, talk to people she knew—and perhaps feared. Maggie blinked slowly, trying to focus her thoughts.

Constantine plopped down beside her and grabbed her hand. "I'm sure he'll call soon. Meanwhile..." He hinged his body to look at her straight on. "I've been wanting to talk to you."

Maggie was instantly alert. In her experience, "I want to talk to you" usually translated as, "Let's talk about something important and potentially awkward."

Maybe he wanted to break up. Maybe he wanted to propose. Maggie could feel her pulse beating in her neck. A mustache of perspiration dewed her lip. She wiped her mouth.

"Hey, are you hungry?" she said springing to her feet. "I'm sure Camille's got—"

"I have something to show you."

He gestured toward a wooden box on the coffee table. It was delicate, intricately carved. And decidedly ring sized.

A wave of anxiety pummeled Maggie. She wanted to close her eyes, to concentrate on keeping her emotions in check. To not, in short, lose her shit.

A proposal wasn't bad news. If she believed the rom-coms Aunt Fiona had forced her to watch all through middle and high school, she should be thrilled at the prospect of Constantine popping the question. Her eyes should grow misty with emotion. She should offer a dazzling smile and a tearful "Yes!" before the cut to the commercial break.

Instead she just felt like running away.

Constantine grabbed the box and cradled it gently in his long, elegant fingers.

"Um, Gus," Maggie stammered.

He held his hand up. "I know what you're going to say. But I couldn't help myself."

Maggie's mouth had gone dry. She licked her wind-cracked lips. She had to say something, to stop him from proposing, to stop her from breaking his heart. Words dissolved on her tongue like the breath in her lungs.

Constantine opened the box and thrust it under her nose. "Look."

She did.

Nestled in the folds of black silk, a battered silver locket winked at her. She sank further into the couch.

Okay, so not a ring. A keepsake? A family heirloom? A flea market score? "What is it?"

"I found it in Aunt Polly's room. She woke up, got restless, so Camille took her for a drive. I went hunting for Kleenex, found some in Polly's room, but ended up dropping the box. When I bent to retrieve it, I spied this little number under the bed." He liberated the locket and dangled it before her. "They got home while I was on my conference call and went straight up to bed. Guess Polly was more tired than she thought."

Maggie took the necklace, trying to process that Constantine wasn't proposing. Trying to decide if she was relieved or disappointed. She could feel him watching her. She opened the heart-shaped locket. It was empty. She turned it over and found a pair of initials. "F+W? What does that mean?"

"Beats me, but I couldn't help but notice that the initials match both of Howard's last names."

Her thumb traced the engraving, feeling the tiny valleys of each letterform. "Foley and Wright. Curiouser and curiouser."

"Maybe it was from Howard's former life, a gift to a girlfriend."

"Or to his sister, although the initials don't match." She turned the piece over in her hand. "I wonder it if it was supposed to be part of the church rummage sale."

"It could have fallen out of the box while Polly was cramming it with her surprisingly extensive collection of scarves."

Maggie thought of the memory card with the photo of Jenna. Two artifacts from Howard's secret life. Both previously in Polly's possession.

Maggie decided to talk to Polly. Of course, talking would have to wait till morning. Newly invigorated by the find, Maggie and Constantine cruised the internet in an information-seeking drive-by.

Maggie finally unearthed information about Sorrento's new club, but didn't learn anything she didn't already know: Gentlemen's blah blah catering to discerning blah blah. She turned up nothing new about Foley or Denning, so decided to turn her attention to the other physician in her sights.

She hopped onto Kenny Rogers' Facebook page. The doctor had shared an article about a trend toward cosmetic injectables among younger women. He'd also uploaded a dozen additional vacation pictures. Sharing his experience or strengthening his alibi?

She switched to Deirdre's Facebook page. The former beauty queen's latest post featured a selfie taken in her bathroom. She held a white silk robe around her narrow frame, sleeves drooping seductively to expose a Victoria's Secret-worthy décolleté and shoulders so shiny she looked like the understudy for the Tin Man. Her lips were parted in a come-hither smile, her forefinger pressed against them in an I-know-a-secret shush. Beneath was an exclamation-infected post:

The secret is out! I'm thrilled to announce that I'm going to be the face of AccentYOUate!

Thanks to the amazing Dr. Kenneth Rogers for doing the right thing!! #blessed #beautifullife #DeirdreHartConsulting

Constantine made the face he used for people who confused *Star Trek* and *Star Wars*. "The face of AccentYOUate? I thought she hated the face they gave her."

She thought back to Deirdre's expression when she emerged from the exam room—triumphant, arrogant—then Rogers'—fearful, resigned. "Maybe she blackmailed him into fixing and then promoting her."

"Blackmail? Over what?"

"An affair with Polly? His murder of Howard?"

Constantine made poo-poo gestures with his hands. "Polly may be a serial monogamist, but the emphasis is on monogamist. She's not the cheating type. And I still don't see Rogers as a killer. As for Deirdre Hart, my money is on money. Maybe Rogers was tired of Deirdre raking his practice over the social media coals and offered to fix her face. Maybe Deirdre saw an opportunity for self-promotion and wanted to sweeten the pot with a modeling gig. Despite the whole rebirth-as-a-consultant shtick, it's clear she still wants to be in front of the camera. She gets her face fixed and ego stroked. Rogers silences his biggest critic and gets out of a potential lawsuit. Win. And win."

Maggie made noises of agreement, but she still wasn't convinced. The theory made sense, but nothing could shake her feeling that Deirdre and Rogers couldn't be trusted.

She went up to bed tired to the bone, the keyed-up energy she'd felt earlier bleeding off until her insides felt hollowed out. She awoke six hours later to the sound of her phone.

She groaned and grabbed the device. A photo of Austin's earnest face filled the screen. She ran fingertips over the crust that had formed at the corner of her lips, slapped her tangled mass of hair from her face, then pushed to answer. "Hey Austin, thanks for calling back."

"No more attacks, I hope?" His voice was high and thin, as though it were being stretched between two points.

"No, thank God. But there have been some interesting developments." Maggie outlined her conversation with Rose, emphasizing Starr's disappearance. Austin gave a long, low whistle that sounded like it was about to morph into something from *The Andy Griffith Show*. "I'll see what I can learn about the missing girl, if she's missing at all. My guess is that she took some time away and forgot to tell folks."

"After she tells her now-hospitalized friend to get help if 'something happens'?"

"Exactly," Austin said, missing the heavy coat of sarcasm. Maggie made a mental note to follow up on her earlier investigative urges to look into Starr's life. "As for the rest of it, I'm not exactly sure where to take it. Jeff and I are both off the case."

"Jeff's off the case?" Maggie didn't bother to hide the surprise—or the derision—in her voice. "What happened?"

"Smarted off one too many times, peeved the captain. Now he's in the same boat I am. Guess what goes around really does come around." Maggie hoped that were true, but had seen karma hold back one too many times. "Anyway, I'll figure something out and get back to you."

They disconnected. Maggie threw back the covers, slid from the bed and walked to the window. Camille's tidy yard wore a shroud of snow.

The clouds, hung over from the previous night's escapades, performed a walk of shame across a sky turned gray by the sun's perfunctory glow.

She considered her options for the day. She wanted to find out more about Starr, but the prospect was overwhelming. Her head had begun pounding again. She once again considered going to the doctor to see if she had a concussion and once again dismissed it. The irony of an unrepentant hypochondriac refusing to seek medical attention wasn't lost on her. Part of her knew that the possibility of a concussion was another uncomfortable possibility she pushed behind the Wall. Part of her worried that she wasn't thinking clearly.

Maggie massaged her temples. She'd tackle a fact-finding mission about Starr later. For now, a visit to Petrosian sounded logical—doable. She could bring him up to speed on Polly's condition and pump him for more information about Rogers.

Maggie showered and threw on a pair of gray pants and a white merino wool sweater her father had brought back from a recent visit to Ireland. She was more of a jeans girl, but somehow felt the need to impress the pharmacist. She chafed against this unbidden need to earn his approval, but found herself looking in the mirror to assess her appearance.

She'd never been one for self-reflection, literal or figurative, and the last time she'd really scrutinized her visage was when she broke out in hives after eating too many strawberries. Now her freckles and dark circles stood in stark relief on her pale face, the stress of the previous weeks tagging her face with unwelcome graffiti: new pimples along her forehead and jawline.

Maybe it was time to give makeup a try.

She unzipped her cosmetic bag and studied the paltry array of tubes and vials, all forced purchases by Aunt Fiona, former coworker Zartar and a very insistent Mary Kay consultant. She pulled out a squeeze tube of foundation and squirted a teaspoon on the back of her hand. It looked like mustard against the milk-white of her skin. She must have bought it as a summer shade, when she forgot her skin tone ranged from Fair to Consumption.

She remembered Polly's assortment of cosmetics and made her way to the older woman's room. She knocked softly on the door. No answer. She walked down the hall, ready to intercept her in the kitchen or living room. The house was deserted.

Her eyes landed on a note affixed to the front of the coffeemaker like a nametag.

Mags,

You looked beat, so I figured you'd want to sleep in. Sam had a few papers for Aunt Polly to sign. We'll be at his office then at the diner for lunch if you want to join us at 11:30.

Love—and I'm not just saying that—

Gus

Maggie peeled off the note, tossed it into recycling and grabbed a cup of coffee. She began to head upstairs, then paused outside of Polly's door.

She knew Polly wouldn't mind if she borrowed some eye cream or concealer. Polly seemed the type to embrace anything that promised to reduce fine lines or crepiness. Whatever that was.

Maggie eased open the bedroom door and switched on the light. A half-dozen bottles stood at attention on the dresser. Maggie evaluated the assembly of potions. She reached for a bottle that promised dewiness—which sounded more like lawn care than a skin treatment—and knocked over a tube of foundation primer, a product that had always mystified Maggie. What was she, a ceiling?

She stooped to retrieve the tiny plastic cylinder and noticed a prescription bottle in the garbage. She frowned and rescued it from the bin. It was small, clearly a sample. She turned over the blue and white bottle. Bold type announced it as Nardil.

Maggie's mind whirred, her internal processor trying to find the drug in her databank.

"Nardil. Nardil." She whispered, an incantation to summon memory.

Her neurons fired, her synapses connected. The answer appeared.

Nardil was a monoamine oxidase inhibitor (MAO) used to treat depression. Maggie didn't remember Polly being diagnosed with, let alone treated for, depression. What she did remember was that the drug could have dangerous side effects for people taking Sinemet.

Chapter 33

Why did Polly have a sample of Nardil? Who had given it to her?

Maggie turned the bottle over again, searching for the prescriber name she knew wouldn't be there. It was a sample, after all, bestowed onto physicians by drug reps peddling their wares. Not that she begrudged her pharmaceutical brethren. It was all part of the business, an operation conducted at the intersection of Cash and Cure.

The obvious answer was Kenny Rogers. He'd already played fast and loose with Polly's health by agreeing to treat her despite the fact that he was better suited for conditions that were skin deep. If he was doing something nefarious with her medications, a sample would be the perfect vehicle. Seemingly innocent. Practically untraceable.

Maggie opened the bottle. Empty. She wondered how many bottles Polly had gone through, the possible side effects she'd suffered. She surveyed the landscape of cosmetics before her, the towers of foundation, the lagoon of serums, then pocketed the medicine bottle. It was time to get ugly.

Maggie stared up at Pine View's tinted glass. The building looked as if it were wearing sunglasses, an aging Hollywood starlet looking for post-surgical anonymity.

Maggie parked in the loading zone out front, tempering her scofflaw attitude with the assumption that her risk of getting a parking ticket was low. The lot was empty, as usual.

She huffed through the building's sleek glass doors and into Rogers' waiting room. Barbara smiled, her lips parting at Maggie's entrance like an automatic door, then scowled. "I'm sorry," she said with a tone that suggested otherwise, "but the doctor is unavailable."

Maggie could feel her neck growing warm, indignation bubbling to the surface. "He'll want to see me. It's about Polly."

Barbara rolled her eyes, but put the phone to her ear. She stabbed the keypad on the base with a silver lacquered nail. "I know you're terribly busy, Doctor," she threw a meaningful look at Maggie, "but that woman is here. Yes, her. She says it's about Polly and that you'll want to talk to her." Barbara listened, pursed her lips, and tapped her silver talons. "Very well." She replaced the handset with more force than necessary. "You can go on back to his office."

Maggie flung open the door that separated Befores and Afters. She wandered down the hall and found Rogers' office open, the doctor sitting in his chair.

Rogers did that half-stand thing men of his generation did when a woman entered the room. He wordlessly gestured Maggie to close the door and take a chair. He steepled long, brown fingers then rested his chin at the apex. He looked as if he was going to give a diagnosis: you have a raging case of can't-mind-your-own-business-itis. Take two steps out the door and never call me again.

Rogers smiled, veneered teeth lining up like an enamel army. "Barbara said you had something to tell me about Polly?"

Maggie produced the bottle of Nardil from her pocket and slammed it on the blotter that covered Rogers' desk. Paperclips jumped. So did Rogers. "What's this?" he asked.

"This," Maggie said, pushing the bottle toward him, "is a medication that's contraindicated in Parkinson's and with the use of Sinemet that I found among Polly's things. It's associated with a host of symptoms, including sky-high blood pressure, agitation and, in women over the age of sixty, hallucinations."

Rogers picked up the bottle and looked over the top of his glasses. "Nardil. Used to treat depression, if I remember correctly." He placed the bottle back on the blotter. "What about it?"

"You're saying that you didn't give this to Polly?"

"The only prescription I write for her is the regimen she began with her neurologist. As for samples..." He held the bottle aloft. "The drug reps who come here peddle wares for that most serious of conditions." He parted his lips in an imitation of a smile. "Aging skin."

"You're her primary care provider, but she got it somewhere else?" Maggie didn't bother holding the sarcasm. "That's a little hard to buy."

"Ms. O'Malley, I have no idea where this came from. Why don't you ask Polly?"

"I will. I just thought I'd start with her doctor." The air quotes around "doctor" resonated between them.

"You've made it clear that you think it's inappropriate for me to treat Polly, but that's her business, just as her treatment plan is. Even if I had given this to Polly, I couldn't discuss it with you."

"But you already said you didn't give it to her."

Rogers grayed. "Even though I shouldn't have told you that, it's the truth. I have no idea where it came from, and I would never give Polly a potentially harmful medication. I'm quite fond of her."

"Maybe a little too fond?"

Rogers' eyes narrowed behind his lenses. "What's that supposed to mean?"

Maggie scrutinized her nail beds. "Sometimes emotions color judgment." She watched him beneath the fringe of her lashes. "Sometimes emotions can lead to mistakes or actions we regret."

He rebuilt the finger steeple. "I don't know what you're suggesting," he said, his voice air-conditioning cool, "but I can assure you that my emotions have not in any way affected my treatment of Polly because there are no emotions other than friendship and concern for a patient."

"Just as your friendship and concern for Deirdre Hart have made her the new face of AccentYOUate? She just announced it on Facebook."

Rogers swiveled in his chair and straightened an already-straight diploma. "We're looking to rebrand."

"Rebrand?"

"We've had a—" he waved his hands as if trying to conjure an answer. "We've had a downturn."

Maggie picked up a figurine of Snoopy dressed as a doctor and turned it over in her hand. It was signed with Polly's distinctive hand. She replaced it. "Murder is bad for business?"

Rogers repositioned himself, crossing one leg and then the other. "In a manner of speaking, yes. But so is an unhappy—and vocal— customer. It's something Howard and I disagreed on—quite vehemently, I might add. I thought it best to appease Ms. Hart. He thought she'd tire of her crusade and go away."

"Instead Howard went away. Permanently."

Rogers brushed an imaginary speck of lint from his trousers. "Indeed."

"So you made a deal with Deirdre. You'd correct Howard's work and allow her to act as your spokeswoman. In exchange, she'd stop her public tirade."

"She was going to put up a billboard about her unhappiness with Howard's work." He shrank in his chair. "And a bus bench."

"Couldn't you sue her for libel?"

"It seemed easier to placate her. Who knows, maybe it'll even help drum up some business. She has quite the following, despite her problem."

Maggie quickly cataloged the possibilities of hidden sins. Meth. Heroin. Mom jeans. "Problem?"

"Her personality."

"Ah." No amount of medical intervention could fix that.

He rose. "I'm sorry I can't be of more help. I do wish you the best of luck getting to the bottom of this Nardil issue. Polly is a dear friend, as well as a favorite patient. I wish her nothing but health and happiness, especially after all she's been through. Please give her my best."

Maggie stood and turned to go, formulating the rest of the complaint she'd file with the medical boards that afternoon, rehearsing the conversation she'd have with Austin, ignoring the possibility that neither would do any good.

"Oh, Ms. O'Malley," Rogers said. Maggie pivoted back around and held her breath, waiting. "If you want to take care of those premature age spots, Barbara can get you an appointment."

Chapter 34

"Age spots, my arse," Maggie muttered as she stalked to the car. She slid behind the wheel and looked in the rearview mirror. Number one, they were freckles. Number two, even if they weren't, she'd earned those damned spots. She'd sooner connect them with Polly's brow pencil than eradicate them.

She sped to Camille's, missing the familiarity of the Studebaker, and parked at the curb. She ambled up the stone steps, logging the fresh tire tracks in the snowy driveway, and wondered if Polly and Constantine had already come and gone. She put her borrowed key into the door. It swung wide.

A spike of adrenaline jabbed her scalp. It snaked along her shoulders, turning the tiny hairs on her arm into miniature weathervanes. "Hello?" she called out, stepping into the foyer. "Camille? Constantine? Polly?"

Silence echoed back.

Maggie crept along the Pottery Barn rug, moving to the interior of the house like every woman in every horror movie. All she needed was a transparent nightgown and a flickering candle.

An odor drifted to her, acrid, familiar. She put her hand to her nose. Was this memory, a trick of the mind given breath by the power of dejà vu, or did she smell blood?

She trailed a hand through her purse and found her phone. She scrolled through her contacts with her right thumb, pressing hard on the case to keep the device from slipping from her hands, to hold onto something she knew was real. Constantine's number rang.

She continued her trek through the house. The smell, which grew stronger with every step forward, was now joined by music. Maggie paused, cocked her head, straining to identify the melody. It was upbeat, childlike and infinitely familiar. The phone continued to ring in her ear. *Come on, Constantine. Pick up your damn phone.*

Maggie paused at the kitchen door, her heart beating triple-time, turning her ribs into a xylophone. Memories of last year—a cratered skull, a bathroom standoff, the unseeing eyes of the dead—joined the horror of awakening alone and afraid and wounded on the stairwell. The memories became battering rams pounding against the Wall, threatening to knock it down and destroy it forever.

Maggie took a lungful of air and pushed open the door. On the dining room table, positioned between the salt and pepper shakers, was a small greeting card-sized speaker that played the chorus of "Santa Claus is Coming to Town." Beneath the speaker was a rock, the twin of the one that had impregnated her windscreen, with words scrawled across its face:

You'd better watch out.

In her ear, she heard Constantine pick up.

"I think you'd better skip the pie," she said.

Constantine and Polly arrived minutes later, concern radiating off them like heat. They gathered in the kitchen and eyed the rock and the speaker as if they were invasive species.

"I guess whoever did this doesn't celebrate Festivus," Constantine said.

"I don't know," Maggie said, feigning calm. "Looks like they've started the Airing of Grievances."

Polly slipped an arm around Maggie's waist. "Constantine told me what happened with the Studebaker." Nothing about the attack in the stairwell. "Have you already spoken to the police?"

Like that would be any help, she thought. "That's next on my list."

Polly shook her head. "I don't understand who would do this or why. Or how they got in. You locked up before you left, right dear?"

"Of course" was already on her lips, but Maggie stopped. She couldn't remember. Not quite. The actions surrounding her hasty departure were obscured behind a red fog of fury as she thought about the medication that had put Polly's health at risk. Or maybe it was the fog that seemed to be at the periphery of her consciousness since the attack. "I think so," she said slowly. "Although I was preoccupied by what I found in your room when I was looking for some cosmetics."

Polly's eyes grew wide. "In my room?"

Maggie fumbled in her purse. For the second time that day, she pulled out the sample bottle of Nardil. She held it flat on her hand as if it was an apple and Polly was a horse. Polly's brows drew together and then up as she read the package. "Ah, yes. My vitamins."

Vitamins?

"Who gave it to you?"

The eyebrows knit once again. "Well, now let me think." She returned her hand to her HurryCane and was silent a few moments before turning her palms skyward. "I'm sorry, dear. I can't remember. Is it important?"

"They're not vitamins. This is a medication that should be avoided if you have Parkinson's and take Sinemet. It can have serious side effects."

Polly gave a little gasp. "Could this be why I haven't..." She searched for the right words. "Why I haven't felt like myself lately?"

"Very possibly, which is why I'm so interested in finding out who gave this to you."

"Oh dear."

The understatement of the year.

"You can't remember anything about where you got it? It's a sample so you probably would've gotten it at the doctor's office rather than Petrosian's."

Polly tightened her grip on her cane. "I'm certain it wasn't Kenny. He hasn't given me anything new, and I trust him implicitly."

Maggie let that one go. "Are you taking anything else? Something Lev Petrosian might not be aware of?"

"Um..." She looked at Constantine for an answer. When he didn't supply one, she said, "I don't think so?"

Maggie's heart fell to her knees. Polly had a chronic illness, recently awoke from a coma, and was likely suffering side effects from a contraindicated medication. It was no surprise the unsinkable Polly Wright was a bit forgetful.

"I'd like to talk with the doctor who treated you when you were—" She wanted to say "incarcerated," but her lips wouldn't form the words. "In the hospital. I imagine they ran a tox screen. It'd be nice to know what they were looking for and what they found." She grabbed Polly's hand and squeezed it gently. "You'd have to call and give permission, or have Sam Graham do so as your authorized agent. Is that all right with you?"

"Anything you suggest is fine. I'll call Sam while you call the police."

Polly shuffled toward Camille's avocado wall phone. She seemed steadier on her feet, more solid. That was a good. Bad medicine or not, she seemed to be holding her own.

While Polly dialed, Maggie dunked her hand back into her purse and retrieved her phone. Two button presses later and Austin's voice was on the line.

Maggie summarized, including her concerns about Rogers.

"Don't know what to say about the doc, but I'll see what I can do. Meanwhile, I'll tell Ted to get over there right away, get your statement, file another report." As if a report was enough to stop whoever wanted to harm her. As if she needed someone to protect her. She thanked Austin once again and ended the call. Constantine looked at her expectantly. Maggie hit the highlights.

"Another report? What do they plan to do, fend off the bad guys with paper cuts?" He ran his hand through his hair and over his face. "I guess it does start a paper trail."

"As long as that trail doesn't lead to my body."

Constantine paled beneath his stubble. Polly replaced the handset and cut into the void of their conversation.

"Sam has all the paperwork from the hospital, including lab reports." She settled into her chair by the window, sunlight turning the little bit of red left in her hair fiery. "He said it looked like a standard tox screen. Alcohol, amphetamines, opiates, PCP." She made a face. "Whatever those are. At any rate, it didn't sound like they tested for prescription or over-the-counter medications. He emailed the reports to you," she looked at Constantine, "so we can see for ourselves."

Maggie ran upstairs and retrieved her computer. They logged into Constantine's email and gathered around Maggie's laptop as if it were a crystal ball. Constantine pointed, clicked and opened four different reports. Just as Sam Graham had said, the screens sought the usual suspects of impairment.

Maggie leaned back and tapped her finger against her mouth. "Would you be willing to give another sample for a new tox screen?" she asked Polly.

"Absolutely."

"I'd like to go through a private lab rather than having Dr. Rogers call it in." She said it smoothly, as if the request to circumvent Polly's physician was perfectly normal. "I have a friend who works at a cutting-edge laboratory. They can screen for pretty much whatever we want."

Polly nodded and got to her feet. "Whatever you say, dear."

"One quick question." Maggie put her hand into her purse once more. "I wondered what you could tell us about this."

Maggie fished the antique jewelry box from her purse and placed it in Polly's hands. Polly rotated it between shaking fingers. "What is it?"

Maggie tried not to look at Constantine. "Take a look."

Polly tried to open the box. Her thumb and forefingers couldn't prize the lid. Maggie did the honors and handed the box's contents to Polly. The older woman smiled at the silver locket dangling from her fingers. "How very charming. Is it for me?"

"We thought it belonged to you. It's a beautiful piece. I thought you could tell us its origin, its meaning." She paused. "What the engraved initials mean."

She pointed to the letters. Polly squinted.

"Never seen it before. As for F & W..." She lifted a shoulder. "I've no idea. If you find something out, let me know. I'd love to have some answers."

Ditto, thought Maggie. "We found it among your things. Maybe it belonged to Howard?"

Polly frowned, the skin between her brows bunching together. "Why would Howard have a woman's locket?" She looked at Maggie. "Do you think this was a gift to another woman? Do you think Howard was stepping out on me?" Polly's face was pale and drawn.

"I don't think that's it," Maggie said quickly. "Maybe it's a relative's. A...sister's." Maggie exchanged a glance with Constantine and fumbled for her phone, for the photographic evidence of Jenna's filial existence. Before she could begin scrolling through the gallery, Polly rose. She was shakier than Maggie had seen recently and swayed on her feet before regaining her balance.

"I'm sorry, dears, but I don't feel very well." She drew her mouth into a flat line. "I think I'll go on to bed."

Maggie opened her mouth, the truth about Jenna, about Howard, about how his past haunted Polly's present on her lips. Constantine caught her eye and shook his head.

His face said it all. Polly had been through enough. Wait until she was better, stronger, to reveal a duplicity more strange and terrible than an affair.

Maggie clamped her mouth shut and watched as Polly shambled down the hall.

Chapter 35

Ted Del Vecchio's arrival coincided with Camille's. Their hostess tried to mask her shock and anxiety over the break-in by pasting on a vacant smile and offering hot beverages. In the background, the Christmas carol continued to play from the miniature speaker. A creepy soundtrack to the latest turmoil.

"I don't understand this," Camille said pacing between coffee maker and tea kettle, wringing her hands. "I just don't understand. Who would like a hot cider or a cup of decaf?"

Del Vecchio was unperturbed, the only sign of surprise a slight rise of his right brow as he examined the terrible tableau on the kitchen table. "You found it like this? Right here on the table, and left that horrible music playing?"

"Wanted to preserve the evidence," Maggie said. "Same reason I took a picture of the rock in the windshield at the hospital."

"Good thinking." He produced a folder from an attaché bag and clicked to arm his ballpoint pen. "Now, tell me about the events in question." Maggie could scarcely keep a straight face.

Maybe he'd like a chronological list.

Del Vecchio listened, took notes, snapped pictures, then gloved up to bag the stone and miniature speaker. "I'll have the lab process these with the other one. Cross your fingers for prints or trace evidence." Maggie was way ahead of him.

After he finished processing the scene, the quartet walked Del Vecchio to the door in a sad parody of a parade. The moment he stepped from threshold to sidewalk, Camille slammed the door, threw the bolt and affixed the chain. "I'll call a locksmith in the morning," she said, her voice defeated and colorless. "Maybe one of those security companies, too." She shook her head. "I just don't understand how this could have happened." She drifted up the stairs, her body curled into a question mark.

Maggie could relate. She had far more questions than answers. Yesterday's exhaustion returned, making her brain feel fuzzy and her body in need of vitamin everything. She collapsed onto the couch and closed her eyes.

Constantine lay next to her. "You all right?"

She kept her eyes closed. "Yes."

He touched her cheek. "It's going to be okay, you know."

Maggie opened her eyes and locked onto Constantine's face. "How? How exactly is 'okay' going to happen? Are we going to put a guard on my Studebaker? On Camille's house? On me?" She wriggled from Constantine's arms and found her feet. She walked to the mantle, fumbled with wrapped hard candies that gleamed like jewels in their cut-glass dish, tried to unwrap one, failed and threw it back. "Are we ever going to tell Polly the truth about Howard?"

"Yes, we'll tell Polly," Constantine said quietly. "When she's ready to hear it."

"No one can be ready to hear that kind of news, Gus. You're just delaying the inevitable."

He looked at his hands. "I know. I just can't stand the idea of hurting her after all that's happened. Just give it time. Please, Mags. We'll get there. I just want to fill in some of the blanks first."

"Like who killed Howard?"

"And who's behind all of this. There are a lot of possibilities and even more questions, but I do know Sorrento has a long reach."

"I'm not convinced it is Sorrento. How would he know I have anything to do with the fact he might spend the next few decades asking if stripes make him look thin? And if he did, wouldn't a guy like that do more than send caveman nastygrams? Seems like he'd want to do serious damage."

"You don't think clocking you on the head counts as serious damage?"

Maggie grabbed another hard candy, successfully freed it from its wrapper and popped it into her mouth. It tasted like lime and loneliness. She spit it into the wrapper. "As bad as that was, it doesn't exactly scream 'professional crime syndicate.' If he wanted me dead, I'd be dead."

"So if not Sorrento, who?"

"What about Kenny Rogers?"

"Still? Just because he's treating Polly?"

"Not just that. There's his obvious crush on Polly, his hidden jealousy of Howard and their disagreement about how to deal with Deirdre Hart. Not to mention the fact that he could very well be dosing her with Nardil or other contraindicated drugs under the radar."

"Okay, so he has access and opportunity. I still think you're light on motive."

"You ever heard of Munchausen syndrome by proxy?"

Constantine got to his feet and took a giant step toward Maggie. "Isn't that where moms make their kids sick to get attention?"

"Yes, although it's not always moms and it's not always kids. It's anyone who has power over another person and the ability to make him or her sick. Children are the easiest targets because of proximity and powerlessness, but there have been cases of adult children making their elderly parents sick. Even staff in nursing homes and home health workers. It's not a long walk to a doctor-patient relationship, especially if that patient is already compromised. Double-especially if that doctor has motivation to control that patient."

Constantine gave her an oh-come-on look. "And Rogers' reason is that he's secretly in love with Polly and wants to keep her close?"

"You could argue that it fits Polly's pattern of failing health. The worsening symptoms, the sleepwalking, the hallucinations. Have you noticed that she seems better than before she was in jail?"

Constantine thought for a moment. "Maybe."

"It could be because she didn't have access to the sample of Nardil. Or, to put a finer point on it, because Rogers didn't have access to her and whatever else he's dosing her with."

"I don't know, Mags. Unrequited love gone bad. Medication mismanagement. It all sounds a little farfetched."

Maggie smiled. "That's the brilliance of the scientific method. You don't have to know. You have to research and discover."

"Research" was at a phlebotomy lab located next to a Taco Bell the following afternoon.

"My friend recommended it," Maggie told Polly as the scent of chalupas wafted through the air. "The lab is just getting off the ground, so the digs are a little..." She watched as a school bus full of hockey players streamed into the Taco Bell. "Unconventional."

She was secretly glad that Constantine was called into work to address yet another IT emergency. She could only imagine the comments. And the side of nachos that he would have insisted on bringing in.

The phlebotomist, a young woman named Kara with long brown hair and smiling eyes, led them past a tower of cardboard boxes to a chair with a built-in arm support. Kara bustled between the chair and a green Formica counter crowded with empty vials, bandages, disposable gloves and a pink sharps container that looked more suited to storing nail polish than bio-hazardous waste.

"The good news," Kara said, nodding at the packing tape nestled against a broom in the corner of the room, "is we're moving. The contract with your friend's lab made it possible. Plus my boyfriend's in real estate." She gave Maggie the ring finger. "I mean fiancé. We just got engaged."

"Congratulations." Maggie and Polly made a show of admiring the ring, a lovely vintage affair with a pea-sized stone that Maggie recognized as an Old European Cut. Her mother had had the same type of diamond in her own engagement ring. Maggie wondered whether Pop had given it to Constantine.

She shook her head to clear her mind. *Right. Focus.*

Kara expertly pierced Polly's skin, drew her sample then wrapped Polly's arm with a self-adherent beige bandage. "Our new location is right next to a Starbucks." She smiled. "Not sure that's an improvement, but at least it'll tame my bean burrito addiction." She labeled the vial and placed it in a stand. "I'll overnight the sample and that, as they say, will be that."

Maggie nodded. "I appreciate it. And I appreciate you fitting us in. Felicity says you're the best in the biz."

Kara waved away the praise. "It's easy with veins like Polly's." She looked admiringly at Polly's arm as if she were sporting the latest "it" accessory. "Seriously, you've got the best veins I've seen all month." Polly glowed at the compliment.

Back in the car, Polly settled her coat around her thin frame and turned to Maggie. "Now what?"

Maggie thought of the sample's journey to her friend Felicity's lab, the paces she'd put it through to see what was lurking in Polly's blood stream, what could slowly be poisoning her.

"Now," Maggie said cranking the car, "we wait."

They arrived at Camille's to find a plate of muffins and a note from their hostess that she'd be back from work in the late afternoon. Maggie took three muffins, put one back to be polite (although knowing full well she'd come back for it later) and offered the plate to Polly. The older woman shook her head. "No gluten, remember? I used to avoid dairy, but discovered the evils of gluten while I was detained." She gave a wicked smile. "Maybe I'll write a book: *The Jailhouse Diet*. As much as I hate to admit it, I do feel better. I guess Howard was onto something with his gluten-free diet."

Maggie had to agree. Polly seemed better, stronger. Her bet: lack of Nardil—and whatever else Kenny Rogers had been giving her—coursing through her veins.

She considered that Rogers wasn't the only person handling Polly's meds. There was Petrosian. The pharmacist filled her pill bottles with essentially no oversight. As the only one behind the counter, he could create any number of dangerous prescriptive cocktails for Polly and no one would know. But it begged the question: why would he do that? Unlike Rogers, Petrosian had no motive to play fast and loose with Polly's meds. He seemed fond of Polly, but not overly so. He didn't seem to hate Howard more than anyone else. He wasn't involved in a strip club or an insurance scam—that she knew of, anyway.

Maggie was no stranger to far-fetched ideas. The weeks since Howard's death had proved that anything was possible. And yet Maggie just couldn't see Levon Petrosian, pharmacist and egg-sharer as anything other than small town druggist and longtime friend.

Maggie watched as Polly took a cup of tea to her spot by the fireplace, a book in her hand. Maggie was once again tempted to bring up the locket, to find out what Polly knew or even suspected. She saw her friend bent over her novel and couldn't disturb her peace. Constantine was right: heartache could wait another day. Maybe longer.

Maggie mounted the stairs with a plate of muffins in one hand, a mug of coffee in the other. She needed a few hours to recharge the internal introvert stores that had been depleted in the weeks since Howard's murder.

She cracked Constantine's door and saw Miss Vanilla happily making the rounds on her hamster wheel. If the animal missed her master, she was either sublimating or had a good way of hiding it. Maggie could relate to either.

Maggie sealed herself inside her room, carried the laptop from dresser to bed and settled against the headboard with her legs stretched out before her. She lifted the mug to her lips. The sharp rich smell nipped at her nostrils and she inhaled deeply. The aroma brought her back to countless college all-nighters and endless days at Rxcellance.

The feeling was at once nostalgic and painful. It was her personal crusade against cancer that had led her to pharmaceuticals. Her career path had fortified her against the distractions of boys, friends and fun, enabled her to delay the development of that little thing people called a life, allowed her to deny its necessity entirely. Now all she had to show for it was a calling she was forced to ignore and a job she was embarrassed to lose.

Maggie pushed the thoughts from her mind and took a mouthful of too-hot coffee, relishing the distraction of the coffee's burning path from tongue to belly. She opened her laptop, quickly read an email from Pop updating her on business (couldn't complain), Ada (still rocking it) and the world (falling apart) and clicked to check the weather. Instead she hit the local news app, which opened to its digital front page. Maggie's finger poised over the X to close it when her eye caught a headline from the If It Bleeds It Leads school of journalism.

"Woman's Body Found."

No photo, just text, but the line sent a fission of adrenaline up her spine.

Maggie placed the mug on the nightstand and tapped the keyboard's mouse. Below the click-bait headline, a woman gazed back, her eyes rebellious and wounded. Maggie gasped, the knife-sharp pain of grief shucking her insides.

Starr. Young, beautiful, missing Starr.

Chapter 36

Maggie studied the photograph. It was the modern equivalent of a Glamour Shot: Soft lighting, diffused filter, the subject bare-shouldered and wrapped in tulle like a present ready to be opened. Starr's eyes were half-lidded, her lips parted in a Marilyn-esque seduction. Above the airbrushed face, a halo of tri-colored hair glinted in the camera's glow. Starr, guardian angel of strippers.

Maggie wondered what she looked like when she was found. Was her beauty intact? Her body covered? Or had she been left naked and defaced, her dignity stolen with her life?

She read quickly.

Hollow Pine resident Laurel Walker, also known as Starr, was found early Tuesday morning in a trash receptacle behind Suds & Suds Laundromat by Les Holmberg, proprietor. Police responding to the scene said there is no risk to the public at large.

Although officers declined to elaborate, public records indicate that Walker had multiple arrests for drug possession and solicitation. Gary Drummond, director of the state's Coalition Against Violence, told The Daily Courier workplace homicide rate for prostitutes is 204 per 100,000, making it not only the oldest profession in the world, but also the most dangerous.

Maggie read the rest of the article, hoping the letters would rearrange themselves into something that made more sense. The facts remained: Starr had died. Starr had been a prostitute. Starr had been a spark of light and beauty as fleeting and enigmatic as her chosen name.

The article didn't say that two women had tried to report her missing. It didn't say that Starr had tried to protect her friend, Rose. It didn't even say how she had died. The piece simply stated that her profession had put her at risk.

Starr as cautionary tale.

Starr as lesson to be learned.

Starr sliced, diced and served up like a Grimm fairy tale to keep readers on the straight and narrow.

It made Maggie furious.

Yes, prostitution could be dangerous. So could stripping. But Maggie knew one of the greatest risks to Starr's life was her gender. Winning the genetic lottery of double-X chromosomes meant greater risk of becoming the victim of rape, domestic abuse, abduction. Take your pick.

She knew firsthand that following the rules and listening to your guidance counselor didn't necessarily guarantee safety. Being a good girl—whether that meant not laughing too loudly or dreaming too largely— didn't mean you'd live a good life. It didn't mean you wouldn't die at the hands of a lover or a stranger or a john.

Maggie closed the laptop and rubbed her eyes. She felt a headache knocking at the base of her neck. It wouldn't take much to let it crawl up her spine and into her brain where it would fester until it rendered her defenseless against light, sound and thought. She never used to have headaches like this. Then again, she didn't used to get hit on the head or live a life defined by danger and unpredictability.

She wondered what her doctor would say if she journaled her headaches. *Today: Four ounces of chocolate, two cups of coffee, one murder. I think the coffee is what pushed me over the edge, but what do you think, Doc?*

Maggie swung her legs off the bed and returned the laptop to the dresser.

So Starr was a prostitute. Not a complete surprise, she supposed. Conventional wisdom held that some of the women who danced at so-called gentlemen's clubs added the horizontal hustle to their repertoire. No, not women. Girls. Because it was always *girls! girls! girls!*, the suggestion of youth, of vulnerability, of the potential for exploitation, advertised on strip club reader boards and the backs of leaflets.

"Girls" danced. "Gentlemen" watched. And sometimes more than watched.

Maggie wondered what had led Starr from the club to the street. If Starr was involved with drugs as a user, a seller or a go-between, the allure of extra money could have been powerful. Yet despite the promise of money, or the protection of a sugar daddy, Maggie doubted the answer was quite so pat. She imagined the path to prostitution could be a circuitous one.

Maggie wondered whether the other dancers at Sorrento's clubs knew about Starr's moonlighting. Or, more importantly, knew about her death. Chances were the police knew where she worked and had gone to interview her coworkers.

Well, almost all of her coworkers. Rose was in the hospital.

Maggie closed the story and dialed St. Theresa's. She asked for Room 217. The ancient voice on the other end cheerfully requested that she hold the line for a moment then plunged Maggie into the Fifth Circle of Hell: more classic rock Muzak.

Just as AC/DC's "Dirty Deeds" got rolling with a female vibrato and an acoustic guitar, a new voice came on the line.

"You're calling for Madeline Hepburn in Room 217?" the new voice asked.

Rose had gone along with the pseudonym. She wondered how she'd gotten around the matter of identification. "Yes."

Long pause on the other end. "I'm sorry, but the patient has already checked out."

Chapter 37

"Checked out?" Maggie gripped the phone. "But how? When?"

"She checked out," Receptionist 2.0 repeated. She was younger than the first receptionist, but lacked her cheer. And inflection. Every word was uniform in length and tonality, premeasured into tasteless, bite-sized chunks like a meal from Jenny Craig. Noun. Verb. Adjective. Repeat.

"Could I please talk to her nurse?" Maggie asked.

"I don't—"

"Gwen. Older, with a bob? She's on the second floor. Please. It's important."

2.0 let out a long, low breath. "I guess," she said, sounding more like a sullen teenager than a hospital employee. "One moment."

This wait was longer. Several minutes later, Gwen's familiar twang came over the line. "She left this morning, Maggie. She was supposed to stay a good bit longer, have some more testing done. Checking herself out was completely AMA."

Against Medical Advice.

"Did she say why she was leaving?"

"Sure didn't. I come in the room to take her breakfast tray and she's putting on boots. Long ones that go over the knee." Gwen paused. "Never seen boots like that before."

The panic that had first announced itself when Maggie read of Starr's murder began to grow, as if feeding on every morsel of ominous information. "Did she leave with anyone? Did anyone come to see her?"

"She didn't leave with anyone, and I don't think she had any visitors."

"But you're not sure."

Gwen sighed. "I'm not going to swear on my mother's grave, no, but I'm almost positive. I didn't see anyone during my shifts, and none of the other nurses made a note of visitors."

Of course that didn't mean that someone couldn't have sneaked in, terrorized Rose, threatened to end her the way he ended Starr. She thought of the stairwell and the smell of dank despair. There were hundreds of places to hide and wait and strike.

"She did seem upset when she left," Gwen said.

"Did she say why?"

"Nope. Just that she had to get out of here."

"Did she go home?"

"I'm a nurse, not a mind-reader," Gwen said in an unintentional homage to *Trek*'s Dr. McCoy. "I don't even know where home is for her. I looked up the address she gave on the intake forms she filled out after she woke up. Of course, I didn't have any way to verify it because we never got her ID from her or you or any other family member, for that matter." She took a long pause. "The whole thing seems awfully strange."

Maggie cringed inwardly and changed the subject. "Which address did she give? Wondering if it's my aunt's or..."

"I looked it up. It was the police station's."

Constantine answered on the first ring. "If you're calling to propose, you're too late. I'm married to my job, although I'm thinking divorce."

"Gus, I've got bad news." She tried to hold her voice steady. She had no idea if it was working.

"IsPollyokay?" He asked so quickly the words nearly became one.

"She's fine." She paused. "Unfortunately, Starr isn't." Maggie took a deep breath. "She's been murdered."

"What? Hang on, let me get someplace quieter."

Maggie could hear Constantine move away from the purr of machinery, his footsteps echo against concrete. She heard a door scream on its hinges and shut with an authoritative clunk.

Constantine puffed into the phone. "I thought you said Starr was murdered."

"I did. She was."

"What? How?"

"The paper didn't state a cause of death, only that her body was found behind a Laundromat."

"My God." The phone was quiet for a moment, then: "You think it has something to do with what happened to Rose?"

"Rose, fraud, other victims of malpractice. Take your pick. The

Sorrento-Denning angle is looking better and better. The newspaper said Starr has a record of solicitation."

"And by 'solicitation' I assume you don't mean selling Girl Scout cookies."

"It shines a new light on Sorrento's clubs. Either Starr was freelancing, or Sorrento's in the prostitution business."

"Not exactly virgin territory for mobsters. It's practically part of the job description, along with drug running and money laundering. What does Rose say?"

"That's a bit of a wrinkle." Maggie took a breath. "She's gone."

"Like, left-the-hospital gone or disappeared gone?"

"Either. Both. I don't know. She left the hospital and gave a fake address. I didn't think of getting her cell number. I have no way of reaching her, no way of knowing whether she's okay."

"I'm sure she's fine." Constantine's voice tapered off at the end, a diminuendo borne from a lie even he didn't believe.

"I hope so. God, how I hope so."

Their call was cut short by Constantine's boss. Mr. Kowolski was a tall man with a short temper and the unshakable belief that IT problems trumped all. A war could break out and his biggest concern would be whether email was up and running.

Maggie did another circuit of the guest room, absently picking up knickknacks, fingers skipping over the smooth glazed surface of a glass butterfly, a silver spoon, a snow globe with a tiny skier schussing down Mt. Caper. She considered calling 911, the non-emergency police number, Austin, then contemplated the past uselessness of those acts. At least Austin was a friend. Ish. She dialed Austin's number. She got voicemail, wondered if he ever answered his phone and left a cryptic message.

She sat for a moment. She needed to do something, to blow off steam, to quiet her mind. She changed into running clothes and laced her shoes, pulling the laces straight and tight, like her mother had taught her the summer she turned five. She looked at her perfectly formed laces and sagged. She couldn't go on a run. It seemed greedy, blasphemous, in the face of Starr's murder, the rush of blood through her veins an affront to the woman lying naked and alone in the city's crypt. Besides, her heart still sat heavily in her chest. She couldn't imagine being able to get enough air to her lungs to power her legs.

But Maggie was a woman of action. Sitting around waiting for something to happen, for someone else to do something, wasn't exactly her style. She had to move, even if it had nothing to do with exercise.

She left the twee sanctuary of the guestroom and bounded down the stairs. Polly's head was bent over her book, the fire lighting the gray that threaded her hair. Polly looked up at Maggie and smiled. "Well, you're red-cheeked and bright-eyed. What kind of adventure are you off to?"

Maggie snagged her purse, coat and keys. "Nothing very exciting. Just running to the store to grab a few things for Constantine. I know he likes Fritos after a long day at the office." Maggie didn't know why she said that. Constantine hated Fritos, insisting that they smelled like feet and his coworker, Lou.

"These little niceties are the secret to a happy marriage. My husband, Merv, was always doing sweet things like that. Unfortunately, he was also doing sweet things for Marianne Daniels. I got a divorce and Marianne got Merv. I think I got the better end of that deal." She turned a page. "Be careful out there." She looked over the top of the book. "You're on someone's list. Who knows what kind of boxes he's checking off."

Maggie fired up the Studebaker and peered through the windshield. Safelite had performed a curbside repair after Del Vecchio had given the green light, giving Maggie a clear view of what was ahead.

She wished clarity of vision extended beyond her car.

Maggie consulted Siri, inputting the address she'd pulled off a press release posted on the internet. The digital oracle proclaimed The Landing Strip, Sorrento's newest altar of the flesh, eight miles away. Maggie steered the car as Siri instructed and began the upstream slog against rush hour traffic. It was only four o'clock, but when the sun set at five, turning the sky to coal and the streets to glass, people took to their cars early.

Twenty minutes later, Maggie's clutch leg was cramping and her neck was firing warning shots over the back of her head. She drove with her knee, rummaging around in the glove box and freeing her spare film canister from a tangle of receipts, McDonald's napkins and ChapStick tubes. She pried the bottle open with her teeth and shook out two ibuprofen tablets.

She swallowed without water, ignoring the warnings she'd

memorized against such unauthorized ingestions just as she spotted an illuminated sign of a woman straddling an airplane. The Landing Strip.

Maggie jerked the car to the right, crossing two lanes of traffic to a chorus of horns and a flight of flipped birds. She waved apologetically. "Winning friends and influencing others," she muttered to herself.

She cruised through the exit, an elongated cloverleaf that she considered a lucky omen, and took a left onto the first street. The Landing Strip stood at the end of a faux tarmac. 36DD was painted at both ends. The dotted line led to an army green building that looked like the architectural offspring of an airport tower and *M*A*S*H* hospital.

Maggie parked at the far end of the lot next to a custom lifted Ford truck, locked the Stude, and threw a glance over her shoulder. She didn't notice any cars following her and the lot appeared crowded but devoid of people. Then again, she thought she had been alone in the stairwell.

Maggie crunched across the icy parking lot and paused at the door, suddenly aware that she had no real plan. Did she expect to march in and start asking about Starr? Demand to see Rose or know her whereabouts? Interview dancers about coercion into cosmetic surgery? She suspected success via those tactics could be filed under "Nope," "Huh-Uh" and "You're Kidding, Right?"

As she contemplated her next move, the door swung wide and vomited out four young men. The first one fell against her, staggering backward into an abundantly endowed mannequin sporting an aviatrix jacket and little else, then righted himself. He stared at Maggie and emitted a low wolf whistle. "Looks like we just missed the next act, boys. Maybe we should get another round." He reached into his pocket and yanked out a wad of one-dollar bills. "I still have lap dance money."

The second man in the queue, a blond mop-top who looked like he belonged in a Swedish version of the Monkees, grabbed Number One's arm. "Come on, Steve-o. If we hurry, we can make happy hour at the pub."

The men stumbled toward the parking lot and piled into the huge Ford parked next to her car. The engine revved and the car leapt from its space toward the faux tarmac. Maggie was pretty sure one of the men yelled something to her about amateur night.

She looked down at her puffy jacket and faded jeans, mystified by the suggestion she was a stripper. But it did give her an idea. Maggie marched back to her car.

Minutes later, Maggie was at The Landing Strip's door once again, hair slicked back, coat gone, shirt tied around her waist, sports bra adjusted to maximize modest cleavage. She bit her lips, squared her shoulders, and pushed through the door. She was met with a wall of voiceless techno beat. It was like stepping onto the set of *Night at the Roxbury.*

The club was packed, tables glutted, the bar clotted with bar flies attracted to its shiny, beer-dotted surface. In the dim light, Maggie could make out a large center stage bordered by airplane replicas and four smaller dancing platforms arranged like the cardinal points of a compass. The seating was comprised of comfy chairs in army green patent leather. The only women in the establishment were the young beauties who strutted on stage. Maggie suddenly felt geriatric.

She set her mouth into what she hoped was a sultry half-smile and approached the bar. The bartender glanced up from the payload of beers he held in his hands. He eyed her mouth then her chest then her mouth. "Help you?" he demanded.

Maggie tried duck lips. She opened them to speak and choked on her own saliva. She hacked into her palm then grabbed a handful of paper napkins from the dispenser. The bartender's face went from surprise to horror. "You okay?" he asked as she blew her nose into the bosom of the illustrated woman on the napkin.

Maggie nodded, tears running down her face. "Fine," she gasped. "Want to talk to person who hires dancers," she gasped, sounding like a caveman. "Looking for job."

The bartender landed the beers and eyed her as if she might be dangerous. "We're not hiring."

Maggie grabbed another wad of napkins and blotted her streaming nose. "Maybe I could fill out an application."

The bartender laughed. "Application? The only application the boss cares about is how the dancers apply themselves to the pole."

Maggie swallowed. "Oh."

The bartender did another sweep of her face and body. "If you want, you can leave your name with Rose. She's been handling new dancers since Nick's been out."

Maggie's heart leapt. Rose was here! She played casual. "Yeah, okay."

The bartender jerked his head toward restrooms marked Pilots and Stewardesses. "In the office, next to the can." Maggie smiled and nodded, trying to find the sweet spot between provocative and professional, and sashayed toward the office. No one looked her way. The eye of every male patron was glued to the dancers or drinks in front of him. That suited Maggie fine.

The door was covered in wallpaper that approximated wood paneling with a sign that read Control Tower. She gave the wallpaper a brisk three raps and pushed open the door, a smile ready for the woman she had visited in the hospital.

A haggard face marked by too much sun and too little moderation stared back at her. Maggie gasped involuntarily.

A peroxide blonde with curls that rivaled Shirley Temple's looked up. The ringlets at her ears bounced like springs. "Help you?" she demanded in the same way the bartender had. Maybe that passed as hospitality training at The Landing Strip.

"I'm sorry," Maggie said, beginning to turn, "I was looking for Rose."

The woman waved her in like an orange-vested flagger on a busy road. "Yes, yes, I'm Rose." She smiled, exposing evenly sized nicotine-stained teeth that reminded Maggie of lemon Chiclets. Several were MIA.

"Uhh…" Maggie looked around the small office as if the Rose she knew would suddenly appear. "I was looking for a different Rose. She's…" *Prettier? Younger? Has all her own teeth?* "A bit shorter."

The woman laughed wetly then started coughing. Maggie felt vaguely vindicated by her own salivary failures. "I'm Big Rose. There are lots of Roses here. Cinnamons, Sugars and Tonyas, too."

"Oh," Maggie said dully. "Right."

A pseudonym made perfect sense. It furthered the fantasy for customers and offered security for dancers. Maggie winced inwardly. Well, maybe not the security part. The shelter of anonymity was only for those who had the expectation of privacy. Of freedom. She cleared her throat. "Maybe you know the Rose I'm looking for? She's about five-two with lavender hair and—"

"What are you…?" Big Rose asked suspiciously. "…a cop?"

Maggie felt her face flame red hot. The telltale dermis. "Me? A cop?" She laughed. It sounded high and thin. "Of course not. Rosie told me I could get work here."

Big Rose's mouth turned down at the corners. She snaked a hand inside her pink kimono and retrieved a lighter and rumpled pack of Virginia Slims. She lit up and squinted at Maggie through the smoke. "You dance?"

Maggie thought of the time she tried Jazzercise. She'd somehow managed to both expose herself and twist her ankle while trying to chasse into a back-ball-change. "Yes. Mostly in college, but I still have a few moves." Maggie prayed she wouldn't be asked to prove it.

The woman blew a gusty billow of smoke and grunted. "Haven't seen Rose in over a week. Bitch hasn't even called in." She harrumphed and put the cigarette between liver-colored lips. "When did you talk to her?"

Maggie picked at a cuticle. "A while ago."

Big Rose slit her eyes. "Mmm." She took another drag then mashed the lipstick-encrusted cigarette into a vintage ashtray inscribed with the name of a health insurance company. Irony in receptacles. "Don't have time for an audition right now. Come back in the morning. It'll be quiet then and you can shake your money maker." She gave Maggie's chest a long look. "You'll get chump change with those, but the lights are low and we can get you implants. Who says inflation is a bad thing?"

She was still cackling as Maggie rounded the bar and made her way to the door. The thrum of the techno-music collided with the beat of Red Hot Chili Peppers' "Aeroplane." Maggie looked for the source of the syncopation: The Pilot's Lounge, a private room partially illuminated by the glow of a spinning disco ball. Beyond the lingerie-clad mannequin that stood sentry, Maggie could see two shapes inside, one prone, the other gyrating. Standard lap dance with a not-so-standard aviation theme.

The music ended. A middle-aged man in an Armani suit emerged. He glanced at Maggie, blotted his hairline with the back of his hand and hurried toward the stage, a fistful of ones in his hand. Maggie bet he wasn't headed for the vending machine.

A moment later, a woman walked to the mouth of the small dark room. She was two heads shorter than Maggie with blue-black hair, round cheeks and a short aviation uniform bisected by a large white arrow pointing from clavicle to crotch. At the tip of the arrow, degraded type proclaimed the area the Landing Strip.

The woman brushed past Maggie.

"Um, excuse me?" Maggie called over the din of the competing music.

The woman turned. In the half-light Maggie could see she was a teenager. *Girls! Girls! Girls!* "Help you?" The question du jour at The Landing Strip.

"I'm looking for someone."

The face closed. "If you want to request a dancer, you pay first." Maggie pegged the accent as Russian.

"No, I don't want a dance."

Bare arms folded across the zipper of her olive gray bustier. She tossed the blue-black bob. "You want a job? Go see Big Rose."

"I'm not here for a job, either. I want to see the other Rose. The one who hasn't been here for a while."

Fear flashed through the woman's eyes. "We're friends," Maggie said quickly. "I haven't been able to reach her. I'm worried."

The girl-woman peered into the Pilot's Lounge then out onto the floor. "We're not allowed to talk about Little Rose."

"Why not?"

Thin shoulders kissed dangling earrings. "They don't say why. We don't ask."

"Who's they?"

"The big bosses."

"Big Rose? Nick? Dr. Denning?"

The girl's mouth hinged open. "How did—?"

"Did you hear what happened to Starr?" she interrupted.

Smoke-lidded eyes glistened then blinked rapidly. "Yes. Terrible." The eyes grew wide. "Is that what happened to Little Rose?"

"No." Maggie took a beat. "At least I don't think so."

"I pray for her safety." She made the sign of the cross. Orthodox, like Polly. "When we last spoke, she told me she's going away."

Maggie felt her pulse quicken. "You talked to Little Rose."

A head bob sent earrings swinging. "She called this morning to say goodbye, told me to say goodbye to other girls, but not the big bosses."

"Did she say where she was going?"

Head shake-shrug combo. "Away." Proper-noun pronunciation, as if Away were a place on a map.

"Little Rose has a car?"

"She takes the bus."

"The bus? Would she take a bus to leave town, to go away?"

"Think so. But I don't want her to go to Away. There are lots of girls here, but Little Rose is my only friend. She was Starr's only friend, too." Her eyes flooded with tears.

Maggie slipped a hand into her purse and pulled out two hundred-dollar bills. It was the last of her money, a holdover from her final paycheck from Madame Trousseau's. She palmed it to the woman. "You should go away, too. This is a bad place."

The money vanished into the bustier, an expert slight-of-hand borne from hours of on the job training. "Thank you. I will. Soon." She glanced at the bar and straightened her abbreviated flight suit. "I need to get back on the floor or they'll be angry." She shuddered.

She walked toward the stage, her trembling walk becoming a strut, a coy smile splayed across her face. Show time. As the teen wrapped a leg around the pole, Maggie realized that she didn't even know her name, real or otherwise.

Siri informed Maggie that the bus station was 4.8 miles away on Dutton Street. A quick look at the GPS map confirmed that it was downtown, a mere block and half from Petrosian's. Maggie checked the time. It was close to six, far from quitting time for workaholics. She could check the station for Rose then check in with Petrosian to see if he learned anything about Polly's neurologist—or anything Polly-related.

Maggie stomped the clutch and ground the car into first gear. She cringed, Pop's words about transmission abuse and expensive overhauls ringing through her head.

She turned onto the cloverleaf and joined the flow of cars pumping along the county's main artery, tail lights glowing hemoglobin red ahead of her. Rush hour had ended, but the highway was still crowded—"progress" an assessment made only by optimists.

Maggie reached for her cell phone to call Constantine, rationalizing that she was practically stopped anyway. Before she could dial, Ben Stein's roll-call emitted from Maggie's phone. She checked the caller ID. A photo of Felicity stared back, her square jaw and signature round-rimmed glasses filling the frame.

Calling with results from Polly's blood test? That was quick.

Maggie pushed to answer. "Hey, there. How's life on the cutting edge?"

"Busy, overwhelming, gratifying. Just as we've previously discussed."

Felicity had the misfortune of being born without a sense of humor, giving her name a sense of irony, like a huge man called Tiny. "That's great," Maggie said. She downshifted as traffic stalled. She craned her neck, trying to see the cause of the snarl, and spotted a couplet of traffic flares. An accident.

Maggie's imagination took hold as she pictured Rose escaping a would-be kidnapper, a police chase with Sorrento-employed Mafiosi, murder-by-vehicle. She forced her mind to stop. It was the mental equivalent of running with scissors. "Did you process Polly's sample?" she asked, turning back to the matter at hand.

"I did. Negative for alcohol, opiates and stimulants, positive for the prescriptions you mentioned, but nothing in copious amounts. I also ran the sample for over the counter meds. Zantac and Tylenol turned up, which wasn't unexpected considering your mention of occasional gastric upset and the usual aches and pains."

"Ah." Disappointment was instantaneous and crushing. She expected something to show up in Polly's sample. More contraindicated medications. An overdose of the right medication. Poison, even. She'd put it all on black and walked away with nothing. It wasn't square one, but it was close.

"There is one thing of note," Felicity said.

"Yes?" Hope burned bright in her chest. Felicity had found something. Now Maggie would know the depths of Dr. Rogers' betrayal and depravity.

"We've been working on a new test here," Felicity said. "A screening to identify various diseases and conditions, including Parkinson's, for which no specific test existed before. It's still in the development stage and we're not even close to bringing it to market, but I decided to run Polly's sample." Maggie heard more shuffling of paper. "It came back negative."

Maggie felt as if she were staring into an abyss, nothing but black below. "Did you say negative?"

"That's right. Polly doesn't have Parkinson's."

Chapter 38

"There must be some mistake."

"Possibly," Felicity said briskly. "As I said, the test is still under development and not 100 percent definitive. But I have to say it's close. More than close. It's very exciting."

Exciting. Not exactly the word Maggie would choose to describe this little revelation. Shocking, maybe. Disturbing, definitely.

"You're sure?"

"As sure as I can be. Sorry if this is upsetting," she said in a surprising turn of humanity. "I know this must be...strange."

Maggie must have said goodbye, given her thanks and exchanged the kind of pleasantries possible with someone who preferred test tubes over people. She hoped so. Her next sentient moment was arriving at the Greyhound bus depot.

Maggie forty-fived into a diagonal spot before the large glass windows fronting the depot. She set the e-brake and cut the engine.

Polly didn't have Parkinson's disease. It wasn't an absolute certainty, but in Felicity's words, close to it.

Polly's waning Parkinson's symptoms suddenly made sense. It wasn't that she was free of a contraindicated medication. It was that she was free of Parkinson's, period.

The idea didn't just make Maggie's head spin. It made her whole world spin. Why would Polly pretend to have Parkinson's? Why would she fake illness, going so far as to use a cane, take unnecessary medication and feign alarming symptoms?

She had considered Munchausen by proxy for Rogers as a way for him to keep Polly sick and compliant and under his care. Maybe Polly had Munchausen proper, a psychological condition in which people deliberately made themselves sick.

But the question remained: why?

Polly didn't strike Maggie as an attention-seeker. Far from it. Polly was a paragon of fortitude, an inspiring example of overcoming adversity, the first to play down her illness and play up her strengths.

Other possibilities came to mind.

A defense against Howard's boorish behavior.

A ploy to catch Rogers' attention.

A money-making scheme in which she elicited sympathy-driven donations.

None of them really fit.

Another idea floated from the depths of her subconscious, evil and infinitely irresistible.

Polly could be faking the disease because it suited her.

It gave Polly a built-in murder defense, rendering her too weak to wield a knife against her husband. Even if she overcame the "disease" and slit Howard's throat, she did it while sleepwalking. A tragedy. A heartbreak. An unfortunate consequence of her illness and the medications sometimes used to treat it.

Polly faking Parkinson's as a murder defense.

The idea was preposterous. Implausible. And absolutely perfect.

A bogus disease would provide air cover for a crime and sympathy during incarceration. It would be an ideal lie perpetuated by a woman who had tired of her husband and verified by a doctor who was in love with his practice partner's wife. Who perhaps loved him back.

Maggie tried to remember when Polly had been diagnosed. It was around the time she married Howard, wasn't it? Perhaps after the honeymoon, both literal and figurative, had ended?

Like Felicity's Parkinson's blood test, Maggie's certainty wasn't 100 percent. But it was close.

Maggie knew she should feel anger, indignation, even fear. After all, it was possible she had been duped by a murderer. Instead she just felt stupid.

She should have spotted the hypochondriasis, fulfilling the takes-one-to-know-one adage. She should have pegged Polly as a fake, recognized the symptoms that waxed with murder and waned with liberation from prison like the phases of a fickle moon. Maggie had been pulled along with those tides, slipping under the black water of Polly's lies, ignoring inconvenient proofs like the anonymous neurologist no one could remember.

Stupid woman, she admonished herself. *Foolish girl*. Overcome by affection for the woman who might become her aunt-in-law. If such a relation even existed.

Maggie put her head on her steering wheel and honked the horn. She started, then leaned her head against the hard, custard-colored headrest and wept.

What would she do? How could she tell Constantine? Her actions had imprisoned his beloved aunt once. Would he still love her if she did it again, this time permanently?

Maggie didn't want to know the answer.

She swiped her fingers under each eye. She had to control herself, to act logically not emotionally. Emotion, affection for Polly, an overwhelming desire to help, was what had gotten her into this mess in the first place. She should have known better. She should have fortified the Wall.

She imagined firing up her cerebrum, channeling all of her energy into the part of the brain dedicated to higher thinking. The oasis of reason delivered her to a few key insights: Polly's fake Parkinson's didn't change the fact that Sorrento had been lurking around the Wright residence. Or that Sorrento's DNA had been on the murder weapon. Or that Howard-aka-Matthew, Denning and Sorrento had been involved in insurance fraud.

In the sea of lies in which Maggie had been swimming, these truths blazed like tiny life rafts in the summer sun. The question was how they tied in with Polly's falsehoods and her disease with benefits.

Maggie peered into the bus depot's sweeping windows. No matter what she had learned about Polly, Starr was still dead and Rose could still be in danger. She'd stick with her plan for now, decide what to do about Polly later.

Chapter 39

Night had turned the bus depot into a diorama illuminating the people within. Maggie swept her eyes across the building for Rose, hoping for a quick location, but the light wasn't that good and neither were her eyes, thanks to late-night reading sessions under the blankets with a flashlight.

Maggie got out of the Studebaker, hit the locks and walked quickly toward the building. She pushed open the glass door and got her first whiff of Eau de Depot: a combination of urine, stale perspiration and salty snack foods. Maggie covered her nose with her hand to stop the nostril assault.

She scanned the depot. The room was a tribute to despair. The interior was gray. Not dove gray. Steel-on-a-rainy day gray. The black and white Linoleum sported faux Art Deco triangles resembling planchettes, turning the floor into a quilt of Ouija boards. Thickets of conjoined leatherette chairs occupied the center of the room like a furniture sit-in, a protest against institutionalized colorlessness.

Maggie scanned the faces. Most were old, weathered, turned colorless like the room, perhaps by proximity, perhaps in solidarity. Hues of a feather.

No Rose in this gray tundra.

She spotted the ticket counter, an outpost at the back of the room, manned by a man in a flannel shirt. She approached.

The man ignored her, paging through a truck magazine. She tapped on the tiny window that separated them. His eyes flicked up, met hers, returned to the magazine. He sighed audibly, the sound carrying through the thick glass and slid the window. "Where to?"

"I'm looking for a friend. I think she may have purchased a ticket this evening."

He turned back to his magazine, began turning pages. "Don't know about no friend. A ticket to Des Moines, that I can help you with."

"She's young, pretty," Maggie continued as if she hadn't heard him, "has lavender hair."

The man twisted his face into a smile. "Sounds like a stripper." He laughed. Maggie did not. He adjusted his commodious lower half on his small high-backed chair. "I just came on a little while ago. Five, ten minutes. Only people I've seen are those in the waiting room." He gestured vaguely. "Plus a kid with a guitar, only he didn't come in to buy a ticket, just to use the john." He scowled at the affront of unauthorized urination.

"You're sure?" Maggie pressed.

The man's deepening scowl said he was. Maggie thanked him and walked slowly back toward the door. As she passed the restroom, a woman emerged from the side marked "Ladies" in the kind of frilly font favored by perfume manufacturers. The woman met Maggie's eyes, recognition then panic darting through them. Maggie took in the woman's small frame, the long black hair, the pixie face, the Duke sweatshirt. The woman turned abruptly toward the row of seats, head down, eyes studying the floor. Maggie stood there, thinking. Processing. Processing. Then: illumination.

Rose.

She'd dyed her hair, changed her clothes, but it was still the same woman who had once lay unconscious in a hospital bed.

"Rose!" Maggie said loudly. The woman stiffened then kept walking. She bypassed the chairs and shouldered open the depot door. Maggie trotted after her, but Rose had already vanished into the night. "Rose, Rose, Rose," she repeated. She felt like Eliza Doolittle hawking flowers in *My Fair Lady*.

Maggie surveyed the street. Commercial mailbox. Abandoned bike rack. Newspaper stands. No Rose. She squinted, scanning the hidden places between buildings where bad things tended to grow. A shift of light, a wink of metal. The buckle on Rose's boots as she jogged down an alley.

Maggie followed, throwing a glance over her shoulder, suddenly aware of the aloneness she shared with Rose, the feeling she was being watched. Followed. Stalked. She put her hand into her pocket and gripped her keys, preparing a makeshift weapon. Wishing it was the first time in her life that she'd done so.

She picked up her pace, edging from canter to gallop, feet slipping on congealing slush, twice clanging into garbage cans. Then suddenly: a presence.

She whirled around, keys ready to strike. Rose stood glaring, feet apart, arms bent at the elbow, ready to run or hit, just like Maggie.

Rose took a step forward, piercing Maggie's personal space bubble. In the feeble light thrown by a window above, Maggie could see she was shaking. Adrenaline? Anger? Fear? All of the above?

"Why are you following me?" Rose hissed. "What do you want?"

"I just want to talk to you," Maggie said, hunching over, trying to make herself as small and nonthreatening as possible.

"I don't want to talk to anyone. I want to get away from here. This town. These people." Her eyes were wild with desperation. "Please."

Rose pushed past Maggie, her ankle turning in her high-heel boot. She yelped in pain, but limped forward, dragging her hurt foot behind her.

"I heard about Starr," Maggie called to Rose's retreating form. "I know what's going on. I know that you work for a criminal, that you're being coerced into participating in insurance fraud."

Rose stopped. Turned around. Her mouth was twisted in pain and anger. "That's not all we're forced into."

Maggie froze. Dread colder than the night took hold of her.

Rose took a step forward. "Some of us wanted the boob jobs, the lipo. Some of us were ordered to get them."

"By Nick?"

"By Nick, by Big Rose, by one of the guys. It didn't matter who said it, we just did it. And we didn't care that we had to get scoped to get the discount. A good deal is a good deal." She looked at the ground, tapped the slush with her boot tip. "But my mama was right. Ain't no such thing as a free lunch."

"They wanted more money?"

Rose laughed. It sounded like something dying. "They wanted more money all right. And they wanted us to make it on our backs."

It was what a part of her had suspected, but hearing it aloud hit Maggie like a truck. "Prostitution?"

Rose gave a mirthless smile. "You make it sound so...sanitized. Like all the girls are *Pretty Woman* call girls and all the men are Richard Gere." She put her face close to Maggie's. "Newsflash: they're not."

Maggie's stomach roiled. "Is that what Starr wanted to tell you?"

Rose covered her mouth, smearing plum-colored lipstick to create a cosmetic bruise beside her mouth. "She wanted to protect me. She thought of me as a little sister."

Maggie thought back to the waiting room at InHance. Starr had a lot of little sisters. "How did you find out?"

"Nadia, one of the girls at The Landing Strip. I'd been calling around, trying to find out what happened to Starr. Nobody answered, nobody called back. Until Nadia. She told me Starr was dead. She told me not to come back. She told me Sorrento's people were looking for me and if they found me, they'd say I owed them for the surgery then increase the interest until dancing wasn't enough to work off the debt."

Maggie remembered the woman with the accent at The Landing Strip. "Nadia's Russian?"

"Ukrainian."

"Here illegally?" Rose crossed her arms like a shield. "I won't tell," Maggie said. "I just need to know."

Rose looked at Maggie, tipped her chin skyward. "So what? She's not the only one. There are girls from Honduras, the Philippines, China. Not everyone has papers. And not everyone is from outside the country. Plenty of local girls, too."

Girls! girls! girls! from near and from far. Exploitation was an equal opportunity enterprise.

Dread seeped into Maggie's bones. Sorrento wasn't just involved in prostitution. He was involved in human trafficking, turning young women—some undocumented, all vulnerable— into his own private inventory. The women—girls—would be easy to control and manipulate. Because of their age. Because of their debt to InHance. And for some, because of fear of exposure in a political climate that was slow to help and quick to deport.

Maggie looked at the world around her. Dead. Frozen. Waiting for cryonic regeneration. She thought of Starr, Rose, Nadia, a litany of other nameless, faceless victims churning through Sorrento's factories of debasement. She thought of the older man in InHance's waiting room pretending to read magazines. He was there to read the women, to make sure they didn't get any funny ideas about freedom and escape. Maggie's heart sat like a stone in her chest. She felt her breathing grow shallow, anemic, beneath its ponderous weight.

Human trafficking was big business and those they sold were getting younger by the day. Maggie had once read that a hundred thousand children were trafficked in the United States alone and that nearly three-quarters of those children were female.

Girls! Girls! Girls!

Money. Money. Money.

Most were too young to have a driver's license. Some were still playing with Barbies.

Maybe this was what had made Matthew/Howard fake his death. Maybe this was what made him a target for murder.

Rose hugged her sweatshirt around herself. "The worst part? There's no end in sight. Sorrento's not there, but Nadia says the business continues. Another day. Another girl. Another john."

"I'm sorry," Maggie said. "I'm so very sorry." The apology sounded greeting card hollow, the right words curried at the right time. She hoped Rose could feel what her words couldn't convey.

Her mind turned again to the man in the InHance waiting room. "Does Sorrento have a second in command? A man he can trust while he's in jail?"

Rose looked at Maggie, rage and pain and fear playing through her eyes. Naked emotion for a woman who'd spent the past few months unclothed. "Yes, but it's not a man."

Maggie took a step back. "What about the man in the waiting room at InHance?"

"Larry?" She spat the word. "He's there to keep everything—and everyone—in line. Sorrento's right-hand man is a woman."

"A woman?" She thought of Big Rose with the cavernous mouth, the sunken cheeks, the appraising stare. So much for solidarity among sisters.

"I believed her when she said she'd help me find a safe place to live. I trusted her when she said Sorrento's club was a good place to work. I bought her lies about discount cosmetic surgery in exchange for routine procedures. Because I ended up in the hospital, I wasn't around to hear that I owed more. That I'd broken the law by having a colonoscopy that I didn't need. That she'd send me home if I didn't do what they wanted."

"She'd threaten to send them home?"

"Whatever home they were running from. Their home country. The house where their mother beat them. The garage where their step-dad raped them."

Maggie let that sink in. Deportation wasn't the big stick for all of the women lured by Sorrento. For some, the institutionalized abuse of prostitution was a step up from what they'd experienced at home. She knew that this wasn't the case for all exotic dancers or for all prostitutes.

She also knew that it was for those under Sorrento's thumb.

"I have to go." Rose adjusted the backpack. It was pink with rainbows and an illustration of Sleeping Beauty. A girl's backpack. Themes about betrayal, stolen kisses and man as savior.

Maggie was rocked by another surge of sickness. "Where are you going?"

"Away." The same destination Nadia had uttered. Rose turned on her heel and headed toward the streetlight.

"Wait," Maggie said. "I need to know how Big Rose lures the girls into the business, how we can stop her. Them."

Rose looked over her shoulder, her face shaded in the streetlight's hesitant glow. "Big Rose? What's she got to do with anything?"

Maggie furrowed her brow. "I thought you said she was Sorrento's right-hand man—woman."

Rose shook her head, now-darkened hair pillowing against her sweatshirt. "Big Rose helps the new hires, does office work, but that's it."

"Then who's Sorrento's second in command?"

"I don't know her real name. We call her Miss Lulu because she's always wearing yoga pants. Like the brand?"

"Lululemon?"

"Yeah."

"Where did you meet her?" Maggie tried to imagine a woman hunting for victims at a yoga studio, luring them with promises of improving their sun salutations.

"Same place all the girls did. At the runaway shelter."

Chapter 40

"The runaway shelter?" Maggie heard herself ask. She felt as if she were very far away, watching her conversation with Rose. "Which runaway shelter?"

Rose adjusted her backpack and looked back at the street. Meeting someone or just eager to leave? "*The* runaway shelter. The only one in town."

Maggie could feel the hair on the back of her neck rise, her subconscious raising the alarm.

"Running Home? In Old Town?"

Rose gave a single nod. "Not everyone there is a runaway. I was just between jobs. And apartments." She gave a shrug. No big deal. "And not everyone is recruited. Just the young ones. The lonely ones."

Maggie filled in the blanks: the vulnerable ones.

A car roared by on the street behind her, kicking up a spray of crystalline slush. Rose flinched then rubbed her shoulders briskly. Shake it off. "My science teacher played a TV show for us. 'Lions on the Hunt' or something. It's the females that do the hunting. Did you know that?" She searched Maggie's face for an answer. "They look for the animals that are young or sick or alone. Then they strike, cutting them off, cutting them down. That's Lulu. She has a talent for picking prey."

Back in the Studebaker, Maggie called Constantine. The phone rang in her ear as she watched Rose hobble up to the depot's ticket window and push something through the miniature gated community behind which the clerk sat, purchasing a ticket to a new Away, the farthest destination money could buy.

Maggie was about to end the call when Constantine picked up. "'Lo?" he panted. "Are you still there?"

"I'm here," Maggie said. "Wish you were."

"That makes three of us, including my boss who's not so happy about paying overtime. What's up?"

"Oh, nothing really. Unless you count me uncovering Camille as Sorrento's recruiter for his human-trafficking enterprise."

A pause yawned between them. "You're joking."

"I wish."

She told him about Sorrento's and Denning's business model of hiring dancers, convincing them to have cosmetic surgeries at a discount, then forcing them to pay the difference with their bodies—all brokered by Camille through the runaway shelter.

Constantine was silent after she finished. Finally he said, "You're saying that yoga pants plus runaway shelter equals human trafficking, all thanks to the work of one of my aunt's friends?"

"I know it sounds implausible."

"Um, try crazy. Not trying to throw shade, Mags, but this is way out there. I'm with you on the human-trafficking angle. That would be right up Sorrento's alley and maybe not too far of a walk down the plank of immorality for Denning since he wasn't shy about insurance fraud and coerced surgeries. But Camille?"

"Yoga pants," she said stupidly.

"Mags," Constantine said gently, "even if someone from the shelter is recruiting and even if that someone is a woman with a penchant for comfy pants, it doesn't mean it's Camille."

Maggie chewed on her thumb and then her lip. "I know."

"Good." Constantine sounded relieved.

"That's why I need proof."

Constantine groaned. "Oh God. No, Maggie, you don't need proof. You need to take a breather. You haven't been yourself since the—since what happened at St. Theresa's. This is taking over your life."

"It should be taking over your life, too," she snapped. "It's your uncle who was murdered, your aunt who was accused."

"Thanks to you," he said tightly.

Something in Maggie's chest gave way.

A silence fell between them, wedging them apart.

"I'm sorry, Maggie," Constantine said softly. "I didn't mean that."

But he did. Maggie knew it with the same certainty she knew Camille was involved.

She watched a bus lumber up to the depot, open its door and expel travelers in a colorful heap of hats, scarves and gloves. She craned her neck to see if Rose had queued in front of the emptying bus, her Sleeping Beauty backpack slung over her shoulder, relief evident in her body language. There was no Rose. The only person waiting was a man with Lucille Ball hair, skinny jeans, and a bolo tie. She hoped Rose had found her Away.

Maggie started the car and slid it into gear. "I'll talk to you later."

She hung up without saying another word.

The streets were deserted on the drive to Camille's, cars and their drivers in states of quasi-hibernation until first light would push the mercury above freezing.

Maggie found herself continually glancing in her rearview mirror. To see if someone was following her. To see where she had been. To take one last look at the city that seemed to be crumbling behind her. Maybe that made her Lot's wife. Maybe that just made her someone who wanted to escape to a time before Starr's murder, Camille's betrayal, Polly's lies and Constantine's judgment.

Forget Throwback Thursday. Maggie wanted a Throwback Life.

Maggie ruminated over the possibilities in her mind. Was she crazy? Maybe. Was she concussed? Possibly. Was she right? She felt that she was, and for once feeling was enough.

The whole thing fit.

Matthew Foley faked his death to get out of Sorrento's and Denning's business when it turned from insurance fraud to human trafficking. He tried to resurrect himself as Howard Wright, but Sorrento found him. The motive? Money and protection. Eliminate Howard as a potential whistleblower so they could continue to sell women—girls—at a tidy profit. Human trafficking was a billion-dollar industry. Add the 1.6 million kids on streets of the U.S., and it was a nice little talent pool.

She wasn't sure how Camille fit into Howard's murder. Had Sorrento located Howard and paid Camille, his new recruiter for his new prospects/prey, to make friends with Polly and Howard? Maggie knew they had met a year or two ago. Her friendship with Howard and Polly had to be more than coincidence, but that seemed too long even for a long game.

Maggie arrived at Camille's bungalow and gazed up at the darkened windows. Polly was probably asleep; Camille was likely grooming victims.

Maggie got out of the car, eased her door closed with a click and picked her way up the icy walk. She slipped the key her hostess had given her into the lock, a gesture of trust that now seemed jarringly out of place, and eased opened the door. "Hello?" she called softly. "Camille? Polly? Anyone home?"

The house returned her greeting with a silence she could almost touch.

Maggie slipped out of her boots, and her stocking-feet whispered over freshly mopped hardwood as she made her way into the home's interior. She peered into the living room. "Hello?" A bit louder this time, with a hint of playfulness, as if she were playing hide-and-go-seek. *Olly olly oxen free!*

The fire was cold. The room, deserted.

She stole down the hall on the balls of her feet, ignoring the cold that bled through the worn part of her socks, and pushed open the kitchen door, gave the same half-loud, quasi-cheery greeting. Received the same gaping emptiness.

Maggie quickly canvassed the rest of the house.

The laundry room with its smell of lavender detergent and stacks of folded slacks—including multiple pairs of Lululemon yoga pants.

The baby blue powder room with its fuzzy toilet seat cover and knit tissue box cozy.

The garage in which Maggie had watched in horror as Polly sleep-drove to wrest a bloodstained knife from the earth. Behind the freezer where Camille stored casseroles to be given to parishioners who'd had surgery or a baby, Maggie found rust-brown paint and a fine-tipped brush. The paint was the color of blood. The brush was the perfect size for writing death threats.

Camille was behind the stone in the windshield and the miniature speaker on the kitchen table. She was also likely her assailant at St. Theresa's.

Maggie unconsciously touched the back of her head. She had imagined the smell of blood on the rocks, but the attack that had robbed Maggie of control and left her feeling like the victim she promised herself she'd never be was as real as the divot at the base of her skull.

Camille Walsh. Graffiti artist. Attacker. Potential accessory to murder. And damn fine actress.

Maggie strode down the hall and opened the first door on the right, the guest room Polly had occupied since Howard's throat had been unceremoniously opened. In the vanilla glow of a vintage Mickey Mouse nightlight, she could make out Polly's prone form on the twin bed, her hair fanning out like a magenta and silver ocean, her chest rising and falling beneath a tower of handmade blankets. The sleep of the innocent. A paradox, considering her fake Parkinson's.

But that was another lie for another day.

Maggie crept up the stairs, past pictorial jaunts down memory lane. Camille's 5K. Camille's trip to the tropics. Camille's thank-you card. Yadda, yadda. And yadda.

She crested the stairs, went to the guestroom she occupied and took a quick inventory. Empty? Check. Everything in place? Check. She closed the door and moved onto Constantine's room, where she reached into the cage and gave Miss Vanilla a scratch behind one tiny pink ear.

She stepped into the small guest bath, gave a quick glance behind a ruffled shower curtain that reminded Maggie of a nightgown from Madam Trousseau's, then walked to the terminus of the hall and the entrance to Camille's bedroom.

The door was shut, but not latched, the metal tang resting against the door frame. Closure for the commitment-shy.

"Camille?" Maggie called softly. Her heart thudded in her ears creating a pulse that reverberated through her body like a dub-step beat. She pushed the door open with her fingers, shaking tips scratching the whitewashed door. "Camille, are you in here?"

Silence spilled into the hall, drawing her in. Maggie stepped into the room and paused to let her eyes adjust and her breathing quiet. Neither seemed to be working. She could scarcely make out the room's furniture, let alone locate incriminating evidence. Her turtleneck felt clammy beneath her arms where cotton and perspiration met.

She considered her options: use the flashlight app on her phone to surreptitiously search the room or turn on the overhead lamp to give the impression of innocent trespass. *Oh, hi, Camille. I just let myself in to hunt for a bobby pin. I'm sure you don't mind.*

She decided to go with the latter. She gave the switch the finger and flipped it on. The room jumped into full relief. Maggie shaded her eyes against the over-bright illumination of the ceiling-mounted fixture. Maggie figured it had to top two hundred watts. Add energy waste to Camille's growing list of sins.

Maggie surveyed the room. It was larger than the other three bedrooms with white-on-white décor and lace-trimmed everything. Midlife crisis meets midcentury traditional.

A roll top desk fronted a large window dressed in flouncy gauze, its wooden roller barricading a mini storage locker of secrets just begging to be breached.

Maggie peeled the desk open. A dozen neatly organized cubbies promised enlightenment and elicited envy. Camille was nothing if not organized.

Maggie went spelunking through drawers and cubbies. The juiciest things she found were a cache of receipts for Zantac from Petrosian's, an appointment card for a lip wax at a local salon and a stash of Fun Size Milky Ways.

Maggie put her hands on her hips and gave the room a three-sixty pan. Vanity. Nightstand. Bed. Nightstand. Closet.

Since Camille was metaphorically in the closet as a yoga-clad madam and accessory to human trafficking, her actual closet seemed a good place to start.

Maggie opened the double slat-topped doors and was greeted with a row of clothes arranged by color, style, sleeve-length or overall length. Fuchsia was a favorite, followed by cerise, berry and a purple-red Aunt Fiona insisted on calling chrysanthemum. The majority of the wardrobe was comprised of button down blouses and yoga pants with a smattering of stretchy polyester slacks and skirts Maggie imagined were saved for special occasions. Maggie could only imagine what "special" meant in Camille's world.

She slid her arms between the clothes and palpated the closet's back wall for a false door. Nothing. She dropped to her knees and batted aside orthotic shoes. She stood on tiptoe and canvassed the top shelf for hatboxes, shoeboxes and strongboxes. She came away with a dust-induced sneezing fit.

She walked to the bed, a full-size Sleep Number occupied by precious pillows and a crocheted throw and peered beneath it. Not even a dust bunny to be found.

She surveyed the room. Two possibilities remained. She held her breath and approached the nightstand to the right of the bed, the side Maggie would have picked for her own. She eased it open and peered inside. It contained a Bible and a tube of lip balm. Maggie fanned through the Bible, envisioning something like Dufresne's chisel in *The Shawshank Redemption* to emerge from the good book's spine or between its onion paper pages. "Dear Warden," her mind quoted by rote. "You were right. Salvation lay within." Instead Maggie found underlined passages about the Golden Rule.

She rounded the bed and opened the other drawer. Inside, she found three sample bottles of Nardil. Maggie wasn't sure how or where she'd obtained them. Camille was a counselor, a doctor of psychology, if she remembered correctly. Maybe she had procured them through her work, as a patient or simply by asking a colleague.

Maggie was running through the possibilities when she felt a presence. A whisper of air. A shift of light. Another heartbeat transmitting a subliminal Morse code.

Maggie wheeled around.

Camille stood with her hand on the doorknob, a frown pulling what Maggie imagined was a freshly waxed upper lip toward her chin. "What are you doing?" Camille asked. Her voice was level, warm even, the gracious hostess always ready to accommodate a guest.

Please, ransack my room. No, really. I insist.

"Hey, Camille," Maggie said, overdoing casual. "I was just looking for a bobby pin." She decided to go with the prepared lie and lifted an unruly hank to demonstrate. She quietly closed the drawer. "Constantine's coming back tonight and I wanted to do something special with my hair."

It was the stupidest of lies. Anyone who knew Maggie knew she dressed up for no one, especially not men. She prayed Camille hadn't taken notice of her renunciation of her au naturel style—or the flush she felt crawling across her face like a crimson news ticker.

Maggie trespasses and lies. Full story at eleven.

Camille's mouth wavered between cordiality and confusion, her mouth pursing then collapsing. "Oh. Yes, of course. I have some right here."

She moved to her vanity and plucked a smattering of hairpins from a tray of hair doodads. Maggie couldn't identify half of them. "They were right here." She nudged her head to the right. "I'm surprised you didn't see them."

Maggie face-palmed, gently, so as not to jostle her head. "I'm such a space cadet sometimes." She smiled inanely and began jabbing pins into her hair. "I'm going for a messy up-do. Really messy. Sort of a Brigitte Bardot number."

"Mmm." Camille smiled, but something in her eyes shifted. A coldness. A question. A calculation.

Maggie became very aware of their physical proximity, of the overbearing silence of the house, of the fact she was quite possibly alone with a murderer.

She had trespassed into Camille's room. Camille could say she was surprised by an intruder in the dark, had acted in self-defense by bludgeoning or stabbing or, God forbid, with a gun that had been tucked in the back of her yoga pants. A terrible accident. A tragic loss. A simple mistake made by an old woman whose night vision had been compromised by the passage of years and reading too many recipes.

Maggie took a step toward the door. Camille matched her stride. "Well, thanks for the bobby pins," Maggie said. "I should be all set now."

Camille took another step toward her. Maggie picked up the pace, passing through the threshold in two eager strides. Camille followed. Maggie walked past the room she had come to think of as hers, resisting the urge to dash inside and throw the lock.

Just act natural. Just act natural. Just act natural.

Wouldn't acting natural mean stopping by her room to put her hair in the up-do?

Probably. But Maggie found herself propelled down the hall. Past the powder room. Past the hall table with the porcelain clock that chimed the "Ave Maria" every quarter hour. Toward the stairs and her very own Away.

Maggie reached the landing. She could feel Camille behind her, hear the soft shushing of feet gliding over deep pile carpet, almost feel each exhalation against her hair. She wanted to turn. Ascertain Camille's proximity. See what expression she wore. Find out if she had anything in her smooth, dry hands. Maggie kept moving forward in a kind of self-imposed death march.

Then, a misstep, Maggie's foot caught on the third stair from the top, tangling in some invisible impediment (an errant thread? a worn spot?), causing her to stumble.

Maggie steadied herself against the bannister, knocking one of Camille's prized pictures from her self-styled ego wall.

The frame clattered to the ground. Maggie pin wheeled her arms to avoid crushing the picture that lay at her feet, clutching the smooth wood railing for balance, the horror of her clumsiness temporarily eclipsing her fear.

Camille stooped, scooped up the frame and cradled it. She ran an exploratory finger around its edges and smiled. "It's fine," she said. "No harm done."

The predatory aura that had billowed from Camille dissipated, leaving Docile Camille, Nice Older Lady Camille, in its stead. Maggie smiled tentatively. "Oh, good. Sorry about that."

Maggie peered at the paper encased in the frame: the thank-you card Maggie had spied on earlier commutes from bedroom to common areas and back again. She hadn't taken much notice before. Now she saw that the thank-you card featured a custom-printed headline:

Thank you, Miss Camille, for taking such great care of us.

Beneath the line, a dozen signatures in girlish names testified to the sentiment. Beneath that, a logo of a butterfly with the words Mariposa Rescue.

Something tickled the back of Maggie's brain. A remnant of memory. A half-formed impression. It was like an itch she couldn't scratch. Annoying. Insistent. Growing.

The scrape of plastic against plaster snapped Maggie out of her reverie. Camille positioned the framed card on the wall, adjusted its position using some kind of internal ballast, then smiled.

"Um, thanks again for the bobby pins," Maggie said, continuing down the stairs. "I really appreciate it."

Camille swiveled her head toward Maggie like a periscope. She narrowed her eyes then squinted them into smiling half-moons, the Aunt Bea act returning. "You're welcome, dear. You don't strike me as the up-do type." She gave Maggie a long look. "It's nice to see you taking an interest in grooming."

Maggie laughed nervously. "Ha, ha, yeah." She looked down the stairs at her current trajectory. Her choices: hang out downstairs with a suspected human trafficker and possible murderer, or head to the local Starbucks for escape and a double shot of sanity.

The temptation was to pick what was behind Door Number Two, to escape to the comfort of venti lattes and eco-friendly seating, but she couldn't leave Polly alone with Camille. Whatever the reason behind Polly's fake illness, she loved her. She'd do whatever it took to protect her.

She decided on Door Number Three: her room. Which meant close passage by Camille.

Maggie climbed back onto the landing. "Whoops. I was so excited I walked right by my room." She turned sideways to avoid brushing against Camille, to make herself as small as possible. Something she had spent most of her life doing in an effort to reduce her presence and importance. She stopped doing it last year and swore she'd never do it again.

Never say never.

"Talk to you later," she said as she slithered past Camille. "And thanks."

She twisted the handle of her door and sauntered into the room, molding her shoulders in a nonchalant slouch, moderating her pace between leisurely and intentional. As she swung the door shut, she could feel Camille's eyes boring into her back.

Maggie leaned against the door and closed her eyes. Perspiration snaked down her back into the waistband of her jeans. She rubbed denim against her L3 vertebra and straightened. She wasn't in her room to hide. She was there to find the evidence she needed to lock Camille up.

Maggie nicked the laptop from the dresser and plopped onto the unmade bed. She fired up the computer and logged onto Chrome.

The name of the organization on the thank-you card Maggie had almost destroyed had lodged in her brain, its familiarity demanding her attention. She input "Mariposa Rescue" into the Google search bar, clicked the link from the results page and waited as the page loaded.

Stock photos of professionally good-looking teens paired with names changed to protect the innocent and stories designed to yank on the heartstrings.

Touching, but not very helpful.

She navigated to the About page where she found the organization's mission statement, history and location. Mariposa was dedicated to helping runaway youth. Mariposa had a history of protecting those at risk. Mariposa was located in Three Rivers.

Three Rivers. Where Matthew Foley—before he was Howard Wright—had lived. Where he'd defrauded insurance companies and co-owned a strip club. Where he'd witnessed or partaken in something horrific enough to fake his own death.

Where Camille claimed she'd never been.

More images crowded into Maggie's mind, this time shining a spotlight on the tchotchkes around the house. The sheep with the "We'll Miss Ewe" sign. The souvenir snow globe that entombed a skier racing down Mt. Caper. A silver spoon with an illustration of the same mountain. Butterfly business cards. A glass butterfly.

Butterfly. Mariposa was Spanish for butterfly.

Camille hadn't just visited Three Rivers. She had worked there at a runaway shelter.

If Camille used Hollow Pine's rescue shelter as a talent pool for Sorrento's club and human trafficking ring, chances were she'd done the same in Three Rivers. A tourist town with transient populations of young people searching for fun would be great proving ground for honing their business model, for stalking new quarry. Maggie's guess: Camille had cut her teeth in Three Rivers then moved to Hollow Pine to help Sorrento expand his opportunity. The American Dream for him. A nightmare for his victims.

Maggie clicked a link to Meet the Staff! No Camille there, but she did find her in the News You Can Use section in a blurb that celebrated her anniversary with Mariposa. It was the occasion memorialized with the thank-you card. It afforded Maggie a look at Camille nearly six years earlier.

Camille was almost unrecognizable. No silver hair fashioned into a sensible cut. No glasses. No roundness of cheek wrought by sampling countless cupcakes and pumpkin loafs. The woman in the article was lithe and honey-blonde.

Maggie opened a new browser window and searched "Camille Walsh" and "Three Rivers." Google informed her that Camille had taken a spin on the local school board, was a member of Christ the Redeemer parish, and had played Martha Brewster in *Arsenic and Old Lace*. Maggie smiled ruefully at that last tidbit. Camille in the role of a nice little old lady with murderous predilections. Talk about type-casting.

Maggie kept reading. Three pages in, she caught her breath.

In the "Milestones" section of the local online newspaper, several couples were featured in various stages of matrimonial bliss: engagement, wedding and anniversary. The first couple featured in the March 2011 issue: Matthew Foley and Camille Walsh.

The locket Constantine found sprang to mind. The initials F & W didn't stand for Foley and Wright, a clever homage to Howard's dueling identities, as originally thought. The letters represented Foley and Walsh. A romantic union commemorated in jewelry.

In their engagement photo, Camille had donned a fishing hat and was reeling Matthew in. Matthew mugged for the camera, his eyes bulging with mock fear as he pantomimed a struggle to get away. Camille grinned maniacally, one hand on her trim slack-clad hip, the other effortlessly pulling back on the fishing rod. The caption read: "Local woman hooks prominent physician."

It was as sexist as it was cheesy.

Maggie pushed down the pun-induced nausea and read the announcement copy. The staff writer breathlessly reported the happy couple's statistics (him: a fifty-five-year-old cosmetic surgeon, her: a forty-five-year-old counselor), hobbies (fishing and knitting, respectively) and plans for the lavish nuptials (the sacrament to be performed by Father Joseph, the reception at the stylish Hotel de Marco).

Maggie enlarged the photo and did the math. She could buy Howard's/Matthew's age. Camille's, not so much. Either she'd lied about her age then or was putting on an older lady act now.

Maggie's mind flooded with questions. How did the two meet? Whose idea was it to use the runaway program as a means to traffic girls? Did Camille recognize Howard as her dead fiancé in the same way that Jenna had recognized him as her long-departed brother? Did she lead Sorrento to him? Was the murder business or pleasure?

Maggie continued searching the internet, as if the answers would pop onto her laptop's screen. She found more articles about Matthew's drowning, an interview with a very weepy Camille and a real estate ad for Camille's house eighteen months earlier.

Eighteen months. After Polly and Howard had married. Around the time Polly met Camille.

The pieces were falling into place. Now Maggie needed to complete the picture. She hoped it would look like the inside of a prison cell.

Maggie closed her laptop and grabbed her phone. Her urge was to call Constantine, but she was angry with him. Or maybe he was angry with her. She couldn't quite remember.

She dialed Austin. She'd already roped him into problem after problem. Time for him to get some success for his troubles.

Voicemail again, this one informing her that he was out of the office for the next three days. Vacation or forced time off? It was impossible to know. Maggie left a message and ended the call. She tapped the phone against her chin, her version of jostling the Magic 8-Ball.

No answer for what her future would hold materialized. Ditto for what she should do to transform suspicion into proof—and then into an arrest.

Then a bolt from the blue.

Maggie suddenly knew exactly what she would do. And how she would do it.

Chapter 41

"You're going to do great," Maggie told the woman standing before her. "Just, you know, be yourself. Ish."

Ada gave Maggie a look. "Oh, I'm not worried about me. I'm worried about this outfit." She gestured to a pair of overalls, a flower-print button-down shirt and a *Doc McStuffins* backpack. "Aren't you overshooting the whole juvenile look thing? I'll look like I'm twelve."

Maggie's chest tightened. "That's the idea."

Maggie had reached Ada at one of Pop's food carts and was relieved that the younger woman was game to take part in her plan.

"I'm in," Ada had said, sounding even more confident than the last time Maggie had spoken with her. "I'm actually starting at the police academy in a few months. It's something I always wanted to do. Now I'm doing it." She paused. "I've started doing a lot of things I've always wanted to do. Anyway, this will be like a preview of coming attractions."

Two hours later, they were in a McDonald's parking lot.

They entered the restaurant via the side door near the restaurant's dumpsters. Ada ducked into the bathroom to change while Maggie ordered a large Dr. Pepper, in part because she felt guilty about using the restaurant's facilities without buying anything, in part because...Dr. Pepper.

As Maggie punctured the lid with her straw, Ada emerged from the bathroom, her long dark hair in a single braid down her back, her pretty face scrubbed of any cosmetic artifice. Maggie took a drag on the straw.

She'd chosen her partner wisely. Ada already looked young. In her current ensemble, she looked younger, smaller. "Predator dressed as prey," she said. "They won't know what hit 'em."

It took Maggie a while to find what she was looking for. Officially, Hollow Pine didn't have a "bad side." The midsized Midwestern city cherished its wholesome reputation, and the police did what they could to turn the sleepy city nearly comatose.

The truth was, every city had a bad side. In Hollow Pine, dark urges were forced underground where they festered then germinated like poisonous mushrooms in the places light didn't reach. Maggie drove by blocks blighted by poverty. Through neighborhoods blind to a child's perpetual bruises or a woman's propensity for sunglasses and full-coverage concealer. Past streets lined with the walking dead of the drug addicted, the unwanted, the lost.

Some of the last group were runaways seeking refuge from whatever torment lived at home. Some ended up under the protective wing of Camille Walsh and the Running Home Shelter for Runaway Youth.

Questions about where she could score some weed led Maggie to an alleyway that backed up to Old Town. It wasn't far from Petrosian's, but it was a world apart from the sanitized existence of medicine and moisturizer and people who gave near-strangers breakfast when they were hungry.

Maggie nosed the Studebaker past the mouth of an alley, squinting into its narrow brick-lined abyss. She saw crumpled sleeping bags, half-open backpacks, legs sprawled so that no one could pass without tripping. Or noticing.

Maybe that was the point.

Maggie parked on a deserted street in front of a ski shop a half-block away. The meter was out of order. Another good omen?

She turned toward Ada. "Any questions?"

"Nope. I'll just act lost and cold and hungry, not to mention young."

Maggie nodded. "I imagine they do their outreach after dark, looking for runaways to shelter." Maggie clamped down on her rising anger. "Or if you're Camille, to sell. Fingers crossed she's working tonight." She nodded at Doc McStuffins. "The phone's ready to roll?"

Ada lifted the backpack from between her feet and placed it on her lap. She peeled back the flap with Doc McStuffins' face. Where her skull would be, a cellphone screen winked. Ada swiped the screen and pointed at the record button on the FaceTime app. "Yep. I'll make sure the phone is behind the eye where it's mesh, turn the backpack toward the subject—as in Camille—and push the button when I'm ready to record."

Maggie nodded. She'd learned about Mac's Screen Recording from Constantine, who used it to record both business meetings and personal-bests on Mario Brothers. "Something feels weird to you, just walk away. Something looks weird to me, I'll call the police. Sound good?"

Ada nodded. "Undercover 101 tonight. The Academy tomorrow."

Maggie wasn't worried. Not until thirty-two minutes had elapsed without a word from Ada.

The arrangement was simple: Ada would initiate the FaceTime call, mute the volume and capture an exchange with Camille during which—God willing—she'd say something that would inspire the police to look into her "rescue" operation. Then Ada would hightail it back to Maggie's car.

The minutes ticked by, first solitary, then in groups of ten. Maggie craned her neck. The sidewalk leading to the alley was visible, but not much else. From this vantage point, Maggie could only see the occasional slumped form drift in and out of the passageway. No telling what was going on inside. No telling if Ada was still in there.

There was also the possibility that Ada had been taken—or worse. It would be no great feat. Ada was small. Alone. Maggie had been so focused on the trafficking of girls, on Camille's betrayal of womankind, it didn't occur to her that the other runaways could be dangerous.

She checked her phone for the millionth time. Maybe she hadn't turned the volume high enough? Maybe she'd inadvertently shut it off?

It was in perfect working order.

Maggie drummed a gloved hand on her steering wheel. She looked toward the alleyway, back at the phone, then back to the alleyway.

"Feck." She yanked the key from the ignition, unbuckled her seatbelt and opened the Studebaker door.

She'd just take a peek, do a quick walkthrough of the alley. In the dark, with her scarf over her head, she'd be unrecognizable. In theory. It was a chance she'd have to take. She couldn't wait while God knew what was going on in the dark.

Maggie began to climb out of the car. The phone buzzed in her hand. A FaceTime request. Finally.

She pushed to answer. A group of men loomed over the phone's camera.

Maggie's heart climbed into her throat. Oh God. She stood, contemplating her next move—call 911? rush to Ada's rescue?—when she heard Ada's voice and the men chuckle appreciatively in return.

They were talking. Ada was establishing rapport. Maggie smiled. Officer in training.

Maggie sat back in her car and watched. Ada had positioned the backpack on the ground to maximize the view of both her alley-mates and the stack of abandoned cups that marked the beginning of the passageway. Now that she was calmer, Maggie could see that the enclave included girls as well as boys. Most shivered in hoodies that were no match for the bone-chilling cold. Some picked at scabs on their faces. All wore masks of indifference that slipped at the corners, exposing the real emotions that pulsed beneath. Fear. Hopelessness. Forbearance.

The phone's mike picked up the slap-crunch of footsteps on hard-packed snow. The hoodies turned in unison, a single organism responding to external stimuli. A shape approached, black on black in the murky light. Maggie strained her eyes, trying to make out a face, a body type, anything.

Humanoid was as good as she could do.

The figure grew nearer, darkness clotting to form a body: narrow shoulders, wide hips, a small head topped with a jaunty tam. Six steps later and Camille's visage swung into view, the phone's camera peering up her right nostril.

Camille smiled. Maggie could see vestigial salad wedged against an incisor. "Hello, everyone," she trilled. "How are you?" A chorus of adolescent grunts drifted to the cell's microphone. "Is anyone hungry?"

She produced two Arby's bags from her coat in a fast food magic trick then flicked on the flashlight app of her cellphone. A trickle of light shone on the bags, rendering the grease spots shiny and translucent. Maggie could practically smell the roast beef and Horsey Sauce.

The faces of the runaways shone in the reluctant light of the phone. Noses quivered in the cold. Tongues snaked out to moisten cracked lips. The masks slipped a little more, hunger and want shining through indifference.

"Of course you are," Camille said brightly. "Probably cold, too." She reached into the bag and brought forth a sleeve of curly fries. She began to distribute. "You get some fries. And you get some fries. And you get some fries."

She was the Oprah Winfrey of sides.

The teens—and tweens—continued the act of ennui, casually taking the golden potato Slinkys. When they thought Camille wasn't looking, they crammed the greasy food into their mouths, greedily licking their fingers.

Camille surveyed the group, hands on hips. "There's more where that came from. Plus a warm bed. A safe place to stay. Where people won't bother you. Hassle you." She looked at each face in turn. "Hurt you."

"Oh yeah?" a boy's voice scoffed. "You gonna make us go to church or some shit like that?"

The others laughed, high and loud. The sound of wounded animals.

"No church or shit like that," Camille said, the old-lady-cursing routine stunning the crowd into silence. "Just a place where you can go until you're ready to move on, whether that's finding your own place or surfing a friend's couch. No hassles. No strings attached."

The slang clanged in Maggie's ears, Camille's diction yet another lie.

"No such thing," a girl's voice rang out. "Always be some strings. Somebody always working an angle." Out of the mouths of babes.

Camille's shoulders touched the base of her hat. "Suit yourself. But here's my number if you change your mind." She passed out cards. Most fluttered to the ground. She turned to leave.

"Wait." Ada stood. The phone's camera tilted, losing Camille, focusing on the ground. "I'm hungry and I'm damn tired of being cold. I'll come with you."

"Anyone else?" She waited a beat. "No? That's okay. I'll be back if you change your minds." She looked at Ada. "Come on, honey."

There was a grate of canvas as Ada adjusted the pack, and a new scene emerged: progress toward the end of the alleyway and away from Maggie.

Maggie's breath caught in her throat. She couldn't remember if they had discussed this part of the plan. Surely Ada wouldn't go with Camille. Surely Ada wouldn't get in the car. Surely Ada wouldn't go like a lamb to the slaughter.

She just might. *And don't call me Shirley*, her mind automatically movie-quoted.

Maggie pushed away the growing dread. Camille wouldn't do anything to Ada. At least, not right away. Rose and the others had lived safely at Running Home before being recruited into Sorrento's clubs, before being forced into slavery. At the absolute worst, Ada would go to the shelter, find out more, then call Maggie to pick her up.

That's what Rational Maggie wanted to believe.

Emotional Maggie, the one she refused to acknowledge even to herself, knew that things didn't always go as planned. People acted unpredictably.

Shit, as they said, happened.

"You been on the street long?" she heard Camille say.

"Long enough."

"Rough out there."

"Mmm."

A pause. The rusk of canvas against cotton as Ada's backpack rode against her shirt. "You look well," Camille said. "Healthy. Clean. Your clothes are almost new."

Maggie breathed in sharply. The clothes were new, purchased that very evening from a farm and ranch store. She hadn't thought to age or dirty them. She hadn't thought of anything other than luring Camille into implicating herself. Was Camille really that observant, that suspicious, or was Maggie reading into things?

"Five-finger discount," Ada said. "From Winfrey's."

"Winfrey's?" Surprise tingeing Camille's words. "Closest Winfrey's is in Collinsburg."

Maggie's heart began jack-rabbitting against her rib cage, hitting, clawing, trying to get out. Blood roared through her ears, drowning out the shallow breathing that made her chest hitch and fall in jerky hiccups.

"Whatever," Ada said with an abundance of teen attitude. "Some department store downtown."

"All the department stores have moved to the mall."

"Whatever," Ada said again.

A new pause burrowed and took hold, broader and more cavernous than the last. "Where did you say you were from?" Camille asked.

"Collinsburg."

"Right. Like where you picked up these clothes."

Something had crept into Camille's voice. A rustle of doubt. A hint of distrust. And underneath it all, something deadly.

"I have a friend from Collinsburg," Camille continued. "I don't suppose you know Maggie?"

"I don't know no Maggie O'Malley," Ada said, boosting the insolence. "How far is this shelter thing anyway?"

Fear sliced like a knife through Maggie. *Oh God. Oh no.*

"Maggie O'Malley?" Camille's voice dripped with mock surprise. "I don't believe I mentioned a last name."

Chapter 42

"Uh." Ada's voice was a single note, a piano key hit by mistake.

"I don't know who you are," Camille hissed, "but I think I know who sent you."

Maggie heard the dull, wet thwap of flesh connecting with flesh. She watched as the phone's camera tilted skyward then pitched earthward as the backpack thudded to the ground. In the phone's eye, Maggie could see a pair of feet, a glimpse of ankles, moving forward, back, side to side in a sick dance.

She didn't know what was going on, but she knew it was bad. Then she heard Ada's voice, a cry that was high then fading.

Maggie was out of the car and on her feet.

She turned, ready to run toward the alley, ready to charge through the gauntlet of strangers who slept and fought and ached in the shadows, when she collided against something. Or, more precisely, someone.

"Oof!"

Maggie batted the lock of hair that had fallen over her eye and stared at the human wall before her.

Jeff Greeley returned her gaze.

"Oh, God," she said, trying to recover some of the wind that had been knocked from her lungs. It felt like sucking tomato soup through a straw. "Am I glad to see you."

Greeley smiled. "That makes two of us."

"A woman is being assaulted on the other side of the alley." She threw her arm out in Ada's direction like the Scarecrow from *The Wizard of Oz*. "I'm pretty sure the person who's attacking her is the same person who murdered Howard."

Greeley didn't move. "You're kidding me."

"No! My friend is being attacked. I saw it happening while she FaceTimed me."

"Just like you FaceTimed Austin when your aunt decided to dig up her weapon."

Maggie was about to remind Greeley that Polly wasn't her aunt when she noticed his face—the sick smile, the dead eyes—and his body—too big, too close, hemming her against the car.

"Hey—" she began, unsure of what exactly she wanted to say. *Hey, you're being weird. Hey, you're in my space. Hey, what's up with the maniacal grin?* She clamped her mouth shut. Swallowed.

Greeley moved closer. "I've been waiting for this."

Maggie stilled. She felt the coldness where her now sweat-soaked shirt clung to her lower back. She smelled Greeley, a combination of sweat and Old Spice and the fragrant remnants of a dinner that likely involved onions and fish. She could hear her breath coming in shallow pants, making her feel lightheaded, as if a tomb were closing over her head. Sealing out the air, sealing in her fate.

"Waiting for what?" she whispered. Somehow she knew she didn't want to hear the answer.

Greeley showed his teeth. Lopsided. Lupine. A wolf closing in on its prey. "So I could finish what I started at St. Theresa's."

Maggie blinked. "But that was Camille," she said almost petulantly.

"That was me, you stupid bitch."

Maggie's vision narrowed along with her breathing, white dots—not stars, why was it always supposed to be stars?—swimming before her eyes. She took a greedy gulp of air, fighting for the oxygen she'd need to speak, run, fight, live.

"You attacked me in the hospital stairwell," she whispered. "You hit me on the back of the head."

"I also made sure your 911 call about the rock through your windshield got lost, but who's counting? I didn't know who was behind all that rock stuff, but I was happy as hell to know I wasn't the only one who hated you."

"But why? Why did you attack me? Bury the 911 call?"

"Friendly suggestions to stop interfering."

"Interfering?"

"Playing detective. Talking to witnesses." He brought his face to hers, close enough for a kiss. "Obtaining surveillance footage. You set a murderer free and made me look bad."

"Polly's no murderer," Maggie said, but there was no heat behind the words, her conviction tempered by questions about sleepwalking, faked Parkinson's and a knife unearthed in the dead of night. She cleared her throat and tried again. "Look, if this is about your job—"

"This isn't about my job. This is about justice. I'm sworn to uphold the law, and that's exactly what I'm going to do. After I get rid of a few obstacles."

Greeley reached into his coat and withdrew his service pistol. He looked at the empty street and then toward the shadowy maw of the alley. "Not a lot of crime in Hollow Pine, or so-called police brutality, for that matter. But things happen. Maybe I go check out those hooligans." He jerked his head toward the homeless teens. "Maybe they get out of control." He leveled the gun at Maggie. "Maybe, in the heat of the moment, I fire a shot and accidentally hit you."

Maggie fought against a rising haze of panic. Her eyes darted to the street that bisected Old Town, to the shops closed against the gloom, to the alley that had once held the promise of possibility.

Everything seemed far away, including hope.

Her mind shuffled through her options. Grab something from the Studebaker and improvise a weapon. Shove Greeley out of the way, slam the car into gear and speed into the inky blackness. Duck under his arm and run like hell.

She doubted she could do much damage with her film canister of medicine or her glove box of paper napkins. The Studebaker wasn't exactly a racecar. That left running. She was good at running.

Maggie could feel her adrenaline gathering, spooling up like the turbo of Pop's souped-up Camaro. She slammed against Greeley, her elbow connecting with his throat, her boot crashing down on his foot. Greeley reeled back, roaring with pain and rage. Maggie bolted.

She'd managed three steps before she felt his hand grab her ponytail. Her head jerked back, pain exploding up her neck and into the gash at the base of her skull.

She felt her feet slip traitorously out from beneath her. She regained her footing and began running again. Greeley's hand pulled again, slamming her to the ground.

She heard something crack. She wasn't sure whether it was ice or bone. She lolled against the cold and looked up at Greeley.

He wagged his gun, an extension of his finger. "Now that was a mistake. You not only wasted my time, you've made me mad." He put his face against hers again. "My wife didn't like me when I was mad. I don't think you will, either."

He placed the gun against her temple, drew it back and struck the side of her face. Maggie felt as if her eye had exploded from its socket. Blood budded like a seedling, pushing upward, sending runners down her face and into her eye.

"People sometimes fall when they're shot," Greeley said, "hurt themselves. Head injuries aren't uncommon. But you already know about head trauma."

He raised the gun again. Another dose of adrenaline dumped into Maggie's bloodstream, surging through her veins. Though blood streamed into her eyes, she sought her next target, her next opportunity. She didn't care that Greeley had the gun. She was going to fight back. She was going to make Greeley work hard at killing her.

She grabbed for the muzzle, missed, pitching forward and slamming face first into the ground. She reared back on her knees and made another swipe. This time she connected with the pistol, fought Greeley's fingers for the trigger.

Crack.

The smell of gunpowder. Her hand thrown clear with the gun's recoil. She grabbed again. Missed again.

Crack.

Maggie fell back as a bullet tore through her arm. She wasn't aware of the burn it left as it burrowed through her skin or the bone that splintered as it tried to stop its path. She just knew she'd been shot. That her choices were running out.

She reached forward and grabbed Greeley around the knees. She pulled. Hard. Greeley fell to the ground with a smack.

She scrambled on top of him, trying to wrench the gun from his grasp. He jerked his hand free and went for another pistol-whip of Maggie's head. She blocked with her forearm, leaned back and brought her knee to his crotch.

His hands went south, dropping the gun. She snatched it from the ground and rolled off him, ready to train the gun on his chest and order him to freeze, as if she were one of Charlie's Angels.

She underestimated his determination. Or she overestimated her ability to injure him. Probably both. He lunged, clutching at then capturing the gun.

Their hands slipped over the pistol, finding purchase, losing it. Then another report from the gun, the biting tang of gun powder.

Greeley slumped into a heap, red blooming through his overcoat, puddling beneath him.

She'd shot him. He'd shot himself. She didn't know which. She didn't know anything other than the reality of a man lying in a heap like a pile of laundry left on the bathroom floor.

Maggie put her head in her hand, overcome with pain and emotion that had finally scaled the Wall. Horror. Terror. Relief.

Then she remembered. *Ada. Oh Ada.*

Maggie spun around, poised to sprint into the alley. Ada stood ten feet away, gathering Camille's hands behind the older woman's back.

Ada looked at Maggie then at Greeley then back at Maggie. "Looks like both of us are ready for the Academy," she said.

Chapter 43

An EMT with a shock of white hair and earrings that bore a striking resemblance to dingleberries was bandaging Maggie's arm when Austin poked his head into the ambulance.

"I wasn't officially working, but heard the call on the radio." Austin surveyed her arm, now shrouded in bandages. "You okay?"

"Fine. But I don't think your partner will be."

He followed her gaze to a stretcher encased in a white sheet. Two EMTs, their mouths set into hard lines, hoisted it on a silent count of three and loaded it into an ambulance. "What the hell happened?" he asked.

"That's what I want to know," a voice said.

Constantine stepped into view. The shirt beneath his jacket was rumpled and polka dotted with what Maggie was sure was ketchup. His face was unshaven, his hair uncombed, his eyes red-rimmed with exhaustion and emotion. She thought he never looked more gorgeous.

"Gus," she said. And promptly burst into tears.

Constantine gathered her into his arms, pushing aside a now very annoyed EMT, cradling her ruined arm, kissing her lacerated and swollen face. "Maggie. Oh God, Maggie, I'm so sorry. Are you all right?"

"She will be as soon as I finish dressing her arm," Dingleberry grumbled. "It's not a mortal wound, but it does need attention."

Constantine stepped aside for Dingleberry, but kept hold of the hand on her uninjured arm, squeezing it as if he was a drowning man and it was his lifeline. "I just rolled into town when I heard the call." He looked at Austin, lifted his shoulders. "Portable scanner. I'm the curious type." Constantine put his other hand on top of Maggie's. "What happened?"

Maggie told them. Constantine's face darkened. Austin's face flushed.

"I knew Greeley was going over the edge, but I didn't know he'd fall this far," Austin said. "He kept talking about the case, how Polly was guilty, how he'd make sure she paid."

"He didn't just want her to pay for Howard's murder," Maggie said, gingerly touching her battered face with her good hand. "He wanted her to pay for breaking up his marriage and exposing him as a batterer. He'd lost his marriage, his case and his pride." She watched the EMT work on her arm. "I guess when you lose everything, you lose it."

The ambulance-turned-hearse by Greeley's body pulled away. No lights. No siren. No hurry. Where Greeley was going, speed wasn't a necessity.

"I'm just glad you're okay," Constantine said, his eyes still worried. "You're the cream in my coffee, the peanut butter to my jelly, the Pam to my Jim."

"I—" She'd choked on her words then kicked herself. She'd been shot, for God's sake. Why couldn't she say what mattered most? "I love you."

"I know," he replied, quoting Han Solo in *The Empire Strikes Back*.

Austin rubbed the back of his neck, kicked at the snow then looked at his hands. "Uhhh...Yeah, I'd best be getting on. I see a lot of paperwork in my future. You can come down to the station after you're all fixed up. Answer some questions. Make an official statement."

"What about Camille?" Maggie asked. "What about Ada?"

"Camille is in the squad car," Austin said, nodding at a black and white. "Evidently your friend overpowered her, tied her up with her own scarf, then came looking for you. She said something about a martial arts class."

Ada. Small but mighty. And full of surprises.

Austin put his fingers through his belt loops. "Officer Schroeder's talking to her now. If what you said is true, Camille is going away for a long time."

"What about Sorrento?" Constantine asked.

Austin shrugged. "Time will tell."

Time did tell. And so did Sorrento.

In exchange for immunity for insurance fraud and pandering, Sorrento agreed to testify against Camille, claiming he could prove that she murdered both Howard and Starr.

Forty-eight hours after Greeley breathed his last, Maggie and Constantine commandeered a booth at Dinah's Diner to debrief, discuss and digest Ruben sandwiches.

"Let me get this straight," Constantine said as he created a moat of ranch dressing around his burger. "Camille, the matronly baker, is the murderer, not Sorrento the mobster?"

"Truth will out—and so will evidence—but it's looking that way."

"And Camille and Howard were engaged?"

"Camille met Howard—who was then known as Matthew—through Sorrento, her half-brother."

"Dominick Sorrento is Camille's half-brother?" His voice had risen at least an octave.

"Evidently Camille let that little detail slip to Austin and company. They dug in and verified it, but I feel like I should have known. There was a woman in that YouTube video of Sorrento you showed me. I knew she looked familiar, but couldn't quite place her. Now I realize it was Camille."

Constantine shook his head. "And I thought I was up on my Mafia trivia. I not only missed that genealogical tidbit but Camille herself in the video. Guess I need to work on my powers of observation. Mob money helps explain Camille's house. It wasn't a mansion, but it did seem pretty fancy for someone who worked for a non-profit. How did Howard—er—Matthew hook up with Camille, anyway?"

"At first, it was just a business relationship. Camille helped broker talent for Sorrento's club with her connections at the runaway shelter. She fell for Howard and vice-versa, and they peppered their courtship with felonies and fraud. Then Sorrento changed his business model and started turning dancers into prostitutes. The younger the hookers got, the more uncomfortable Matthew-slash-Howard became. When he realized he couldn't get out yet, he faked his death, leaving his grieving fiancée Camille behind."

Constantine chewed on that, and his sandwich, for a few moments. "So how did Camille find her long lost love after all these years?"

Maggie took a long drag on her Dr. Pepper. "Polly told me Howard used to drop her off at the church for bingo and their baby blanket ministry for the hospital. My guess is Camille spotted Howard and recognized him for the same reasons Jenna did. Oh, speaking of Jenna, she changed her story."

"To what?"

"The truth. Austin said that she'd been hiding out ever since she talked to us, terrified that she'd end up like her brother. When she saw the news about Camille and Sorrento, she decided it was safe to come out—and come clean. She went down to the station and told the cops that she knew about the insurance fraud at InHance and had suspicions about the dancers. When Matthew died, she figured Sorrento had engineered the accident. When we told her about Howard and his murder, she realized that her brother had faked his death only to have Sorrento make it real. Except that it wasn't Sorrento."

Constantine took another bite, chewed thoughtfully. "I still have trouble seeing Camille as the killer. I mean, I get that she was pretty annoyed when she discovered that Matthew was still alive, but so annoyed that she decided to kill him?"

"Don't forget we're talking about a combination of business and pleasure. Camille was devastated by Matthew's death. Imagine how furious she'd be when she discovered he'd gotten remarried and was living the high life while she grieved. Add to that the risk of Howard discovering that Camille and Sorrento had expanded their operations into Hollow Pine, and you have the very real possibility of blackmail or tattling to the police."

"And the plotting began."

Maggie took a few fries from Constantine's plate. "I think Howard saw Camille during one of his chauffeuring sessions for Polly. He panicked, wrote that note in his date book that got the police so interested in Polly and started planning his escape to Barbados. Unfortunately, Camille had already laid the trap."

"Which was what exactly?"

"This is an ongoing investigation," she said, channeling Austin, "so I guess we'll have to let Sorrento fill in those blanks. My theory: once Camille realized that her dead fiancé was alive, she tried to elicit Sorrento's help in making him dead for realsies. Maybe Sorrento refused, figuring Howard was too much of a coward to be much of a risk. So Camille took Sorrento's car and did the deed, probably with a knife swiped from Sorrento's own kitchen, which would have already had his prints and DNA. Not too big of a trick if she wore gloves and had access to Sorrento's property, which she likely did."

"Blood's not thicker than water?"

"Maybe she thought that whole half-sibling thing gave her a loophole. And since Sorrento is set to testify against her, it seems to go both ways. In any case, Camille had to be furious when she discovered that Matthew was alive and her own half-brother wouldn't do anything about it. Long story short: she killed Howard, tried to pin it on Sorrento, then killed Starr, figuring the police would guess that Sorrento's reach exceeded his jail cell."

"But no proof that Camille had anything to do with Starr's death—or that Sorrento didn't."

Maggie nodded. "True. We'll see what happens. My bet is that Camille will go up on a murder charge, Denning will be prosecuted for insurance fraud and pandering, and Sorrento will no longer be the slippery don without a record."

Constantine pushed his plate away and folded his hands across his chest. "Okay, all of this makes sense. But I still don't understand the whole thing with Polly. The hallucinations. The sleepwalking. Her digging up the knife in her yard."

"The hallucinations and sleepwalking aren't too hard to explain. Polly was already a sleepwalker. She also had a variety of medications on board, which could have both exacerbated her parasomnia and set the stage for hallucinations. Petrosian pulled up Polly's purchase history. Over the past year, she had been a regular consumer of Zantac, which Camille was buying for her."

Constantine shrugged. "Tummy troubles. It happens."

"Zantac can cause or worsen hallucinations, especially in women who are over sixty and sometimes in conjunction with certain medications."

"Like those for Parkinson's."

"Polly's cocktail of meds, some of which were contraindicated, was just the beginning. She was also being dosed with a powerful hallucinogen."

Constantine's eyes grew wide. "A hallucinogen? Like what?"

"Nutmeg."

Constantine used an imaginary shaker. "Nutmeg, nutmeg?"

"I've been doing more research, looking for other hallucinogens. Then I remembered: *Orange is the New Black.*"

"The TV show or Camille's latest fashion statement?"

"The show. On *Orange*, some of the prisoners use nutmeg to get high. Nutmeg contains myristicin, similar to mescaline, which the body converts to a psychedelic. It's also enjoyed a resurgence among teenagers looking for an organic high. I remembered riffling through Camille's cupboards, seeing her vial of super-concentrated nutmeg oil. I started thinking how easy it would be to incorporate hallucinogenic doses into Polly's diet, both with nutmeg oil and ground nutmeg."

"So Camille watches Netflix or hears runaways talking about their nutmeg highs then hatches a plan to gaslight Aunt Polly?"

"Don't forget her degree in psychology. She likely studied psychopharmacology, which could have informed her knowledge of both artificial and natural psychoactive compounds."

Constantine pulled his plate close again and gave a handful of French fries a ketchup bath. "The Baked Baker. Camille does the old cookie-baking-granny routine, but loads her cookies with a hallucinogen designed to make those who consume it rant and rave."

"She was careful about who consumed it. If you remember, she had a stash of goodies just for Polly, claiming they helped her adhere to a special diet."

"Now that you mention it," Constantine said, "I do. She probably counted on Polly not being able to detect the nutmeg because she'd been losing her sense of taste and smell for years. Add in the medication, and you get a smorgasbord of alarming behaviors: fantasies, delusions, paranoia. It even explains why she seemed better after she got home. She wasn't exposed to Camille's nutmeg overdose or Zantac while incarcerated, and she'd sworn off gluten—and any baked goods potentially containing nutmeg—after she got out."

Maggie nodded, but didn't say anything about the faked Parkinson's. She wasn't ready to broach that topic. Wasn't sure if she'd ever be.

"I guess the good news is that Howard wasn't a philandering creep."

"That we know of. Despite the rumors, there's no evidence of him having affairs. On the other hand, there's plenty of evidence that he was an ass."

"Touché." Constantine reached for his Reuben and mowed down one side in three large bites. "As far as the knife goes, I like the theory that Polly was sleepwalking the night Howard was killed and came across Camille burying it in the yard. Her subconscious logged the event then compelled her to dig the knife back up several days later. She literally dug up the answer to who killed Howard. We just didn't realize it."

Maggie played with her sandwich. "At least we have some answers—and some progress. The trafficking ring has been shut down. The bad guys—and gal— are headed to jail."

"We'll see if Sorrento is slippery enough to get out of this one."

Despite the evidence and the plea bargain, Maggie could imagine Sorrento wriggling out and going on to new crimes, fresh victims. It was a sobering thought.

Constantine slid to her side of the booth and pulled Maggie close. "Lawbreakers caught. Polly home. Justice served. Now you pledge your troth to me and we'll call it happily ever after."

Maggie tucked her head beneath his neck and hugged him tight. Thoughts of Polly, of doubts, of the kinds of secrets that came between people streaming through her mind. She couldn't help but wonder why Polly had faked Parkinson's. She couldn't help but think the answer couldn't be good.

As much as she loved movies, Maggie had never been much of a believer in happily ever after. Especially for herself.

Chapter 44

She also wasn't a big believer in long goodbyes. When it was time for her to head back to Collinsburg, she kept her farewell hug to Polly brief.

Constantine's aunt was back in her own home, Camille's abode now transformed into a crime scene. For once, Polly looked at home among the opulent furnishings. She stood to inherit a great deal from Howard's estate. It seemed she was getting used to the idea.

"Constantine should beat you by an hour," Polly said in her home's grand and gilded foyer. "He said he was going to swing by work on his way into town, but I doubt he'll be long." Polly abandoned her cane and gave Maggie a surprisingly strong hug. "Thanks for everything. Without you, I'd be wasting away in jail. Without you, I would have never known about who Howard really was or who I could really trust." She shook her head. "I still can't believe this whole thing with Camille."

Trust. Lies. Not knowing what someone is really capable of. Maggie could relate. She forced a smile. "You're welcome."

The snow had begun falling again, miserly flakes that fell from the sky like dandruff of the gods. Maggie penguin-stepped toward her car, her footsteps dampened by the thin layer of snow that clung to tree and earth with parasitic fervor. She didn't want to risk falling onto her arm, which still ached and wept into the bandage beneath her coat, or onto her bruised and swollen face, which sported hues of blue, yellow and green. Part of her was grateful to have something other than a potential head injury to worry about.

"I've been thinking about what you said about Kenny being my doctor," Polly said when Maggie was a few steps away. "Maybe I should go to a neurologist. I've been feeling better, but you never know."

Maggie wondered if she'd see a fake neurologist for her fake Parkinson's. "Good idea."

"He asked me out, you know," Polly blurted. "Kenny. The other day. We've been friends for years. Maybe it's time I found out if there's more than friendship there."

Maggie nodded but said nothing. She gave a final wave to Polly with her good arm, feigning an intimacy she didn't feel. Then she drove down the snow-dusted street and tried to drive the questions from her mind.

It didn't work.

Minutes later, the Studebaker turned onto the streets that led to Petrosian's pharmacy as if pulled by an invisible magnet.

She told herself she just wanted a bottle of Dr. Pepper and a pack of gum for the road. She told herself she wouldn't bring up Polly and her faked illness. What purpose would it serve? Polly had suffered in her own ways. If she wanted to put a medical label on it, who was Maggie to judge? It wasn't as if Polly were guilty of anything terrible.

Was she?

Maggie found Petrosian at his computer eating a pastry.

He shot her a look, put the pastry on a white saucer, and dusted his hands. "It's nazook," he said in a tone that seemed vaguely accusatory. "My wife makes it. Quite delicious."

"I'm sure it is." She fingered a box of Claritin, pulled cough drops from the shelf then replaced them. "I'm leaving town," she said at last. "I just wanted to thank you for all of your help. With Polly."

Petrosian glanced up from his pastry. "You are welcome."

"Polly doesn't have Parkinson's," Maggie said in a rush, unsure why she was telling him this, but unable to stop herself. "She's faking."

Petrosian's eyebrows rose above the rim of his glasses. "And you say this why?"

"A friend of mine is developing a diagnostic test. She used it to run Polly's sample. It came back negative. The test isn't an absolute, but her symptoms seem to have disappeared—or at least improved—ever since..."

"Since...?"

"Since she got out of jail. It just seems sort of..." She studied a display of cold medications. "Convenient. And now she's talking about possibly dating Kenny Rogers. It just makes me wonder."

Petrosian pleated his arms against his lab coat. "I see."

He came down from behind his pharmaceutical perch and approached Maggie. Away from his pulpit he seemed smaller. Older.

"It's possible Polly was misdiagnosed," he said.

Maggie wanted to suggest Munchausen syndrome. Instead she raised her eyebrows.

"I finally located Polly's neurologist," Petrosian continued. "A retired doctor by the name of Hayes. He retired early because he'd been plagued by malpractice cases."

Maggie sank into the chair of the blood-pressure machine. "Malpractice."

"Mostly misdiagnoses."

Maggie processed this. "You're suggesting Hayes misdiagnosed Polly."

"It's certainly a possibility."

Maggie's mind skipped over the past weeks. Research. Observations. What she knew. What she thought she knew. She considered new possibilities based on what Petrosian had told her. Misdiagnoses. Misprescriptions. Parkinsonian symptoms.

A theory emerged.

"What if Polly has Lyme disease?" She whispered it, as if speaking too loudly would create a torrent that would blow the seeds of this new idea into the wind.

Petrosian drew his eyebrows together, white caterpillars above his eyes. "Lyme disease," he repeated.

"It's called the Great Imitator for a reason. It's an impersonator of other diseases, including MS, Lupus, ALS and..." She gave Petrosian a meaningful look. "Parkinson's. It starts with a rash, *erythema migrans*, often in the shape of a bull's-eye. But the rash goes away in time, and not everyone has that textbook presentation. In rare cases it can develop into neuropsychiatric Lyme disease with symptoms that look a lot like Parkinson's: tremors, difficulty walking, and trouble with balance, swallowing, speaking. Hayes may have had a track record of misdiagnoses, but he's not alone in missing Lyme. It's a complicated— and controversial— disease."

Petrosian's brows lowered. "Some doctors believe chronic widespread symptoms are an autoimmune response rather than persistent infection. That can make diagnosis and treatment difficult."

"But not impossible. It can be confirmed with a Lyme titer and treated with a multi-week course of amoxicillin or tetracycline. Neither antibiotic guarantees success, but it's a step in the right direction. Lyme disease symptoms wax and wane. Polly is going through a good spell, but without treatment, her symptoms will return."

She was suddenly glad that Polly was planning to see a neurologist and that Kenny Rogers was close by.

Petrosian massaged his chin. "Lyme disease. It never occurred to me. Guess I'm getting old."

Maggie wanted to put a hand on his shoulder. Resisted. Petrosian didn't seem the hand-on-the-shoulder sort of man. "Neuropsychiatric Lyme is rare. Once she was diagnosed with Parkinson's, we all continued to follow that line of thinking. Add in the cocktail of drugs she was on, and her symptoms were even more confusing."

Petrosian smiled. She was surprised to see how natural it looked. For the first time, she noticed the pharmacist's well-worn smile lines. "I like you, Ms. O'Malley," he said. "And I don't like people."

Yeah, no kidding.

"If you need a job," he continued, "a change of scenery, maybe you could think of working for me. I know you're overqualified, but maybe you'll like it." He shrugged. "You could even take classes at the university and become a pharmacist yourself."

A job back in pharmaceuticals. On the human side. The idea had appeal. Helping people was what had gotten her into the field in the first place. And it wasn't like she had a job to go back to. Maggie smiled. "Mr. Petrosian, are you offering me a job?"

Petrosian frowned back, mock seriousness belied by sparkling eyes. "Only if you're accepting."

Maggie thought about new starts, new possibilities, a life away from the shade of the past. Maybe Constantine could quit his job and move to Hollow Pine. Maybe they could make a home together.

Maybe she'd ask Constantine to marry her.

Maggie clasped Petrosian's warm hand. She looked into his face and saw the future. "I am, Mr. Petrosian." she said. "I most certainly am."

© TaguePhoto.com

KATHLEEN VALENTI

When Kathleen Valenti isn't writing page-turning mysteries that combine humor and suspense, she works as a nationally award-winning advertising copywriter. *Protocol* is her debut novel and the first of the Maggie O'Malley mystery series. Kathleen lives in Oregon with her family where she pretends to enjoy running.

**The Maggie O'Malley Mystery Series
by Kathleen Valenti**

PROTOCOL (#1)
39 WINKS (#2)

Henery Press Mystery Books

And finally, before you go...
Here are a few other mysteries
you might enjoy:

SHADOW OF DOUBT

Nancy Cole Silverman

A Carol Childs Mystery (#1)

When a top Hollywood Agent is found poisoned in her home, suspicion quickly turns to one of her two nieces. But Carol Childs, a reporter for a local talk radio station doesn't believe it. The suspect is her neighbor and friend, and also her primary source for insider industry news. When a media frenzy pits one niece against the other—and the body count starts to rise—Carol knows she must save her friend from being tried in courts of public opinion.

But even the most seasoned reporter can be surprised, and when a Hollywood psychic shows warns Carol there will be more deaths, things take an unexpected turn. Suddenly nobody is above suspicion. Carol must challenge both her friendship and the facts, and the only thing she knows for certain is the killer is still out there and the closer she gets to the truth, the more danger she's in.

Available at booksellers nationwide and online

Visit www.henerypress.com for details

KILLER IMAGE

Wendy Tyson

An Allison Campbell Mystery (#1)

As Philadelphia's premier image consultant, Allison Campbell helps others reinvent themselves, but her most successful transformation was her own after a scandal nearly ruined her. Now she moves in a world of powerful executives, wealthy, eccentric ex-wives and twisted ethics.

When Allison's latest Main Line client, the fifteen-year-old Goth daughter of a White House hopeful, is accused of the ritualistic murder of a local divorce attorney, Allison fights to prove her client's innocence when no one else will. But unraveling the truth brings specters from her own past. And in a place where image is everything, the ability to distinguish what's real from the facade may be the only thing that keeps Allison alive.

Available at booksellers nationwide and online

Visit www.henerypress.com for details

CIRCLE OF INFLUENCE

Annette Dashofy

A Zoe Chambers Mystery (#1)

Zoe Chambers, paramedic and deputy coroner in rural Pennsylvania's tight-knit Vance Township, has been privy to a number of local secrets over the years, some of them her own. But secrets become explosive when a dead body is found in the Township Board President's abandoned car.

As a January blizzard rages, Zoe and Police Chief Pete Adams launch a desperate search for the killer, even if it means uncovering secrets that could not only destroy Zoe and Pete, but also those closest to them.

Available at booksellers nationwide and online

Visit www.henerypress.com for details

IN IT FOR THE MONEY

David Burnsworth

A Blu Carraway Mystery (#1)

Lowcountry Private Investigator Blu Carraway needs a new client. He's broke and the tax man is coming for his little slice of paradise. But not everyone appreciates his skills. Some call him a loose cannon. Others say he's a liability. All the ex-Desert Storm Ranger knows is his phone hasn't rung in quite a while. Of course, that could be because it was cut off due to delinquent payments.

Lucky for him, a client does show up at his doorstep—a distraught mother with a wayward son. She's rich and her boy's in danger. Sounds like just the case for Blu. Except nothing about the case is as it seems. The jigsaw pieces—a ransom note, a beat-up minivan, dead strippers, and a missing briefcase filled with money and cocaine—do not make a complete puzzle. The first real case for Blu Carraway Investigations in three years goes off the rails. And that's the way he prefers it to be.

Available at booksellers nationwide and online

Visit www.henerypress.com for details

CPSIA information can be obtained
at www.ICGtesting.com
Printed in the USA
BVHW011356221020
591611BV00016B/342/J

9 781635 113419